THE
CHILDREN
OF THE
AMULETS

BOOK ONE
THE JOURNEY

NICK PEMBERTON

The Children Of The Amulets

Book One: The Journey

Copyright © 2013 by Open Tomes

Photography by Shelley Spence

Cover design by Anna Pemberton

Artwork by Rachel Pemberton

First Printing: May 2013

ISBN-978-0-9879620-1-0

www.childrenoftheamulets.com

www.opentomes.com

The Binding

Let time remain still,

And this complete you,

May the wind remember,

When she is ready.

Let the silence guide you,

And this complete you,

May time return her,

When you are ready

- Deciphered from the engravings on the original amulets by
the first of the docents

Chapter 1

The Invitation

When the girl was born, in the place of her parent's first meeting, Canace smiled in her long sleep. The wind will remember, she thought, and for the first time since her sister had left, the spirit of Canace felt whole. I will go to the girl, she whispered. It is time - It is time.

Jenny stumbled and froze as people raced past her, running ahead of the advancing wall of fire. The ash and soot whirled around her and she coughed roughly. Above the wind and roar of the flames sirens blared and a helicopter rattled across the haze.

It can't land, she thought, *it can't see what it's doing.*

A gust of wind blew the flames toward her and she felt her face tingle and tighten under the heat.

Crack! She spun around toward the sound to see burning needles raining down from an exploded tree on the scattering people. They clawed at their hair and beat their clothes, stumbling away.

The smoke billowed up, darkening the sky, and the town was lit by the eerie red glow of the fire. Jenny squinted across the Bow River toward her street.

I've got to get home - Dad will know what to do.

She turned toward the bridge and bolted, jumping over people and passing cars - her red hair flying out behind her. Ahead of the bridge a line of flame launched itself across the road and Jenny held up her arms to break through.

Faster!

She ran so swiftly the flames couldn't touch her and she screamed, bursting through the dense smoke.

What the-?

She stopped and stared, her eyes darting about.

Where am I? Where's my house?

There were no houses, no roads, no river - everything had vanished. She was surrounded by a ring of flames like a noose tightening in on her.

She backed away from the nearest flame and tripped, falling to the grass. She smelt something new - pungent and bitter.

My hair!

She gasped, her lungs burning with the smoke and heat. She curled up in a ball and closed her eyes.

I'm going to die.

Suddenly the heat stopped, the crackling and crashing around her ceased and the air cleared.

Jenny opened her eyes and sat up. The flames still roared and the smoke poured toward the sky, but something spared her patch of grass. She squinted, looking at the edge of the flames. Something was there, something moving, a white blur capped in red swirling around her.

A patch of the wall of flame was parting, a dark rectangular field forming in it. The white blur kept zooming around the edge and in the dark rectangle a girl appeared. She was dressed in a long white robe and as she walked, her hair spilled around her side - the same red hair as Jenny's.

She reached out her hand and helped Jenny to her feet. Jenny wiped her eyes to clear them. The girl was exactly like her. It was like looking in a mirror reflected on a wall of flame. The girl still held her hand and Jenny trembled in her grip.

'Who are you?' Jenny cried. 'And what has stopped the fire?'

The girl smiled and looked at the edge of the flames, where the white blur still flashed around them.

'It is the wind, my sister. It is you.'

As soon as she said it, the white blur froze and Jenny saw another girl, identical to the first, standing and looking at her. The girl didn't flinch as the flames roared past her and the searing heat returned.

'You, my sister. Save yourself.'

The girl released Jenny's hand and vanished. Jenny stared frantically around and screamed as the flames drew close. Just as they reached her toes and the burning started, the world went dark; the heat and the noise vanished.

It was pitch black in her bedroom, still the middle of the night. She was soaked in sweat and panting hard.

That same nightmare, she thought desperately. Why, why, why?

She sat staring out the window making sure all the houses were still there. The street lamps glowed dimly and for once Jenny heard no sounds - no birds, no cars, and most importantly no people. With everyone asleep the voices that she heard in her head, the voices of everyone around her, were silent.

She lay back slowly, breathing gently and letting the lingering fright of the nightmare leave her. Willing herself to be calm, she let the sound of her heart and the steady rise and fall of her breath wash over her.

What if everything stopped? she thought.

She held her breath and listened to her body - she couldn't stop her heart's beat, but she could will it to slow down.

I can control my breathing, though.

With slow, deliberate thoughts, she breathed in, held it, and breathed out. Silence. Breathe in. Pause. Breathe out.

If I fall asleep, will I keep breathing?

She stared at the ceiling, trying to ignore the rhythm of her lungs. She tried to think about something other than her breath, shifting frantically over the events of the last few days. Her best friend Sarah's twelfth birthday, the horrible trip her family had taken back to Calgary, the noise of everyone around her.

It was no good. She kept returning to her breathing, to the controlled pace. She frowned and slid out of bed. She padded over to the window, staring up at the peak of Sulpher Mountain, brightly lit by the moon.

Why are there always two girls?

The dream was so vivid, so frightening and always the same.

What does it mean?

Jenny sat on the bench in her window, staring up at the peaks. She couldn't remember when the dreams first started, but she could remember when they got worse: just after they had moved to Banff, five years before.

'We're moving,' Jenny's mother had announced.

The Greysons were sitting quietly around the dinner table, thinking about the horrendous day they'd just been through.

'What?' her father exclaimed. 'What are you talking about?'

'You know exactly what I'm talking about, Donald. We are moving. Away from here. Away from Calgary.'

Jenny looked at her mother and then her father. After a few moments of concentrating on each, she knew that once again she was the reason for their fighting.

'Don't you think that's a little rash? That maybe you're over-reacting?' her father asked, his voice low and even. 'After all, it's not the first time it's happened, and I'm sure as she grows older, she'll...'

'Oh come off it! She was catatonic! She couldn't walk, or speak - it's not getting better, it's getting worse!'

Jenny put down her fork and got up.

'Where are you going?' her mother said. 'We're talking about you, you know.'

Jenny looked at her but said nothing, and then started to walk away.

'You come back here at once, young lady!'

Jenny whirled around, a look of anger blazing across her blue eyes.

'I need to be alone, *mother*,' she hissed. 'I thought you knew that!'

Her two brothers looked at each other, smirking behind their hands.

'It's not funny - how would you feel if it had happened to you?' their father said. 'We've got to help her, all of us.'

'By ruining our lives?' her elder brother Tom said. 'By leaving home?'

Their mother sighed and stared out the window toward the distant mountains.

'She's not getting better, boys. She's already seven, and her doctor thought this would have stopped by now. We have to do something.'

'But why do we have to move?' Tom pleaded.

'It's the people,' their father said. 'She's having a lot of trouble being around people. They, um, frighten her somehow. That's what happened today.'

'But she's been to the mall before,' Tom continued. 'What's so different? Why did she freak out?'

'I wish I knew, Tom, really I do. But I think your mother's right. We have to get her away from here.'

'So our lives get wrecked, all because of her?'

'They won't get wrecked!' their mother shouted.

Tom stared at her, a frown framing his face, but said nothing.

'Where are we going, Mommy?' Mark, Jenny's five year old brother, asked.

'Banff,' she replied.

Two months later, on a warm July afternoon, the Greysons left Calgary, their van stuffed to the roof with precious possessions and headed west toward the mountains. Jenny smiled as they passed beyond the city bounds and looked straight ahead.

'This is great!' she said.

'Yeah, wonderful,' Tom grouched. 'I hope you're happy.'

'I am. No more crowded malls, no more horrible people.'

'I thought you liked the mountains, Tom,' their mother said from the front seat.

'Well sure, to visit. But what is there to do? It'll be boring!'

'You just wait, I'm sure you'll make new friends, and besides, Calgary isn't that far away. We'll still visit.'

Tom sat in silence, staring out the window.

Jenny looked at him, concentrating on what she sensed from him. His mind was reeling with anger and frustration, most of it directed at her - he blamed her for everything that was happening, for ruining his life.

'It's not my fault, you know,' she said to him.

'Of course it is,' he snarled. 'You and your fits. Your temper, and your spells.'

'But I can't make it stop!'

Tom crossed his arms and turned away, staring out the window.

'Too bad you weren't better at running away. Maybe then I'd still be at home!'

'Thomas!' his mother yelled, shocking their father almost off the road. 'That's quite enough out of you!'

She turned to Jenny and tried to smile.

'It's not your fault, dear. You can't help being who you are.'

Their new house lay on the south side of the Bow River, up a small street that had to snake its way up the slope of a mountain. Jenny couldn't remember a time in her life when she felt more relaxed and happy. It was an easy place to be alone, so long as she stayed away from Banff Avenue, the main street in town and the place where most of the tourists flocked.

At the foot of their street, stretching along the south side of the river, there was a large park and Jenny had already found many secluded spots where she could read or play with no one interrupting. She went almost every day, winding her way along the edge, making sure she was alone before settling in.

When she got to the park it was empty so she walked past the children's area, slowly moving across the field toward the sandbox. She sat on its edge, staring into it, trying to imagine what it would have been like to live in a castle. Even though she was seven, she still loved playing in sand, still loved to build structures, towns, roads and fields.

The peace of her solitary building, being able to ignore all the sounds, all the intrusions around her, was the best part of building sand-worlds. Using a bucket that someone had left, she started making small towers, pretending they were buildings that lined the streets.

On the smaller lanes she used her hands to create houses for people to live in, scooping the sand up and mashing it into mounds. A small gust of wind blew the sand from her hands and the sun glinted off it. She picked some of it up and held it high above her. She tilted her head and looked up at her hand, letting the sand fall slowly through her fingers. A satisfied tremor shook her as the sand cascaded down. She tried to wrap herself around the column of sand and found that the glints weren't always where they were supposed to be - they moved as the wind gently shifted. Over and over again she scooped up the sand and poured it past her watching eyes, trapped by the sensation.

She was so absorbed in what she was doing that she didn't even notice the child approach. Emerging from the trees, he walked quickly and silently over to her. He looked slightly older than she was and had a pale, almost alabaster skin. As he sat down beside her, she looked away from her pouring sand and nearly jumped out of her skin.

He held his hands up in front of him, reaching timidly toward her. She looked at him and frowned through squinted eyes. He had on dark boots, close to black which rose above his shins almost to his knees, an old grey pair of pants and a white shirt. He had a black robe or cape thrown behind him and around his neck was a small but beautiful medallion, with a glowing gold core. It was the only thing about him that had any color - everything else was grey, or black, or pale.

He looked at her sand village and smiled, crouching down to look at the buildings she'd made with the bucket. She concentrated on him, not sure why she couldn't hear anything from him - if she wasn't looking at him, she'd never have known he was there. He didn't say anything, instead leaning back and resting on his arms, watching her and her village.

A sound from across the park startled her and she turned to see what it was, knocking over one of the bigger castles she'd built. Her face fell when she saw the damage she'd done and she reached for the bucket to rebuild it. She was stopped by the pale boy, who held up his hands and shook his head.

Gesturing at her to sit down, he turned to the ruined castle. He held out his hands, palms down and waved them gently over the sand. As if drawn to a magnet, the sand began to trickle together, piling itself up like it was trying to reach him. He tilted his head and moved his hands around the pile, poking the air around it with his fingers, shaping turrets in the air.

6

The sand rushed to fill in his work and within moments a new castle stood gleaming in the sun, intricate in detail. The boy withdrew his hands and looked over at Jenny.

She had a wide smile on her face and giggled as he sat back. She looked at him and then bent down to look at what he'd made, admiring the window impressions, the turrets and the gate.

When she looked up, he was gone. She sat up straight, searching for him and found nothing.

She jumped to her feet and stared around. She couldn't see anything of him, no footprints in the sand, nothing. She closed her eyes and listened. She could hear children in the small playground, still hear the large swings creaking but her companion was gone. She turned slowly, listening and stopped. Opening her eyes, she stared at the woods across the field. He went that way, she was sure but no sign of him remained.

'Hi!' a voice behind her said.

Jenny flinched and spun around. Standing to one side of the sandbox was a girl with dark black hair, cut in a bob, smiling at her.

'I'm Sarah - you're the new neighbor, huh?'

Jenny concentrated on her and then smiled.

'Sarah Tomiyama, right?'

Sarah frowned.

'Um, yeah, I guess...'

'I did it again, didn't I?' Jenny said. 'I always do, you know, I say things I hear, never know when to stop, it's just, well, that's your name, right?'

'What do you always do?' Sarah asked, smiling.

'I always go too fast. At least, that's what my older brother says.'

Sarah rolled her eyes.

'Yours too, huh? Older brothers suck. I hate mine.'

Jenny nodded, looking at the ground.

'So what's your name?' Sarah asked.

'Oh, sorry. I'm Jenny. Jenny Greyson. We just came here - from Calgary.'

Sarah glanced toward the sandbox.

'Hey, did you build this?' she said, looking at the castle, 'It's amazing!'

'No, I, well I built a castle, but it broke, and then this boy came...'

She paused and looked around, then back at Sarah.

'Did you see him? He went into the woods, just before you came - you must have seen him.'

Sarah shook her head.

'Sorry, I didn't. Maybe I know him - what did he look like?'

'Well, he's a little older than us, I think. He wore gray pants, and a sort of cloak or cape - a black one, and his skin was totally white - no color at all - even his eyes were colorless.'

Sarah thought for a moment.

'Must be a tourist. Sounds like one of the weird ones my mum warns me about - not too many people wear cloaks in the middle of summer.'

'You mean they do in the winter?' Jenny laughed.

'You won't believe it,' Sarah replied. 'We get all sorts of people here. So c'mon, do you want to meet my friends?'

Five years later, on the first nice day after Sarah's twelfth birthday, the two girls were walking slowly down their street toward the park. The late June air was still crisp and dew hung on the leaves around them. As they stepped from the shadow of the mountain, they felt the warmth of the sun on their backs.

'So what happened to you in Calgary?' Sarah asked.

Jenny shuddered at the memory of her family's recent trip, a trip that was supposed to be fun - visiting old friends, shopping and dinner at her grandparent's house.

'I don't know,' she mumbled.

'Tom seemed pretty mad at you,' Sarah continued. 'He said you ruined the trip, as usual. What did he mean?'

Jenny paused, staring up at the peak that rose above the Banff Springs Hotel. How could she explain the voices? The shouting, frantic din of everyone's minds? The painful, driving urge for silence?

'I ran away,' Jenny whispered. 'I hate that place. I hate the people.'

'Me too. But why run away? Just ignore them, like they ignore you.'

'I can't. The noise was too much.'

'Then plug your ears next time,' Sarah laughed.

'Yeah right, that wouldn't look weird at all,' Jenny replied.

'So was it the same as before?'

'Before when?'

'Like before you moved here.'

Jenny shrugged and started walking again.

'I don't know. I don't remember that.'

'Your mum said it was. She told me to keep an eye out.'

Jenny crossed her arms across her chest and walked faster.

'She doesn't know what she's talking about,' she said fiercely.

'So what did she mean?'

Jenny spun around and glared at Sarah.

'Drop it.'

'Drop what?'

'All of this. Just forget it.'

'Whoa - Ok - whatever. I'm just trying to help.'

Jenny's shoulders sagged and she shoved her hands in her pockets.

'I know. But you can't. No one can.'

They walked the rest of the way to the park in silence. The sun had risen higher in the sky and the sidewalks were starting to dry. Wisps of steam rose from the field and drifted away toward the river. Across the field, people were running in and out of the woods.

'Park Tag!' Sarah exclaimed. 'C'mon!'

They ran across the field toward where their friends were playing. A dark-haired boy came over, grinning, and tagged Sarah on the shoulder.

'Sarah's it!' he screeched, bolting into the woods.

'Hey, no fair David - why didn't you pick her...'

She turned to where Jenny had been. She was alone.

'Jenny! That's just as bad!' she yelled before sprinting off, looking for someone to catch.

When Jenny took off, she ran deep into the woods and found a massive tree surrounded by some low-lying brush. She crouched down and leant against the tree, sure she wouldn't be seen.

She listened to the others, trying her best to stay quiet. Sarah was moving loudly through the woods, trying to flush someone out. Jenny peeked around the tree and saw Sarah in the distance, looking in the wrong place. Marty was somewhere dark, somewhere near the river - she glanced that way and smiled. He was behind the fallen tree, sure that he couldn't be found.

Too easy, she thought.

David was harder - he wasn't staying still. At first glance, he'd gone the opposite way and it took Jenny a moment to sense where he was - he was creeping along the opposite side of the woods, close to the path, crouching low to stay hidden from view. She could tell he was doing his best not to laugh.

She sat back down and hid since Sarah was drawing near. There was no way that she could make a run for it if Sarah got too close, so she sat as still as possible, keeping her mind and body quiet.

As Sarah walked past her, Jenny heard a distant crack like the snap of a small tree. It was followed by angry voices, using words she couldn't make out. She stood up and turned to look. David was standing about one hundred yards away, in the middle of the path, holding up a toy car. He was surrounded by several older boys and Jenny could feel his fear as the boys yelled at him.

She and Sarah started walking toward them and as they got closer, they could hear David's desperate apologies. Jenny felt a sudden, deep anger at the older kid, and took off toward them, running as fast as she could. Sarah stopped and stared, stunned at how fast Jenny was going - faster than any athlete she'd ever seen.

The older boys had their backs to her but David could see her coming and his eyes widened. The largest of the boys noticed his reaction and turned around just as she arrived.

'Jenny!' Mike Sinclair exclaimed. 'Where did you come from?'

'Back there,' she said, indicating with her head without taking her eyes off him. She knew he was furious and she could see why. David was holding a broken model car, one that had a large antenna mounted on its rear spoiler. Mike had the controls in his hand.

'Then go back. This doesn't concern you,' he said, turning back to David.

Jenny walked over, reached up and put her hand on Mike's shoulder.

'You leave him alone,' she hissed.

Mike whirled around on her.

'What do you mean?' he yelled. 'Get out of here!'

'It was an accident, Mike, and you know it,' she continued. 'He didn't mean to step on it.'

'So what? He did and he's gonna pay. Now get lost!'

Jenny walked over and stood beside David. The older boys towered over the two of them.

'No,' she said.

He stood still, staring at her through furrowed brows for a long moment and then lunged at her. Everyone gasped as Jenny vanished. Mike clutched at his side and turned around. Jenny stood behind him, her arms crossed, watching.

'I said leave him alone!'

Mike let out a low grunt and then charged at her again. This time she crouched down and leapt into the air, kicking him on the head before landing behind him. He fell to the ground, face first and got a mouthful of needles and mud. He stood up, beside his friends and wiped the needles away.

'C'mon, guys, get her,' he snarled.

They all advanced. She stood still for a moment, staring from one to another and then ran right at them. As if hit by an invisible force, all of them went hurtling back and smashed to the ground or into trees. They got up slowly, their eyes widening as they backed away before turning and running.

As soon as they were gone, Jenny started trembling, her shoulders sagging and she looked at David.

'Are you all right?' she asked, her voice quaking, 'Did they hurt you?'

He merely nodded, looking from her to the retreating boys and back.

Sarah and Marty came over but said nothing. As she looked from one to the next and concentrated on them, she knew she'd done something that scared them and as she thought back on the fight, she began to understand.

'Jenny,' Sarah said, 'what just happened?'

'What do you mean? I told them to leave. They wouldn't.'

'Yeah, but how did you do all that?'

Jenny's eyes squinted up.

'I - I don't know. I mean, they were going to hurt David, so I just -'

She paused and stared at her feet before looking back up at her friend.

'I just made them leave.'

Sarah shook her head and turned to the others.

'OK, guys - Jenny's 'It' for trying to get herself killed!' she yelled.

Jenny started counting and they all took off.

As the game continued, an old man stepped out from behind a tree and moved off into the woods. He walked swiftly, with the speed of one much younger and as he got further away, he faded from view and then disappeared. Jenny felt a twinge in the back of her mind and whirled around on the spot where he had just been.

No one ever saw him which was just as he intended.

He reappeared in an eerie, outdoor space, a small stage in front of him with no obvious backdrop and a bonfire burning to its left. His clothes had changed to magnificent dark blue robes, laced with gold inlay and he walked past the fire towards the front row of seats that faced the stage. The seats were hewn from the rock and went up and away from the stage for some distance - there were perhaps one hundred seats in all.

As he looked up at the seats, shapes began to emerge on them, forming first into swirling, vaporous clouds and then into a mist that focused into human outlines. The shadows became whole and the seats filled with people. They were each dressed in grey or light brown clothes that hung softly on them, a black shawl or cape draped over their shoulders and they were all wearing bright medallions that hung from a gold chain around their necks.

The people were from all over the world, all shapes, sizes and color. They sat in silence, watching the old man at the front, waiting to hear what he had to say. The medallions around their necks glowed brightly in many different colors.

In the front row of seats three impossibly old figures sat, two men and one woman, wearing robes that matched those of the old man. They were surrounded by others of varying age yet obvious importance and their robes had many inlays of gold and silver and were far brighter than the masses that rose in the seats behind them. The three elders rose slowly as the old man approached.

'What news, Exeter?' the woman said in a lilting voice that hinted at an Irish background.

'I have seen her again. She is...' he paused, looking for the right words, '... quite gifted.'

'I would think that's a good thing,' she replied.

'Well, yes, my lady, I agree, but I have not seen such power in one untrained before. She is already able to sense the thoughts of others, and she has some remarkable physical abilities. What is even more unusual is that she is using them well.'

He went on to describe the fight he had just witnessed and as he did, ghostly images of it appeared on the stage. He pointed out how easily Jenny rose in the air when she jumped over one of the boys, how she seemed coldly calm in the face of what should have been overwhelming odds against her.

When she rushed at the boys and they burst away from her as if hit by an invisible hammer, the three elders watching gasped. A murmur rose from the assembled crowd as well and a low swell of voices drifted down as they discussed what they had just seen: a chaotic, swirling mist around Jenny, one that seemed to lash out at the bullies as she ran past.

'You see?' the old man said.

'Indeed,' the older of the men said, 'That is highly unusual - great caution is required.'

'There is more, Exeter?' the old woman asked.

The old man looked at her, his face a mask of confusion.

'There is. She has had visitors. I cannot say who they are, but they resemble us.'

Several people in the front row of seats leaned forward. One of the standing elders looked hard at the old man.

'In what way?'

'They dress the same, that much is certain. I found it very hard to see them - they seemed to flit in and out of vision. They were very pale, almost no color at all, except...'

He was cut off by the woman.

'Except what? Are they bound? Could you see them?'

He nodded slowly.

'Yes, my lady, I could. Very bright they were as well, and pulsing, just as here.'

The voices around rose, some almost shouting. The three elders turned and held their hands up and instantly a silence fell. They turned back to the old man and stood thoughtfully for a moment.

'It is not possible to say what this means,' one of the men said, 'but it is very obviously a signal.'

He turned back toward the front row of seats where some sat watching him closely.

'It is as some of you have predicted. However, we will not know for some time yet. Do not make undue judgments.'

'Undue judgments?' a man several rows back said. 'Sir, this may not be what you think either - these pale beings are a warning, I'm sure of it.'

'Sure of what, Vladimir?'

'And the girl,' Vladimir continued, 'She is not like us - we all saw what she can do. She and the pale beings have made contact, yet we barely see them. What does that tell you?'

'Nothing at all,' the old woman in the front replied. 'It is a mystery, but nothing more, as the Docent has just said. The girl is gifted, that we have seen. We should concentrate on what we know, and leave speculation to its own devices.'

The Exeter cleared his throat.

'There is the question of matching!'

'Indeed. This will be a challenge for you old friend, no doubt of that.'

The Docent paused and smiled. 'But you have always been the best at what you do, we all have full confidence in your choice. Have you seen the boy lately?'

'No, sir, I've been a bit preoccupied. I will soon.'

'Good. Now then, the real question is the young lady you've presented today. Visitors like those you've alluded to are one thing, but there are far more sinister things in this world.'

'And,' added the old woman, 'there are many who may have noticed.'

'I agree.'

The elders turned to face the crowd, staring slowly from one to another. The people seated nodded or twitched and then slowly dissolved away into the same mist they were when they arrived, drifting away from the seats and over the plains that surrounded them.

When they were all gone the three elders and the Exeter remained.

'Shall I proceed?' he asked them.

'I would advise great caution in this,' one of the men said.

'But we cannot ignore her!' the woman exclaimed.

'No, we cannot,' he replied, nodding at the Exeter, 'let's just hope *they* do!'

Jenny's home was a small, wooden house, painted blue and white and had a covered verandah on the front, where her parents often sat to read the paper or simply talk to friends.

She and Sarah were walking back up the street after the game in the park had died down and Sarah was still buzzing about the fight.

'So come on, Jenny, tell me what happened!' she urged.

'I told you, I'm not really sure. I hate those boys, and I got mad, is all.'

'Yeah, you just got mad. C'mon,' said Sarah.

'Well you'd have done the same!'

Jenny stopped walking and stared at Sarah. 'Wouldn't you?'

'Sure!' Sarah laughed, 'If I could. Not everyone can just jump over people, you know - or vanish.'

'I didn't vanish! What are you talking about?'

'At the start - we all saw it. One moment you were there, standing in front of him, and the next you're behind him. How did you do that?'

Jenny paused for bit, thinking back to the fight.

'Well, I just ran. Nothing else.'

Sarah snorted and set off again.

'C'mon, Jen. I've never you seen you move that fast, even in races at school. You were going faster than a car!'

'I was not!'

'Yes you were. Everyone there saw what you did, and none of us have ever seen anything like it. What's going on?'

Jenny sighed and looked up at her friend.

'I don't know. It's like something inside me snapped.'

'But you've been mad before. I've seen you yell at your brothers. What's so different now?'

They'd reached Jenny's house and stood at the foot of her walkway, talking on the sidewalk. Her parents were sitting on the porch and heard snippets of the conversation drifting up from the street. When Sarah left, Jenny came trudging up the walkway.

'So what was that all about?' her mother asked.

'Nothing.'

'Something happened, Jenny, for Sarah to be so upset. What was it?'

She told them all about her morning including what had happened to David. When she was done she slumped down in a chair opposite her parents.

'You're certain there's no more?' her father asked, leaning forward.

'No Dad. Nothing.'

He raised an eyebrow and glared at her, his eyes never leaving hers.

'Tell me again how you managed to get all those boys to leave, yet there isn't a scratch on you?'

'I don't know,' she blurted. 'They kept trying to hit me and stuff, and I just moved. They fell down a lot.'

'Jenny,' he whispered, 'I know that's not what happened. Tell me what really went on.'

He crossed his arms and leant back, staring over his glasses at her. Her fists clenched together and a red glow spread across her cheeks.

'No!' she yelled, leaping up and running into the house.

A glass sitting on the table cracked and shattered, spilling its contents. Her mother stood up and peered down the street, sure that someone had thrown something at them. Her father didn't bother and sat staring at the broken glass, a long-forgotten tremor running up his spine.

That evening there was a hockey game on television and the family gathered to watch it together. It was one of the few times that they were allowed to eat in front of the television and they usually ended up with hamburgers and french fries.

The game started off well but by midway through The Flames were taking a beating, and they started to lose interest. Jenny changed into her pajamas and went down stairs. She sat in front of the fire, staring into it.

When her mother came back in, Jenny crawled over and sat on the sofa beside her. She slowly leaned over and curled up in a ball and put her head on her mother's leg. Her mother stroked her hair and she slowly fell asleep, no longer bothered by the day.

About an hour later, her father came down and found them both asleep. He nudged his wife and bent down to pick Jenny up. He carried her up to bed and placed her in it. She was still in her house coat which he carefully removed, making sure she didn't wake.

He sat on the edge of her bed, watching her sleep, lost in memories of her birth and the difficult childhood she'd had. After a while, he put his hand on her head and closed his eyes. One minute later, he sighed, took his hand away and left, closing the door behind him.

His wife was watching from the hall.

'Well?' she said when he came out.

'Well what?'

'Tell me what you saw.'

He looked at her and just nodded. Her face wrinkled up and she walked away to their bedroom, her shoulders shaking.

On Monday morning, Jenny was the first up, trying to avoid running out of hot water midway through her shower.

When she was finished, she stood in her housecoat in front of the sink drying her hair. There was a small radio on the counter and Jenny smiled as one of her favorite songs blared out. She started dancing, forgetting about her hair and twirled around the little room.

She caught sight of her reflection in the mirror as she spun, the housecoat twirling with her and grinned. *One day I'll be a famous dancer!*

A knock on the door jolted her back to reality.

'Hey Jenny,' Tom yelled, 'that's not a dance hall, and there's a line up here!'

Jenny stopped and returned to the sink to finish her hair, a red glow spreading across her normally pale skin. She shut the radio off.

'I'll be out in a minute,' she stammered.

She looked at herself in the mirror and hurriedly brushed her hair out. Grabbing her toothbrush, she set to work, still watching her reflection. She bent over the sink to rinse and shrieked when she looked up.

Attached to the mirror was a letter, in a dusty old envelope, with her name written on it in a formal, hand-written style.

Chapter 2

The Jump

When they put them on, Canace and her sister felt wonderful, and the sounds around them became whole. But when they traveled from home, away from the mountain, Canace grew tired, overcome by the song. Her sister took her arm, and guided her to silence, where she remains.

When she plucked the letter from the mirror, Jenny noticed that it wasn't held there by anything at all. The mirror had no mark on it from where the letter had been, no tape, nothing.

The paper looked old with a yellow tinge to it and was frayed around the edges. Her name had been written with a fountain pen in an old script. The letter was warm, as if it had been sitting in a plate warmer.

She turned it over and looked at the seal, made with a thick purple substance that had a picture stamped in it. The seal was wax and the picture in it was something she'd never forgotten, the medallion that the strange pale boy from the park had had on five years earlier. It was a wavering circle with two criss-crossing hatch bars across it that looked like frozen flames surrounding a diamond shape in the middle.

She turned to the door, unlocked it and headed out past her brother, still looking at the image in the wax. He said something about how long she had taken but she wasn't listening. She went into her room and sat down on the edge of her bed. Using her penknife, she carefully lifted the wax off the envelope and put it on her bedside table.

She opened the envelope and read the letter:

Dear Miss Greyson,

We have been watching you for some time. You are, we feel, a most promising candidate. Please go to the large fir tree in the park, the one you always climb with your friends, on the night of November 2nd and, at 9:30 PM, climb it. When you get to the top, jump.

'We look forward to meeting you.'

Jenny laughed out loud and read it again. She figured that someone was playing a joke on her. She crumpled the letter up and threw it in her wastebasket.

She got dressed when she saw the clock, not wanting to be late for school but still hungry enough to want a big breakfast. As she pulled her sweater on, she caught sight of the wastebasket and shuddered.

The letter sat on top of the other things in the bin, completely unharmed. It was as if she'd never scrunched it up.

She bent down and picked it up, staring at the paper, looking for signs of her crumpling. There were none so she tried to tear a corner off it. She couldn't harm it: it was like trying to rip metal. She went over to her desk and grabbed her scissors and tried again. Even they couldn't break it.

She crumpled it once more and held the balled up paper in her hand. It got warmer and then unfolded, returning to its untouched state. She read it again, this time more seriously. When she was through, she hid the letter, the envelope and the wax seal in her desk.

She wandered slowly out of her room, heading for the stairs, her mind racing with what the letter might mean. Maybe it was from that pale boy she'd seen years ago - certainly the image in the wax implied that. She started down the stairs, staring at the boots near the front door. They reminded her of the boots he had worn - tall and dark.

An excellent candidate for what? She turned at the bottom of the stairs and headed down the hall toward the kitchen.

Could it have anything to do with those girls in my dream? She opened the door to the kitchen and walked in, squinting at the morning sunlight that played across the white-tiled floor.

'Where've you been, dear?' her mother asked, rushing a bowl of cereal over to her. 'Your brothers are nearly done!'

Jenny sat down and started eating.

'Jenny?' her father asked.

She jerked her head up and looked at him.

'Answer your mother's question,' he said.

'I'm sorry, what did you ask?'

'I said, where've you been?' her mother repeated. 'You were a long time getting ready today.'

Jenny nodded, still thinking about the letter, wondering why she was being asked to jump out of a tree.

'I couldn't decide what to wear,' she finally mumbled.

Her brothers both laughed.

'It doesn't look like you thought too hard about it,' Mark said.

'Yeah,' laughed Tom. 'You always wear that green sweater - what was the big decision?'

Jenny didn't answer, spooning cereal into her mouth and staring out the window. Her brothers sat snickering at her. Tom leaned over and waved a hand in front of her face.

'Hello? Anyone home?'

Mark laughed but Jenny ignored him, turning her head away.

'Does anyone have anything exciting planned for the day?' their mother asked.

Jenny shook her head, looking down at her cereal.

'Yeah right,' scoffed Tom.

'What do you mean?' their mother asked.

'She's definitely got something exciting coming. Several of them, I bet.'

Jenny looked up at him.

Did he know about the letter? Maybe he left it to get me in trouble.

He smirked at her.

'How long do you think it will take for Mike Sinclair to get back at you?' he asked.

She shuddered.

'What did he tell you?' she asked.

'I didn't talk to him,' Tom replied. 'Everyone knows about what you did so you better be careful.'

Jenny stared back down at her bowl and ate as quickly as she could. Tom kept laughing then grabbed the phone and called one of his friends.

When Jenny finished, she got her things and ran out the door. Her father followed behind and stopped her.

'What was that all about?' he asked.

She shrugged at him.

'Nothing'

'Jenny, it wasn't just nothing. Tom's right - you be careful, OK?'

'I will be.'

'And I don't just mean of Mike Sinclair. You be careful what you say to people - careful of what you know.'

She frowned at him.

How does he know that? she thought.

He went back inside and she turned away, walking up the street. Her thoughts drifted back to the strange letter. Why had it told her to climb a tree and jump out of it? And who was watching her? She glanced around, trying to figure out if she was alone. Two nights ago she'd had the nightmare about the two girls again and when she woke up, she was sure someone had been in her room. She couldn't go back to sleep that night and now, with the letter's arrival, she was sure she was being watched.

When she got to Sarah's house, it was dark and quiet. She walked up to the door and just as she went to press the doorbell, a tingling sensation in the back of her head told her to stop. She stared at the wooden door, painted white and felt Mrs. Tomiyama looking out the peephole. Jenny stepped back and waved.

The door opened gently and Sarah's mother stepped out on to the porch.

'Good morning Jenny,' she said. 'I'm afraid Sarah's sick today and won't be joining you.'

She stood with her hands folded together in front of her.

'Oh, I'm sorry,' Jenny said. 'Nothing too bad?'

'No, nothing much - just a nasty cold. She'll be back at school in a couple of days.'

'Uhm, ok, well tell her to get well soon - for me, I mean, from me.'

Mrs. Tomiyama smiled and turned back toward the door.

'I will, dear. Give her a call after school, she'd like that.'

Jenny tried to smile and went back down the stairs and out the gate.

No Sarah, she thought. *Why today? What if Tom was right, what if Mike does have something planned for me?*

She ambled slowly up the street toward the entrance to the schoolyard. Without Sarah to distract her, she could feel the excitement and nervous energy all around her. At twelve years of age, she and Sarah were in their last year at the junior school and there were many younger kids who still arrived with their parents. Immediately next to her school and sharing the same playground was the senior school, where Mike and his friends would be.

She climbed the stairs up into the playground, bracing herself. Kids were yelling greetings to each other and running in many directions. Jenny looked around for signs of the older boys and then started walking slowly toward the main entrance of her building.

She did her best to avoid the sounds all around her, staring at the distant door and trying not to think of how alone she was.

Don't listen she thought. *That's how you get in trouble.*

She concentrated on her steps and looked down at her feet to make sure she kept them moving.

There's Jenny!

Startled, she whipped her head up. No one was looking at her.

I wouldn't want to be in her shoes.

She tried to ignore the voices, the way everyone else seemed to and kept walking.

I wonder when he'll get her!

The voices were all different and floated to her from many directions. Every time she looked up, no one was looking at her - no one was paying any attention to her.

They think I don't know what they think of me she thought.

A gnawing pain started in her stomach, a nervous feeling that she couldn't contain.

Mike said she was toast - man, this is going to be sweet!

Jenny winced and started to go faster, not quite running, but no longer walking.

I'm almost there she thought.

'Where are you going?' a boy's voice said out loud.

Jenny looked up and saw about ten kids gathering in front of the main entrance to the junior school. She didn't know any of them but they clearly knew her.

Where are the yard monitors? she thought.

'Didn't you hear him?' another boy said.

'Uhm, yes,' she mumbled.

'So where are you going?' the first boy said again.

Jenny didn't answer, instead just pointing at the door. Everyone burst out laughing and more kids stopped to watch. She tried to find someone she knew but every face staring back at her, laughing silently, belonged to a stranger. They were all jeering at her and then someone started chanting her name.

'Grey-son! Grey-son! Grey-son!'

Other kids picked it up and the chant grew to a roar. If Mike hadn't known where she was before, he sure would now. Jenny put her hands over her ears and screamed. The kids laughed again and returned to the chant. Jenny turned and looked desperately around for help.

Then she saw him - Mike was at the edge of the crowd, pushing his way toward her.

Jenny turned back toward the outer school yard and ran, faster than the wind, heading toward a clump of small fir trees in the far corner. The kids stopped chanting, stunned at her disappearance.

She sat on a low branch, three trees in and almost completely hidden. The crowd of kids was starting to break up in the distance and other kids were arriving, filling the playground further. She was shaking with fear and anger and tears were streaming down her face.

Staring through her tears, she thought she saw Sarah. She wiped her eyes on her sleeve and looked again. Far across the school yard, in amongst the yelling kids, stood a Japanese girl. She had on tall, dark boots, grey slacks and shirt and around her shoulders she had a black cloak. She was facing away from Jenny, toward the entrance to the school yard and not moving. The cloak billowed out from her, as if blown by a strong wind.

But there is no wind, Jenny thought, looking at the kids around the girl - their jackets hung loosely off them as they ran around.

The girl turned toward her and Jenny gasped - the girl was completely pale - no color at all. The girl smiled and started walking toward her. None of the other kids in the school yard paid her any attention as if she wasn't there. She kept walking, her cloak blowing behind her, undisturbed by the commotion around her.

When she drew near, Jenny saw a flash of green around her neck, coming from a round object on the end of a gold chain. It was the only thing about her that was colorful.

'Hello, Jennifer.'

Her voice had no tone to it but it wasn't a whisper. It was more like wind rushing through grass.

'Who are you? How do you know my name?' Jenny said, wiping her eyes.

The girl stood at the edge of the trees and then slowly stepped in, coming over to stand beneath Jenny.

'I was called Midori once. You may call me that if you wish. And we all know your name, Jennifer.'

She gestured for Jenny to climb down and waited while she did.

'So I, uh, don't understand. Why are you here?'

Midori turned around, looking at everything around her.

'To be somewhere now, I would have to be from somewhere else. I am not.'

Jenny frowned, puzzled by the strange answer. She looked at Midori's necklace and the medallion that hung from it, the only colorful part of her. She noticed the bands that ran across it and saw amongst the markings the same symbol that she'd seen on her letter. Midori followed her gaze and smiled.

'Jade Green - a beautiful color,' she said slowly. She held it up and looked into the green glow. After a few moments, she lowered it again and returned her gaze to Jenny.

'Did you get it?'

'Get what?' Jenny asked, trying hard to hear Midori's thoughts or even sense her presence, staring at the necklace the whole time.

'The letter.'

Jenny snapped her head back up and looked in the girl's eyes.

'You left it? On my mirror?'

Midori shook her head slowly.

'No. I do not know how it got there.'

'But you know ...'

'I do.'

'So what does it mean?'

'We want you to come, Jennifer - need you to. We haven't got much time left and you are the reason. Please come - things have begun - you've felt them.'

'What things?'

'I can say no more. Just remember the letter.'

Midori started to fade and Jenny could see right through her.

'Wait, don't go! I don't know if I...'

Midori reached out and put her hand on Jenny's shoulder. It was icy cold and sent a tingling electric shock crawling through her.

'You've got to go back there, back to those people - don't let them bother you so much.'

'But they're so mean sometimes. And their voices, they're just...'

'Overwhelming? I know. It was that way for me once.'

'Really!' Jenny exclaimed. 'How do you stop it? What should I do? Can you help me?'

Midori smiled and it sounded like the wind was happy.

'You are so much more than them. Don't forget that. And don't forget the letter, Jennifer.'

'But why do I have to jump out of a tree, why can't I just come with you now?'

'Because he hasn't gotten his yet.'

Jenny frowned.

'Who hasn't? Got what?'

'Enough questions, Jennifer. I must go and so must you. Remember the letter.'

'Midori! Wait!'

Midori grinned and started walking deeper into the trees. She was fading away and when she was quite transparent, she turned back to Jenny.

'I know her,' Midori said.

'Know who?' Jenny replied.

'Your sister, with the red hair - I know her. Remember the letter.'

As she said it, she faded completely from view and Jenny was sure she saw a mist drift away into the trees, a jade green mist that shimmered away into nothing. She stood for some minutes watching the trees, puzzling over everything she'd just heard.

She knows her. My sister. Maybe those dreams are real.

The ring of the school bell broke her concentration and she turned and sprinted back toward the door.

For the rest of the week, Mike Sinclair tried to get at her whenever he saw her in the playground. With so many other people around, he didn't do much more then threaten her and by the end of the week, he started to tire of it. When the weekend arrived, Sarah invited Jenny for a sleep over. After a huge pizza and pop dinner, they settled in their pajamas in front of a movie.

'So what should we go as?' Sarah asked.

'To what?' Jenny asked, puzzled.

Sarah gave her a mock punch on the arm.

'Halloween, you creep!'

'Oh, yeah, well - I'm not going this year.'

'What!'

'No, really, I'm not. I sort of hate it.'

Sarah crossed her arms and stared at her, an amused smile spreading across her face.

'Since when? We had a blast last year.'

'Maybe you did.'

'Jen, hey, what are you hiding this time?'

'Well haven't you noticed what people have been saying about me? How they all think I'm a freak?'

Sarah's mouth dropped open and she shook her head.

'Some people even want Mike to beat me up,' Jenny continued.

'Like who? I haven't heard any of this.'

'Everyone. Even Marty thinks I have it coming'

'What are you talking about?' Sarah gasped. 'He would never say that.'

'Well he thinks it. Everyone does.'

'C'mon - you don't know that.'

Jenny stared at the floor and said nothing.

'Right?' Sarah continued.

'I dunno. Maybe,' Jenny whispered. 'It's getting hard to tell sometimes. But I still don't want to go out for Halloween.'

'Too bad. If you don't go, I won't go, it'll be no fun. Besides, this'll be our last year. Let's go out with a bang!'

Jenny tried to smile.

'Ok, but not for very long. People are - weird, you know, on Halloween?'

'Of course they are - that's the point.'

'Well it's, I don't know, I don't like it.'

Sarah put her hand on Jenny's bouncing knee to slow her down.

'It'll be fun - I promise. You need to learn how to relax!'

'No kidding,' Jenny sighed. 'Easy for you to say.'

After school on the day before Halloween, Jenny wanted to get home to finish her costume. She bolted out of the classroom when the bell rang, not waiting for Sarah or anyone else to catch up. As she approached her locker, she saw a note sticking out of the grill. It was a badly drawn picture of her with a black blob on her head. It read simply 'We'll get you.'

She ripped up and threw it in the garbage then headed out the door to the playground, walking across it toward the small path that led to her street.

They all hate me she thought to herself. *They wish I was dead.*

When she got home, she went straight to her room to work on her costume. She'd found a pair of boots to wear that were a dark gray, almost black. She had a gray pair of pants and a shirt and she sat on her bed working on a black cloak to wear over top.

What about the medallion? she thought. *Where will I get one of those?*

That night she sat awake in her bed, reading the letter again and thinking about Midori. The letter was as warm as the day she'd found it and the letters on the page sometimes shimmered like they were melting. She'd stare at them and they'd snap back to form but it made her uneasy - she wondered if the letter was trying to tell her something else.

The letter's instructions both scared and excited her - she wanted to follow its instructions, to heed Midori's call. She lay on her back, staring out the window at the moonlight bouncing off the mountains. They always seemed closer to her at night.

Why can I suddenly run so fast? Why are people's thoughts getting easier to hear? Something's changing she thought to herself. *Midori knows what it is - she knows what's happening to me. If I go, maybe she'll tell me.*

On November 2nd, she knew she'd find a way to be in that tree at nine thirty in the evening.

The next night Jenny tried again to get out of going and it took Sarah a long time to change her mind. She reluctantly agreed to meet up in front of Sarah's house at seven thirty. When she left, there were lots of children out on the streets. Jenny didn't want to run into any of them so she kept close to the houses, moving in between hedges, over fences and behind trees. Some little kids spotted her and one burst into tears when he caught sight of her face.

Jenny smiled behind the hood. The white makeup was working - no one knew who she was so she could do anything. Sarah's house was at the far end of the street, near the school so Jenny had many gardens to creep through. As she emerged from behind one hedge, she nearly ran into a gang of kids going up to the house she was passing. They screamed when they saw her and she let out a violent, loud hiss, clutching at them, before she ran from view. She could hear their nervous laughter falling behind her.

Up ahead, Sarah was lurching around what looked like an oversized teddy bear.

That must be David's idea of a wolf, Jenny thought.

They hadn't seen her coming, as she was still two houses away, slinking close to the buildings, away from the sidewalk. She grinned and held up her arms under her cloak, forcing it to billow out and ran at them with a loud and guttural growl.

She ran so fast that she seemed to be a dark blur and before either of them could turn to face her she was on them. Sarah screeched and ran and David stood stock-still with fright. Jenny burst out laughing and Sarah stopped, realizing she'd been tricked. She turned and came back.

'Oh my God, Jenny, *that* was incredible!' she exclaimed.

'Yeah,' said David, finally, in a shaky voice, 'how did you sneak up on us like that?'

'I didn't! I ran!' she replied, enjoying his discomfort.

David and Sarah looked at her.

'From where? We didn't see you coming,' Sarah said.

'That's because you weren't looking the right way,' Jenny laughed. 'I was sneaking along the houses not the sidewalk!'

'Man!' David said. 'That was scary!'

Marty finally came rambling over and for the next hour, the four of them wound their way through the neighborhood, scaring some kids, amusing others and collecting lots of loot. Jenny had sewn large pouches inside her cloak, making it easy for her to carry her stuff. David had a plastic bag and both Sarah and Marty were carrying shoulder bags.

It started to drizzle and the umbrella Marty had brought turned out to be useful - to Marty and Sarah. Jenny decided to just use her hood, not minding the odd drop of water that hit her face and David simply didn't care about getting wet, saying wolves were used to it. They'd wandered far from their street and were returning along one of the bigger roads, satisfied with the night's haul.

As they turned on to David's street, they saw a gang of younger kids returning. They were talking excitedly to each other and didn't pay attention as they stepped into the road to cross.

Jenny and her friends watched in horror as a car slammed on its brakes, skidding across the slick pavement towards the kids. Sarah started to scream but Jenny stared straight at the car, clenching her fists.

Just as the car was about to hit the first child, Jenny unclasped her hands and quietly said 'Stop.'

Instantly the car did, like it had run into an invisible brick wall. The driver's eyes were staring in horror at the kids in the street, all of whom were staring back. Sarah was still screaming.

When they regained their composure, the four of them hurried over to see if the kids were injured. The driver got out of the car, still shaking and came to see as well. No one was hurt and almost no one knew what had happened, how the car had suddenly stopped.

Jenny did know and was trembling, scared of what she had done. She thought back to something Midori has said: *You are so much more than them.* She looked at the car, still sitting where she'd blocked it.

Maybe I am.

The image of the car screeching on its tires and then suddenly stopping stayed with Jenny for the rest of the night. After they'd all gone home and she'd taken off her costume, she stood in the bathroom, washing the makeup off her face. She stopped, staring at the spot where she'd first seen the letter. She had no doubt, no matter how scared she was, that she would go - she had to find out what was happening to her.

On Sunday morning, she decided to go to the park to check her route one more time. When she left her house, she felt the cold air biting at her but the sky was clear and the wind was barely moving. She could see the snowcaps on the mountains in the distance and felt a calm come over her. Something stirred deep within her, a feeling of ancient familiarity, of belonging. She smiled as the feeling enveloped her and was certain she heard the distant peaks calling her, reassuring her, with the same words, carried on the breeze: *This is your home.*

She reached the entrance to the park. It was still early; no one would be here yet. She walked slowly down the center path, heading for the tree where she had been told to jump. There was a small pond near the entrance just to the right of the children's playground. The town stocked it with big, lumbering orange fish. It had a small stream leading from it that ran alongside the path.

The path crossed over the stream on a narrow wooden bridge. As she walked over it, she looked down through the cracks to see if any fish went past. If they did, she had to go back to the start of the bridge and try again. It was a game she and Sarah used to play and it sometimes took them hours to cross. This morning there were none, the water being too cold for the fish, so she crossed without stopping.

On the other side a large stand of trees sprang up. The path had to wind its way through them which made it the best place to lose someone during park tag. Once she walked out of the trees there was a long stretch of the path that headed through a field toward the swings, fort and sand box.

Seated on one of the benches beyond the trees was an ancient old man, dressed entirely in gray. He was stooped over as if watching something on the ground but Jenny was quite sure he was watching her. She tried to listen to him, to hear his thoughts but found him silent.

He was watching her but not for any reason that she would have guessed. He smiled, knowing where she was headed: The tree - she wanted to make sure one more time. He'd seen her do this same walk several times over the last week, although he'd been careful not to be seen by her or anyone else. Today it didn't matter if she saw him - today they might get to meet - if she made it.

Jenny hurried past to the tree which was just off the path behind some bushes. She stood at the base, staring up the trunk, trying to decide how to climb up. The tree leaned out towards the path, towards the light and had lots of branches. The top was a long way up, and while she and her friends had climbed it before, it was far too high for a jump.

Jenny gathered her jacket around her shoulders as the wind picked up and headed back home.

The rest of the day dragged on and on. She was thinking about the evening adventure and that made everything else boring and slow. Dinner was a big Sunday meal, a tradition in her family. They ate in the formal dining room and had to stay for the whole meal. Her brothers hated it, especially having to use linen napkins. Jenny liked it because it usually meant that at least one of them would get in trouble and she could, for once, enjoy their discomfort.

When dinner was finally over and the plates all cleared from the table, she was able to go. She quietly got her coat and boots laid out in the back stoop off the kitchen and headed to her room. She changed into her blue flannel pajamas and sat watching the clock. She knew she needed half an hour to get to the park and climb the tree.

By nine her brothers were watching something awful on television with their father and her mother was in the big bathtub unwinding before bed. Jenny tucked the letter, which felt even warmer than the day she had found it, in her sleeve and snuck down the stairs. She got to the kitchen and was just putting on her boots when the lights from upstairs came on. Panicking, she ran out the door without her coat.

She was instantly cold and snuck in to the garage to see if there was anything there to wrap up in. She couldn't go back because her brother, who had come to get a soda from the fridge, would catch her and she'd be back in her room before the trip even began. She found a tired, worn blanket, full of holes and wrapped it around herself. It gave her some warmth but smelled moldy and old.

She hurried down the street and into the park. There was a slight breeze and it was cold. It was also dark and the small path lights didn't go far into the gloom. As she crossed the footbridge, she didn't bother to look down, making her way into the winding trees. The light was even less and the trees seemed massive and frightening, leaning towards her and hissing in the breeze.

She came out of them, passing the swings, which were swaying and creaking. Finally she came to the tree and looked up. It was the same tree but in the dark it seemed huge, impossible to climb. Determined to go on, driven by Midori's words and her recent experiences, she started to climb.

As she did, the blanket slipped off her shoulders and she was left with just her boots and pajamas.

The breeze was getting stronger and she was getting cold. She kept climbing, sure the tree was growing as she did, making it more difficult. She was tiring and didn't know how much farther she could go. She reached the top and looked at her watch. Nine twenty-five - In five minutes, she had to jump - or forget the whole thing and go home.

She crouched down, trying to use the few needles that were left at this time of year as a barrier to the wind. Could she jump? She looked down, thinking to herself that she must have finally gone crazy - she was going to kill herself if she did. She looked again at her watch: Nine thirty. Time to go.

Without thinking, she stood up and grabbed on to a branch that was sticking up to steady herself. *On three*, she thought.

One.

Two.

Three.

And she jumped.

Chapter 3

Paul Green

Even though she could be the wind, Canace was only one half:
Her sister was the rock, the means by which she measured.
When their parents were lost, the sisters wandered; Canace, the
speed, and her sister, the guide. Watch out! Her sister would
cry, they are close! But Canace went on, with the wind.

After Jenny jumped the old man gathered himself together and headed down the path. He knew he had little time, that he had to move quickly and check the other. As he walked into the thick trees, he began to fade, moving into the shady gloom of the forest where he vanished.

He reappeared at the edge of a dimly lit square in the heart of London, England and saw the boy standing alone, looking at a dark patch of grass just in front of him.

Ah Mr. Green he thought, *have we convinced you?*

The twelve year old boy, Paul Green, stood in the middle of the square, staring into the monstrous bonfire that raged in front of him. The heat bounced off his cheeks, making his skin recoil and stretch itself thin. The flames reached to at least twice his height, the sparks traveling high into the night air before finally fading out.

The boy raised his hand and looked at a letter. He moved the paper up slowly and then back, shaking his head. The old man tried to imagine what he read there, what the fire he feared would look like.

We need you, Paul he thought.

The fire burned brightly in the middle of the square, casting a flickering yellow-orange light that danced across the Victorian terrace houses surrounding it. He saw the boy look back at his grandparent's house, on the far side of the square, hoping that one of them might be coming to stop him, to pull him away from the inferno.

No one was there.

The boy straightened, breathed deeply and closed his eyes. He stuffed the letter into his coat pocket, and shuddered. His lips curled and he stepped forward, disappearing before his feet touched the coals.

The old man turned around immediately and bolted from the square.

There's no turning back now - they have met.

It was nearly four years earlier when Paul was eight that his father was killed. He was burned to death after a beam collapsed on top of him as he lay unconscious on the floor. When it hit his father and the inferno erupted, Paul sat up in bed sweating. He threw off his covers, stood up and walked over to the window, staring out at the modest houses that surrounded him. He looked up at the cloudy sky and his anger at his father's absence, at his missing Paul's karate trial melted away. It was replaced by an overwhelming feeling of loss, a sense that something important, something irreplaceable, had just been taken from him.

At midnight, still sitting in the window, Paul heard the doorbell ring. He heard his mother jump from bed, heard her bustle to get a dressing gown on and hurry down the stairs. He went over to his door and cracked it open, staring at the two men talking to her, their uniforms crisp, their caps held stiffly at their sides.

The grim sadness that he felt washing up the stairs told him something terrible had happened, and he knew, when his mother collapsed, that it had to do with his father.

In the days before his father's death, Paul's only focus was his upcoming karate trial. He was going for his brown belt, something that had taken him two and a half years to build toward. His deftness and natural instincts had caught the eye of several of London's sensei. The brown belt trials involved far more than the simple katas that he'd had to master so far; he had to prove himself as a fighter.

Paul tried to get to the dojo as soon as he could after school. Three days before the trial, his mother dropped him off early and he found the dojo dark. He changed into his gi and sat down in the small waiting area. When his sensei came in, minutes later, he smiled.

'Early today, aren't you Paul?'

Paul grinned up at him.

'My mother had an appointment and had to drop me early. I don't mind.'

'Neither do I, it will give us a chance to work on your sparring.'

They bowed at the entrance and stepped into the dojo. After a few stretching exercises, his sensei stood up straight.

'We'll work on your blocks to start. Are you ready?'

Paul nodded and concentrated on him. He was moving slowly, back and forth, rocking back on his heels. Paul felt the tension building across from him and crouched down.

Here it comes! Paul thought, feeling the change in his opponent.

His sensei darted forward and whirled around, startled to find Paul coming at him from behind. With no time to think he reacted and knocked Paul flying back against the wall.

'Oh, Paul, my apologies,' he said running over.

Paul picked himself up and winced a little. *Why didn't I see that coming?* he thought.

'That was an impressive dodge,' his sensei continued, helping him up. 'How did you know to do that?'

'Your feet,' Paul replied, avoiding the truth. 'I've seen that pattern before.'

His sensei frowned.

'Obviously you need to spar with more people than just me. Not everyone moves the same way - remember that at the trials - you will not know your opponent as you do me.'

Ben Green's funeral was held at the large Anglican Church near Paul's grandparent's house. It was filled to capacity - Ben was a man that many, many people loved and they came from as far away as Australia to say their goodbyes. They started to arrive shortly after the announcement of his death, taking over the arrangements, letting Paul and his mother Emma be together, helping them absorb what had just happened.

'Mum?' Paul said, looking into the living room where she sat. 'May I come in?'

She glanced up, her eyes swollen and held her hand out.

'Of course, darling. Of course.'

He walked over and stood in front of her, looking down at her tear stained face.

'We have to go soon. The car's arrived.'

'I know dear.'

'Are you all right, Mum?'

'I'll be fine. And you?'

Paul shrugged and his collar popped out from underneath his sweater. Emma stood up and tucked it back in.

'Let's have a look at you,' she said, putting both hands on his shoulders.

As soon as she touched him, Paul felt the panic inside her, the urge to scream, to run.

'Come,' he said, taking her hand and guiding her out. 'They'll be waiting.'

Emma grabbed him into a hug, resting her chin on his curly brown hair, so like his father's. She held him for a full minute and then released him, drawing a sharp breath.

'You've got his strength,' she whispered. 'Remember that when we're in the church.'

He frowned, and looked up at her.

'I'll try.'

His uncle opened the door to the car when they arrived and they drove in silence to the funeral home where they would accompany his father's casket on its trip to the church. They gathered together with his grandparents and family and set out, three long black cars heading for the church.

They arrived just as the last of the mourners went in. The pallbearers were already there and one after another, they came over to greet Paul and Emma. Paul shook hands with each and when he reached the last, a man named Clive Eby, he hesitated. Clive was nervous and as he looked at him, Paul knew why. Clive Eby had been in the pub the night Ben Green had died.

'Paul...' Clive began, leaning over.

'It's all right, Mr. Eby. I know.'

Paul reached out his hand. Clive smiled and took it, shaking firmly. Paul's eyes widened under his grip and he staggered over. Clive immediately let go.

'Oh Paul, I'm sorry. Don't know my own strength sometimes.'

'Yes, uhm, sorry, what?' Paul stammered. He looked around, not sure where he was. He thought he could see tables in a pub, a warm fire beyond the hearth, people talking and laughing. He shook his head, staring at his father's coffin.

'I'm fine, sir,' he finally managed. 'Is it time?'

'It is. Are you ready?'

Paul watched as the coffin was removed from the hearse and carried toward the main entrance. He stood beside his mother and walked slowly behind it, staring at the pattern in the polished wood.

What was that? he thought. *I saw Dad - he was there!*

When they walked into the church, Paul knew that everyone was looking at him and at his mother. She was staring down at the deep red carpet, her body contorted with frozen grief. Paul knew she was struggling to keep going, could see that her legs were walking in a forced, rigid step, as if they wanted nothing more than to run back out the door.

He reached out, took her hand and thought of calming her. He thought of his father, his smile, his laugh and willed her to do the same. He felt her hand relax, saw her walk straighten and looked up at her.

'Ok?' he whispered.

She nodded, still clutching his hand and followed her husband's casket to the front of the church. For the next hour, the sense of absence in Paul, of loss, worked its way to the surface, driven home by the readings, by the hymns, and by the prayers.

At the graveyard, standing next to the coffin as the final sacraments were read, he stood crying, wondering how such a wonderful man, the only father he'd ever have, could be taken from him so soon. As the coffin lowered and the first small clumps of earth followed, he turned and ran, unable to stand the grief he felt pouring from everyone around him. His uncle went to follow but his grandfather held him back.

He came to a stop fifty yards later and sat down on a small bench, still crying. He heard a faint whisper, like a sealed door opening and looked up. On the other side of the small road that wound through the graveyard, an ancient man stood. His clothes were grey and worn threadbare, and he leaned on a thick, black cane as he walked over. Around his neck he wore a gold chain and on the end of it, a small blue stone hung, glowing under the gold bands that held it. He walked over and sat down beside Paul and looked back at the new grave.

'You will never stop missing him, Mr. Green,' the old man said.

His voice was deep and to Paul it sounded like it might be on either side of him, like it was bouncing around him.

'I know.'

'Neither will any of his friends. Neither will your mother.'

Paul looked up at him and stared into his eyes.

'I can't feel you,' he said, frowning and wiping away a tear.

The old man's eyes widened and he held his hand out.

'Are you sure?' he asked.

Paul reached out and took his hand. It was cold, but firm.

'I feel your hand,' Paul said, 'but not you. Why is that?'

'One day, perhaps, I'll teach you. But not yet. Do you feel them?'

He gestured toward the people gathered around the grave. Paul saw that his uncle and grandfather were still looking at him, making sure he was in sight.

'Yes.'

'Right now, you need them, Mr. Green - be with them, let them help you.'

He stood up and put his hands on his back, before leaning over to grab his cane.

'Don't forget any of him,' he said, 'Don't forget his voice, his hands, his eyes. Promise me that.'

Paul nodded.

'I shan't,' he said.

The old man's eyes glanced away and he put his hand on Paul's shoulder.

'Looks like I've got to go - We'll speak again, one day, I'm sure.'

Paul tried to smile.

'We will,' he whispered.

'Will what?' his grandfather said, walking across the grass. 'Who're you talking to?'

Paul looked around, trying to find the old man and saw no sign of him. His grandfather sat down and put his arm around Paul's shoulders. Paul leaned in and closed his eyes.

'No one,' he whispered, 'No one, Gran'dad'

In the months after the funeral, they'd tried to stay in the house. It seemed so empty without Ben Green. His friends no longer came to visit and Paul felt increasingly angry with him, like his death had been his own fault. One night, as Paul's mother was tucking him into bed, his feelings overtook him.

'Why didn't he just get out of the way?' he demanded.

'Who do you mean, darling?'

'Dad. Why didn't he leave? He didn't even know them.'

Emma sighed heavily and sat back down on the edge of his bed. Paul had just asked the exact same thing she had asked herself, hundreds of times since.

'Mum?' he prodded. 'Why didn't he just go?'

'I wish I knew, darling. It's just that your father...'

'But don't you always think that? When you're crying?'

She flinched and looked away.

'I don't know, Paul. A lot of times - I wonder what he was thinking, why he stayed. It's what he always did. Your father hated to see people treated unfairly, to see them defenseless. I believe that's what happened.'

'I felt it happen,' Paul whispered. 'I knew.'

'Come off it, how could you? You were asleep.'

'I can mum. The same way I know when you're sad or crying.'

'Paul, please, you can't, that's impossible.'

He looked at her, and held out his hands.

'May I show you?'

She reached out, and took his hands. She felt something warm wash through her, something intensely focused on her. She opened her eyes and saw that Paul was looking right at her.

'This is how it happened,' he said.

With a dizzying rush of air, she found herself standing in Paul's room at night. A different night. He was asleep, in his bed. She watched him for a moment, and then he suddenly sat up, looking at her.

'There's something's happening to him,' he whispered.

The scene switched to a crowded, smoky room. It was the pub to which Ben had gone. Paul was holding her hand, beside her, and looked asleep. She stared around, trying to find Ben. Paul pointed to the door and it opened.

Her husband came in and headed straight to the bar, where a friend was sitting.

'Ben!' his friend exclaimed, 'Finally made it, did you? Here, sit down - first one's on me.'

The bartender placed a Guinness in front of Ben without asking. He nodded his thanks, clinked his glass with his friend and turned around to lean on the bar and survey the room.

'Who're those gits then, Clive?' he asked, pointing at a group of loudmouthed men sitting in one corner.

'Never you mind them,' Clive replied, 'They're leaving, soon I hope. The way I hear it, they got thrown out of the stadium today, and they're in a foul mood.'

They watched as one of the men stood up, stumbled over his chair and lunged toward the bar. He leaned heavily against it, waiting for his next pint, before heading back. He tripped over a bag as he passed by a young couple and then turned, yelling at them.

The couple drew back, trying to ignore him. The bartender started moving toward them just as the rest of the disgruntled men stood up. They headed toward their friend, shouting loudly. The couple rose, trying to leave. They were surrounded by the group.

Ben and Clive put their pints down and walked over to the couple. Ben started gesturing toward their table. His voice was calm. The bartender joined him.

Suddenly one of the men took a swing at Ben. He stepped aside to let it pass. Another smashed him over the head with a chair. He crashed to the floor, unconscious. The fight spread, men standing up, bleeding from blows. In moments the entire pub was awash in the brawl. Amongst the shouting, the punching and the crashing, Ben lay inert. What looked like a pint glass came sailing across the crowd into a lamp, knocking it over. The spilt oil ignited.

As the fire erupted and the crowd began screaming, the scene disappeared. Emma was sitting in Paul's room, no longer holding his hands. Paul was crying.

'Paul, what happened? How did you...'

'I couldn't stay. I couldn't watch. It hurts so much!' he wailed.

She reached out and hugged him. His sobs slowed down, and he settled into his pillow. His eyes closed and he fell asleep. She sat back and looked at him, quite unable to understand what she'd just seen. It had seemed so real, she had felt people rush past her towards the fight, she'd seen Ben go to their defense. Why hadn't she heard what they were saying? Maybe they knew Ben. Maybe there was a reason that they went after that young couple.

She slowly got up, tears running down her cheeks and walked to the door, shutting the light out as she did.

As the darkness fell, Paul shifted in his sleep and looked up at her.

'Don't ever wash his pillow, Mum,' he whispered. 'Will you promise?'

One month later, Emma put the house up for sale and rented a flat near her parents. Paul knew the area well, since he spent lots of time at his grandparent's house. The house sold in a bidding war between three potential buyers and four weeks later, they walked out the door for the final time.

Paul didn't look back as Emma drove them away. The trip was swift and they snaked their way into London past Victoria station to the square where his grandparents lived. They would be staying with them while their belongings were in transit. Paul loved his grandparents' old house, since it had so many interesting things in it, particularly the big attic.

There was a back stairway that ran from the third floor where Paul usually slept, to the attic. The stairs were narrow and had old, worn out wooden treads which creaked.

When he arrived, he gave his grandfather a quick hug and he headed straight up, to be alone. Emma put down her bag and started after him.

'Let him go, dear, it's his favorite place to be. He's perfectly safe.'

'I know,' Emma sighed. 'I used to spend hours there too. It's just that Paul has been acting so strangely lately.'

Her parents looked at each other.

'We've noticed. He seems so *withdrawn*.'

'Ever since Ben died, he doesn't want to play with other children, or even be near them. He says he hears too much, *feels* too much, when he does.'

'What's that supposed to mean?' asked her mother.

'Well, at first I thought he was just being odd, really, as he does go through phases like that. But then, the strangest thing happened one night when I was putting him to bed. He grabbed my hand, and I swear, I thought I was at the pub when Ben died. Paul was there too, and we saw the whole thing.'

'You what?'

'Saw it all. Paul somehow *showed* me what happened. And then... Wait, here he comes. I'll tell you later.'

Someone was running down the stairs and a moment later Paul burst into the room.

'Look what I found!' he shouted, holding a small, colorful box.

'Oh, Paul, you weren't supposed to find that so soon,' laughed his grandmother. 'We were going to give you that as a sort of house warming present. It won't be much of a surprise now, will it?'

'How did you find it?' his grandfather continued. 'We thought it was so well hidden.'

'Well,' Paul replied, looking away. 'I don't know, it just seemed, I guess...'

He broke off and looked around. 'Might I play with it now?'

'Sure,' they both said at once and he turned around and ran up the stairs.

'Well,' said his grandfather, 'that's him settled then. How about a drink?'

Two years later an old man returned to his home, London, to visit Paul. He took his time, enjoying the walk down the edge of the Thames, admiring a view he'd seen countless times over the years. Every time he came back, he noticed the changes that no one else seemed to care about: the water had risen an inch, the banks near the tower had fallen back again and the boats were becoming impossibly congested.

He loved walking here. Large, busy streets lined the shores and people bustled about him. London still seemed as familiar to him now as when he'd first seen it, as a boy, some three hundred and forty years before. This day was bright and warm, in the heart of May and all of London seemed to be outside enjoying what the sun had to offer.

He was known as the Exeter, a name he couldn't remember being given or even who had given it to him. It was a title he'd come to earn, from years of observation and success. He'd grown up in a different London than lay before him now and yet it still called to him, still felt as if this was his home.

Late that afternoon as he wandered away from the river, a sudden movement caught his eye. The city was settling into the long lazy drift towards sunset and children were running home after a game of capture the flag. Paul was amongst them and the Exeter watched as Paul said his good byes and headed home for supper. The Exeter fell in behind him on his walk back home.

Paul could sense someone watching him and kept whirling around to look. Every time he did, the Exeter was nowhere to be seen, vanishing at the first sign of a turn. He asked Paul questions, in a language so old that even the Exeter had no idea what it was or where it came from.

'What is your name?' he whispered.

'Paul.'

'How old are you?'

'I'm ten and a half.'

'Why are you talking to yourself?'

'I'm not, although I can't see you.'

Paul knew the questions were real but he couldn't tell where they were coming from.

'Can you hear me?' the Exeter asked.

'Yes,' said Paul, 'of course I can. Why can't I see you?'

The Exeter didn't speak out loud, instead standing directly behind Paul and smiling.

'What are you laughing at?' asked Paul, spinning around.

The Exeter vanished but kept speaking.

'Have you ever talked to me before?' he asked.

'Maybe,' said Paul. 'And I've talked to others - people just like you.'

'When?' he asked.

'A couple of years ago, at least. It was straight after my father died, after his funeral. Somebody used to talk to me when I was going to sleep. Sometimes I would hear voices when I was playing in the attic.'

The Exeter fell silent, wondering who had visited him. Perhaps the Docent - it would be just like him.

They drew close to Paul's house and the Exeter prepared to leave.

'I have to go now. Perhaps we'll talk again,' he said.

'We will.'

The Exeter snapped to full attention: this was a complicated boy, one who would require close observation before any further contact.

Paul arrived home and climbed the stairs to his house. The Exeter turned away and walked quickly up the street, once again fading as he went. Paul opened his door and then stopped. Concentrating as hard as he could, he tried to sense the person who had spoken to him on the wind. He felt a familiar tingle in the back of his mind and he turned, looking right at the place the Exeter had been. He saw a faint shimmer, nothing more, which faded away under his gaze.

Paul loved playing football and had since he was a young boy. He and his friends played in an intra-mural league in London. Five of them had been together, on the same team, since he was seven and at the age of twelve, five years later, they were one of the tightest lines in the league.

On a late Saturday afternoon, in the north end of the city, they won another match and after the post game celebrations, they headed for the tube and home. They loved to stand as close to edge of the platform as possible, letting the blast of air from the lead carriage buffet them as it shot past.

They clambered onto the train and stood in the opposite doorway, laughing about the game.

'So how did you know?' Sam asked Paul.

'Know what?'

'Well, what they were going to do! Why'd you pull back just then?'

Paul grinned, looking at his friends.

'Ah they always do that. Hadn't you noticed? They burst up and then drop. Every time.'

'So?' Charlie said. 'Lots of teams do that. How'd you see it?'

'It's their halves. They don't keep up,' Paul replied, fidgeting.

'Maybe they're tired. I mean, we're pretty fast, really.'

'No, no - they all fall back - just a bit. That's when I did it.'

His friends nodded, thinking back on the play.

'We won because of that, you know,' Sam said.

Paul looked at the floor.

Across the aisle, seated in the middle of three benches, the Exeter watched the scene play out. *He's perfect* he thought. *He's got them all convinced.*

Paul felt a gnawing sensation in the back of his mind as he talked to Sam and he looked up, toward the old man, before looking away.

Oh no Paul thought, as a feeling of anxiety hit him. *Not again.*

He stiffened, eyeing everyone around him. His friends were still talking about the game, and as the conversation died down, Paul watched his friend Cedric move back, distracted by something to his right.

Cedric leaned away toward a group of people who looked like tourists. He stood still and then slowly reached down, into a women's handbag and removed her wallet. He stashed it in his jacket and walked back to his friends.

'Excuse me!' said a man in a loose, brown suit. 'Young man!'

He grabbed Cedric and reached for the wallet.

'What do you think you're doing?'

Cedric froze and Paul could see the color rising on his face. His friends stepped back, trying to crush themselves against the carriage doors.

'I said, what are you doing?'

The man held the wallet up in Cedric's face and the owner caught sight of it.

'Hey!' she yelled. 'Where'd you get that?'

'From this one's jacket' he replied. 'He's just pinched it!'

The old man watched Paul breathe in sharply and step forward. He put his hand on the man with the wallet.

'Did you collect the change too?' he asked.

'What?' the man said, turning to him.

Paul brushed Cedric with his hand, pointing toward the opposite door.

'When it fell out of her bag - I'm sure I saw some coins roll away.'

The man looked toward the door.

'No, I'm - I guess I missed that. Thanks.' he said.

The woman took the wallet and they both stooped down looking for the change. Paul went over to the rest of his friends and asked them to help search. After several minutes, no one had found anything and slowly stood up.

'Must have been mistaken,' Paul said.

'Well, no matter,' the man replied, turning back to the woman. 'Anything else fall out?'

'No, thanks,' she said, returning to her friends.

The train pulled in to the next stop and the old man watched Paul and Sam get off. When the doors whisked closed and the train lurched forward, he felt an involuntary shudder travel through him.

Paul and Sam tromped up the stairs from the tube to the foyer of Victoria station, beyond which lay the train bays. They walked out into the outside air and waited for the signal to cross.

'What's wrong?' Sam asked.

'I dunno,' Paul groused. 'Nothing.'

'Leave it alone,' Sam said. 'I already know.'

'Know what?' Paul said, looking up in alarm.

'Your Dad - it was four years ago today, wasn't it?'

Paul sat reading by himself in his room. He got up and began poking around a set of shelves. He stopped, noticing that the things on his desk weren't quite where they'd been left. He walked over to it wondering if his mother had been snooping again.

He opened it, looked in and frowned at its contents. Sitting on top of his papers was an old envelope, frayed around the edges, with his name written across the front.

He picked it up and it felt as if it had been left in the sun. He turned it over, looking for clues. On the back, he found a seal made of thick purple wax.

He slit it open and read it.

Twice.

The contents didn't make sense.

Dear Mr. Green:

We have been watching you for some time, and are now convinced that you are ready to help us. On the evening of the 2nd of November, go to the square outside your grandparent's house. You will find a bonfire burning there. At precisely 9:30 PM, step into it.

We look forward to meeting you.

It was the strangest letter Paul had ever seen. He read it again, shocked that someone would ask him to go near a fire. He tossed it back on his desk and wandered away, thinking about his father.

The Exeter decided after Paul hadn't looked at the letter for a week to visit him once more. He spoke to him softly that evening as Paul was falling asleep.

'Did you read it?'

Paul turned over, startled at the voice.

'Who's there?'

'We've spoken before. Over two years ago after a game of capture the flag.'

'Where are you?' Paul asked, sitting up and looking around.

'Nowhere that you can see me. I noticed that you're quite good at football.'

Paul kept turning his head trying to find the speaker.

'I just play, like all the others.'

'No, Paul, you don't,' said the Exeter. 'You listen to others, you know what they're feeling, what they want to do. You know it, and you act on it.'

Paul smiled.

'Who are you?' he demanded.

'The person who left you the letter. Read it again Paul. It's not a prank. We really do want to meet you.'

Paul felt a cold breeze brush past him and then the room fell silent.

When he woke up the next morning he went over to his desk, grabbed the letter and re-read it. The words were just as frightening as they had been the first time and the letter still felt warm.

Paul sat at his desk debating whether or not to say anything to his mother or his grandparents. They wouldn't understand it, he thought, they'd just tell him someone, probably Sam, was playing a bad joke on him. He tucked it into his book bag and went downstairs to breakfast.

As October drew to a close, Paul's anxiety built. He was walking to school, thinking about the letter and its impossible request.

'No one will notice.'

Paul didn't even flinch.

'I wondered when you'd be back. You know it's too dangerous for me to go.'

'Not everything is as it seems, Paul. I'd have thought you knew that by now.'

'But how am I going to manage it?'

'You'll find a way. You know you can - you can convince people of almost anything.'

'I didn't mean that - the letter told me to step into a fire!'

'Did it? Well, just remember what I said - not everything is as it seems - look right through it.'

As he sat in his room, doing his schoolwork, his mind kept drifting to the letter, to the bonfire. The wind-voice had put curiosity above his fear and he knew he was going to go.

On the night of November 2nd, he watched a movie by himself on the television and then went to bed. After the house was silent and dark he snuck out of his room and down the stairs.

He put on his coat, slipped the letter into his pocket and gingerly opened the door. He pulled it shut and walked down the short flight of stairs to the street. It was cool out, so he gathered the coat around him, setting off for his grandparent's square.

As he walked, a woman came rushing around the corner. He slipped behind a parked car before she could say anything, hiding in silence. She looked around, startled by the near collision, and then by his sudden disappearance.

When she finally moved on, Paul set off again, looking at his watch. Nine-twenty - he had ten minutes to go. The square was just ahead on the other side of the street. He stood between two parked cars and waited until there was no traffic. He darted across the street and into the square.

He immediately saw the fire. It was huge, burning right in the middle of the clearing. Sparks shot from five-foot flames and the wood crackled loudly. A couple walked across the square right past the fire and didn't seem to notice it.

Paul walked slowly over and stood ten feet away from it quaking with fear. The heat was overwhelming and he held his arm up to shield his face from the inferno. He fished the letter out and re-read it. He glanced toward his grandparent's house. Then back. He closed his eyes and stuffed the letter back in his pocket.

C'mon then he thought.

As he stepped into the flames, he opened his eyes and was astonished by the sight. The fire and the square had vanished, all of London, with its cold wind, dark shadows and noisy cars, had gone. In its place there were some distant mountains, snow-capped, with a river running from them. It wound its way past the spot where he was standing towards what looked like a small stage, surrounded by stone seats. Paul started walking over to it and noticed that he wasn't alone.

Walking quickly, her arms wrapped tightly around her shoulders, was a red-haired girl in blue flannel pajamas.

Chapter 4

The Beginning

When they were born, her parents rejoiced. Twins! They shouted with joy. Canace was born second, and rushed after her sister from the moment she could walk. That they survived their birth was a miracle, but what followed was legend, and though the story was lost through the ages, Canace knew its discovery was near.

As soon as she jumped Jenny closed her eyes and screamed, waiting for the horrible impact. She was sure the drop to the ground would be swift but when she didn't hit, she started doubting herself. She wasn't falling. There was no rushing air, nor were any branches scratching her as she fell through them.

How can this be? she thought. *What's happened, where am I going?*

The tight grip that had held her when she jumped released her and she opened her eyes. Banff had vanished, the mountains had disappeared and she stood in an unfamiliar grass field. The air was cool and without her blanket she started to shiver.

'But I'm not hurt,' she whispered out loud. 'I'm ok and I jumped out of a tree. I must be nuts.'

In the distance, she saw a campfire and a small stage nearby. She set out for it, shivering and noticed a tall, curly haired boy heading there as well. She broke in to a run heading straight for him.

'Hey!' she said. 'Do you know where we are? I mean, what just happened? Where *are* we?'

'I've no idea,' he replied. 'I've never seen anything like it.'

He looked at her, and saw her shaking.

'Here,' he said, taking his coat off and wrapping it around her. 'You look half frozen.'

'Thanks,' she replied, wrapping the coat around herself.

'All right now, then?' he asked.

'Warmer, yeah,' she said, 'but where are we?'

'It looks like the high country, perhaps northern Scotland?'

'*Scotland?*' Jenny said, 'How could that be?'

'Well, I mean, it looks like it.'

He paused.

'How could it be? I don't know. One moment, I'm standing in front of my grandparent's house, and then this...'

Jenny concentrated on him, listening to what he wasn't saying.

'I jumped out of a tree,' she said matter-of-factly. 'And landed here. And you, that fire, wow, I don't...'

'How could you know that?' he exclaimed.

'Oh no. I'm sorry, I just thought, you know,' Jenny said, trailing off and looking toward the bonfire.

'Maybe we should go that way,' she whispered, gesturing with her head.

'Yeah, sure,' he said.

They walked in silence for a few minutes.

'I'm Paul, by the way. Paul Green.'

'Jenny Greyson,' she replied.

'From America?' he asked. 'Your accent...'

'Canada. Banff, actually. You?'

'London.'

'Really? Wow! Isn't it humongous?'

'Yeah, I guess. Bigger than ... Banff, did you say?'

Jenny laughed.

'Only by a few million. Banff's tiny. Never heard of it?'

They arrived where the fire burned, to the left of a small stage. Row upon row of stone seats rose in front, curving gently to each side. The sky was as dark as when they'd left their homes, and they drew near the fire's warmth.

Paul crouched down and stared into it, frowning.

'Is something wrong?' Jenny asked.

'What?' he said looking up at her. 'No, no, not with the fire. - But have a look at the stones around it.'

The fire was set in a ring of stones. The stones where placed evenly apart, all the way around and were all rectangular. A second set of rectangular rocks lay across them, forming a perfect ring around the flames.

'What about them?'

'They look so familiar. I just can't figure out why.'

Jenny concentrated on him, trying to figure out what he meant.

'Maybe you've seen a fireplace like this before,' she said.

He sat back and stared at the flames.

'This isn't safe.'

Jenny looked at it, letting the heat warm her up.

'Safe?' she finally said. 'It looks ok to me.'

'I don't think so,' he replied. 'I can't believe someone would leave a fire like this unattended. Too dangerous. They'll be along shortly, and then we'll get some answers.'

'I hope you're right,' she sighed. 'The weird thing is, I can't feel anyone else.'

Paul turned and stared at her.

'What do you mean?'

'You know what I mean. You're the same. Isn't that why we're here?'

'I don't know why we're here. You can feel people too?'

'Yeah,' she nodded. 'All the time. More than I'd like.'

'Wow. I thought I was the only one.'

'Me too,' she said, watching the fire's light. 'Guess not, huh?'

They sat in silence, staring into its depths, where the embers lay glowing. The flames licked along the surface of the logs but the wood itself didn't burn.

'Hey' Jenny said, tilting her head to look at him.

'Yes?'

'Any idea how to get home?'

'How do you mean?'

'Well, we were told how to get here, right? But not how to go back.'

Paul shuddered and looked back at the fire.

'I don't know, really,' he said.

Jenny got up and walked over to the first row of seats. She sat down on the rock chair closest to the fire. It was surprisingly soft for rock and fit her well. She looked over at Paul trying to get a better sense of him.

He was completely blank.

Paul was doing the same thing with the same problem: he couldn't sense her feelings, or even her mood. He could feel an extraordinary power emanating from her. If he wasn't looking at her, he would never have guessed she was a young, redheaded girl.

She felt like a king or an emperor and Paul thought there was something else, something hidden within her that seemed truly ancient.

He gave up and stared back into the fire. The instant he did, Jenny breathed in sharply.

'How did you do that?' she asked.

'Do what?'

'Um, it's a little hard to explain. You know what we were talking about earlier?'

'You mean how we can feel other people near by?'

'Yeah,' she replied. 'Well, I couldn't sense you at all just now. It's like you weren't there. And then you were again. How did you do that?'

Paul smiled. 'I stopped trying to read you.'

'That's all?'

'Pretty much. It was weird though. Usually I can tell what someone is feeling, what mood they're in. With you, I couldn't tell at all.'

'So it was the same for you as it was for me - just a blank wall?'

'Sort of. I don't know how to describe it - you weren't blank, but you weren't, well, normal.'

'Tell me about it!' she laughed. 'No one thinks I'm normal, especially since I make mistakes all the time, telling people things I shouldn't know. Do you?'

'I don't think so - I try not to do much with it,' said Paul.

'Really? I can't stop.'

Paul hunched over, looking at her, before replying.

'No, it's true. I don't use it. People tend to ... react when I do.'

'Like when you showed your mother that fire in the pub?'

Paul's mouth dropped open and he stared hard at her.

'See what I mean?' she continued. 'It happens to me all the time. I know stuff people would never tell me.'

'Hey, wait a minute,' he said, sitting back and glaring at her. 'Like what?'

'Like how you feel about your father - I know when he died you were mad at him, and you feel guilty because he knew that - about missing the Karate trial?'

Paul's head fell and he stared at the earth in front of him. How did she know? He'd never told anyone, not even his mother, how he felt when his father left that day. He remembered fighting with him about it, begging him to stay and fly up for his meeting the next morning but he'd never told another soul.

'How could you know that?' he whispered.

'I don't know, it's like I can see the scene, just the way you could. I know how he died - doing what he always did, trying to help others.'

A long moment of silence hung between them. Paul could tell, just hearing her speak the words and remembering that horrible night, that she really knew what he'd been through - that she had read his mind and memory.

'I've just always been able to sort things out that I see, or hear, or even feel about other people,' she said in a hushed voice. 'It's frightening sometimes, and it makes me very lonely. Most people get angry when I start talking to them about something they never told me, secret stuff about ...'

She stopped talking in mid sentence and stared at the stage. It had started to glow an eerie blue and the trees behind it seemed to slip together into a tight curtain. Paul sat down on one of the chairs and watched with her.

The blue glow kept pulsing and the curtain of trees swayed in the wind. Faint music wafted towards them, carried through the brush and voices started to chant, growing louder and more frantic. The smoke from the fire started to twirl and dance towards the stage, gathering itself together.

The voices were repeating a word, or a phrase over and over again. It sounded like a hissing, long whisper - 'XXXXTRRRR, XXXXTRRR'. A loud rumble started from deep beneath them, coming straight up. The smoke grew dense and formed a twisting cloud, whirling around a shape.

Everything stopped.

The smoke, the music, the voices, even the fire, disappeared. The stage sat bathed in a warm yellow light, like sunlight and in the middle of the stage a strange man stared back at them. His was a craggy, wizened face with tufts of white hair sprouting above it. He had bright green eyes and a billowing black cloak wrapped around him, under which they could see a dark blue robe. As soon as he saw them, he smiled and practically ran off the stage toward them.

'Wonderful to finally see you both together!' he beamed. 'I've been waiting years for this moment!'

Jenny sat frozen by his sudden appearance.

'Who are you?' Paul asked. 'Did you bring us here?'

'In a fashion, yes, I did.'

'Can you take us home again?'

'Again, in a fashion, yes I could.'

He paused, a smile on his face and his eyes twinkled as he looked from Paul to Jenny.

'But I won't.'

Jenny's eyes widened.

'Why?' she whispered. 'I think maybe I should go back.'

51

'I have a proposal,' the old man said, sitting down on the edge of the stage. 'You hear me out, and then decide what to do. After all, you're here, aren't you? Pretty weird way of getting somewhere, don't you think?'

Jenny cocked her head and stared at him.

'You're one of the guides, aren't you?' she asked.

He laughed, a deep, rolling laugh that shook his whole body.

'No, Jenny, I'm not. And you're letting that talented mind of yours get into things it shouldn't - again.'

He stood up, walked back over to them and held his hand out.

'Let me tell you why you're here. *How* you got here I'll explain later, once you're ready and have been introduced to the others.'

'Is Midori here?' Jenny asked. 'She said she knew what was happening.'

The old man looked at her and she felt a tingle in the back of her head.

'Midori?' he replied. 'Not anyone I know, I'm afraid. Now what's next? Ah yes, the letters...'

'Did you write them?' Paul asked.

'Technically no, Mr. Green, I didn't write them. I'm not sure who did. But I did place them where only you would find them. That you were able to read and follow them is much more interesting, don't you think?'

'I don't understand,' Jenny said, glancing at Paul. 'They were just letters.'

'Did you bring them with you?' the old man replied.

Paul pointed at his left coat pocket, in which Jenny found his letter. She pulled it out and scanned it.

'Hey!' she said. 'This is the same as mine. I thought you were told to step into a fire!'

'I was,' he said, taking the letter from her and reading it with a frown. 'See?'

'They are both the same,' the old man chuckled. 'You just read them as you want to - it's part of the test to see who gets here and who doesn't - as well as what frightens you.'

'Frightens?' Jenny asked, puzzled.

'Absolutely. I understand that Paul hates fires and you, despite living in the mountains, are afraid of heights.'

'But my friends and I climb that tree a lot.'

'Ever done it by yourself?'

Jenny shuddered.

'No,' she whispered, at which the old man just smiled before asking Paul to bring him the letter. He had the two of them gather round him to read it together:

'You are cordially invited to join us on November the 2nd, at 9:30, at the Gathering Common, to begin your journey. The Common is easily found by approaching the infinite fire. Follow your best judgment out of your home, and take the first leap of faith you find. You will begin your journey once you've arrived. Once you've met each other, ask the Exeter what to do.'

'Are you the Exeter?' Jenny asked.

'That's my title - what they call me when they forget my name. Which happens more often than I'd like.'

'So what's your name? So we don't forget,' she continued.

'It's rather long, and, if you don't mind my saying it, not something you're ready for. I think, for now, that you should call me Ornolt - that's the first part of my name, and the only part that's easy to say out loud.'

Ornolt stood up and took the letter over to where the fire had been. 'You're not supposed to keep the letters, of course. Now, Jenny, you dropped yours, when you jumped, so I picked it up after you left.'

From beneath his cloak he fished out her letter and put it on top of Paul's. He placed them both in the fire's ashes and stood back. The letters twisted themselves into tubes, and began to expand, growing longer and getting a rough surface. They stacked themselves and changed back into wood and, just as they looked like perfectly ordinary logs, burst into flame. The fire looked exactly as it had when they'd first arrived.

A gust of wind blew across the plain, fanning the flames of the fire. The moon had risen high above them and Ornolt hadn't stopped talking.

He told them that he belonged to a group of people who shared a common bond - not of blood relation but of their sense of what surrounds them and by the way in which they shared their experiences. He called them his ordered family, with names that couldn't be pronounced who had been drawn together for centuries. He told the children to think of members of this order as distant relatives, cousins they had not yet met.

'The order found me in the exact same way it found you,' he continued. 'With letters sent from the infinite fire. I found mine under my bed and it took me a whole day to figure out what it said.'

'So why does it send letters to people?' Paul asked. 'Why don't you just come and introduce yourselves?'

'Because that would be too easy. You have to overcome something to get here, a fear that to any normal person would be very real and insurmountable but which to you is an illusion. Take me, for example. I couldn't read, so the letter would normally be impossible to decipher. But I badly wanted to change my life and I knew, if I stared at it long enough, I could read it. And that's exactly what happened.'

'What did it tell you to do?'

'I'd rather not say, to be honest. It still frightens me.'

'Wow,' Jenny whispered. 'Worse than jumping out of a tree?'

'Or into a fire?' added Paul.

'To me, yes, far worse. But as you can see, I made it. And now, as the Exeter, I get to help choose new recruits. Like you two.'

'How did you do that?' Paul continued.

'Well, you've already noticed that there's something special about both of you. That something calls to us - we're drawn to it as iron is to a magnet. My job is to decide not only who belongs with us, but who should come with whom. It took me years to match you two up.'

'Match us?' Jenny whispered. 'What's that mean?'

'Hopefully you'll soon find out. And trust me, it's a good thing. I'm skilled at what I do - I can tell what I need to know when a child is not much more than four years old. That's what makes me the Exeter - I can sense people's qualities right away.'

He noticed Jenny concentrating on him.

'Miss Greyson, there's something else I can do that you may find troublesome. When I want, I can shut my mind off to everyone and everything. No one in the order can read me, especially newly arrived, precocious girls who have always been able to know things about people.'

'Do you mean me?' she asked.

'Quite so.'

Jenny smiled.

'You were born over three hundred and forty years ago, in London, England,' she said. 'Your parents died when you were ten, defending you - people wanted to kill you, said you were an - abomination - what's that? Anyway, you joined the order shortly after that.'

Ornolt leapt up, open mouthed and stared at her. He walked away and stood alone, muttering to himself. When he finally returned, his smile had returned.

'I've just been told to be very careful with you, Jenny. No one has ever done that. Now then, where was I?'

He scratched his head and sat down again.

'Ah yes. The Exeter asks questions of people, and, from their responses, decides if they have any potential, whether they're honest, and whether they're lonely enough. That's what I do, and I've talked to both of you over the years.'

'You're one of the voices, aren't you?' Paul exclaimed, leaning forward. 'The wind voices that I could hear but never see?'

'Not at first - I didn't start talking to you until you were ten. You're one of the few, Paul, in all my years of observing, who's been aware of me. I was so fascinated by that that I came back many times to check on you. Others of the order came as well; some before me. You thought, I think, that we were ghosts, didn't you?'

'At my grandparent's house - you used to tell me what to do, where to find things. Why did you do that?'

'Well, we didn't really,' Ornolt said. 'You just were so good at sensing other people that you heard us talking. Later on, if you survive the adventures that lie ahead, you'll find that people in our order tend to talk about things in a jumbled way, talking about things as if they've happened just before they do.'

Paul eyes widened, but he said nothing.

'Are you saying,' Jenny asked, 'that those pale children, like Midori, are from the order as well?'

'Is that who she is?' Ornolt said after a long pause. 'I'm afraid we don't know exactly who they are, it's very troubling, and makes it even more important that you understand why you're here, and why you must do what's ahead of you. It's the only way you'll ever get home, but more importantly it's the only way to us, to the order.'

She could tell he was disturbed by her pale companions, a reaction that surprised and frightened her.

'What do we have to do?' she asked nervously. 'To get home, I mean.'

'You have to find your amulets, and bind with them if you can - when you do, the journey will begin,' Ornolt answered.

'Amulets? What journey?' Paul asked.

'You will find out about the amulets soon enough. I hope I have made the right choice with you two. If I have, your fate will be completely in your hands.'

'Our fate?' Jenny said, 'Does that mean we might not make it?'

'Absolutely it does,' Ornolt replied. 'But I have a good sense about these things. I think you'll probably be fine - you'll get through.'

He paused and looked at the brightening sky before returning his gaze to them.

'There's something else you should know. We can help you two, more than anyone else in the world possibly could. We're just like you and know exactly what you've been through. If you make this journey, if you succeed, you will discover a joy, a way of living unlike anything you've ever experienced.'

Smiles crept across their faces.

'You'll learn more about the order soon enough, and meet many more of us as your journey progresses. I'll let them speak for themselves, and instead tell you more about how you got here - how we found you.

'The gift you have is something we all share, and, as you will find out very soon, we have a way of traveling to times and places where that gift exists.'

He paused, looking at Jenny.

'Is something wrong?'

'I don't know,' she replied, glancing around the common. 'Can you tell us where we are? I have a very strange feeling that we're not anywhere real at the moment - that you, this fire, everything around me is just a dream.'

'It's very real, Jennifer, and you'd better get used to thinking that. Most people have no idea how to get here, but believe me, if I threw a rock at you, it would hurt. If Paul went and jumped in *that* fire, he'd get burnt. It's important that you know that. You can't ever let your guard down, here, or anywhere else. You might get caught, or worse, killed.'

'Killed!' she exclaimed. 'By what?'

'All manner of things,' Ornolt grumbled. 'That's something else you'll find out about your gift, about the amulets - you will become aware of many new and dangerous things.'

'Then shouldn't we just go back?' she said. 'Before it's too late?'

'It already is too late,' he replied. 'Especially for you.'

He turned away and stared at the fire before continuing.

'I know this is hard for you to accept right now. I mean, that letter sounds like gibberish, doesn't it? And my rambling must sound frightening. But you'll see, soon enough, that there are places that people like you know how to get to, when you put your minds to it. You're a special person and so is Paul. It's time you learned what that means and how the order can help you.'

It was well into the morning and as the air warmed under the rising sun, they could see more of where they were. In the distance, the mountains swallowed the eastern sky. They were jagged, with snow-capped peaks and from where the Common sat, there was no way through them. The river that ran past was fed from the mountains and flowed to the southwest. They could just make out the signs of a settlement in the distance.

Ornolt fell silent, to give them time to think about what they'd heard so far. Jenny tried to read more from him. He was a great judge of character and could tell almost immediately if a child had the gift. He had been watching her for years, waiting for the right moment to invite her. She knew that the order was ancient, that it had seen many, many generations grow up to influence the world and that it patiently picked those who could join. She found no hint at all of why the order existed, or when it had started and she wondered if Ornolt just didn't know.

'Ok guys,' Ornolt finally said, 'I think we'd better get going. We've got a long day ahead of us, and we didn't get any sleep. Of course you could probably manage without it but when you get to be my age, sleep is an important part of the day.'

He stood up and stomped his feet, as if to shake out cobwebs.

'It's been awhile since I had to walk anywhere. Wonder if my feet still know how to do it?'

He winked at them and walked over to the stone-ringed fire.

'Well come on then,' he said when they didn't follow him. 'We've got to find your amulets as soon as possible. That can be tricky, you know.'

As they stood up they felt an enveloping warmth and looked at each other. The clothes that they had worn were changing to much sturdier, more comfortable garments: Tall black-leather hiking boots, grey slacks and shirts, and warm wrap-around black cloaks just like Ornolt's. Slung low over their shoulders was a small carry-sack.

Jenny looked at Paul and stifled a scream. Apart from his skin, which looked quite normal and flush with color, he was dressed exactly like Midori and the pale boy she'd seen at the park.

Ornolt smiled, unaware of Jenny's revelation and raised his hand up in front of his face. He blew softly on it and reached into the fire, rummaging around in the coals. When he pulled his hand out, he had two sturdy walking sticks, one for each of them.

'Here you go,' he said. 'These are going to become like a third leg. If you ever feel tired, lean on these, and they'll lend you the strength that bore them. They're not bad in a fight either!'

He handed the sticks to them and set off at a brisk pace down the path that led away from the common.

The terrain was rough but with their new boots and hiking sticks, they kept a steady pace. Ornolt's features were smoothening and softening and as he marched ahead of them, he looked no more than fifty years old.

Whenever they looked down at the stream, it was empty, like a dark swimming pool. It was strange that a place with as much natural beauty as this would have such a sterile stream. It should have rocks, Jenny thought and sticks and lilies - even fish. Suddenly they appeared, emerging from under small leaves or around rocks that sprang up from nowhere. The water was perfectly clear and looked cold. When her eyes followed its course back towards the mountains, it was the color of a summer sky, a color she remembered from streams and lakes around her hometown in the Rocky Mountains.

She thought again about Midori and the boy in the sandbox. Why was she dressed like them? What could it mean? Was she going to become one of them, colorless, alone, not knowing where she was from? Or was the order meant to stop that fate? Were the pale children still on their journeys unable to find their way home? She shuddered again looking back toward the mountains.

She remembered a place she had gone as a young girl that had a tall waterfall which sent incredible blasts of mist into its bay. As she glanced back at the river, thinking about that mist, a heavy fog rolled in from the woods to the north.

'Jennifer, do be more careful!' exclaimed Ornolt.

She had no idea what he meant and shot a questioning look at Paul.

He shrugged at her and fell back into the rhythm of the walk. He'd been hiking since he was a young boy and really liked his new boots and clothing. When they'd started, the air was cold and crisp and the cloaks had warmed them against it. After they had been walking for a while and begun to heat up, Paul felt the cloak lighten, hanging loosely off his back like it was made of silk.

He was so caught up in the hike that he didn't notice the mist and almost walked right into Jenny.

'Where did this come from?' he asked.

'A good question' said Ornolt. 'It isn't often that fog would come in on a morning like this. There's not much of it either.'

'I was just thinking about the time I used to spend in the Rocky Mountains,' Jenny said. 'I used to see a mist there, near the waterfalls that was just like this. It's strange, the way it came in right then.'

Ornolt remained silent.

'Well, it's gone, as fast as it came,' said Paul. 'It's like that quite often in the countryside really. You'll be walking along, cursing the stuff, wishing it was gone, and then, poof, it vanishes. Happens all the time.'

'More often, I'd imagine, than you think,' said Ornolt.

They continued on, slowing to step over fallen trees or to dodge around large boulders in the path. The sun was climbing steadily in the sky and the wind had disappeared. Even though they'd been walking for hours, the settlement remained firmly planted in the distance.

Ornolt slowed and then turned to face them.

'This is going to be a little harder than I thought. It's one of the problems with these paths - they never know when to stop. We're going to have to rest here for a moment and then we'll have to leave the path behind.'

'Why would we do that?' said Paul. 'We'll get lost or end up walking in circles!'

'That,' said Ornolt, 'would be a great deal more progress then we've made so far.'

He looked at each of them and they heard him ask a question even though he didn't open his mouth.

'Why have we stopped? Why is the path the same? *Where are you going?*'

His voice came from all around them and they huddled closer together. They thought about what he'd asked, particularly about the path. How could it be the same path? They'd been walking for hours and the Common was nowhere to be seen.

Ornolt was just looking at them and they kept hearing the question echoing all around them: '*Where are you going?*'

'I think we should go there - to that settlement,' Paul said, pointing off into the distance. 'We need somewhere to sleep tonight and we don't have any tents or sleeping bags or anything.'

'There is no settlement,' Jenny whispered. 'There's nothing there. We have to keep going, don't we?'

Ornolt's face burst into a radiant smile. 'You see it, don't you Jenny. It's right on the tip of your tongue. I can't tell you what it is but I can help you see it. Look again!'

She looked back towards the settlement. It was still there, shimmering in the heat built up from the sun. Then it started to fade. The more she stared, the more it disappeared.

'What do you see?' asked Paul. He looked and saw only the same distant image - what looked like a gate and a few small huts on the bank of the river.

'Nothing. It's gone,' said Jenny.

'What?' he exclaimed. 'It has not! It's gotten bigger! I can see docks and boats going into it and a market in the middle, with hundreds of people milling about...'

He stopped as the image started to wobble. Jenny was looking at him, her eyes boring into him. He had a sense of unease and felt that same cold power simmering about her. He shuddered and turned away, looking back at the mountains.

'What do you see?' asked Ornolt.

'Nothing,' Paul replied. 'It just vanished.'

'No,' said Jenny. 'It never was there. It wasn't real.'

Chapter 5

Of Amulets, Guides and Gates

When they had passed their twentieth year, Canace and her sister wandered through the north, through the bitter wind, and across the straits to the new world. It was harsh, and cold, and they struggled for warmth, for life. They were drawn to a land of mountains and lakes, and there, in the comfort of the cave-peak, they slept for two years, where for them, time remained still.

'Do you understand yet?' Ornolt asked.

'Understand?' Paul asked.

'What just happened. You did see a village, right?'

They both nodded.

'So where is it? What happened to it?'

'It didn't feel real,' Jenny answered. 'It's like this whole place is made up. The rocks, the fish in the stream, all of it.'

'Very close,' Ornolt said. 'Once you find your amulets, you'll understand.'

'What are amulets?' Paul asked.

'They are going to become the most important thing you have, if they choose you.'

The sky above them started to fade and the deep blue color washed away, turning whiter and whiter.

'Go that way,' Ornolt said, pointing toward the forest that ran back from the river.

The trees were thick - pine and oak - and ancient. The trunks looked ragged, like they'd been blasted by a sand storm - large swaths of their bark were missing or ruptured. The canopy above was a mix of needles and leaves, woven tightly together, preventing the sun's light from hitting the forest floor.

When they took a step toward the trees, the children noticed a change right away. The trees, like the sky, were fading away, first losing their color, the canopy turning gray. Then their trunks started to blur - they could no longer see specific trees and the whole forest began to melt away.

'What's happening?' Jenny cried, turning back toward Ornolt.

He stood with his arms crossed, staring at the forest.

'Nothing yet,' he replied, 'although you may be having trouble seeing it that way. This is the first real challenge - to find your amulets. Look at each other.'

Jenny's face and hair were losing all color and slowly disappearing, as was the ground beneath them. She looked at Paul and could barely tell where he was.

'Ornolt, help!' she said, 'I can't see!'

'That should not matter,' he said. 'Find your amulets without your eyes. Or your ears, or your nose. Prove yourselves. Use that part of you that let us find you in the first place.'

'Now go. Work together and find them.'

'But what if we can't?' she asked. 'What happens if we don't?'

'Then you fail.'

The image of Ornolt faded away and the children were left in silence. Jenny looked at Paul and could barely see him. She walked over to where she thought he was.

'Can you still hear me?' she said.

'Barely,' she thought she heard.

'Ok - listen, I can still feel your presence - can you feel mine?'

'Yeah.'

'And I can still hear your thoughts. You'll have to lead. I'll listen to you and follow.'

There was no reply and she realized with a jolt that she couldn't see anything - the world had gone a unified white.

'PAUL!' she screamed.

She heard nothing. She breathed slowly, willing herself to be calm and started searching for him. In a few moments she found him, already moving. She walked toward him, concentrating on his presence and began to hear him.

I think we should go toward the trees.

He turned to where he thought they were and headed that way. She followed him, holding her hands out in front of her. They walked for several paces before Paul abruptly stopped. Jenny walked right into him - she thought.

I've just hit a tree - I guess they're still here. I hope you are.

He hadn't felt her collide with him.

They're controlling this she thought to herself. *We can feel some things but not others.*

Jenny, let's go into the trees. Put your hands on them. Follow me. We'll pick our way through.

He moved off to her left. She gingerly followed him, grasping for trees as she went. They moved slowly for several minutes, stopping momentarily and searching the ground with their hands. They felt nothing - no needles, no soil - the ground didn't exist.

Paul moved away and Jenny concentrated on him again. She had trouble finding him - it was as if his presence was spreading out.

Jenny, if you're there, something's weird. I can feel something else. Can you?

She cast her mind about and found what he meant. Far ahead of them and moving. It was coming rapidly toward them. She turned toward it and stared into the blanket of white.

Then she felt a shaking sensation in the ground and heard a rushing wind - where was it? In the whiteness that surrounded them, a dot appeared, growing bigger as the noise increased.

She thought she could see the outlines of trees as the dot came toward them.

I think we better hide!

Paul's thoughts were panicked. He must have seen this as well. She tried to answer but before she could, the image changed again. It looked like a large, molten rock was hurtling toward them and they saw it leave burning holes in the trees that appeared in its path.

Jenny, run!

No! she thought *No, Paul this must be it.*

He hadn't moved and she could still feel his presence. She lifted her arm and pointed at the rock, which had shrunk in size and looked like it was about to slam in to her. When she thought it was no more than two feet from her face, she held up her other hand and shouted 'STOP'

Immediately it did and with a rush of sound and energy, the world reappeared. They were standing in deep woods on a slight slope. The rock continued to hover in front of Jenny and Paul looked at her in amazement.

'Can you hear me?' he said.

'Yes!' she exclaimed. 'Do you think we've found the right thing?'

'Indeed you have, Jenny,' Ornolt said, stepping out from behind a tree. 'Well done.'

He reached out for the rock, which had shrunk to the size of a grapefruit. He turned it over and over, examining its surface.

'Ah,' he said, 'here we are.'

He placed the rock on the ground and stomped on it. It shattered as if it were made of glass and vanished. In its place lay two gold necklaces with blue ornaments on the end. The ornaments were held to the necklace by fine gold bands on which a stream of engravings had been etched.

The Exeter frowned and bent over, staring at the blue ornaments. He scratched his head and sat back.

'Is something wrong?' Paul asked.

'I'm not sure,' Ornolt replied. 'They are amulets, certainly, but they feel different, older somehow.'

'I don't understand.'

'No, I'm sure you don't. These are the first amulets you've seen, after all. And they're here, which must mean they're for you. Here, let's just check something.'

He picked up a stick from the ground and poked it toward the necklaces. As soon as he did the stick burst into flame.

'Well, that's certainly right,' he said. 'So let's see. Each of you, pick one up.'

'But surely we'll get burnt?' Paul asked.

'No, no - I'm certain you won't. Now, quickly please. They won't wait very long.'

The children bent down and reached toward them. They felt no pain even when they wrapped their fingers around the ornaments. They stood back up, holding them out toward Ornolt.

'Those are your amulets. They are identical to each other, a unit. They know when they are near each other, need to be near each other. Just as you do. Take these amulets, place them around your necks, and bind with them.'

The children did as he asked and placed them around their necks. Immediately the amulets started to glow, a soft blue light under the gold bands and they felt a great feeling of relief, of happiness, wash over them. All around them there was a soft light moving through the trees and into each amulet.

The Exeter let out a deep sigh and stepped toward them, placing a hand on each of their shoulders.

'Never forget this,' he murmured. 'Even in your darkest moments, the amulets, and what they hold, will give you all the strength you need, just as long as you let them.'

He stepped back and they looked at each other. Paul felt the tension in Jenny evaporate. She no longer seemed to be a distant power but rather a companion, a channel for what he felt. Jenny felt herself relax, accepting that Paul was far more aware of others than she. The bond that they shared through the amulets was tighter than anything they'd felt before. It was a beginning, a new life where they knew the experiences of the world would make sense, where the unexplainable differences could finally be shared.

The Exeter turned and walked away. They followed him, tucking their amulets under their cloaks as they did.

'Did you feel that?' the old man asked.

He stood at the edge of the stage of the common staring at the woman next to him.

'Yes I did. Like a cold breath, wasn't it?'

'Indeed. Those two amulets look different - I just can't place how.'

They looked back at the stage, watching Jenny's amulet as she put it on.

'Look at the glow - it's brighter somehow.'

'And the trees - look at that!' the old man exclaimed.

The forest through which the children had come was healing - the bark of the trees, damaged by centuries of amulet arrivals, was smoothing over and the canopy above was growing lush. The burn marks disappeared and the holes in the trees filled. The two figures watched, fascinated, as all signs of the amulet's passing vanished.

'Something new, I'd say,' the old man murmured.

'Maybe,' she agreed. 'But we better be careful. Let's gather more people for the observation of their first steps. I'd like more eyes on this.'

As they were marching through the forest, Jenny bounced her amulet in her hand.

'Does that happen to everyone?' she asked.

The Exeter smiled at her. 'Almost everyone. Some, as I said, never find them, and don't go on. They aren't matched. That, thankfully, doesn't happen often.'

'So do they really go blind?'

'They loose all their abilities, yes. They return home, broken, incapable of continuing. It's a truly awful thing!'

'But Ornolt, can't you tell? Doesn't the order know?' asked Jenny.

'Not exactly. I am usually very good at matching the groups - that's what I do, but, we've never figured out where the amulets come from - what they are. We know that the amulets are very important, that they somehow focus us, bring out our abilities, and unite us. Why they choose who they do is still a mystery.'

'Do you have an amulet?' Jenny asked.

'Yes,' he replied.

'Can I see it?'

He stopped and turned around.

'I doubt it. I'm not part of a team, as you no doubt have figured out, and so my amulet is not, hmmm, what's the best way to describe it...'

'Here?' Paul suggested. 'Real?'

The Exeter smiled.

'An odd way to put it, Paul. But no. What makes you say that?'

'Well,' he mumbled, 'you don't seem to have a necklace on, not that I can see. And I can't feel anything about you that is attached...'

'He's not, Paul,' Jenny interrupted. 'He's not like us. After all, he's three hundred and forty years old. I think he is an amulet, as much as a person can be.'

'You're right Jenny,' Ornolt replied. 'My amulet and I have for a very long time been one and the same. Its part of what it means to be The Exeter. Sometimes it is visible, sometimes it is not. But I can always feel it.'

He paused, looking up through the trees towards the sky.

'Come along now. We haven't got much time. We need to leave the common before the day's out.'

The children looked at each other, frowning. They'd left the stage at first light and had been hiking for hours. They were surrounded by a dense forest and climbing up a steady slope, away from the river. The air was thinning and getting cooler, which caused their cloaks to thicken around them.

Jenny looked down from the trees and followed Ornolt, putting her boots in his footprints. The forest floor was bare earth and she wondered where all the leaves and pine needles were. With as many trees as surrounded them, the ground should have been covered in them. Even as she thought this, she heard a soft crunch under her foot and looked back down, shocked to see twigs, acorns and needles appearing all around her.

'That was you, you know,' Paul said.

'What was?' she asked.

'The ground. I'm sure you've just changed it.'

'Don't be ridiculous,' she exclaimed. 'How could I?'

'I don't know. But you did - I think it's just like the village, before.'

Ahead of them Ornolt was listening. They were drawing close to an important realization.

'I've been thinking,' Paul continued. 'Ever since we put on these amulets, I feel stronger, more sure of myself. That's because of you.

'I've never been able to follow anyone's feelings so closely. It's part of the puzzle. I knew you were thinking about the ground, about what should be there.'

Jenny stared at him. 'Why would the ground change because I wanted it too?'

'Maybe you were only seeing what you wanted to and not what really was there.'

'Oh come on. Are you telling me that even though I can see trees all around me, if I just want to see it wrecked they'll all fall down?'

Ornolt whirled around and ran back toward her.

'Jenny, no! Stop!'

But it was too late. She'd raised her arm, in a sweeping motion, gesturing at all the trees around them. A great cracking could be heard and the trees started to lean in many directions, toppling as their roots let go. Branches were ripped away and rained down ahead of the trunks.

'Run!' shouted the Exeter.

They turned around and fled back down the path, jumping over rocks and darting about trees. Their cloaks were flying out behind them as they plunged away from the chaos. Great concussions of sound caught up with them as the trees hit the ground.

Just as quickly as it had started, it stopped. They turned around, panting and stared back up the hill. It looked like a twister had touched down in one small place. Every tree had fallen in a circle of about one hundred feet. The sun's light shone brightly through the canopy on a scene of utter devastation: nothing was left.

Jenny stood frozen with horror. Paul and Ornolt looked back in amazement.

'I don't - I can't have done that,' Jenny whispered, so quietly the others barely heard her.

Ornolt frowned, rubbing his beard thoughtfully.

'I must say, it's far more than I expected. Far more. There should have been a single branch perhaps, or a carefully aimed set of cones. We'd better get a few things sorted out, young lady.'

He started back up toward the circle of fallen trees. Paul followed him but Jenny stayed rooted to where she stood. Ornolt went back and took her hand.

'Come on, Jennifer. You have to face this. You have to find out what happened.'

On the stage of the common, the scene played itself out for all those who sat in the rock seats watching. They had arrived as soon as the children had been bound, summoned by the two who had felt the cold sense of dread from the children's blue amulets.

'This cannot continue!' a man several rows back shouted. 'Those trees were real! That should not have been possible!'

'Calm, please, Ucheen,' the old man said, standing up from his front row seat. 'She is strong, I agree, but there's no need to do anything.'

'No need, Docent?' Ucheen stammered. 'I can't believe you're saying that - not one of us could ever do what she just did. The Exeter is not the right one for them anymore.'

Voices floated down in agreement.

'Perhaps,' the Docent replied. 'Yes. You are right.'

'So we'll stop them? Pull them out now?'

'Absolutely not. It is time they met their first guide and since you are so keenly interested in them, I believe you should be that one.'

Chuckling erupted around the seats and Ucheen looked back at the stage, which showed the children and Ornolt approaching the fallen trees.

'Me? Why me? They should be stopped, not catered to!'

'That is enough. You need to go now. Agreed?'

He looked around at everyone. They stared back, nodding in unison.

Ucheen snorted.

'Fine, I'll do it, since you all seem to think it's right. What form?'

Ornolt and the children got closer to the trees and as the dust settled, Jenny felt herself calming. She knew that in some way, she had done exactly what she had thought to do. She had cleared away everything in her gaze. She didn't know how, and, try as she might, she couldn't make anything like it happen again. She pointed at leaves and willed them to move - they didn't. She looked to the canopy of the surrounding trees, wishing they would reach out and pick up their fallen comrades - they didn't. Why had she been able to then?

Absent-mindedly, she fiddled with the amulet, on the end of its chain. It felt warm and reassuring.

They reached the fallen trees, and Ornolt paced around them, looking for something. Paul had not said a word, and was uncertain of what he'd felt as the trees had come down. Like Jenny, he knew she'd been the reason they'd fallen. He'd felt an intense burst of power from her when she'd swept her arm towards the trees and, as it passed by him, only the amulet's connection to her had stopped him from falling as well. He hadn't expected the scope of the destruction but had known as they ran that it would be enormous.

Eventually, the Exeter stopped poking about the fallen trees and came back to Jenny. He crouched down and met her gaze.

'What do you feel?' he whispered.

'Shock, I think. I didn't mean to do this. I still don't believe what's happened.'

'But you do see it, don't you?' he prodded.

'Yes.'

'You know it cannot be undone.'

'I don't know. Perhaps.'

'No it can't.'

He turned to Paul.

'What do you think happened, Paul?'

'I've no idea. I've never seen anything like it.'

'But,' said the Exeter, 'you must have felt it. You must have known something was going to happen. The two of you are matched, after all.'

'Yes,' he said simply. 'I felt it.'

'So did I!' said a high pitched, raspy voice behind them. 'Not only that, but I felt my whole world coming down!'

They whirled around and saw a large black bird perched on top of one of the fallen trees. It was staring at them, resting on its tall legs, its black wings shuddering with anger.

'Ah,' said Ornolt. 'Your first guide. Good luck then.'

He turned and walked swiftly away from them, fading from view as he went between the trees then vanishing altogether.

Jenny and Paul stood open-mouthed watching him fade. Ornolt had left them alone in this strange world, alone in the midst of Jenny's destruction. Neither one of them understood what had happened.

They didn't have long to think about it.

'Oh close your mouths, you twits!' squawked the bird. 'Ornolt wasn't going to help you anyways!'

The children whirled around and frowned at the bird, noticing for the first time how large it was.

'Who are you?' asked Paul.

'Doesn't much matter, now, does it, Paul-ee,' squeaked the bird. 'Your little girl-friend here went and destroyed my home, obviously trying to kill me!'

'I meant no such thing,' Jenny burst out. 'It was an accident!'

'Some accident, you destructive moron. Now shut up and listen. I was sent to be your guide for the next few minutes, so pay attention. I might even tell you something useful. Might.'

It fell silent save for the angry swooshing sounds that came from its wings as they adjusted themselves and its red eyes snapped from one child to the other, glaring at them with a barely-contained contempt.

'I don't think I've ever seen a worse team here before, and that's saying something. Ornolt has gotten really careless, picking you two. Why'd you go and do this, girl?'

'My name's Jennifer - most people call me Jenny or ...'

The Raven cut her off.

'I don't care what your name is. As far as I'm concerned, you're another careless twit and I'll call you what ever I want. I can't believe they're letting you continue.'

Jenny felt her anger building, pushing away her initial fear of the bird.

'You should watch your mouth, little one,' she said.

'Or what, little Miss Mad gonna knock me down?'

'What are you doing?' Paul asked it.

'Oh look, he can talk,' the bird said. 'And why should I answer you? You obviously don't matter at all. Unless you can clean up after her little 'accidents'.'

'C'mon Paul,' said Jenny, 'This isn't helping - let's try and find our way out of here!'

'Sit down!' the bird screeched. 'Or you might get hurt.'

'What could you possibly do to hurt us?' Jenny exclaimed, her temper rising further. 'We're much bigger than you.'

The raven stopped twitching, stopped all noise and movement and stared at her with its nervous eyes. 'You'd do well, young wench, to mind what you say, and to whom you say it, in a land as strange as this. Has it occurred to your small mind yet that I may be a great deal more than just a bird? Have you ever, in your short, miserable life, met a talking raven, or any talking animal, for that matter?'

That shut them both up.

'I thought not. You still think this is some sort of game, don't you? I assure you it is not. You came here of your own accord, by figuring out how to read those letters, and then actually doing what they said, even though it might have killed you both.

'Now that you're here, you better figure out how to survive. There's no way else to get home, and no way else to live. Ornolt's gone, and believe me, he's not coming back. I'm not inclined to help you any more than I have to, since you willingly destroyed my home.'

'I did not!' Jenny interrupted. 'I didn't know you were there, and I certainly didn't know I could do something like this!'

'Nor did I,' said Paul. 'We mean you no harm.'

'Oh shut up, you great twit!' the raven said to Paul. 'You're here, which is surprising enough. You'd better grow a spine if you want to get through the rest of this. Oi! Cut that out!'

The bird turned back to Jenny. 'There's absolutely no point trying to read anything from my mind. Like I said earlier, what makes you think I'm just a bird! Every time a team comes through they try that feeble trick.'

It settled its wings in again. 'Sit!' it said.

'What?' they both said.

'I said *sit*,' it repeated. 'We've a lot to get through. Pull up a tree; as it turns out, there's plenty available. Oh, and put those stupid walking sticks of yours away in your bags. You don't need them just now.'

It waited while they settled themselves.

'Now then. If you were listening to Ornolt, you would have noticed that the last thing he said to you was that I was your first guide. Much to my dismay, he was right. Since I'm your first guide, I'm going to have to lay out some basics for you, and given the way you've acted so far, you really need it.

'You're now on a journey, whether you like it or not, with only one goal in mind - find your way back to the common. It's the only way you'll ever see your homes or families again. Doing so will require you to do a few things you've never done in your lives so far. Like think.'

It paused for a moment, snickering.

'What's so funny?' asked Paul.

'Well, young twit, I was just thinking how much fun it would be to give you the wrong instructions. I could send you to the far corners of the earth on a useless adventure, and you two would probably never know I'd done it.'

'But you won't,' said Jenny. 'You can't.'

'Very good. The wench seems to have been listening. I'm surprised. All right then, here's the real thing. All your lives you've both been able to do small things that others can't do. That's always bothered you, and made things often quite difficult. Am I right so far?'

They both nodded.

'Good. Well, from now on that changes. You absolutely have to use all your skills here, and further, you must work together to get through this. If you do, the promise that Ornolt spoke of will come to be and your lives will become far more than you ever thought possible. If you don't, you will lose something.'

'Lose something?' asked Paul. 'Like what?'

'I actually don't know. Maybe a foot. Maybe your lives. I've never been told what happens. None of that really matters at all. Just work together, figure out what you're doing, and you'll be fine. Perhaps you'll even come back and fix this mess up. Not that I put much faith in that, as you've so far proved to be complete nitwits.'

'Why are you being so rude to us?' asked Jenny.

'Because I thoroughly disapprove of you, and of your continuing participation.'

'I think you're scared of something,' she pressed. 'Maybe of us.'

The raven stared intently at her. 'You, young wench, have a lot to learn. Perhaps we should start now.'

Jenny gasped and stared all around her. She stood up, quivering with fear and continued darting glances back and forth. Paul tried to get up and help but found he couldn't move. Jenny was starting to shake, a tremor that ran through her entire body. She stumbled backward from where the bird was perched and tripped over a fallen tree. She fell to the ground and curled up in a ball, holding her hands to her ears, letting out a low wail and twitching.

The raven watched her closely, and didn't move.

Suddenly it all stopped. She sat up, breathing heavily, still rubbing the sides of her head.

'Perhaps,' the raven said quietly, 'you will be more careful about who you insult. I am a guide, for now, and will not hurt you. At least, not permanently. Now get back here, sit down, and listen to what I have to say.'

Jenny hurried over.

'What happened to you now, wench, was a small taste of what I can do, particularly when I'm not forced to look like a bird. One day, perhaps, you'll learn how to defend yourself against it, but for now, be more cautious.'

Paul reached out to Jenny and gave her a small hug.

'Are you all right?' he asked.

'Yes. I'm fine. I - I'm just, surprised is all. Maybe a little bruised.'

She was rubbing her side where she'd hit the ground.

'Now listen up,' said the Raven. 'I've got just a little bit more for you. If you're good, we'll be done soon.'

The two children sat up and looked back at it.

'The amulets that you found earlier have several purposes. They act as a sort of homing beacon that can help you find each other when you're lost. This usually only works over short distances, about two or three miles, although their true range has never been tested. Don't expect it to work from different continents. They glow as they get close to each other. Take them out and try it now.'

They withdrew their amulets from beneath their cloaks and held them close to each other. They were glowing a strong blue. Jenny stood up and walked away from Paul, and as she went, the amulet started to dim. She stepped behind a tree so that she couldn't see Paul, and held the amulet up. As she moved it slowly back and forth, its inner blue core glowed at different intensities. Moments later, she returned.

'You'll also note that the amulets get warm when you approach two things: A guide, like me, and a gate. Now guides have only one purpose: to help you with whatever your current task might be. My task, telling you the basics, is the simplest thing a guide has to do, so, if you actually pay attention, you'll understand exactly what I'm saying.

'Other guides cannot be so straightforward, since you are here to learn as well as to survive. In fact, sometimes the only way you'll be able to tell whether what you're hearing, or seeing, or reading is a guide or not is by checking your amulets. They will both be quite warm when you check them.'

Paul held his amulet tightly in his hand. It didn't feel very warm at all.

'How come mine's not warm now?' he asked.

'It's because the amulets only warm up when they first get near the guide. Believe me, if they stayed as warm as they get all the time you're near us, you'd find them too hot to wear.

'Now, I also mentioned that they get warm near gates. You've actually already run in to a gate, although, knowing you two, you have no idea what I'm talking about.'

'I think I do,' Jenny said. 'The letters. My jump. The way we got to the common.'

'Very good. Perhaps you can think after all. That was a gate, although quite a special one, since it was able to open up without an amulet near by.'

'But Guide,' said Jenny. 'It was near an amulet - The Exeter was there for both of us.'

The raven sat quietly for a minute.

'That, little wench, is a most interesting thought. Imagine that, from you. Well, well. Perhaps those gates weren't so special after all.'

Jenny smiled.

'If I may continue: the gates are essential to you while you're here, as they let you travel great distances in very short times. Sometimes, they are the only way to get out of whatever place you are in. I suggest that whenever you find a gate, you take it.'

'How exactly do we do that?' asked Paul.

The raven shrugged.

'It's different each time. If it's a door, walk through it. If it's a plate of food, eat it. You'll figure it out. Now remember gates only go one way - you can't turn around and go back. They also sometimes put you in places you don't necessarily mean to be. Have your wits about you when you go through, if that's possible.'

They both grinned at the bird, getting used to its mannerisms and waiting for it to say more. It didn't.

'Well,' said Jenny, 'what do we do now?'

The bird looked at her.

'Leave, of course, you thick-minded dolt. I'm through with you.'

It turned around and flew away over one of the trees.

They stood up and without speaking started back up the path that Ornolt had originally been on. Paul was in the lead with Jenny traipsing along behind. The path was climbing steadily up, towards what looked like a rock cliff.

'Paul, are you hungry?' asked Jenny.

'Not really, you?' he replied.

'Well, maybe a little. We haven't eaten since this morning. I could do with a burger, you know and some fries.

'Uhgh that sounds awful. I think ice cream would be better. Cool us down a bit, it would.'

Jenny stuck her tongue out. 'I imagine the kind of ice cream you'd get here would probably have some horrible flavor, like 'Damp Forest Floor' or 'Bag of Hair'.'

Paul laughed, joining in. 'How about 'Dehydrated bog-butter'.'

They kept walking, making up dumb names for ice cream and came to the bottom of the rock cliff. They couldn't see the top since the rock leant back as it went up.

'Well, do you suppose we climb this?' asked Paul.

Jenny looked around and then shook her head.

'Nope. Look, I think the path continues this way.'

She was pointing to her right along the lower edge of the cliff. The ground was clearer there so they set off. They continued for some time before Jenny jolted to a stop, grabbing at her amulet. It was warming up.

'Paul,' she started.

'Mine too,' he said.

They looked around. All they could see was the path, continuing along the rock, some trees and the ground cover.

'Perhaps we missed it,' Jenny said.

'Maybe,' said Paul. 'Let's go back - the amulets will cool off if we go the wrong way.'

They turned around and headed back slowly, looking everywhere as they did. After just a few yards, the amulets grew cold.

'Nope,' said Jenny, 'it's got to be the way we were going.'

They turned back and felt the heat return to the amulets. Ahead of them in the side of the rock cliff they saw a small, dark cave. They inched toward it and looked in. It was pitch black.

'This must be it,' said Paul. 'Let's go.'

'We should check if anything's in there first,' Jenny said, stopping him.

She paced around, looking for any sort of sign of animal life - footprints, droppings, even scrapes on the trees. She didn't see a thing.

'C'mon,' said Paul, 'there's nothing here, and the amulets are still quite warm. This has to be it. We just step in, and see what's in there.'

Jenny picked up a large stick and threw it in to the cave. It landed about six feet in and stirred up dust. Nothing happened.

'Ok, there can't be anything there. Let's go.'

Paul stepped forward and went up to the cave. He peered in, looked back at Jenny and smiled.

'I think it's safe - let's see where this goes. Sink or swim, eh?'

He stepped in to the cave and instantly disappeared. Jenny grabbed her amulet and held it up. Its glow had disappeared. Alarmed at being left alone, she rushed into the cave and just like Paul, she vanished.

Chapter 6

An Ancient Reaction

While Canace could not bear to leave their mountain home, her sister delighted in the world. She traveled through the gates, to times and lands neither could ever imagine. She absorbed all that she saw, learned all that she was offered, and, on her return to their home, passed what she knew to Canace.

He sat alone on a windswept, smooth log looking west over the line of mountain tops at the setting sun. From a distance he looked much as any man would. He was tall, with long legs hunched to one side. He wore brown and grey robes that looked like they were made of cheese cloth and his head was almost completely wrapped in a scarf of the same material. He was hunched to his right, his elbow resting on his knee and his hand holding his head up.

He shifted, lowering his hand and the skin of his face swirled in color, changing as the sun set. He stood to stretch, rising up to almost ten feet in height and paced back and forth in front of the dark cave behind him. He was a sentry, watching for anything that might approach the cave. His job was to convince whatever approached to leave, preferably without being seen. It had been his job for nearly four hundred years and until two days ago, he'd been happy to do it, content with the peacefulness of the mountains.

It was a warm night, still well above freezing, which at the top of a mountain as large as this was a welcome change. The color bursts to the west as the sun set should have brought a smile to his face but instead he scowled. Something had changed in the world, something that threatened to expose his kind once again, if not their very existence. The morning assembly, deep behind the mouth of the cave, in the great hall, wasn't something he'd soon forget - the tension in the room had made the air thick and as he'd sat on the rock floor amongst the others, no one said a word.

'It has been nearly two thousand years,' their leader bellowed from the top of the stairs that rose from the front of the great hall to the smaller chambers behind them. 'Two thousand years since we've paid any attention to the humans. This morning, I have to tell you we must change that. We can't stay hidden any longer!'

Whispers started floating through the air, rising to shouts as the listening crowds absorbed what had just been said.

'You have the right to know why and I will tell you in a moment. But first, look around you! What do you see?'

Heads turned, staring at each other and at the surrounding hall. On every wall, except where there were doors, small alcoves had been carved, each about one and a half feet tall and wide.

'Each of those chambers should be filled. But they're not. Each of those chambers should have a glow to them. But they're dark. But it wasn't always so! There's not many in here alive who would remember but we used to regularly add to our collection, bring new light glowing to one of those chambers. Who here remembers that?'

Less than a third of the crowd nodded and grunted in acknowledgement, smiling at the memory.

'We haven't hunted them, my friends, because they grew too strong! They figured out how to talk amongst themselves, using the amulets! They could feel us coming and vanish before we even got close!'

Their leader turned and paced back and forth in front of them.

'We haven't been able to harvest their amulets for a very long time! Why is that? Why do the amulets not respond to us as they do to them?'

He stopped and stared, waiting for an answer. None came.

'That's right. No one knows. I don't think even a full blown member of the human order could tell you. Even when fully bound to their amulets, they have no idea how it happened, or where the amulets come from. Yet come they do! And they lend their extraordinary power to the humans!

'But you all know that. You don't need to hear me rail against the humans once again. We all know that we made our fragile peace with them millennia ago and for the most part, not one of them knows where we are. I'd be willing to gamble most of what I own in saying that almost every member of the order doesn't even know about us.

'So why are we talking about this now? Why am I so angry?'

Another pause, more staring at each other.

Their leader stomped his feet and walked over to one of the alcoves. He held a two foot stick in his hand.

'Here's why!' he yelled and thrust the stick into the alcove. Immediately it burst into flame and he was forced to drop it before getting burnt himself. The crowd was on its feet in an instant, turning toward the doors.

'Stay where you are,' their leader bellowed. 'You are quite safe.'

He waited while they settled down.

'There's not one of us who has ever seen that happen. Not one. Some of us can remember over three thousand years and this has never happened. We've always been able to approach our collection, to pick up the amulets. Even when they went dark over a decade ago, we could still handle them.'

'So what has happened?' a voice shouted from the crowd. 'What has changed today?'

'A new pair of recruits is what happened,' he stated flatly. 'The order has found another pair of youngsters to join them. Nothing too extraordinary in that, right?'

Nods came in waves across the crowd.

'Wrong. One of our observers was lucky enough to be there when these two children were bound to their amulets. They found their way into the woods quickly, even without their normal senses. They seemed to talk to each other without speaking. The girl could follow the boy with no eyes or ears to help her.

'When they found their amulets, the trees and landscape healed. Completely. No sign of any amulets passing was left. And the instant that they were bound, our collection in this room started to burn us. There has to be a connection between all of this. The one they call the Exeter found the new amulets to be 'curious'. That has to mean something.

'And then there's the girl. There's something about her that is different, but we can't quite place it. She's certainly very strong - she was able to knock down a large number of trees with one gesture. But our observer thought her presence, the sense he had of her, was familiar.'

He paused again and then sat on one of the stairs.

'Thoughts?' he asked. 'Suggestions?'

'Has anyone been to the wall of inscription since this happened?' someone near the front asked. 'Perhaps it will have changed as well.'

Their leader paused and smiled.

'An excellent idea. Let's go at once.'

When she stepped into the cave, Jenny felt like she'd been grabbed in a vice. She didn't think she was moving but she could tell she was no longer in the forest, no longer even in the cave. She looked down at her amulet, still clutched tightly in her hand and saw the blue glow return.

I must be catching up with Paul, she thought.

She tried to look around and discovered she couldn't move - she couldn't even turn her head. Concentrating as hard as she could, she stared ahead, trying her best to see. All she saw was utter darkness, punctured by the amulet's glow. It was no longer warm, so she supposed that they had passed beyond the gate.

Where am I going?

It was so different than the gate that had brought her to the Common. That gate had happened instantly - as soon as she had jumped from the tree, she had landed on the grass and started walking.

Her thoughts were abruptly interrupted by the end of her journey. She felt something warm and soft all around her; something strangely wet. She opened her eyes and realized where she was - deep under water.

Feeling a sudden panic, she started trying to swim to the surface but found she couldn't - she didn't even know where the surface was. Her lungs were starting to hurt her. She realized she was in a lot of trouble - so deep underwater with no air.

Think, she told herself. *There has to be a way.*

With her lungs fit to burst she forced herself to be calm, to be still. She opened her eyes. High above her, she could see shafts of light bursting through the surface of the water, sending great beams sparkling toward her. Staring around, she saw nothing - just the dark blue of distant, deep water. She realized she was standing on the bottom of whatever body of water she'd ended up in.

Her mouth started to leak air as her lungs forced themselves to empty.

I've got to breathe! she shouted in her mind.

Then she noticed something. The amulet in her hand was bubbling hard. It was pouring out air which was rushing away in large, sloppy bubbles towards the distant light. She blew the rest of the air out of her lungs and stuffed the amulet in her mouth. Concentrating hard, she breathed in through her mouth without opening it and found her lungs filling with welcome, wonderful air.

She slowly looked around. Her eyes were not suited to underwater use and although the salt of the sea didn't bother her, almost everything appeared to be in a fuzzy haze. Just ahead of her, she saw what looked like a human, dressed in heavy swimwear and thrashing madly about. She rushed over and as she grew closer, she realized that person was Paul.

She grabbed him by the shoulders, found his amulet and stuffed it in his mouth. Moments later he stopped thrashing. She continued to hold his shoulders, looking him in the eye while he figured out how to breathe.

'Oh my God!' a panicked voice said from all around her. *'I almost drowned!'*

It was Paul's voice but he wasn't opening his mouth.

'How did you know, I was so scared, I...'

Jenny removed her hands from his shoulder and immediately the voice stopped. She looked at him and held her hand to her ear. Even though the water made her eyes fuzzy, she could tell he was still twitching and still having trouble adjusting to this strange way of breathing. She couldn't talk to him but knew somehow that he could talk to her.

He calmed down and reached out, taking her hand.

'You have to be touching me, or I have to be touching you, for you to hear me...'

Jenny wanted to ask him how but found she couldn't. Instead, she pointed with her free hand at her mouth and shrugged.

'You can't yet,' said Paul's voice, *'We can't do the same things as each other, remember?'*

She nodded.

'Good,' he said. *'For now, just nod or shake your head. I'll know. Shall we try and find a way out of here?'*

She shook her head but then burst into a fit of bubbly giggles. Paul took her hand again.

'I'll take that as a yes. Look over there - it looks like the land slopes up. Let's go that way'

Paul let go of her hand and started out. Their boots were heavy and awkward so Jenny tapped him on the shoulder and reached down to take hers off. She did the same with her socks and her cloak and stuffed them in her bag. He followed suit and they set off once more.

The water was warm and bright. Sea water, Jenny thought. When she'd been struggling with the amulet, she'd tasted a strong salt, so this must be the ocean. Somewhere south, she imagined but where? As they walked, they got closer and closer to the surface. It was a sandy ocean bottom with little plant life or anything else remotely alive.

Jenny looked behind her into the deep blue of the ocean depths and shuddered. She'd read a lot about sea creatures but couldn't remember ever having been in an actual ocean and was frightened of what might be there. She turned back and concentrated on just following Paul.

To her immense relief, they emerged in shallow water, their heads breaking the surface. She took the amulet out of her mouth and breathed in the warm, wet air. Paul did the same.

'You all right then?' he asked.

'Yes, fine thanks!' she replied. It was absolutely wonderful to be out of the water's walls and breathing again. The warm air and sun on her back felt even better.

'Where are we?' she asked.

'I've no idea,' said Paul. 'But I like the feel of it. Warm air, warm water, no ravens!'

Jenny laughed, started looking around and did her best not to scream. She'd caught sight of the land, of the beach and of the people staring back at them. Paul and Jenny stood in the shallow waters of a vacation resort -

all the people on the beach were sitting on beach chairs or towels, with drinks and food in plentiful amounts around them. Waiters in bright, flowing sarongs drifted amongst the tables, clearing away used glasses and dishes, and delivering new drinks.

The passage that led down from the hall was dark and steep. It had been carved out of the granite rock centuries ago and was clearly made for beings far smaller than those who were stuffing themselves through it now. They went in single file, bent over to nearly half their height, carrying oil based torches that cast little light against the dark stone walls.

Progress was slow, particularly on the stairs which for them were more like ladders - they had to turn their feet sideways and lower themselves slowly down. The dust on the floors was thick and they walked as slowly as they could, trying not to disturb it.

The three of them paused, breathing slowly and let the air catch up with them.

'Do either of you know how much farther we have to go?' the front man said.

'No - we come down here so rarely that we've never accurately measured it.'

'I wonder why - it's such a pleasant journey!'

The trailing man, who hadn't spoken the whole time poked the man ahead of him and gestured ahead.

'Let's go,' he grunted. The swirls in his face were slower than the other two and he walked like one much older than he looked.

They set out again and came to a long, dark staircase. The bottom of it was not visible in the weak light of their torches.

'One at a time,' the trailer said. 'No point losing all of us to one slip.'

The other two glared back at him.

'Been here before?'

'A long time ago, yes,' he replied. 'These stairs are near the end. Very tricky.'

The lead man began his descent, taking each step slowly. He stopped about half way down, some thirty feet below the others.

'The wall is different here,' he called back. 'Something's in the rock.'

'Like crystals?' The trailing man asked. 'They glow a little, yes?'

'Maybe. I'll keep going.'

He continued slowly down and faded from view as the stairs went forward.

'I'm at the bottom!' he called back, his voice echoing off the walls.

The second man started down, going slowly as well. He was far taller than the first man and was forced to hunch down as he went. When he was ten steps down, as he reached his leading leg down to the next step, he felt a cramp start in his supporting leg. The pain went from a dull ache to a sharp, stabbing pulse which made him twist around and grab at his calf. He lost his balance as he did, falling on his rear. He started to slide down the stairs, one jarring bounce at a time. He sped up as he fell and the cramp became sharper.

With a loud crunch he landed at the bottom of the stairs, his head bouncing off the ceiling as he tried to stand up. The lead man steadied him and he panted in pain.

'I've broken it,' he winced, holding one foot off the ground.

'You're sure?'

'Yeah - unbelievable. The return trip should be a delight.'

'Is he alright down there,' called the last man.

'No, get down here. He's broken something.'

'Great,' the last man mumbled. 'Here we go.'

He turned around and went down the steps as if he was on a ladder, keeping one hand on the stairs as well as his feet. With the other hand he held his torch above him, feeling his way down step by step. He arrived at the bottom minutes later.

'Let me see,' he said, crouching down in front of the injured man.

He wrapped his hands around the man's foot and pressed gently. A sharp wince told him he'd found the spot.

'Believe it or not, this isn't too bad. We'll wrap it, and you'll be able to put enough weight on it to get back. Sit down on the bottom steps and wait here.'

'No way. I didn't come all this way to miss out on this.'

The other two glared at him.

'Fine,' the trailing man finally said. 'Sit down and let's get this wrapped.'

He tore a strip off his shirt sleeve and wrapped the man's foot as tightly as the pain would allow.

'Alright, you two, there's something ahead that you haven't been told yet,' he said. 'There's a barrier coming that we put up to prevent this place from being disturbed.'

'What sort of barrier?' the injured man said. 'Will I be able to get through?'

'We all will - don't worry. It's a stone wall that we'll have to break through.'

'With what?' the lead man said. 'We didn't bring any tools for that!'

'We won't need them. There's a spot on the wall, near the bottom left as we approach it, which can be wiggled loose. Once it's gone, the wall can be collapsed into that spot. It's not as strong as it looks.'

'So why is there?'

'To protect what lies behind it. People who come down here when they shouldn't just see that wall, and the fake inscription on it, and go back, none the wiser.'

They moved slowly forward and the air started to brighten. The walls had more and more sparkling crystals in them, long veins of color that picked up the light from their torches and bounced it back. Streaks of blues, greens and reds became greater than the dull granite and they felt as if their torch power had tripled. They came to a bend in the tunnel, and as they passed by it the ceiling rose up above them, letting them stand at full height.

'The wall should be just ahead.'

They walked a few more paces and came to a huge pile of rubble. The lead man turned to look back at the last man.

'You mean this wall?' he said, pointing at the rubble.

'What do you think?' the last man hissed. 'Something has happened here that we should have known about.'

He walked forward and looked at the rubble. He pushed a few rocks away from the left side and stood back up.

'Look at that,' he said. 'Whoever did this got through without collapsing the wall.'

'There's something else,' the injured man said. 'Look at the rubble.'

'What about it?'

'It was smashed apart, no doubt of that. From the other side!'

He was right - the crumbled rock lay in a scattered pattern coming from where the wall had stood toward them. Whatever had gone through the wall had used enough power to reduce most of the stone to dust.

'Let's go,' the older man said. 'Go slowly, and be careful. As far as we knew there was no other way down here, and we built that wall centuries ago.'

'And judging by these rocks,' the injured man said, picking up a larger piece of the rubble, 'this happened fairly recently. These splits in the rock look new.'

They stepped through and let the old man take the lead. He took a few steps and held up his hand.

'Look there!' he exclaimed, pointing at the ground.

The dust was thick and hard packed, clearly undisturbed for thousands of years. Snaking through the middle of the dust, leading toward the rubble, were a pair of human footsteps. The person had not been wearing any footwear and had small feet, even for a human.

'This is not possible,' he said. 'There has never been a human in here.'

'Why didn't we see any footsteps back there?' the injured man asked. 'It's just as dusty.'

'Good question,' the old man grunted. He followed the footsteps back toward the rubble, being careful not to disturb them. They led right up to where the wall had been, where they stopped. The last two prints were beside each other, facing what would have been the wall.

'Did they just vanish?' one of them whispered.

'Looks like it,' the old man said. 'C'mon, let's get to the real wall. And don't wreck any of the human-child's footsteps.'

'You think it was a child?' the injured man asked.

'Or a very small adult. Maybe a woman?' the old man replied, following the footsteps back.

They came to another wall, this one filled with crystal - almost no granite was visible. In the middle of the wall, in gold lettering, something had been inscribed but they could not read it. The characters were not in any alphabet they recognized and were a mixture of symbols and pictures.

The footsteps that they had followed to the wall appeared to come right out of it - one of the prints only had the front half of the foot - the other half looked like it was beneath the wall.

'Does this wall move?' the injured man asked.

'I don't know,' replied the leader. 'We have never managed to get past it, although we have tried. It sure looks like it can from that footprint. Let's get back - we must decide what to do!'

They made their way carefully past the footsteps and then past the ruined wall. They fell into a slow rhythm, allowing the injured man to keep up. The stairs back up seemed impossibly steep, and as they climbed and the crystals in the rock faded, their passage grew dark. After nearly an hour of stooped, difficult walking, they found themselves back in the familiar halls of their home.

They made their way through to the large gathering hall, where all the amulets lay quiet and dark.

No one was there.

They walked slowly around the edge of the hall, almost to the tunnel leading back toward the cliff face entrance when a voice stopped them.

'What did you find?'

They whirled around. The man who had spoken to the full assembly, their leader, sat on the wide steps, watching them.

'You were gone a long time,' he continued.

'We found footsteps, sir. Human footsteps.'

'What!' the leader exclaimed. 'Where? Down near the wall?'

The expedition's leader nodded and stepped forward.

'Yes sir. Though not our wall. That has been destroyed. From the inside. Near the original wall.'

'Destroyed? How?'

'Unknown. An explosion perhaps? There's almost nothing left. What's stranger still, sir, are the footsteps. They look like they come right out of the walls, and then ...'

He paused, looking at the two who'd been with him.

'And then, they stop.'

'Stop? Where?'

'At the spot where we built our wall. It's as if they destroyed the barrier, and then vanished.'

The leader stood up and paced back and forth.

'There has to be a connection,' he finally muttered. 'The new recruits. The amulets burning us. And the wall. It's far too many coincidences at once.'

He paused, scratching his head.

'We need to learn more,' he whispered. 'We need to watch those new recruits, we need to bring them here, we may even need to kill them.'

'But what of our peace with the humans?' the old man who'd been to the walls asked. 'Won't that make things insufferably difficult for us?'

'They can't know it was us,' replied their leader. 'We're going to need our invisible observers to help us here. No human has ever been able to see them. They're perfect.'

His pacing quickened.

'I'll deal with it,' he continued. 'In the meantime, not a word of what you found. It will disturb too many people.'

He gathered his cloak around him and strode away, following the path towards the mountain peak entrance.

A woman sitting on the edge of the beach noticed them and shrieked. A man nearby looked at where she was pointing and sat up.

'Oi! You two! What do you think you're doing?' he shouted. 'Get out of there, before you drown!'

Jenny grabbed her amulet, wondering if this might be another guide but it was cold in her hand. She tucked it under her soaked shirt. She and Paul waded slowly out of the water and stood looking at the couple.

'Do your parents know where you are?' the woman asked.

'Not exactly,' Paul answered. 'They're just down there, around the point. We should be getting back to them.'

'Where are you from?' asked the man.

'Sorry?'

'Your accent,' the man continued, his voice softening. 'You sound English.'

'London,' Paul replied. 'And, uh, this is my sister, Jennifer. C'mon, Jenny, lets go!'

Paul took her hand.

'Don't speak, or they'll know you're not my sister.'

She turned to follow but the man stopped them.

'London? Well this is quite a vacation, then. Hawaii's a long way from home, isn't it?'

'We're on our way to Sydney,' Jenny said, 'to visit our Aunt. My mother's sister. It's our first trip! We went through Canada, took a bit of tour.'

Paul stared at her. Her voice was different. She sounded more like his mother than like herself.

'Really? That's where we're from - you'll have a great time!' said the woman. 'How long are you staying here?'

'I don't actually know,' said Jenny. 'Did Mum tell you, Paul?'

'No, but I don't think it was for very long. A few days, I expect.'

They turned up the beach, walking away.

'Where are you going?' the man called after them. 'There's nothing around there - just a bunch of cliffs. The hotel's back that way!'

'Thanks!' said Jenny. 'I guess we got all turned around, swimming.'

The man and woman looked at them and frowned. When Jenny caught sight of Paul she realized what was wrong: They still had their hiking slacks and shirts on with heavy bags slung over their shoulders and had just walked out of the ocean. Not wanting to explain themselves, they hurried away towards the hotel.

Once they were out of earshot of the man and the woman, they let out a sigh of relief.

'That was great!' exclaimed Jenny.

'Great?' Paul said. 'I dunno - I thought we were in deep trouble.'

'Well, yeah, I guess.'

'So what was so great about it?'

Paul could sense how excited Jenny was.

'Just talking to them. I never do that!'

'You never talk to people?' Paul asked. 'Never put on accents? It sure sounded to me like you do.'

'Nope. I'm usually too shy. Dad does the talking, or Sarah.'

'Really,' he laughed. 'That's not what I've seen. Ever since I met you, you talk all the time.'

'Maybe it's these,' Jenny said, holding up her amulet. 'Maybe it's this new world we're in.'

'I'd say we're the ones who are new,' Paul said. 'This place looks pretty real to me.'

'I know,' said Jenny. 'And those people seemed normal too; it was easy to read them.'

'Yes,' said Paul, 'it was. I think this really is Hawaii.'

They walked slowly down the beach, ignoring the stares from the people lying on towels and chairs. They rolled their hiking slacks and sleeves up, trying to look like the other kids around. The amulets were quiet and hidden. Paul turned, walked away from the water and sat down.

'What are you doing?' Jenny asked.

'I'm sitting!' he grinned. 'C'mon, we've been on the go all day. We've no idea what we're doing, it's supposed to be cold, it's supposed to be a school night, and I just want to enjoy it. I'm sure my gran's going to wake me up at any moment and tell me to get out of bed.'

Jenny walked over to Paul and pinched him on the shoulder.

'Ow!' he cried. 'What was that for?'

'To prove you're not dreaming. You'd have woken up.'

She sat down next to him and watched the surf slowly rolling up the beach. It was wonderfully peaceful, the sound, the smell and the surf. She looked back at Paul.

'So do you really think this is real? Well, not here, I mean Ornolt, the raven, everything else?'

'I don't know. I know we're still here, together and we still have the amulets.'

Jenny fished hers out and stared at it.

'I wonder what it says.'

'On the bands?'

'Yeah - it doesn't look like normal writing, does it?'

'Nope,' he replied. 'Something older, hieroglyphics maybe. So what did you feel when you put it on?'

'Like a thick blanket was lifted off of me. I felt so - free, lighter, you know?'

'Kind of. I felt a little frightened at first, like I should turn and run. It didn't last long and when it passed, I thought I could feel everything around me.'

'Everything?' she asked, her nose wrinkling up. 'Like the trees, even?'

'No, just a hum really. A sort of sense of what was there.'

Jenny picked up some pebbles and threw them slowly into the ocean.

'So what about underwater? You know, the talking?'

Paul leaned on his knee and stared at the water.

'I was terrified,' he finally said. 'And then you stuffed my amulet in my mouth, just when I was going to breathe in water. All I could think was 'thank you, thank you' over and over again - and you heard me.'

'It's different than the way I hear people's thoughts. It was your voice, what you wanted to say.'

'Mmm, I know. But I've never done that with anyone else.'

'So how did you know you could with me?'

'I didn't - not until you reacted - I knew you heard me, and I figured out how. It's like the way I can show people things.'

'You mean like your mother? The way you showed her your Dad's death?'

Paul glared at her.

'I hate that you know that, you know.'

'I'm sorry, I just hear things, all the time, and I... Hey, what's wrong?'

Paul had stopped glaring at her and Jenny saw his eyes widen as he looked past her. He held his hand close to the ground and pointed behind her. Jenny turned to look and saw what was bothering him. Two children, perhaps eight years old, were standing about fifty feet away from them. They had on the clothes of the order just like Jenny and Paul and both had glowing red amulets around their necks. Their faces looked washed out and white, their hair was gray and they stood staring at Paul and Jenny.

'What are they?' Paul whispered.

'I don't know - but I've seen people like them before - back home.'

'Really? What did you do?'

'Well the first time, it was a boy, and he...'

She stopped as the two young children turned and walked away from the water, toward the street that ran along the edge of the beach. No one on the sand paid any attention to them, as if they couldn't tell they were there.

'C'mon,' Jenny said, putting on her boots and standing up. 'I think we should follow them.'

Paul followed her lead and they ran across the sand, trying to catch up with the pale figures. When they had nearly reached the street, they saw the children disappearing into the crowded market that lay on the other side. Paul stepped onto the street when the light changed and was about half way across when he noticed that Jenny wasn't with him. He looked around and saw her standing on the edge of the road.

'Hey, let's go,' he said, returning to her, 'We're going to lose them!'

Jenny grabbed his hand and stepped forward.

'Ok,' she mumbled, her eyes darting about.

They went across and as they headed into the market area, Paul felt Jenny's grip tighten. He concentrated on her and felt an overwhelming anxiety hit him - she was terrified.

'What's wrong?' he asked her.

'Nothing,' she replied, tightening her grip further as she stomped toward the market.

'No, there must be something,' Paul started.

'There isn't!' she yelled at him and Paul felt a burst of energy sweep over him and a litter box behind him burst open.

'Yes there is,' he said quietly. 'I can tell, remember? What's happening?'

Jenny sighed loudly.

'It's the people,' she finally said. 'I can't stand being around them - They make me ... nervous.'

Paul grabbed both her hands and stood in front of her.

'Ok, I think I know what you mean. You know what I do? I pretend it's something else.'

'Like what?' she asked, her eyes twitching back and forth.

'I don't know - did your mother ever brush your hair when you were a kid?'

She stared at him, her blue eyes boring into him.

'Yeah, so?'

'Did you feel a tingling all over your head when she did?'

She nodded.

'Pretend this is the same - all those people, they're just...'

'Brushes?' she laughed, her hands finally relaxing.

'Sure, brushes - whatever works.'

He let go of her and saw that a small crowd had gathered around them, watching their strange exchange.

'Hungry!' he said loudly, 'Why didn't you say so. Let's go find ...'

'Burgers!' she finished.

They hurried away into the market area and through the sliding glass doors of the mall that lay behind. It was packed with tourists and stalls selling all manner of souvenirs, trinkets and useless junk. They looked around, trying to find the pale strangers. The mall was a long, rectangular building that had two levels. Escalators ran between them in the middle and they saw another set of doors at the far end.

'Anything?' he asked.

'Yeah, lots,' she replied.

'The kids?'

'No brushes - there's a lot here.'

'So where did those kids go?' he persisted. 'I thought I saw them come in here.'

'I, uhm, didn't notice,' she mumbled.

'Maybe they went out the other end.'

They walked through the mall and wove their way through the crowds. Jenny was once more holding Paul's hand tightly as they walked out the far doors which opened onto a large street with three lanes running in each direction. A small strip of grass and benches divided it in the middle. About one block along, they saw the dividing patch widen where a series of statues stood.

'Over there,' Paul said. 'Let's climb up that pointy one and look around - we'll have a better view.'

'Ok,' Jenny said.

As they crossed toward the middle, she let go of Paul's hand. They hurried across the grass to the statues and climbed up, trying to find any sign of the pale children.

'Do you see anything?' Paul asked.

Jenny was higher up than him, looking down a long section of the roadway. She could see busy crowds on either side, going in and out of shops, hailing cabs and loading trunks. What children she could see were all with parents or older siblings - none of them looked like the pale strangers.

'Not a thing,' she finally replied. 'You?'

'I thought I had - but I was wrong. They've just disappeared, I'm afraid.'

A loud squawk from a car startled them.

'Hey you two,' a policeman said, leaning out the window. 'Get down - what do you think you're doing?'

They sheepishly climbed down.

'Sorry, sir,' Paul said.

The officer waved dismissively at them and moved off with the traffic. The children wandered toward the closest bench and sat down.

'We've missed them,' Jenny sighed. 'I wonder where they were going?'

'I don't know. On the beach, they seemed - happy, didn't you think?'

Jenny stared at him.

'You read that?' she asked.

'Well, sort of. They felt hopeful, happy - like they knew us. Didn't you feel that?'

'No, sorry. I don't think I'm much use here.'

'Why?'

'It's the same thing - the people. Too much hair brushing, I suppose.'

'So what is it, really, about the people? Have you always had this trouble?'

'Yeah, forever. It's why we live in Banff.'

'Because it's so small?'

She nodded.

'I was born in Calgary - which is much bigger. Whenever my parents took me anywhere, I would go a little nuts. Screaming about the noise. Right before we moved to Banff, I started blacking out around crowds.'

'Wow,' he said. 'That bad, huh? I can't imagine it.'

'It's like everyone talking at once - all these sentences pour over me, all mixed up, in different voices. You can't cover your ears, or close your eyes - nothing works.'

'Is it the same here?'

'No,' she said, after a long pause. 'It's better here. Maybe the people are different.'

'Or maybe it's something else,' Paul said, fingering his amulet. 'Maybe these help.'

'Maybe,' she said, 'I hadn't thought of that. It is easier, and, hey, look!'

She pointed across the street. On the other side, near a small laneway, the two pale children stood hand in hand.

'Let's go,' Paul said.

They hurried across the street and dodged their way among the crowd, heading for the lane. They felt the heat of the sun beating down on them and both of them started sweating. Their boots had lightened and looked like sandals sticking out under their slacks.

When they got to the lane and turned into it, they saw the two children again, far ahead of them, heading inland. They started running down the lane and saw that it threaded between the buildings, crossing several main streets as it did. The pale children remained far ahead of them and looked like they were just drifting forward - their feet didn't move.

When they approached a break in the buildings, a car came screeching around the corner and bore down hard upon them. The lane was narrow and they had nowhere to go. Jenny screamed, grabbed Paul's hand and ran as fast she could back the way they had come.

The car screeched to a halt and the driver squeezed out, staring in bewilderment at where the children had just stood. He leaned down and looked under his car and then at the walls around him. There was no sign of any impact, no sign of the children. They had vanished right in front of him. Scratching his head, he turned and inched his way along the side of the car, climbing awkwardly back in to the driver's side. He drove off slowly, looking everywhere for the children.

Jenny and Paul watched the car emerge from the lane from the safety of the doorway that Jenny had stopped in, some three hundred feet away.

'That was too close,' she said, breathing heavily.

'How did you do that?' Paul asked, still amazed they'd escaped.

'What?'

'Run like that. Do you know how fast we were going?'

'I, uhm, no. But I think it's something else I can do, you know, like the mind stuff?'

'Not really,' he replied.

'It started happening back home, just before I got the letter. My friend Sarah started noticing it a lot - she said that when I ran, sometimes she could barely see me.'

'Huh - cool. And it worked on me.'

'Wow - yeah I guess it did. I wonder if anyone saw us?'

'Besides the driver? I hope not.'

He stepped back into the lane, and looked around. Far ahead, several blocks away, he could see the two pale children. He pointed them out to Jenny and they set off again, slowing down when they came to the streets. When they got up to where the children had been, the lane emerged into a wide square in which trucks and delivery vans were parked.

On the far side of the square, they saw them again, standing near a truck, pointing at the back of it.

'Do they want us to get in it?' Jenny asked.

'It sure looks like, doesn't it?'

They walked around the edge of the square, trying to avoid eye contact with the people who milled about the vehicles, loading or unloading goods. When they got to the truck, the pale children were gone. Jenny peeked in the back and saw that it was empty.

'Should I?' she asked Paul.

'Yeah,' he said, 'this feels right. Let's go.'

They climbed in and crouched in a corner. The truck was a covered pickup with canvas sides supported by sturdy bars above. It was empty except for a few wooden crates near the cab. The driver returned and climbed in to the cab without noticing his stowaways. The engine rumbled to life and the truck made its way out of the square, heading out into the busy street.

'Where do you suppose we're going now?' asked Paul.

'I've still got no idea,' smiled Jenny, 'but it's better than walking.'

Just as she said this, the traffic thinned out and the truck sped up. She crawled over to the crates and poked inside. With a squeal of delight she realized that they were full of fruit. She threw some to Paul and they dug in, leaning against the sides and grinning at the taste.

The truck rolled along for hours, and when it finally did start slowing down, they peeked out at a totally different scene. They were in a small, rural village and when the truck pulled into a small gas station, they hopped out and snuck away. They made their way along the side of the road, away from the few stores that formed the main street and headed out toward the countryside.

'We don't have anywhere to sleep, you know,' Jenny whispered. 'And I'm getting really tired.'

'I am too,' Paul said. 'Maybe we should sneak around back of one of those barns over there, and wait the night out.'

'Good idea,' she said, bouncing her amulet in one hand. They were walking along a dirt road, near what looked like a cornfield. They followed the road around the edge of the field and came to an old, abandoned barn.

They snuck through the fence, walked over to the barn and peered in. Nothing was there, so they slowly opened the door which creaked loudly on its old hinges. Once they were inside they closed it and looked around.

'What time is it?' Paul asked.

'I don't know - maybe eight?' she replied. 'I don't care either. I just want to sleep.'

She climbed up on an old cart that was sitting at the end of a caravan and spread her cloak out as a bed. Using her bag as a pillow, she lay down and closed her eyes. She was asleep moments later.

Paul kept poking around, unsure of his surroundings. He'd never been in as hot a place as Hawaii and yet here he was, with someone he'd barely met, inside a strange building. He couldn't help wondering what came next.

After a while he grew tired so he crawled up onto the cart and copied Jenny. He lay down on his back next to her, staring at the ceiling. He concentrated on her and felt her absolute calm. The turmoil from the mall was gone and he allowed the peace that flowed from her to lull him to sleep.

As he drifted off, he marveled at how great it was to have met her - someone as different from others as he.

Jenny had the deepest sleep she could ever remember. When she woke up she couldn't remember where she was. She'd turned over in the night and was looking right at Paul's back. It was morning and the sunlight was glittering through the trees. With a start she sat up - they'd been inside when they went to sleep. She looked around, her eyes adjusting to the light and noticed they were moving.

The cart was lumbering slowly along, the last of several, being pulled by a small tractor towards the slowly approaching mountains. The driver hadn't noticed them and the barn had long since disappeared.

She tapped Paul on the shoulder and watched as he blinked himself awake.

'Shhh!' she said, her finger to her mouth.

'I think we're really lost now!

Chapter 7

The Accident

Though they lived in their mountain home, found through the cave-peak, for decades, Canace and her sister remained the same, beyond age. Her sister continued to travel, to explore the world, and was captivated finally by what she found: In the land between their northern home and the great jungles of the south, she came across a boy who knew her for what she was.

The stage of the common fell dark as the children drifted off to sleep. For those watching their journey so far this was a chance to reflect on what they'd seen. The people seated in the chairs started to stand, stretch and walk about the surrounding fields. The infinite fire burned steadily, its light bouncing off the glittering amulets that walked past.

Three members of the Order walked together toward the nearby river. When they got there, they sat at its edge, watching the moon's reflection on the rippling surface of the water.

'I am not comfortable with this,' one of the young women said. She had on a glowing gold amulet that matched the woman sitting next to her. The third person shifted with a wince, showing his age.

'With these stones?' he asked. 'Or with what we've just seen?'

'Yoshi, please,' she replied. 'You know exactly what I mean. Something's just not right with this whole thing.'

He nodded slowly.

'I know, Sasha. They are getting help, and it's not from us. They seem to know exactly which way to go. By tomorrow they'll have found the word-rocks. That would normally take a very long time, and several gates.'

The second woman stood up and looked into the stream.

'It's like they were following someone,' she said.

'Who?' Yoshi asked.

'It was hard to tell. Did you see those strange children on the beach?'

The others shook their heads.

'They were pale, as before - and I thought I saw amulets.'

'*What?*' the others said together.

'You really didn't see them?' she asked.

They shook their heads.

'Then we're in trouble - something has gone terribly wrong. We must warn the others.'

They leapt up and ran back to the common.

As the cart lumbered along, Jenny waited for Paul to fully wake up. The barn that they'd snuck into the night before was nowhere to be seen. Judging by the nearby mountains, they must have been riding in the cart for hours before they had woken.

The road they were on was tight-packed dirt and gravel and looked like it had been oiled several years ago. It was just wide enough for two cars and it wound along the edge of a vast plain with forests rising up the foothills on the other side. The edge of the forest was lined with volcanic rock cliffs, forcing the road to twist its way along them.

'Where are we?' Jenny asked when Paul finally sat up.

'I've no idea,' he replied. 'Besides Hawaii, that is.'

'I wonder how long we've been moving?'

'Or why we didn't wake up.'

Jenny turned to look toward the driver.

'I guess he didn't notice us either. This is really weird, Paul.'

'No kidding. Everything that's happened is. Like yesterday. Who were those strange children? And why did they make us get in that lorry?'

'I've been thinking about that. You remember I told you I'd seen them before?'

'Those children?'

'No, not exactly. But I've seen children like them. Back home in Banff. The first one, the boy, was right after we moved, and he could make things happen - he built a sand castle without touching the sand.'

'I don't understand.'

'He just waved his hand over the sand and it sort of followed him. And then he disappeared.'

'So what did you do?' Paul asked.

'Nothing. I couldn't find him. But you know what was weirdest?'

'What?'

'When he was sitting beside me, I couldn't feel him, or sense him, or hear him. If I wasn't looking at him, I'd never have known he was there.'

She paused, watching the road slowly fall away behind them.

'It was the same yesterday. I couldn't sense those children at all.'

'But I could,' Paul said. 'They're not like anything I've seen before.'

'Well, yeah.'

'No, no - I mean they were old, Jenny. They felt really, really old. And happy.'

Jenny shivered and pulled her cloak on, wrapping it tightly around her. The material thickened itself and she sat hunched under it, letting it warm her up.

'You said that before,' she continued. 'Happy. I wonder what that means?'

Paul shrugged and fingered his amulet, thinking about those the children had worn. The red glow had seemed so out of place against their grey clothes and faded faces. The road ahead started to wind out of sight, wrapping around a tall rock cliff. Paul tried to look ahead, to where the road emerged again and felt something cold, something dark run past.

'Did you feel that?' he said.

'Yes,' Jenny whispered. 'Something's happening.'

They were in the last cart of seven, pulled by a dark green tractor. All of the carts were empty and bounced loudly over each bump in the road. The tractor reached the curve ahead, swinging to the right and they watched each cart follow. The turn was so sharp that after two carts, the tractor could no longer be seen.

Jenny reached over and grabbed Paul's hand and felt it trembling as well. The air grew cold and harsh and while there was no wind, not even a breeze from the moving carts, Jenny could feel the goose-bumps on her skin rise up. Something was coming toward them and while they couldn't see it, they could feel it - a calculating force was changing - something.

Their cart was starting to turn the corner, catching up with the tractor. They saw that the road straightened momentarily before bending back to the left through a small tunnel. They strained to look past it but saw nothing - the field's vegetation was too thick and high to see beyond.

When they entered the tunnel, their sense of foreboding grew even more and as the light faded, Paul noticed something he hadn't seen before. All around Jenny there was a faint, blue mist, the same color as the glow of their amulets. It swirled about her, small currents moving up and back and he could see that when she looked at something, the mist momentarily focused as well.

'Jenny, what is that around...?'

He was cut off by the blast of an air horn ahead of them where the tractor and first few carts had emerged from the tunnel. Both children squinted against the light as their cart emerged and as their eyes adjusted they saw the impending disaster. An immense eighteen wheeled truck was careening toward them, moving far too fast for the small road they were on and had no way of stopping.

They both screamed as the tractor tried to veer aside, off the road but couldn't. It was struck head on and the driver was sent careening into the field. The truck had locked its brakes and they could hear the tires grinding away at the gravel surface, unable to get enough grip to slow down.

Paul couldn't take his eyes off the massive grill of the cab as it tore its way through the carts in front of them. They were lifted from the road and shattered, the wood splitting and peeling aside. He couldn't see the driver of the truck even though he could see the steering wheel. He turned toward Jenny and started to scream and then stopped.

She was standing up, staring at the truck barreling toward them. He saw her arms rising slowly from her sides, her palms held forward and rigid. The blue mist that had been only faintly visible in the tunnel was glowing brightly and the currents were all rushing along her arms, gathering into a bright ball in front of her hands.

When the truck was no more than two carts away, she suddenly arced both hands to the right, toward the rock. Paul saw a blue ball of light shoot from her hands toward the truck, wrap itself around the cab and hurtle it into the rock face.

With a buckling crash the truck jolted to a stop, the cab crushed flat against the cliff. The cart they were in was untouched, the only one not damaged and it slowly tilted forward, resting at an angle on its connecting arm. As soon as it did, Jenny crouched down and grabbed Paul.

'You alright?' she whispered, her arms shaking.

'Well, uhm, yeah,' he replied, staring at her. 'What, just, I mean, what did you just do?'

'I don't know. That truck was going to kill us, wasn't it?'

'Maybe,' he said, 'I guess.'

'So I had to stop it.'

'But how? What was that blue mist around you?'

She frowned at him.

'What mist? What are you talking about?'

She paused, hearing a faint hiss from a deflating tire. With a gasp, she turned around, staring into the field where the driver of the tractor lay.

'C'mon!' she cried. 'We've got to help him!'

They leapt out of the cart and ran over to him. He lay in a broken heap. His legs bent unnaturally back and a large metal rod stuck out of his belly. His eyes were closed and they could see he was barely breathing, his chest rising with his shallow breath. Jenny crouched down beside him and stared at his face.

She concentrated as best she could, trying to read his mind. She didn't expect to find anything but what she got was the exact opposite: chaos. It was as if every memory he had was coming to the surface, fighting for recognition, knowing it was never coming again. She tried her best to sort out the images: Children running, a fishing boat, an old woman, birds. She got nothing at all that helped her with a name.

'Paul,' she cried, 'come here - I need your help.'

He rushed over and knelt down beside her. An ambulance screeched up and two paramedics jumped out, running over to them.

'See if you can get through to him,' Jenny said to Paul. 'Tell him to think of his name, his family.'

Paul reached out and took the man's hand. It was cold and damp. He could feel a sense of total panic rushing from the man, of fear. Slowly, quietly, he started trying to reach him. He said the same thing over and over again. 'I'm here - tell me your name. I'm here - I'm Paul. Tell me your name.'

Jenny waited, listening to the calm coming over the man. The images were slowing down and starting to rest on just a few - two small girls and a name card sitting at a dinner place setting. Jenny could read it and knew who it was.

'Paul - his name is Jeffrey Sampson,' she said. The paramedics near her frowned at one another but wrote down everything she said.

Paul continued, this time using his name. 'Jeffrey - I'm Paul. Please wait. I'm Paul, Jeffrey. Can you hear me?'

To everyone watching, Paul wasn't saying anything, just holding the man's hand and looking at him. One of the paramedics started to move toward them but stopped when the man let out a loud moan.

'He's trying Paul!' exclaimed Jenny, 'He's trying! Keep talking to him.'

As Paul did, the man tightened his grip on Paul's hand. Paul was still sending the same message: 'I'm Paul, Jeffrey - Can you hear me?'

Suddenly the man's eyes opened and he looked right at Paul. His voice, barely a whisper, said 'Yes, Paul.'

Jenny could still sense the panic in him. 'Jeffrey, I'm Jenny - can you hear me?'

'Yes.'

'If it hurts to talk, don't - I can hear you anyway. The twins will be fine. Shannon will be fine.'

At the sound of his wife's name, the man smiled and closed his eyes.

'*Find them,*' he thought, '*tell them I love them.*'

'We will,' Jenny said. 'You're going to be ok - the ambulance people will take care of you.'

'*No,*' came his thoughts, '*I feel it. I'm not - but that's OK - you'll tell them, you said so, I'll be...*'

The thoughts stopped. His eyes were closed and his breathing slowed. Jenny and Paul bowed their heads, knowing he'd left. The paramedics dived in, trying to revive him.

The children stood up and stepped back. Slow, small tears leaked down their faces as they absorbed the death that lay in front of them.

The paramedics sat back, wiping the sweat from their brows. One went over to the ambulance as two police cruisers and a fire truck arrived. The other turned toward the children and Jenny started talking as soon as she was close.

'His name was Jeffrey Sampson. He's forty-six years old. His wife's name is Shannon. He lives just back there and has two twin girls, age eight. He's a cane farmer and was on his way to tend some fields.'

Jenny went on while the policemen and paramedic listened. Paul put his hand on her shoulder and she stopped, turning to him with a puzzled look on her face. The paramedic stepped back and returned to help her partner.

'I, uhm, well he...' Jenny stammered.

'Did you know him?' one of the officers said.

'Not directly,' Paul said, stepping in front of Jenny and looking right into the policeman's eyes. 'I think he works for my father, in the fields just ahead.'

'In the cane fields?'

'Yes,' Paul continued. 'I'm fairly sure.'

'Did you witness this? The crash?'

Jenny saw that the paramedics had moved the body into a shiny black bag and were zipping it up.

'Uhm, not directly sir,' Paul said. 'We had climbed up over that rock there, above the tunnel, and were on our way back when it happened.'

Jenny concentrated on the two officers and was amazed at the acceptance she found - they believed every word Paul was saying.

'That's a pretty bad cut you've got there on your shin,' one said, pointing at Paul's left leg. 'Perhaps you'd better let them have a look at it.'

Paul looked down and saw a long gash just above his ankle. He nodded at them and walked slowly over to the ambulance. Jenny started to follow, but stopped, staring into the cane fields. She felt the same cold presence that they'd felt on the cart and knew something was lurking there, watching them. She hurried over to where Paul sat, on the back of the ambulance, wincing as one of the paramedics dressed the cut on his leg.

'Did you feel that?' she whispered to him, cocking her head toward the fields.

'Yeah,' he replied, glancing over. 'We're not alone, are we?'

The paramedic finished with his bandage and rolled his pant leg back down over it.

'Try that out,' he said, helping Paul up. 'Put a bit of weight on it - how's it feel?'

Paul walked back and forth, amazed that he felt almost nothing.

'Feels great,' he said. 'Thanks!'

Another fire truck and ambulance arrived and the children could see they were trying to get into the cab of the truck. They worked slowly, tearing the sides of the cab off with a giant, claw-like machine. The children started walking toward the cane fields to investigate what they'd been sensing.

'Hey you two!' one of the police officers called out. 'Hold on. I need your names, please.'

Jenny stared at them and then at Paul but he just smiled.

'What for?' he asked.

'Because I asked you. You were witnesses to two deaths. I have to get statements from both of you.'

'I'm Paul. Paul Green.'

Jenny started to open her mouth but Paul put a hand on her shoulder.

Just tell the truth, Jenny. Trust me.

'Jennifer Greyson,' she said, spelling out her last name.

'And why were you here again? Something about climbing?'

'That's right,' Paul said. 'We were just over the tunnel, back there.'

The officer turned to look where he was pointing. He saw a sharp, tall rock wall above the tunnel and frowned.

'You were climbing there?' he asked.

'Uhm, yeah,' Paul continued. 'We weren't having much luck though, so we gave up.'

'And then we were just going to walk back home,' Jenny continued, 'but...'

'But what?' the officer asked. 'Where were you going to walk to?'

Jenny could tell he didn't believe her.

'Well, back the way we came. I've never been here but Paul says it's a nice walk.'

Paul rolled his eyes, feeling the disbelief washing off the man.

'What she means, sir, is that...'

The officer held up his hands.

'Enough, please. You weren't really climbing, were you?'

The children looked at each other but said nothing.

'That's what I thought. C'mon, both of you. We'll take you back to town, and call your parents. Whatever you were doing, I'm sure they're worried about you.'

At the sound of his words, Jenny stepped toward Paul, grabbed his hands and ran. The officer yelled, spinning around, trying to find them. His partner ran over and they started combing the area, searching for the vanished children.

When the children disappeared, the members of the order who were watching all started shouting at once. They rose from their chairs, some angrily debating, while others made their way down toward the front of the stage, gathering around three senior members, who were having a debate of their own.

'Chantal, I am telling you, it had to be a gate.'

'Docent, it could not be. They don't yet know how to create gates - it requires one of us to do so.'

'Then what was it? Where have they gone?'

'I don't know - yet. We need to put our heads together and search them out. Concentrate on their amulets - I'm sure we'll find them that way.'

She pointed at four people and nodded at them. They hurried over to the front of the stage and grabbed their amulets. The stage started shifting rapidly from scene to scene around Hawaii, trying to find the children's amulets. The people debating each other in the seats slowed down, watching with increasing dread as the stage searched without any luck.

'Perhaps a wider area?'

'No, it is something else - if I didn't know better, I'd say the children are being hidden from us.'

The Docent spun around and stared at the four stage searchers.

'What do you mean, hidden?'

'Well, sir, something else is there, I'm sure of it.'

The Docent walked over and stood beside them, watching the search. Chantal joined them.

'What are you thinking?' she asked.

'I think we should watch what just happened again. Everyone, listen please. Concentrate as hard as you can on the moment the children disappeared.'

They all sat down and stared at the stage. Their amulet's glow increased and the image on the stage wobbled, changing back to that of the children talking to the police officer. When Jenny grabbed Paul's hand, the Docent held up his arm.

'Stop,' he barked.

The image on the stage froze and they all gasped at what they saw - Jenny looked like she might be running but her speed was astonishing - she had already moved at least fifty yards from the officers when the Docent had called out.

'She's just running?' someone asked.

Several people started to chuckle, while others remained silent.

'Isaac,' Chantal called out. 'You are worried about something else, aren't you?'

'I am,' he replied from two rows back. 'Running is one thing, and it is impressive, but have you all forgotten how the truck stopped? Can anyone here do what that girl just did?'

'It is not unheard of,' Chantal mumbled.

'Then who? I've never seen it.'

The Docent held his hand up and leaned toward Chantal.

'You have another idea?' he whispered.

'No, not yet. But I've been thinking, as we watch them progress, that we may be pushing things too much.'

'What do you mean? We've got to see what they can do, and they've got to find their way here.'

'Maybe. But what else is watching? Why can't the stage find them?'

He shook his head and then looked up at the others.

'Listen, all. They can't have run far, so let's find them, and start to really challenge them.'

'I disagree,' a voice called from the back. 'Enough is enough. Pull them out, before she gets us in more trouble than we can handle.'

Voices joined in agreement and got louder and louder as they did. The Docent walked over to the stage and climbed up on it, holding his hands up for silence. It was a few moments in arriving and when it did, he stood still, staring up at the people around him.

'We cannot pull them out. If we do, we'll lose the only chance we're ever going to get.'

'To do what?' someone called out.

'Control her.'

Jenny finally slowed down about one mile down the road. She and Paul were running as hard as they could and it had taken them only a few seconds to cross the distance. When they stopped, they were both panting hard. Paul guided Jenny off the road and into the cane fields before they sat down to rest.

A few minutes later, they heard the sound of engines approaching and the ambulance passed them. Their sirens were silent; they were no longer in any hurry. The police cruiser followed a short time later, moving slowly, both officers glaring about as they passed.

When they'd finally caught their breath, they stood up and peeked out of the cane field. They could see a small town ahead from which the emergency vehicles had come.

'Let's go there,' Jenny whispered, 'and try to find out where we are.'

'I don't know,' he answered. 'Those people are going to spread the word quickly about us and what we just did.'

They were sitting twenty feet back from the road, looking at the cliffs in the distance.

They sat for a few minutes, listening for any more approaching vehicles. When none came, they stood up, picked up their bags, slung them over their shoulders and turned towards the road.

They both screamed when they saw what was standing there.

It was a man but like none they'd seen before. His skin was a sallow grey, his eyes were sunken and tired and his clothes old, tattered and worn. But his voice, when he spoke, was young and bubbling with energy.

'Jenny Greyson. And Paul Green. I've been watching you since you arrived. Very impressive, I must say.'

He was blocking the path back to the road and showed no sign of moving.

'Who are you?' Paul asked.

'Me? What do you mean? You've learned all about me. You've been *taught* about me, briefed on my exploits, convinced of my worthlessness.'

The manner in which he spoke made them shiver, as if his words were wet, or oily. They drew back from him, slightly repulsed. He was standing up straight and was tall, towering over both of them. When they didn't reply, he continued, slightly taken aback.

'My name, as much of it as can be said out loud, is Aloysius Strumn - a name you have no doubt heard, and fear.'

Jenny and Paul looked at each other and then back at the man, shaking their heads.

'Well no, actually, we haven't,' said Paul. 'Ever.'

'Why should we have heard of you?' Jenny continued.

Aloysius Strumn smiled, a slow, crooked smile with a glint in his eyes.

'How delightful!' he said. 'You haven't been told. There may be hope yet!'

He bound toward them and shook their hands gravely. Jenny flinched when he grabbed hers.

'Come, sit, I'm so pleased we're going to get to know each other.'

His voice still rang of something off-color, something neither Jenny nor Paul could place. His eyes darted between them, nervously, like he was hiding something. Jenny and Paul sat down and looked at him.

'Excellent!' he exclaimed. 'Now then, let me tell you about myself. My name, as I said, is Aloysius Strumn, and I...'

'I'm hungry!' Jenny interrupted.

Paul glared at her but Aloysius Strumn just smiled.

'Then you should eat, young lady. Hunger does not promote an open mind!'

He turned around and reached into the canes behind him, rummaging for something. When he turned back, he had a basket full of bread, fruits, jam and juice. Paul and Jenny looked at it in amazement and then tucked in.

'One day,' Strumn continued, 'you'll understand how easy it is to find what you want, if you know where to look. Or perhaps how to look would be a better way of putting it. Mmmm, yes, that probably would be best. Now then.'

'I am, like you two, a little bit different than most people...'

'Yeah,' snickered Jenny, 'we noticed. Nice clothes.'

'Jenny!' Paul hissed at her. 'What are you doing?'

'Don't worry Mr. Green,' said Strumn. 'She can't help it. It's me. I have this effect on most people. I tend to disrupt people - in fact, I tend to disrupt almost everything. Well, everything that needs it.'

He broke off, casting his eyes slowly around.

'What are you looking for?' asked Paul.

'Nothing much, young man!' he replied. 'I just need to be cautious. They won't want me talking to you two, that's for sure!'

'Who won't?' Jenny asked.

'You know - the order. Those meddlesome twerps think they know the way things should be, but they really don't. They're quite sure I'm the source of everything that ever goes wrong. I *cause* everything to be wrong, to hear them speak.'

'Do you?'

'No. In fact, quite often it's just a matter of perspective. What they might think is wrong, or evil, I might think is actually exactly right. Take that accident you just saw, for example. Nasty business that.'

'Yes,' said Paul, 'it was. We almost got hurt and then that poor man died!'

'I know,' Aloysius Strumn replied. 'I know. Two men died actually. You really have got to learn when not to interfere. They'd have found out soon enough who Jeffrey was and you two, if you'd just shut up, could now be searching about in that town over there for whatever it is you're supposed to find.'

Jenny was looking at Strumn with increasing suspicion. She couldn't quite place what was bothering her and found him almost impossible to read. It was as if he wasn't there.

'The accident had to happen. Terrible thing, yes, but it was necessary. I saw no other choice.'

'Are you saying,' said Paul slowly, 'that you had something to do with it?'

'That you caused it?' Jenny added.

'Well, it depends how you look at it. I didn't actually cause it, that fool of a truck driver did. He could have made it much cleaner.'

Jenny and Paul were shocked and Strumn was getting more agitated, his hands practically flapping in front of him.

'Now look children, you do not understand. Events happen. Jeffrey was going to die very soon, I knew that. It was just a matter of how, and in my opinion, going out like he did is far more humane than dying slowly of an incurable disease.'

'What are you talking about?' Jenny asked. 'How is a tragic accident like that a humane way to die?'

'Well, everyone is going to feel very sorry for him, don't you think? I mean, he was the good father, the good farmer, off to the fields, loved the twins, loved Shannon, wanted the best for them. Dying of cancer was not the best for them, especially here.'

'Cancer?' exclaimed Paul. 'How do you know all this? And what exactly have you just done?'

'Well Paul, I'm like you, like Jenny, only far older, and far better at it. I've found, over my long years, that it is best to bring on the inevitable.

If a tree is going to fall,' he continued, looking sharply at Jenny, 'it's best to just bring it down. Likewise with Jeffrey: he was going to die soon anyways - my way was faster.'

'Why did you leave them?' she interrupted.

'Leave who?' he frowned.

'The order. You left. Or,' she paused, 'No, wait, were you asked to leave?'

Aloysius Strumn glared at her.

'So you lied - you have been told of me' he said.

'No,' said Jenny. 'You're just not as good as you think.'

Strumn smiled again, a slow, crooked smile.

'Very good Jenny! I'm even more impressed. You've still got quite a bit to learn, but, I think one day you'll be very good at this. You should stay with me.'

He turned to Paul. 'You both should. I could teach you far faster than is customary.'

'Teach us what?' asked Paul.

'Dear boy, have you not realized why all this is happening to you? Why it is that you're not back in London, with your mother and grandparents? You're being taught who you are, what you can do!'

He suddenly stopped and stared past the children, into the cane field. Rising slowly, he walked over to the edge.

'Something wrong?' Jenny asked.

Paul put a hand on her shoulder.

Something's there he thought to her. *He can feel it. Something's watching.*

Strumn picked up a broken piece of cane and threw it into the brush. It stopped in midair, bounced back and fell to the ground. Strumn turned back toward the children.

'I can't believe you're still here,' he whispered. 'They should never allow this!'

'Who shouldn't?' Paul asked.

'Shhh,' Strumn hissed. 'You're being watched by more than just the order.'

The children's eyes widened.

'By what, then?' Paul continued. 'It's right there, isn't it?'

Strumn shook his head.

'No, it moved when I threw the stick. I can't find it. But I will tell you this, and if any member of the order is watching, they should know this too. What's watching you, if I'm right, is very old and very dangerous. The order should pull you out right now.'

He turned, grabbed the basket and dashed into the cane, fading from view before he finally vanished. Jenny and Paul looked at each other, astounded at his sudden and unusual exit.

Chapter 8

Are We Alone?

When she returned from her journeys, Canace's sister brought back all that she was given: rugs, pots, paintings, and exotic foods. Canace worked hard, using the strength of the wind that was in her, to make their home adjust, and the mountain hollowed itself before them.

'Let's get out of here,' Paul said. 'Which way?'

Jenny looked around and then pointed toward the cliffs.

'Better avoid the town, I think,' she said.

'But what about Strumn? What he saw?'

She looked around, trying to sense anything around her.

'I can't feel anything here - you? You're better at this than me.'

Paul stopped and closed his eyes. He stood still for several seconds and then looked at her.

'Nothing. And when Strumn felt something, so did I.'

'You're sure?'

'Yeah - let's get moving. I want to get out of here as soon as we can.'

They picked up their gear and started walking. It was hard work moving through the fields and they left a trail behind them of broken cane, footprints and dust. After an hour they finally broke out of the cane. The mountain loomed large in front of them but the village was nowhere to be seen.

They headed for a small stream that was flowing along the side of the mountain. When they got there, Jenny kicked off her boots and waded in.

'Oh!' she shrieked. 'It's cold!'

'Great,' said Paul, 'I'm roasting.'

He took off his boots and joined her. Jenny reached down and cupped some of the water to her mouth.

'Is that a good idea?' asked Paul.

'Sure,' Jenny said. 'It's just rainwater I bet. I drink out of streams like this back home all the time.'

Paul drank some as well before they got out and sat down, letting their feet rest and dry in the sun. Once they were, they set off again, following the stream. After a few minutes of walking, they noticed their amulets were warming up.

'Gate or guide, do you think?' asked Paul.

'My money's on guide,' said Jenny.

'What money? We could use some of that. Get a nice hotel room, some food, some sleep.'

Jenny smiled. 'Wouldn't that be great? We could let everyone know we're safe, go back to the beach, have a swim, some dinner, watch TV all night and then sleep all the next day!'

'I think I've seen enough of that ocean,' grinned Paul. 'C'mon. Let's find what's causing these things to heat up.'

They walked towards a small waterfall that fed the stream. When they got there, the amulets were almost too hot to touch. They looked around, expecting someone to walk out of the shadows, or for another cave to appear. Nothing did happen and the amulets began to cool off.

'Guide,' said Paul.

'I agree,' said Jenny, 'they stay warm for gates, and cool off for guides. Isn't that what that idiot bird said?'

'I'd watch that,' said Paul. 'Remember what it did to you.'

She shuddered and rubbed her side. They started poking around among the rocks and trees, searching for the guide.

'I can't believe it' said Jenny, exasperated. 'There's nothing here, and there's so much to ask!'

'No kidding. Like where are we?' he replied. 'Or why are we doing this?'

'What about buying food, or finding somewhere to sleep?'

As soon as she asked, the rock face beside the waterfall rippled and words began to appear on it:

'*To buy food, or find shelter, just use money.*'

'Paul!' said Jenny. 'Look!'

She pointed at the rock. He did, just as the words began to fade.

'Wow!' he said. 'It's like it heard you.'

'Perhaps that's our guide.'

'Well, why doesn't it keep going?'

'*Because you didn't ask.*'

The words appeared as soon as he had asked and faded away right after.

'Ah,' said Jenny. 'I think I get it. You have to ask a question, and it will answer. Watch. Will you answer all our questions?'

'No.'

'Why not?' she demanded.

'*Not all questions have answers. Not all answers should have questions.*'

'That's nice and confusing,' grumbled Paul. 'It told us before to just use money. That would be nice. Where are we supposed to get that?'

'*You already have it.*'

They looked at each other in confusion.

'Where do we have it?'

'*Look in your bag, when you need it.*'

Jenny reached for her bag and looked in. Her cloak was stuffed in so she removed it. Nothing else was in there, including her walking stick which she knew she'd put there earlier.

'There's nothing here. Are you sure?'

'*You don't need it.*'

The words were already fading.

'What do you mean?' she asked. 'Of course I do!'

'*When you need it, you have it. Now, you don't need it.*'

Jenny was starting to get annoyed. Paul was rummaging through his bag.

'What I need,' he fumed, 'is a bit more to eat. I didn't get enough of that...'

He stopped and pulled his hand from the bag. In it was an apple.

'How did this get here?' he asked. The words appeared immediately.

'*You need it.*'

'Ok, ok,' said Jenny. 'That makes sense! The bag can give us things we need. Will it give us anything?'

'*No.*'

'What will it give us?'

'*What you need.*'

The words faded out and no more appeared. Paul took a bite of his apple and went over to the stone wall, running his hand over it.

'Where did you go?' he asked. There was no response.

'I suppose that's it, then,' he said

'I think so,' said Jenny. 'Maybe we should go. I'd really like to get to a hotel, and phone home - let everyone know I'm ok.'

'How are we going to do that?' Paul demanded. 'Remember last night? We hopped a ride in that Lorry! We're a long way from the beach.'

'Oh yeah. That could be a problem. What we could use now is a map.'

'So,' he said. 'If you need it...'

'... look in the bag!' she exclaimed. She opened her bag again and pulled out a map. She stared at it for a while before setting it down.

'I've no idea where we are!' she said.

'Spread it out, lets have a look,' said Paul.

They laid the map out and stared at it.

'Look,' said Paul. 'There's the village you said Jeffrey was from. There's a road, and mountains - that must be where we are.'

'If that's true, we're no where near the beach!' said Jenny.

'Well, let's see. If we follow the road this way, here's the next town - that must be where the ambulances were from. If you keep going, the road comes to a bigger road - perhaps a motorway...'

The sun was high in the sky and they threw their cloaks over their heads to ward off its heat. The cloaks changed again, becoming lightweight with a reflective, metallic surface. After another long, hard trip through the cane fields, they came back to the road. They set off towards the town where they assumed the ambulances had come from, hoping not to run in to the police.

They heard an engine in the distance and saw, as it came around the corner, that it was a bus. Waving frantically, they rushed toward it. The driver stopped and opened the door.

'You're a long way from anywhere,' he said pleasantly.

'Can we get a lift?' Paul asked, reaching his hand out. 'To anywhere?'

The driver looked puzzled but took his hand, shook it and then smiled.

'Sure, I'm going to Kaunaoa beach - bit of a trek.'

'Does it have a hotel?'

'Absolutely - have a seat.'

They did, right in the front.

'Paul,' Jenny whispered. 'How did you do that?'

'I thought you already knew,' he teased.

'Well, not like that. What did you do?'

'I've never really known - I just, talk, you know? And people listen.'

'Cool,' she said as the bus started off. 'I wish I could do that.'

She stared out the window at the passing fields, before lying back against the cushion and drifting off.

Paul tapped her shoulder some time later.

'Jenny' he said. 'We're here!'

She opened her eyes and looked out. A small, white hotel stood ahead of them. The bus driver had already gotten out, letting other passengers off. They climbed out and dashed away before he noticed they were gone. When they entered the lobby, they felt a cool blast from the air conditioner. Several people were staring at them and they were instantly aware of how strange they looked. They got in line for reception and stepped up as soon as they could.

'May I help you,' said a small man behind the desk.

'Yes please!' said Jenny. 'Do you have any rooms available?'

'Young lady, I'm afraid that while I may have rooms, I cannot give one to you!'

He spoke in a smug way, pleased to be able to rebuke her.

Paul stepped in front of her and placed his hand over the man's.

'You can give one to me, though, can't you?'

'Y- yes,' he said, faltering, not knowing why he was saying it. 'Please fill out this card.'

He handed Paul a registration card. He filled it in, using his uncle's name and address.

'What sort of room would you require, sir?'

'A suite please, two rooms, with an ocean view. Non-smoking, obviously.'

'Quite,' the little man replied. 'Let me see what we have.'

Jenny did her best not to react to Paul's conversation. She could tell from the hotel clerk's mind that he thought Paul was an adult. The people in line were trying not to laugh and to stop herself, she turned and stared at the clock above the counter.

'Here we are, sir, room 412 - how many keys?'

'Two, please,' he said.

'Certainly. I'll need an imprint of a credit card, please.'

Without hesitation, Paul reached in his bag and drew out a credit card, which he handed over. When their registration was complete, they headed up to their floor, found their way to their room and opened the door. What they saw made them both gasp - the room was beautiful, with a westerly view of the ocean, a terrace and two bedrooms. Jenny rushed in to the bigger one and collapsed on the bed.

'Dibbs! You get the crap room!'

Paul walked in, smiling. 'So did you like that down there?'

'Sure did!' she said, 'You're a good mimic. But that clerk was pretty weak minded. He's too busy thinking about his date tonight to pay attention to us.'

'Well,' said Paul, 'it worked. We'll get a great sleep tonight. Let's go for a swim.'

'Shouldn't we call home first?' she said. 'I really want to let my parents know I'm ok.'

'It's still too early in the morning there,' he replied, pointing at the clock. 'We will soon. C'mon.'

'Well what about bathing suits?'

'No problem,' he said. 'Shall we go shopping first?'

They went down to the lobby, wound their way through the tourists to the hotel's general store, and found swimsuits, toothbrushes, and pajamas. They put everything on their room tab, went back upstairs to change and headed for the pool. Jenny dipped her toe in and looked back at him.

'You ready?' she asked him.

'Almost. I wouldn't mind warming up here in the sun for a bit first.'

He reached in to the beach bag they'd bought, grabbed some sun lotion and started putting it on.

'Here,' he said, handing it to her. 'You look like the burning type. Better get some of this on.'

'I did upstairs - see ya!' she cried, turning around and diving in. She was amazed at how warm the water was - like jumping into an enormous bathtub. She swam back to the edge, near Paul.

'C'mon, lazy, this water's really warm!'

Paul leaned down to test it and she grabbed his arm to pull him in. He returned to the surface, spluttering and smiling and tried to push her under. She dove down and swam away, heading toward the waterfall. Paul burst away, caught her and then splashed her as he went past. They got to the waterfall and sat down underneath it, feeling the water falling around them.

'So, what do you suppose we do next?' asked Paul.

'Eat,' she said, looking around at all the people and their food.

'No, I didn't mean that, I meant what's going to happen next?'

Jenny leaned back to let the water splash her head and emerged moments later.

'You know what?' she said. 'Maybe we should just go home. We've got some money now, so we could just buy some tickets and go, right?'

'I don't know if we really can,' he replied. 'That credit card came out of the bag. What if it just disappears? What if someone tries to stop us?'

'You mean like the order?' Jenny said. 'They haven't helped us yet. We're on our own.'

'But that's sort of the point, isn't it? We're supposed to find our way back to the common - that's what they said.'

Jenny crossed her arms, letting the water pound down on her back.

'Don't you feel, like, abandoned?' she asked. 'Weird?'

'Well, yes, of course,' he said. 'But I also feel like we're doing quite well. I mean, I can sense so much more than I used to, because of the amulets.'

'I know. Me too. Hearing people's thoughts is getting easier all the time.'

'And what about your speed? That was quite a run earlier. And the way you stopped the truck from hitting us?'

'I didn't even know I could do that,' she replied after a moment.

Paul looked at her and saw the faint blue aura around her, shimmering slightly in the sun.

'I can see it,' he whispered.

'See what?'

'You're surrounded by something that only I seem to see. It's, I don't know, it looks like a blue glow. The same color as these,' he said, holding up his amulet.

'Really?' she said, stretching her arms out, trying to see what he meant. 'I can't see anything.'

'Well I can. But it's very faint.'

'What do you think it is?'

'I don't know. Maybe it's just you - maybe I can sense something of you that no one else can. But it's what stopped the truck.'

'*What?*' she exclaimed.

'It was. When you held your arms out, I saw it - it got really bright, and then when you yelled at the truck, the mist stopped it.'

'Wow.'

'No kidding. I bet we're supposed to figure out how.'

She nodded and slipped back into the water. She dove under and swam slowly across the pool. She looked at the amulet, hanging heavily on the end of its chain and noticed it wasn't bubbling. Only when I need it she thought, her head breaking the surface. Maybe that mist is the same. She climbed out of the pool, spread her towel out on a chair and leaned back on it, letting the sun warm her.

Paul arrived moments later and did the same.

'Do you know something else?' he asked, turning to look at her.

'What?' she said her eyes still closed, basking in the sun.

'I'm really glad I met you.'

Jenny grinned.

'Me too.'

They lay in the sun for a while, as it lowered in the sky. When others started to leave and the poolside concession closed, they packed their things and headed to the lobby.

'Hey,' Jenny said, grabbing Paul's arm, 'I want to get some more clothes - for tonight I mean. We can't wear our hiking gear to the restaurant!'

Paul chose light, conservative shorts and a polo shirt, and Jenny an Aztec patterned sun dress. When they got back to their room, they cleaned up and sat down in front of the television. Paul fell asleep almost at once, since he hadn't slept on the bus and Jenny watched TV until it became too boring.

She headed out to the terrace and watched the sun descending toward the westerly horizon. She leaned on the rail smiling and watched the boats drifting across the setting sun's reflection. They looked tiny and with the orange glow behind them all she could see was their black silhouettes. She sat down on one of the chairs and sighed, the smile slowly disappearing. A few minutes after the sun's disk dropped below the horizon, she stood up and walked back in to the room, glancing over at Paul, who was still slouched over, sound asleep.

'Here, lean over,' she whispered, lowering him onto a cushion. 'You're going to hurt your neck like that.'

She went over to the small desk in the living room and started reading the hotel's booklet, trying to figure out how to call her parents. She picked up the phone and, following the instructions, dialed her home in Banff.

The phone line clicked and hissed a couple of times and then started ringing. She waited for someone to answer and then heard the click as the receiver was picked up.

'We're sorry - all the lines are busy. Please try your call again later.'

Jenny hung up, and stared at the desk, her head in her hands. How could there be no lines? She knew her phone number and had dialed it properly. Something was definitely wrong.

At seven she finally woke Paul up. 'Hey, c'mon - dinner'

'Leave me alone,' he grumped, slowly waking up. 'I'm not hungry.'

Jenny poked him in the ribs. 'Paul - Let's go.'

As he sat up he noticed her mood - she was trying to be light but had a dark cloud hanging over her.

'What's wrong with you?' he asked.

'Nothing,' she said.

'C'mon Jenny, you know I can tell. You're upset about something.'

'Yeah maybe,' she sighed. 'I'll tell you at dinner.'

'Ok - let me go get changed,' he said, heading off to his room.

'And hey,' he said, turning back and grabbing her hand. 'Relax. We will figure this out.'

Jenny tried to smile, watching him leave, before turning to her mirror and tying her hair back in a bun. She looked at the yellow flowers that were on the counter and remembered what Sarah did to her hair. She picked one and pinned it into the bun. When Paul returned, he looked at her and raised an eyebrow.

'Wow! You look, well, great,' he said, trailing off.

'Thanks,' she mumbled, heading toward the door.

They went down and found the restaurant. They told the host that their parents had gone to another restaurant and that they would like a table just for themselves. He led them to one near the window, overlooking the beach. Paul stepped behind Jenny's chair and held it for her and then sat down in his chair.

'Hey,' she said. 'Why did you to do that?'

Paul smiled. 'Consider it part of your training. To be civilized, one must pay attention to the details. Chivalry, unfortunately, has been forgotten.'

'What are you talking about?' she laughed.

'Chivalry. Common decency. You've quite a bit to learn, I'm afraid.'

'Yeah right. Let's just eat.'

Paul whispered something to the waiter and then ordered fruit punch for both of them. While they waited, they watched people arriving for their meals and let the feeling of happiness that surrounded them pull them in. Minutes later the waiter interrupted the children's laughter with their drinks and a plate of deep fried ringlets.

'What is this?' Jenny asked.

'Calamari, of course,' Paul replied. 'It's squid. Quite delicious.'

Jenny wrinkled her nose in disgust. 'I hate squid.'

Paul looked at her. 'You've never tried it.'

'I have so.'

'When?' he asked.

When she didn't answer he stabbed a piece with his fork, dipped in salsa and popped it in her mouth.

'Chew,' he said.

'It's great!' she exclaimed, a smile spreading across her face.

'No kidding,' he said. 'So what was happening back upstairs? When you were so upset?'

'I tried to phone home, you know, to tell everyone I was ok.'

'And?'

'I couldn't. Something's wrong with the phone lines.'

'You're sure you did it properly?'

'Yes. I tried several times. It kept saying there were no outgoing lines or something and I don't know what to do.'

'Let's finish dinner and I'll try my mother when we go back up.'

They finished as soon as they could and headed back to their room. Paul started reading through the phone instructions, doing some calculations.

'You know what?' he said. 'I can't call right now - it's still too early.'

'What?'

'The time zones, you know - everyone will still be asleep. Let's call first thing tomorrow.'

With a sigh she sat down on the sofa.

'I guess you're right. I'm getting tired anyway - I think I'll go to bed.'

Paul watched as she went to her room and closed the door. Since he wasn't tired, he sat in the living room watching TV. He couldn't believe how many channels there were and how almost all of it was awful. As he flipped, he came across a newscast and stopped.

On the screen were pictures of the accident from that morning, obviously taken after they'd left. The reporter was talking about the awful deaths, with pictures of the two men, and giving details about their families. Paul considered going to wake Jenny but froze with the next words:

'Police report that there were details of the crash with which they were very troubled and that they were seeking two children in connection with the accident.'

A police artist sketch of Jenny and him appeared on the screen and while it didn't look anything like them, he didn't like the fact that their encounter with the police was making headlines on television. Paul watched as they continued describing the circumstances of the accident:

A routine morning, clear skies, no inland fog or other visibility hazard. Jeffrey Sampson was traveling along the northwestern edge of the cane fields, when he was struck head-on by a large truck. The truck had bounced into a rock cliff, killing the driver on impact. Sampson had been thrown clear of the tractor and died a short time later. The circumstances of his death were suspicious, police report, saying only that the two children on the scene knew things that they could not have known if they hadn't been involved.

When the report ended, Paul switched off the television and thought about what he'd just learned. He assumed they were still being hunted and the longer they stayed, the more likely they were to be caught. The sketches didn't look like them but he was sure the two police officers and the paramedics would recognize them right away. If the bus driver or any of the hotel staff saw this report, they might turn them in. He went to bed wondering how to tell Jenny that they couldn't stay any longer at the hotel.

The next morning Jenny rose with the sun. She peeked into Paul's room and saw that he was still asleep. She sat down at the desk with the phone and tried to call her parents again. Her face fell as she listened to the voice in the receiver.

'You have dialed a number that is not in service. Please hang up, and try your call again.'

'*What now?*' she thought, '*I can't have dialed the wrong number.*'

She tried once more and got the same result so she dialed directory service in Banff. After a few rings, an operator came on the line.

'Residential or Business?' she asked in a bored tone.

'Um, residential please,' Jenny said.

Hearing a child's voice, the operator softened. 'Sure, dear. Who would you like to find?'

'Greyson - Donald Greyson, on Roselawn Street,' Jenny replied.

'Ok - just one moment.'

Jenny could hear a tapping sound while she waited.

'I'm sorry - I'm not finding that. Could you spell the last name for me please, dear?'

'G - r - e - y - s - o - n.'

'Nope, I'm not getting anything. Are you sure it's in Banff?'

'Quite sure. Umm, I'll call back. Thank you.'

'You have a good day, dear. Thank you for calling.'

Jenny stood up and stared out the window at the morning sea. She felt a frantic urge to move, so she scratched out a note for Paul, pulled on her bathing suit, sundress, sandals and sunglasses and headed out the door.

The swimming pool was deserted when she went by and there wasn't a cloud in the sky. The sun was rising on the far side of the island, leaving the beach in shade. The tide was out and strange things had washed up on the sand - Jellyfish and mottled green plants. She walked down to the edge of the water and then along it towards a small stretch of rock that rose at the northern edge of the beach.

The early light rose over the ocean and she saw no sign of anyone else. While the voices in her mind were as peaceful and quiet as they'd been in many years, she couldn't shake the feeling of dread she felt. As she wandered along, she watched the gentle surf washing the beach. Her footprints were being slowly erased and when she looked back toward the distant hotel, there was no sign of her passing.

She came to the rock and sat down on it, pulling her knees up to her chest and resting her head on them, just watching the water. She pulled out her amulet and looked at it. The blue glow was quite faint, since Paul's amulet was far away. She stared through it at the water, watching the light patterns from the sea bounce through it, thinking again about the phone and her parents.

She didn't even hear him approach.

'Good morning, Jenny,' an oily voice said behind her.

She nearly jumped out of her skin in surprise and whirled around to see Aloysius Strumn standing there. He was looking at her in a strange way, as if he was trying to look through her.

'Um, Hi,' she said. 'I didn't hear you come up.'

'I didn't,' he said. 'I don't always walk. I don't have to.'

He paused.

'I was just thinking about you two - wondering how you were holding up?'

The way he said it gave Jenny the creeps. She was quite sure he was hiding something but she couldn't tell what it was. He sat down beside her and began idly lobbing pebbles into the water, checking his hands after each throw.

'So,' he asked, 'did Paul tell you about your new found fame?'

'I don't know what you're talking about,' she said firmly.

'Then he didn't tell you. You were on TV last night.'

'On TV?' she gasped. 'What do you mean?'

'Well, not you exactly but a rather poor drawing of you. The police want to find you Jenny, and Paul.'

'But we've stayed out of trouble - we've been really quiet and good.'

'Yes, my dear, I've noticed. You've been enjoying yourselves, haven't you?'

'I guess,' she said. 'But there's been some weird stuff. We have to be careful.'

'Of course you do,' Strumn replied. 'Of many things, several of which most people never hear of.'

'Like you?' she blurted.

'I'd imagine you already know the answer, Jenny. I see things differently than most people, and do not suffer scum gladly.'

Jenny gulped.

'So what do you do - just kill people?'

'Oh no - I don't kill, despite what you may think. I merely disrupt people's choices. What they do with that is up to them - if they do nothing, they might get killed.'

He paused for effect.

'Or they may change - for the better.'

Jenny looked at him. Strumn was fidgeting more than usual and seemed to be having a hard time sitting down.

'What do you mean 'change'?' she asked.

'Well, young lady, this is where I'm most misunderstood. I disrupt people, those most in need. I don't kill them. For some, certainly, this leads to death, like poor Jeffrey yesterday, but, as I said to you then, that was a much kinder death.'

'I still don't think you have the right to decide that!' Jenny exclaimed.

'But I agree, my dear, I don't have - nor do I.'

'Then what does?'

'Fate - circumstance - the finer workings of time, who knows?' he said. 'I am a small part of that. One which most people, particularly those in the order, *abhor!*'

He practically hissed the words out and his whole body was shaking hard. Aloysius Strumn was most upset, Jenny could tell and while she still couldn't read much out of him, she could feel a sincerity flowing off him.

'So you still didn't tell me what you meant by 'change'.'

'Ah, well, think of it this way. When a boat is traveling on calm seas, it can usually find its way fairly easily. But, in rough seas, many course corrections are required to get it to its destination. I provide course corrections to those in rough seas. I do not, however, provide the destination.'

He stood up, pacing back and forth.

'For example, yesterday I ran in to a young thief. He's perfectly healthy, has a reasonably happy family life - he doesn't need to steal. I would have guided him into the hands of much worse thieves, who would have either slit his throat, or scared him onto a saner path. Either way, there'd be one less thief to worry about.

'Unfortunately I was too late, and he was caught, handed over to the police. It is likely he will become even more hardened against authority, and pursue, upon his release, a more reckless path. I only ever get one chance to disrupt, so he's now a lost cause.'

Jenny couldn't decide how she felt about Strumn. His methods were quite alien to her and yet he knew so much about her and Paul. She wondered why he seemed so eager to talk to them and whether he would help them - whether that was wrong.

'You are wondering, just now, why the phone won't work?' he asked.

She shuddered. While she often did that to others, no one had ever read her thoughts and thrown them back at her.

'Y-Yes,' she stammered. 'It was so strange. I know my own phone number, and it didn't work.'

He paced back to her.

'I have to go now, Jenny, as I'm needed elsewhere, and judging from that little trinket round your neck, Paul is close to finding you.'

He pointed at the amulet and its increasing glow.

'I'll leave you with this thought: Not everything you see here is entirely real, no matter how much it may appear so to you. Try, if you can, to separate the real from the - *placed.*'

He turned and walked into the sea. By the time he was up to his waist, he was transparent and by the time his head went under, she couldn't see anything but the current marks of his passing.

Paul came dashing across the beach, panting and stopped in front of her.

'Where have you been? I've been worried sick.'

'You're sweet when you're being a twit,' she smiled. 'Didn't you read my note?'

Paul paused. 'What note?'

'The one I pinned to the door.'

'I didn't see any note,' he mumbled, looking down at the sand.

'I just - wanted to get some fresh air, and I'd had enough sleep.'

Paul knew she was hiding something, so he looked at the ground and saw all the footprints, many made by feet much bigger than hers.

'Who where you talking to?'

'Aloysius Strumn. And he had some interesting things to say.'

'Like what?'

'Well, I don't think he's actually that bad a person.'

'But Jenny, he *killed* that man yesterday.'

'You know, I don't think he did. There's more to him than that.'

They returned to their room where Jenny tried to phone her parents again with the same result. It took Paul longer to figure out how to dial from Hawaii to London but eventually he heard the other end ringing.

He also got an answer. The man at the other end of the line was clearly not his mother or his grandfather and he was quite irritated at having to answer. Paul patiently explained that he must have dialed the wrong number and confirmed with the man the number he had dialed.

He slammed the phone down and stomped over to the terrace. Jenny joined him and put a hand on his shoulder.

'Are we alone?' he asked, looking back at her.

'I don't know,' she whispered. 'But I do know that Strumn said that not everything we see is real. He called it *placed*.'

'Placed? I wonder what that means.'

'Perhaps the phones have been tampered with just to make us think something strange is going on.'

'Yeah, so what do we do?'

'Well, what if we go there?' she replied.

'Where?'

'Home. Banff, or London. It would be pretty hard to hide a house, don't you think?'

'Yeah, good idea!' he said. 'But I think that the only way out of here is the way we came. Through a gate.'

He walked back toward his bedroom but then suddenly stopped near their fireplace, holding his amulet.

'Look at this Jenny,' he said.

She did. In the fireplace which not a minute ago had been dark and cold, a fire raged. As she approached, her amulet started to heat up.

'Do you think it's a gate?' she asked.

'I'm afraid it might be - again.'

'And will you be ok, you know, with the fire?'

His face fell but he nodded.

Jenny looked down at her feet and her beach sandals. 'I guess we'd better change, and figure out what to do.'

A few moments later, they were dressed in their travel clothes with all their new belongings stuffed in their bags. They were standing in front of the fire, wondering how the gate was supposed to work.

'What do think?' asked Paul. 'Is it real?'

Jenny held her hand out close to the fire. It was warm but not scorching hot.

'It doesn't feel quite like a normal fire - it's more like...'

'This isn't a good idea,' he stated. 'There has to be another way.'

'No, it'll be fine,' she replied. 'It's sort of like the fire at the common.'

She opened her bag and found that everything she'd put in it was gone, all except her walking stick. She pulled it out and Paul did the same.

She went over to the fire and poked it with the stick. It didn't change at all; no sparks, no disturbance of the flame. When she tried to poke one of the logs, the walking stick sunk right in.

'It's like how you got here,' she said. 'We have to step in.'

'Are you crazy?' he said. 'We'll get burnt! Maybe even killed!'

She reached out her hand and stuck it in. She pulled it back out with no damage.

'I'm quite sure,' she said.

'Well, ok,' he said, 'but this time we go together. Let's just hope it takes us close to home! I want to figure out what's going on.'

Holding each other's hand, still talking about where they hoped to be going, they stepped into the fire and disappeared.

Chapter 9

Where the Gates Go

Their amulets were their completion, and to Canace and her sister, they marveled every day at what they had been given. For two years they had slept, in their mountain-cave, safe from the cold, from the thirst, and from the hunger. When they awoke, their bond was stronger, and at their feet, glowing a bright blue and waiting to be worn, were the originals, the first of an unbroken line.

When the children emerged on the other side of the gate, their first instinct was to turn around and jump back in. The fire was gone, the warmth of Hawaii and the comfort of their room lost.

The gate had dumped them in the middle of a raging snowstorm, in a bitterly cold, isolated place. They couldn't see more than ten feet in front of them and the driving wind started caking them with cold, icy snow.

Paul flung his arms up in front of his face and sat down, curling up into a ball. The snow began piling up against him and he started to shiver. He wanted to open his mouth and scream, but couldn't - his jaw was too cold to respond. He glanced up and saw Jenny, her arm braced in front of her, staring at something.

He stood up and struggled over to her. The wind whipped his cloak against him so he drew it tight. When he reached her, he grabbed her arm and froze. His sense of her had changed. It was as if there were two people standing in front of him - the Jenny he knew and someone else, an ancient memory struggling to the surface.

When she had stepped out of the gate and the snow and wind had hit her, she had instinctively known they were in trouble. The air had a numbing bite to it that was familiar and the speed of the wind, the amount of snow that had hit them told her this was a mountain storm.

She saw Paul crouch down and just as she was about to do the same, just as the panic was going to hit her, she heard a familiar voice, carried in the snow.

'It is the wind my sister - it is you.'

She staggered over, a dizzy, nauseous feeling washing over her. She'd heard the words before, so many times, in the nightmare of the two girls. She looked up, expecting to see the snow replaced by fire and was hit in the face by a blast of wind and ice.

'Watch the wind - watch what you are doing.'

She heard the voice this time as she did people's thoughts and smiled. She gathered her cloak around her, throwing part of it over head, concealing most of her face. She held her other hand out in front of her and studied the snow patterns on the wind, saw where they were coming from.

'That's it, my sister. You remember, don't you?'

Jenny nodded. The snow was blowing hard along the line of the land and as Paul put his hand on her arm, she felt the voice recede. The snow didn't swirl at all and she realized it was driving up a steep slope, one with no trees or any other vegetation. This was a mountain storm and they were in a terrible place: a peak that rose above the tree line.

'Jenny!' Paul yelled in a barely audible voice. 'Where are we?'

She turned her head slowly toward him, feeling the last of the nausea disappear.

'I'm not sure,' she yelled back. 'But it's definitely a mountain top, and we've got to get out of here!'

'How?'

'Follow me - hold my hand, and go slowly.'

He nodded, brushing the snow off his face.

'Pull your cloak around you like me,' she yelled.

He did, and noticed how it had changed - it had become heavy black wool, woven so tightly the snow and wind couldn't get through it. He held it closed with one hand and held hers with the other.

Jenny watched the wind again and chose a path leading away from the storm. They moved down the side of the mountain, pausing after each step to catch their breath. Even though they were moving slowly, they were panting, their lungs working hard at such a high altitude. Jenny felt the tremors in Paul's hand and concentrated on him, feeling the turmoil.

'Hey,' she panted, turning around and looking at him through her cloak. 'We'll be fine, ok?'

'What about that!' he said, pointing at the snow ahead of them.

Jenny turned to look where he was pointing. The wind was rushing at them, blowing the snow with it. Something wasn't right about it - a huge gap, like a bubble, moved slowly across.

'Is that caused by the wind?' Paul shouted.

'I don't know,' she replied. 'I've never seen anything like it.'

They looked again, trying to find the strange bubble but it was gone. Jenny turned around, leading them further down. After half an hour's descent, they saw the tall shadows of trees loom out of the storm. They could see the snow driving over them, the outer edge of the trees bending against the wind's strength.

They fought their way toward the trees, their faces nearly numb with cold. They felt the snow back off at the edge and then, as they moved deep into the woods, the air slowed. It was still bitterly cold, but the snow, ice and wind were held back by the thick trees. Jenny guided them to a tightly formed grove and they sat down beside each other, drawing near for warmth.

They sat in silence, letting the canopy protect them until their shivering died down, their breathing slowed and the feeling returned to their faces.

'Well!' Jenny exclaimed. 'The beach was better than this!'

'Oh my god yes,' Paul said. 'I've never been in anything as cold and harsh in my life!'

'I doubt many people have,' she replied, her voice lowering. 'That was very dangerous. We could have been killed.'

'So how did you know what to do? Is it always like this in the mountains?'

'No,' she said, shaking her head. 'I mean, there's always winter storms. I've just never gotten caught in one like this.'

'Never?'

'Not on top of a mountain.'

'But you seemed so, I don't know, confident. Why?'

'I wasn't. I actually felt sort of sick, and then, there was something else.'

Paul stared at her, remembering what he'd sensed.

'There was someone else,' he said.

'Yeah,' she replied. 'Did you hear her too?'

'No. I just, when I grabbed you, someone else was there.'

She stared deep into the woods, watching some of the snow flakes that broke through the canopy drift to the ground.

'The voice said things I've heard before.'

'Like what?'

'It said the wind was me.'

Paul shuddered, staring where Jenny had stood. He thought he felt something watching them, something moving around them. He tried to find it and saw nothing.

'The wind was you? What's that mean?'

'I don't know, that's just it. This girl, in a nightmare I used to have, would say that to me and then, I - hey, what...'

Paul stood up and pulled Jenny up with him.

'Something's here.'

'Where?' she asked, whipping around. 'Maybe we did see something out there!'

'I'm not sure. I can feel it.'

Jenny concentrated on the trees around them and felt nothing.

'Are you sure?'

'Absolutely. We're not alone.'

'I can't feel anything.'

'I think we should go - right now!'

She nodded and they set off once again down the mountain. Jenny led the way and Paul followed, glancing about, sure that something was with them. The trees still groaned and creaked as the wind whipped them, forcing the children to jump out of the way of falling branches.

'This is the worst storm I've ever seen!' Jenny exclaimed.

'How long will it last?'

'I don't know. I hope not much longer - the trees can't take it.'

They fell silent again, the rhythm of walking taking over. Jenny could feel Paul's nervousness about their surroundings and when she concentrated on him, she was surprised at how much easier his thoughts were to hear. Something had changed in her, back on the mountain peak; her abilities were getting stronger.

Was it because of the girl's voice? she wondered

Sasha leaned back from the stage, where she had watched the children's descent. She was frowning and mumbling.

'Something wrong?'

She turned toward the speaker, the old man they called 'Docent'.

'I'm not sure. I thought I saw something in the snow.'

'Show me.'

She clasped her hand around her amulet and closed her eyes. On the stage, the children's journey down the peak replayed. The wind was hammering them and they both had their hands in front of their faces, fighting through it.

'There!' she said, opening her eyes and freezing the image.

The bubble in the snow was clearly visible. It looked like the snow was rushing around it, as if it was solid.

'What is that?' she asked.

The docent stood frowning, rubbing his beard with one hand.

'It could be something to do with the storm,' he mused. 'But I doubt it.'

He paced back and forth in front of the image.

'What happens to it next?' he asked. 'Does it move, or vanish?'

Sasha grabbed her amulet again. The scene on the stage resumed and they watched the bubble move slowly across the peak, fighting the wind, getting away from the children's line of site.

'That's deliberate!' she exclaimed.

'Yes it is,' agreed the Docent. 'I wonder what that is. Keep an eye on it and your mind open. See if you can get any sense of its presence.'

The snow slowed gradually and as they descended further, the trees became larger and further spread out. The air, while still cold, was easier to breathe and the children found themselves warming up.

'You're still worried, aren't you?' Jenny said.

'It's the strangest feeling. I'm sure we're being watched.'

'By what?'

'That's just it - I don't know. It's not like anything I've felt before. I can't tell if they're afraid, or angry, or anything.'

'There's more than one?'

'Yeah. All around us.'

Jenny walked quietly for a few minutes, listening to Paul's thoughts, trying to find what he had felt.

'Maybe you're sensing animals,' she suggested.

'Animals? Up here? Like what?'

'Birds, deer, elk, bear - lots of animals live here,' she replied.

'I didn't, I mean - shouldn't we be able to see them?'

'Not if they don't want to be seen. Wild animals don't like us.'

'Well, maybe then. But the weird thing is, I think we're being followed. Would animals do that?'

Jenny shook her head and shuddered. The storm had almost blown itself out and they could see small patches of blue sky appearing above the canopy. A few moments later, Jenny held her hand up, signaling a stop.

'I think we're coming to the edge of the woods,' she said. 'We'll have to be really careful.'

'Why?' Paul asked. 'Will the storm get stronger out there?'

'Maybe,' she replied. 'But that's not what I'm worried about. I remember my dad saying the only reason a forest stops on a mountain is that there's nothing for it to grow on.'

'Yeah? No soil, that sort of thing?'

'Worse - no ground. We need to watch out for cliffs and landslides. Don't go near the edge, ok?'

She slowly moved forward. Just ahead of her, the trees came to an abrupt end. She walked up to the last one, reached out to it and looked beyond. She gasped at the view. Paul caught up and looked at what she was seeing.

They were staring out from a vantage point few people ever got to see. They had reached a rock cliff, several thousand feet to the bottom, where the mountain continued to descend away from it. It stood at the edge of a massive valley, one that stretched far away to the horizon. The storm was still working its way across and the snow and wind it left behind shrouded the view.

Far below them they saw a thin, crystal blue lake and it looked like a river flowed away from it through the valley.

'Where are we?' Paul whispered.

'I've no idea,' Jenny replied, shaking her head. 'I've never been on a mountain top like this, other than sulpher mountain back home.'

'Is it like this?'

'A bit. The mountains look sort of like home, I guess.'

'But you don't recognize them?'

'No. This is a big valley, though. Maybe even a pass.'

'A what?'

'A pass - a way through the mountains from way down there. The roads go through passes. We've got to find a way down.'

'Not down the cliff, surely?' Paul asked.

'No - let's head along the edge.'

She turned and started to follow the trees along the ridge. The valley below stretched as far as she could see and the peaks that rose on the other side formed a long line, a border to a vast stretch of unbroken wilderness. She guessed that the ridge they were on followed a similar pattern, which meant there must be a gentler slope down ahead of them.

'Paul,' she said, turning to look at him. 'I think - Oh my God - Don't move!'

Paul froze and stared at her.

'What's wrong?' he cried.

'I told you not to go out there - that's not rock you're standing on!'

'Then what is it?' he said looking at his feet.

'It's just ice and snow. If it breaks...'

'Jenny, no - what do I do?'

She looked back at the forest.

'Don't move a muscle. I'm going to try and find something to reach you with.'

She hurried into the woods, looking for a small sapling or a fallen branch to reach him.

'Anything?' he called.

'Shh!' she said. 'Even noise might break it!'

A crack pierced the air, a sharp, loud snap that came from several yards away. Jenny ran back to the edge of the trees nearest Paul and took off her cloak.

'Here, catch this,' she said, throwing toward him. He grabbed it and they heard another ominous crack.

'What's this for?' he asked.

'Tie it to yours and then throw one end back!'

He nodded and brought his around. He tied them firmly together and gathered the material together, then threw it toward her. It landed two feet in front of the tree she clung to. She leaned over to grab it but couldn't quite reach it. She lay down flat on the tightly packed snow and stretched toward it. Paul remained as still as he could, watching her. She reached her hand out and just as she was about to grab it the ice shelf crumbled. Paul stumbled back toward the edge.

She watched in horror as the white ice peeled away to the left of her, the cracks in it shooting forward toward Paul. He was struggling to get some sort of balance, his legs bent forward and his arms flailing.

'Paul!' she screamed as the ice beneath him vanished. She pointed at him and whipped her arm back toward the woods and he went flying back into them, crashing hard into a tree before collapsing on the ground. The rest of the ice shelf let go with a horrendous crash and Jenny had to cling to the tree nearest her not to go with it.

She pulled herself back from the edge, leapt to her feet and ran over to where he lay.

'Paul, talk to me!' she cried, bending down and shaking him.

He groaned and rolled over. He had a large cut across his forehead and his nose was bleeding. She reached down and hugged him.

'Paul, I'm so sorry - I didn't mean to hurt you!'

He looked up at her, his eyes blurry, before reaching up to his forehead.

'I'm, Paul, Oh my God, I didn't think, I just...'

'You just saved my life,' he said, cutting her off. 'That's what you did. If you hadn't thrown me here, I'd be at the bottom of that cliff!'

'But I didn't mean to hurt you - I just wanted to pull you back, and then the ice let go, so...'

'Yeah,' he said, tenderly touching his forehead. 'But you saved me - somehow. What was that, anyway?'

'I don't know,' she sighed, sitting down beside him. 'I have no idea what just happened.'

He stood up, untied her cloak from his and wrapped hers around her.

'Whatever it was, thank you.'

She looked up at him, blowing some hair out of her face.

'Next time, listen, ok?'

'I will, I promise. And next time you throw me, please be gentler!'

Jenny stood up and walked back into the woods, before turning and heading slowly along the line of the trees. Paul followed, carefully putting his feet in her footsteps.

'So it felt like a powerful vice,' he said.

'What did?'

'When you saved me. It felt like something grabbed me in a vice.'

'Did it hurt?'

'No. Well, the tree did. But the grip didn't.'

The edge they were following was uneven; large sections of the cliff had eroded away, and they were forced to climb back up the mountain to skirt the edges of long-forgotten land-slides.

'I wonder what it is - how I do that,' she continued.

'I didn't get much of a chance to watch this time.'

'So you didn't see that mist, like before?'

'No,' he said staring at her back. 'And I can't see it now either.'

She held her arms out in front of her and looked at them, trying in vain to see something. After a few moments of searching, she gave up and they set off again, following the line of the trees. It took nearly an hour before they finally reached a gentler slope. The forest thinned out as they approached and then started to descend into the valley. They followed it and after another long hike they came to a flat, snow-covered plateau.

They walked across the snow to the edge where a massive boulder sat. They climbed up on it and sat down, resting and staring across the valley.

'Turn around,' Jenny said with a smile.

'Why?' Paul said, doing so anyway.

'Look at that cliff. We were up there.'

He looked up, craning his neck back to see the top. It looked gigantic, towering above them.

'We couldn't have been that high up,' he said.

'Yeah, we were. And look back that way - look at the snow-line along the edge.'

He did and saw a point where the snow looked like it had been ripped away.

'Is that what I think it is?'

'I think so,' she replied. 'That's where you were standing.'

'My god,' he breathed. 'That's frightening.'

'I know.'

She turned back toward the valley and pulled her knees up tight wrapping her cloak around them. She felt the sun warming it up and let the heat seep into her. They were much closer to the valley floor, no more than a thousand feet up. The gentle, wooded slope continued beneath them to the river. She looked up at the sun, trying to gauge the time.

'We'll have to keep moving,' she said.

'I know,' Paul replied. 'It's going to get cold again, isn't it?'

'Very. We've got to find shelter. Maybe down by the river. Maybe we'll find a cave, or something.'

'We might. Let's just rest a little more - my feet really hurt - are you hungry?'

She nodded and stared down the valley. From a long way distant, she heard the haunting sound of a train whistle.

'I love that,' she whispered. The sound echoed off the mountains, quieting with each repetition, the whistle repeating itself several times. She listened to the sound as it faded out.

'A train?' Paul asked.

'Yeah. It reminds me of home. I love hearing it at night, when I'm in bed. It makes me feel cozy.'

'You realize what it means, right?'

She stared at him, listening to his thoughts.

'You're right!' she exclaimed. 'We've got to find it. It might be shelter!'

He glared at her as she stood up and she realized what she'd done.

'Sorry,' she said sheepishly.

'It's ok,' he replied.

She stared down the valley, toward where she thought the sound had originated. She followed the river as far as she could see, and thought she saw something.

'Look there,' she said, pointing. 'Do you see something over the river?'

'I think so - it looks like a trestle bridge.'

'Yeah - could be a train bridge or a road. Either way, we've got to go there.'

Paul hopped down from the boulder and then turned to help her down. The hike down to the river bed was steeper than the descent from the cliff but the lower they went, the better they felt.

'So why here?' Paul asked.

'What, the gate?'

'Yeah - why did it dump us in a snow storm? On the top of a mountain?'

'Who knows?' Jenny answered.

'Well there's got to be a reason. That's two gates we've been through and both times the exit sucked!'

'I never thought of that,' she said. 'Why underwater? Or in a snowstorm?'

'Do you think it was on purpose?'

They'd nearly reached the river and could hear it flowing over the rapids.

'Who'd do that?' she asked.

'Well, I was thinking more about what Strumn said to you. About things being placed. Maybe the gates are too. Like a test.'

She stopped and stared at him.

'What?' he said.

'Well, when we stepped into the fire - the gate, we were talking about Banff.'

'Hey, you're right. Maybe the gates listen to us?'

'Or something,' she said, looking at her amulet.

They had reached the river which, while frozen at the edge, was wide and fiercely flowing in the middle. On each bank, large ice blocks and sheets made the walking treacherous so they climbed back up into the woods and started walking along the river's edge toward the train bridge.

Paul felt exposed and kept glancing behind or across the river.

'Something still there?' Jenny asked.

'Yeah - Maybe. I don't know.'

'I wish I could tell.'

Paul held his hand out toward her.

'Can I try something?' he asked.

'Sure.'

He put his hand on her shoulder and thought about all the things he sensed around them. Jenny sagged as Paul's feelings surged into her - it was as if she was looking through his eyes, hearing with his ears and sensing things the way he did. She reached up her hand, putting it on his and staring around.

'See?' he said

'Wow,' she replied, still holding his hand in place. 'They're all around us, aren't they?'

'I think so.'

'C'mon,' she said, pulling him along. 'We can't do anything about it. Let's just get to that bridge - we can't be out here when the sun goes down.'

They started off again toward the bridge. When they finally reached it, their legs ached from walking in the snow and their faces felt frozen solid. The bridge was a metal trestle bridge and they saw two lines running across it. They clambered up the side of the embankment and stared across the shining rails.

'Two lines,' Jenny whispered.

'So?'

'There wouldn't be two lines all the way through - one of these must be a siding.'

Just as she said it, she heard another whistle on the other side of the bridge. The track curved sharply to the right several hundred feet back from the opposite edge. The train was not yet in view but they could hear the low rumble of the diesel engines approaching.

They stepped back into the trees, and watched as the lead engine rounded the corner. Its whistle blew again and it sounded massive, the pitch strong and piercing. It was moving slowly, crawling across the bridge and past them at not much more than a runner's pace.

There were four engines followed by a series of tank cars. Beyond them came a long line of car transports. The train was slowing down and as the first of a set of box cars arrived, the brakes brought it to a squealing stop, each car bumping into its predecessor with a loud clang.

'Why are they stopping?' Paul asked.

'There must be another train coming the other way.'

'Ah, ok. Let's get on!'

'What, on the train?' she exclaimed.

'Yeah - look, some of those cars look open - and empty!'

She looked where he was pointing and saw what he meant - several of the box cars looked deserted, almost run down. Their brown paint was peeling off, rust surrounded the hinges and faded graffiti was splashed across them.

'I guess no one would see, would they?' she said.

'Not out here - c'mon!'

They sprinted out of the woods towards the nearest open car. When they drew close to it they realized how high up it was. Paul could barely reach the floor. He gave Jenny a boost up and then she turned to help him. They stood up and walked in to the cavernous space. The car was huge and almost completely empty. A wooden pallet lay at one end and several bundles of paper lay near it. The floor was metal, badly scratched and cold.

They walked over to the other side and looked out toward the front of the train. It curved away from them so they couldn't see the engines.

'I wonder how long it's going to sit here?' Paul asked.

'Yeah - I'm cold already!'

'Maybe we should try and get to the front - get some help.'

'Would they help us? Or just pretend to until we get wherever this is going?'

'I don't know. What do you want to do?'

'Stay here. If we close one door and just leave the other open a bit, the wind won't be too bad.'

'Ok,' Paul said, walking over to the door they'd come in. He leaned hard on it, barely moving it.

'Here, give me a hand.'

Jenny came over and they both pushed as hard as they could. With a loud, metallic groan, the door slid slowly closed. Just as it clanged shut, they heard the whistle of an approaching train.

A few minutes later, their car was buffeted by a train going past them. They hurried over to the open door and looked at the silver gleam of the passenger coaches that shot past them.

'I bet they're warm,' Jenny said.

'Me too. And they probably have food.'

'And TV. Maybe even beds.'

Paul could feel her spirits sinking and smiled at her.

'C'mon, we've got this whole car,' he said. 'Let's make the best of it.'

'How?'

'Well, these cloaks will keep us warm, the bags will feed us. We'll wait it out, see where we're going.'

He stumbled slightly as the train jerked to a slow roll.

'See? Moving already.'

'They're quite bold, aren't they Docent?'

'Indeed. And I'm quite tired. This seems like a good time to return home and rest.'

The few members of the order who sat watching the stage nodded and watched as the old man they called the Docent stood and walked away past the infinite fire, fading into a grey mist and vanishing.

'Why are they letting them stay on the train?' a young man asked.

'My best guess,' Sasha said, 'is that it's the only possible way they'll stay warm overnight.'

'But what about tomorrow?'

'What are you so worried about?'

'You do know where that train is going, right?'

The train moved slowly along the tracks, hugging the side of a mountain on a precarious perch. The children peeked out of the door and marveled at the view before pulling back from the wind. The sun was starting to set, throwing a deep pink over the bottom of the few clouds that remained. When it dipped below the western mountain tops, the sky turned a dark, cold blue.

The temperature inside the car began to plunge and the children sat huddled together in the least drafty corner, both cloaks wrapped around them. Jenny's teeth were chattering, and Paul couldn't stop the shivering that ran through his body.

'How are we ever going to sleep?' Paul asked.

'I don't kn-know,' Jenny stuttered. 'I've never been so cold.'

'Maybe we should move around a bit.'

'I think that would be worse. I'm not moving!'

'What we really need is a heater,' Paul said.

'Yeah - and blank-k-kets, and food.'

The car was dark and the only light they had was from the glow of their amulets. The blue light they cast sent long shadows behind them but didn't reach the opposite end of the car. Jenny stared into the gloom and thought she saw a light.

'Paul,' she chattered, 'L-Look there.'

He squinted toward where she was pointing and saw what she meant. The light was a gold colour and started getting brighter. It split in two and grew stronger still. They saw, in the gold light, two faces - grey faces, hidden behind hoods.

'Who are you?' Paul called out.

The faces came forward and they saw two children, dressed just like them, holding hands. One held his finger to his mouth and motioned for Jenny and Paul to stay seated.

The pale strangers turned toward the far end where they'd come from and held their free hands up. A light appeared on the wall and a bench popped up from the floor. They walked over and sat down. They then stared at Jenny and Paul.

'They want us to do something, I think,' Paul said.

Jenny concentrated on the two strangers and was surprised to find she could hear them.

'They're showing us what to do!' she whispered.

'What do you mean?'

'They keep thinking about the common - and what we saw.'

'So?'

Jenny held her hand up and thought about her fireplace at home. She stared at the corner across from them and thought how it might look if it was with her now. An image of it appeared briefly then faded away. The pale children stomped their feet and held their clasped hands up, pointing at Paul.

'I think they want us to do something like they did,' Paul said, watching them.

'Yeah - maybe. Here, take my hand. Try to imagine a fireplace right over there.'

'What?'

'The stream, in the common. Remember?'

'It was empty,' he cried, 'and then we changed it!'

'Exactly. Maybe we can help ourselves like that here.'

Paul stood up and held his hand out. Jenny took it and they stared into the corner. Paul imagined his grandparent's fireplace and Jenny thought about her own. The wall across from them started to crackle and spark but no fireplace appeared.

'Maybe we have to think of the same thing,' Jenny suggested.

'Ok,' Paul said. 'Let me show you what I'm thinking of.'

He poured an image into her of his grandparent's fireplace. They turned back and concentrated, watching as a fireplace appeared on the wall and a fire burst to life within it. The light and heat hit them immediately and they rushed over to it, holding their hands out to absorb the warmth.

'Wow!' Jenny said. 'It worked!'

'It sure seems real, doesn't it?' Paul replied. 'Shouldn't we be careful? What if the train catches alight?'

'It won't - don't worry. What about something comfortable to sit on?'

She took his hand and started thinking of a sofa, trying to send the image to Paul. He looked at her with a puzzled expression on his face and then concentrated with her. A large rounded sofa began to appear. When it was finally solid, they thought it was too close to the fire, so they pushed it back and sat down.

'This is incredible!' Paul exclaimed. 'I mean, really magic! How are we doing this?'

'Let's ask them,' Jenny said, turning toward the pale children. They were no where to be seen, nor was the bench they'd been sitting on.

'They're gone,' she said.

Paul stood up and walked over to where they'd been. There was no sign they'd ever been there. He came back and sat down again, holding his hands out toward the fire.

'It's cold over there,' he said.

'Well not here,' she said, reaching into her pack and pulling out a sandwich. 'I say we eat, then sleep.'

'What about the fire?' Paul said.

'What about it?'

'Won't someone notice a burning box car? Or at least all the smoke?'

'Maybe the smoke isn't that much, or maybe only we can see it,' she suggested.

'Maybe. I guess it doesn't much matter. If they do see it and stop to investigate, we'll just have to make a run for it.'

The fire had died down so he went over to the wooden palate and started pulling it apart. He brought the boards back and stacked them by the sofa, before carefully placing a couple onto the fire. When he turned back toward the sofa, he saw that Jenny had wrapped herself in her cloak and fallen asleep.

He sat and stared into the fire, thinking once more about his earlier near accident on the cliff. How had Jenny saved him? There must be something more to her that she didn't yet fully understand, something that let her move things without touching them. He looked at her and saw, between the bright flickers of the fire, a faint blue glow all around her. It wasn't moving the way it had on the tractor and he assumed that it was because she was asleep.

137

His eyes began to droop so he copied her, using a sofa cushion for a pillow. He drifted off watching the fire.

When he woke up, the fire had died down to just a few coals and he saw the first hints of daylight poking through the crack in the door. He stood up and stretched and saw that Jenny was still asleep. He grabbed more wood and took it over to the coals. They were too small to light the boards so he grabbed some paper from the bundles at the far end and used them to get a flame. He added the boards and when he was satisfied the fire wouldn't go out, he went over to the door and peeked out.

The train was still in the mountains and moving at a fair pace. They were on an embankment that ran down to a four lane highway, following the same path they were. There were no cars on it but he could see a large green sign in the distance. As they drew near, he started to see some white markings. When they were close enough to read, he nearly shouted.

He ran back over to Jenny and shook her shoulder.

'Hey, Jenny - wake up!'

'What's the matter,' she said, rubbing her eyes.

'It's morning, and we're traveling along side a motorway of some sort!'

'Cool,' she replied. 'So what?'

'So we just passed a distance sign. It said we're a hundred and eight kilometers from Banff!'

Chapter 10

Banff

Canace's sister was so taken by the boy, and his fascination with her and her amulet, that she wanted to give him her gift. Canace went deep into the mountain beneath their home, to the chamber of crystal veins, and brought forth a beautiful purple core, around which they fashioned an amulet, much as their own.

'Banff? Are you certain?'

'Absolutely. Those tracks don't branch before Banff.'

'Then we've got a real problem. They absolutely must not go there. We must alert the senior members - too bad the Docent already left. I guess we'll have to go wake him up.'

'True enough. We'll have to get Chantal and she can summon anyone else she needs. How long have we got?'

A short, pudgy man stood up near the right side of the stage and came over to them.

'At the rate that train is going, and given the weather ahead, it won't reach Banff until the next morning.'

'You're sure?' Sasha asked.

The man nodded firmly. Sasha fished her amulet out from the folds of her robe and held it tightly in her hand, staring at the space just beyond the infinite fire. The others watched as a tunnel of light appeared, shimmering into existence with a bright flash. Sasha walked quickly into it before it snapped shut.

In an instant the tunnel reopened and Sasha came back, the Docent and several other members following after her. The seats that surrounded the stage started to fill in with the outlines of people, misty at first, then slowly gaining shape and color. When they were completely restored, they started talking in a low, urgent babble.

The Docent held his hands up and waited for silence.

'Well, my friends, we have a challenge. We should, of course, have seen this coming, were we not so blinded by the rapid progress these two children have made.'

139

He paused as another bright flash occurred, Chantal appearing from within it.

'She's trying to go home, I hear,' Chantal said with a smile. 'This should be interesting.'

'Interesting! How can you call it interesting?' Ucheen cried.

'Because it is,' Chantal replied. 'I can't remember the last time a candidate managed to land a gate so close to home.'

'But surely we're going to pull them out? It will be chaos if she gets there - if anyone recognizes her!'

'It may or may not be,' the Docent replied. 'We have nothing to base that on. For her, certainly, it would be traumatic.'

'Then what do you suggest?' Ucheen asked.

The Docent leaned over and whispered to Chantal, who nodded in agreement.

'We can't pull them out. As noted earlier, if we do, they will be permanently lost to us. They are fully bound to their amulets, and if they don't learn our ways, right now, they never will. We must let them continue until they find their way back here.'

The Docent paused, thinking.

'All right,' he finally said. 'We'll have to handle this as best we can. We need every one of our influencers on this. There are going to be many people who recognize Miss Greyson and we must convince them they are wrong.'

'Or prevent that recognition entirely,' Chantal said. 'But first, is …Ian still standing in for her?'

Several people nodded at once.

'Good. Someone must warn Élan what's coming. She's the best imitator we have, so let's make sure she's ready.'

'I'll go,' Sasha said. 'I've seen her in action before - she once had to stand in for a Russian ambassador, in the middle of a negotiation in the Far East, and she was *better* than the original - she's more than up for this.'

'She's never faced this sort of challenge before,' Ucheen said. 'There are not just the two children to worry about, after all.'

'Don't worry - he hasn't noticed,' Ornolt said, arriving in a hurry from the right side of the stage.

'Sorry I'm late,' he added.

'How do you know?' Ucheen demanded.

'I found him, I trained him after his first absorption, and I helped him make his life choice. I know him, and I know he hasn't noticed.'

Ucheen grunted and sat back down.

'All right then,' the Docent said. 'I want one of you, Isaac perhaps, to be on the Greyson family. They must not recognize her, no matter what. I'll handle her friend, Miss Tomiyama. Ornolt, take Liu and Carl with you to shadow the children and alert us the moment they get near the town.

'We'll need at least two influencers to trail them within the town - where are our Canadian friends?'

He looked up into the seats and found a middle aged couple.

'Ah there you are. You've been to Banff, right?'

They nodded.

'Good. Blend in and make sure no one reacts to the children's presence.'

'What about their amulets?' the woman named Liu asked. 'Won't they react?'

'They absolutely will. But the children won't know what that means. All right, is everyone ready?'

A murmur of assent drifted down.

'Good. Exeter, what's the best place to arrive in Banff - you've done it a few times lately.'

'The forest in behind the park - no one will see us, and it lets us get to the rest of town very quickly.'

'Remember, everyone - blend in. Change into North American winter clothes and hide your amulets. The children mustn't see them!'

Ornolt waited for everyone to change their appearance and then strode from the Common, into a dark, misty fog. He faded and then disappeared as the rest of the interception party followed.

'Really? Banff?' she squealed.

Paul nodded with a smile on his face. Jenny leapt up and ran over to the door of the boxcar and stared out at the passing scenery.

'This is great!' she exclaimed. 'I can't wait to get there! Everyone will be so excited - Sarah's going to love you - she's a sucker for accents.'

'I guess everyone there sounds like you, huh?'

'Pretty much. It's a small place. I wonder what time it is?'

'Early, early,' he replied. 'The sun's not quite up yet.'

'So how far did it say we had to go?'

'One hundred and eight kilometers. And since we're moving quite quickly, we've probably already done ten of those.'

Jenny looked out the door again, looking for something familiar. The train was moving away from the road, climbing higher up the side of the embankment, before splitting away onto the far side of a long, narrow lake. She could see a road sign on the side of the highway but it was too far away to read. A tractor trailer crawled along the road, going in the opposite direction, its headlights casting a yellow glow ahead of it.

The road disappeared as the train swung around a smaller mountain and she stepped away from the door, her face nearly frozen.

'It's still really cold out!' she said.

'I noticed,' Paul said. 'And very dry. I hope it warms up.'

'Oh it should once the sun comes up. It's still just barely November, after all.'

The train suddenly shuddered and they could feel it starting to slow down.

'We must be getting close!' Paul said.

'Yeah, I guess,' Jenny sighed.

'And?'

'I don't think the train's going to stop.'

'Why not?'

'They usually don't - no reason to.'

'Well I hope it's going pretty slow when we get there!'

'Yeah, me too - we might have to jump!'

Paul shivered and drew his cloak tight around him. The train continued to slow and then it lurched to the right. They hurried to the door and looked out. The train was passing over a switching, as the tracks split in two.

'Another siding?' Paul asked.

'Yeah, or maybe we really are getting close. The old train station does have more than one track running through it.'

The blast of the engine's whistle rang out and they listened to it echo off the surrounding mountains. Minutes later, the car they were in rolled over a level crossing, the signal lights flashing and the bells ringing.

'We're close!' she said, her eyes twinkling. 'I know where we are!'

The train was slowing down even more.

'Hey,' Paul said, looking back into the car. 'What about that?'

She turned and looked where he was pointing. Their fire was just about out; only a few dim coals remained.

'I guess we better get rid of it,' she replied.

'How?' Paul asked.

She didn't answer and stood staring at the fireplace. Paul felt the same cold presence he had when they first met at the common, a feeling of unease which made him step back from her. He saw the faint blue aura around her intensify and then flash. The fireplace and sofa vanished and all that remained were the few broken bits of the pallet they hadn't burned. Jenny turned away and sensed Paul's anxiety.

'It's a lot harder to do that,' she said.

'What's harder?'

'To destroy what you've built. I didn't want to.'

'Well it had to go, I guess.'

'Yeah.'

'So what's so hard?'

'I don't know - it's like - you can't just let it go, can't just wish it, like when we made it. This took - focus.'

They went back over to the door and pulled it open again. The air outside was still freezing. In the distance, they saw a highway.

'Oh, wait a second,' Jenny said. 'The other side!'

She leapt across the car, Paul close behind. The opposite door was far tougher to move and after a hard push, it slid open.

'There it is!' Jenny cried, pointing way ahead. 'That's the station!'

The train was crawling along at a jogger's pace.

'We'll have to jump,' Paul said.

'Yeah,' Jenny said, standing at the edge. 'Ready?'

Paul nodded and they leapt from the car, landing with a hard thud in an embankment of snow. They rolled down the other side and hopped up. Paul brushed the snow from his face and shook himself off.

'You all right?' he said to Jenny.

'Sure am!' she said, drawing a deep breath. 'It even smells like home. This is great!'

'So where to?'

She pointed toward the station house.

'That way, and then into town. It's a bit of a hike.'

'Couldn't be worse than yesterday. Let's go.'

With a small whoosh of air, Ornolt appeared in the deep woods behind the park. One after another the other members appeared, before the gate finally snapped shut. Ornolt lead them to the edge of the trees and stared out across the field. It was still early in the morning, and cold, so there was no one around.

He took Isaac and Sasha aside and pointed out the street where the Greysons lived. They nodded and headed out across the field. Sarah's house was just up the street from there, which he pointed out to the Docent. The other four who remained followed him back through the woods, taking a short cut to the bridge that crossed the Bow River.

They hurried across into town, where they split up again. Carl, Liu and Ornolt headed toward the train station, sure that the children would get off there, while the remaining couple went to find some breakfast, to get a sense of the people who lived here.

'Hey, what's that?' Paul asked, holding his amulet up.

'They're pulsing,' Jenny said. 'I wonder what that means?'

'That bird didn't say anything about pulsing.'

'Didn't they pulse once before? Around Strumn?'

Paul frowned, trying to remember.

'Maybe,' he finally said. 'Think he's here, too?'

Jenny's eyes widened.

'I hope not! If he is, he'll be up to no good!'

'We better keep an eye out then.'

They kept walking, heading down a tree lined street. No cars went by and Jenny glanced around, frowning at what she saw.

'Paul,' she said. 'There's something weird here.'

'Like what?'

'Well, the snow. Something's not right about it.'

He reached down and picked some up.

'Feels normal to me. Cold, wet - you know, icy.'

'That's not what I meant,' she said, shaking her head. 'There's too much of it.'

'I thought you said it snowed a lot in the mountains!'

'Well, yeah, but this stuff's been here a while.'

'So?'

'So it wasn't here when I left. And that was two days ago.'

Paul swiped at the ground with his feet, chipping away at the ice layer below it. The embankments of snow that ran along side the street looked like they had several layers to them and he could see the crystal-like structure of the older ice underneath the surface powder.

'You're right,' he said. 'This *has* been here a while. What do you make of that?'

'I don't know. Ice doesn't form like that in one night - it takes a lot of melting and re-freezing.'

'Was it this cold when you left?' he asked.

'No - not even close. I wonder what's going on?'

She looked away from the embankment at the sound of an approaching engine and looked toward the centre of town.

'We're a long way from my house - let's get going.'

Paul looked at her and smiled and then brushed some snow off her shoulder.

'Or,' she said hesitantly, 'Are you hungry?'

'Famished,' he replied.

'Well see that restaurant over there? They've got the greatest pancakes. We go there for Sunday brunch all the time.'

'Lead the way.'

They walked briskly toward the diner and when they reached the front door, Jenny stopped again.

'What's wrong?'

'I don't know - another weird feeling.'

'Like what?'

'Like we're being watched. Or followed.'

'I wouldn't be surprised' he said, opening the door. 'And I don't care. It's warm in there, and it smells fantastic!'

They walked in and looked around. The place was almost empty, with just two booths occupied. Two large men in flannel checkered shirts with base ball caps sat at one, sipping coffee. They didn't even look up when the children passed them.

'Do you know any one?' Paul whispered.

'Nope,' Jenny said. 'But like I said, this is nowhere near my house.'

'I thought you said Banff was tiny.'

'It's not that small,' she said, rolling her eyes. 'C'mon - let's get a seat near the fireplace - I'm still freezing.'

They sat down at a booth on the inner wall across from a small fireplace. A gas flame licked its way along a ceramic log, casting little heat. The entire room looked brown - the wallpaper was a swirling yellow pattern on a dark background and dim lights hung from the walls. Beyond the fireplace lay another room, which was roped off. The kitchen behind them had one man in it who looked up when they sat down and whistled at someone they couldn't see.

Moments later a large, middle aged waitress ambled over.

'Well good morning,' she said. 'Why are you two up already?'

'Early risers,' Paul said with a smile.

'Huh. I guess so. You shop at the same store, too, I see. Hungry?'

They both nodded.

'You know what's best here?' the waitress continued. 'The pancakes.'

'I know!' Jenny said. 'They're the best in town. Really fluffy.'

The waitress paused, looking at her.

'You been here before?' she asked. 'I don't recognize you.'

'All the time. My family comes here for Sunday brunch. It's great!'

'I must be getting old then - I just can't place you. What's your name?'

'Jenny Greyson, we live on the south side...'

'You're Donald's daughter? Huh. I guess I never looked that closely. So what'll it be?'

'The pancakes,' Paul said, 'And lots of syrup!'

The waitress smiled and walked over to the kitchen. Paul watched her go, and then glanced back across the room. The two men were still talking, and he got a sense of fatigue from them, of resignation. He looked further on, and saw a dark haired couple, both reading the paper. He couldn't sense anything from them, no mood, not even their presence.

'So do you know her?' he said, turning back to Jenny. 'That waitress?'

'Not really. I've seen her before, but I don't know her name or anything.'

'What about those guys? Or those two reading the paper?'

'Nope.'

'I can't feel them,' he whispered. 'Can you?'

Jenny looked across at them and concentrated.

'Yeah. They're bored. I guess the paper's not that interesting.'

'Huh. I wonder why I can't?'

'Maybe you can't sense everyone. That happens to me a lot. Or at least it used to.'

Their pancakes arrived moments later and they fell silent, eating as fast as they could.

'Delicious!' Paul exclaimed as he finished first. 'You were absolutely right.'

'Told you,' she replied.

When they were finished, Jenny reached in her bag, looking for her credit card. She couldn't find it but did find two twenty dollar bills. They walked over to the till, where she saw a small sign that said 'cash only'.

'Interesting,' she whispered to herself.

'What is?' the waitress asked, giving her change.

'Sorry, nothing. Just talking to myself.'

They headed back outside and although the sun had risen above the mountains, they felt the cold seep back in. They gathered their cloaks around them and walked as fast as they could toward the centre of town. Jenny was anxious to get home and looked around eagerly for someone she knew.

'Hey,' she said. 'See that man over there? Near the newspaper box?'

Paul looked where she was pointing.

'Yeah. What about him?'

'He's one of my teachers.'

'So let's go so hello!'

'What for?' she asked.

'To see if he knows you.'

'Of course he will,' she laughed. 'Why wouldn't he?'

'I bet he won't,' he replied. 'C'mon.'

They walked across the street and over to the man. He was leaning on the wall, looking at his watch and then staring up the street.

'Hi Mr. Roland,' Jenny said when they got close.

The man looked at her and frowned.

'Uhm, good morning. I - sorry - you must be a former student of mine. I have a terrible memory for names.'

Jenny froze and stared at him.

'Are you ok?' he asked.

'Do you know someone named Jenny Greyson?' Paul asked, stepping in front of Jenny.

Mr. Roland's face lit up.

'Yes, indeed. One of my best students! An uncanny mind for mathematics. Why do you ask?'

'We're, uhm, cousins of hers,' Paul continued.

'From England, I'm guessing?'

'Yes sir.'

'So how do you know my name?'

Paul paused.

'I think you're in a class photo she has. When we got here, she was showing us her year book from last semester, pointing out her friends.'

'You mean Sarah. She doesn't have any other...'

He stopped, catching sight of someone on the other side of the street.

'Sorry, kids, I've got to go,' he said. 'I'm meeting my fiancé for brunch. Say hi to Jenny for me!'

He hurried across to where a woman stood waiting for him. Paul grabbed Jenny's arm and guided her away, up the street toward the river.

'See?' he said when he was sure no one else would hear. 'He didn't know you. Something's definitely going on here.'

Jenny didn't say anything and had a nasty frown on her face. She stomped away, ignoring everyone on the street, heading towards a large, old bridge that crossed the river.

'Hey, slow down!' Paul said.

'Why?' she asked.

'Because. I want to figure out what's going on before we go to your house.'

She stopped and whirled around, glaring at him. He could feel the anger pouring off her and saw, even in the broad daylight, the blue mist starting to build around her.

'How are we going to do that?' she demanded.

'Well look, you obviously know these people, but they don't know you. The only possibility I can think of is that someone's interfering.'

'It better not be Strumn.'

'I doubt it. You remember that couple at the pancake place?'

'Yeah.'

'They're following us. They're about two blocks behind us. Don't look - it'd be too obvious.'

'But how could they do this? How come Mr. Roland didn't know me?'

'I don't know, Jen. Just please, will you trust me?'

She smiled and her shoulders dropped.

'Ok.'

'Good. If we were in London, I bet you'd have to do this for me.'

'Maybe. But it sucks.'

'Well you're doing great so far. So here's what I think: we're being followed by people we don't know, who might be part of the order, or might be friends of Strumn's. We've seen some very strange things already, like those pale children.'

Jenny nodded but said nothing.

'I think that so far, it's a warm up. Something much bigger is waiting. Can't you feel the tension around us?'

'Yeah, and you know what else? I can still hear everyone's thoughts here. They're the same as they always were.'

'Except?'

'Except around us. They see us, they see me - and they suddenly change. Like a switch going off.'

'See! That's what I mean. They know we're here.'

'Well, I bet they couldn't do this to my family. Or my friends.'

'What about your teacher?'

'That's different. Sarah will know me.'

They continued walking while they spoke and reached the south side of the Bow River. They crossed the stone bridge and stood in front of a T shaped intersection. Directly across from them stood a square turreted building with a Canadian flag flying on a small flagpole above it. It reminded Paul of some of the buildings in London, with its white stone framed windows and old grey bricks.

Jenny suddenly grabbed him and pointed to their right. He looked along the road and saw three kids their age walking toward them. The two boys were talking about something urgent, their hands gesturing madly, their words pouring out as quickly as they could speak. Jenny was ignoring them and looking at the girl behind them. Paul knew right away who it was: the dark hair, the sparkling black eyes - it had to be Sarah.

Before he could stop her, Jenny ran up to her friends.

'Hey guys!' she said. 'Cold one today, isn't it?'

The three kids stopped and stared at her.

'I guess,' one of the boys said. 'Are you from around here?'

Paul could see Jenny tense and hurried over.

'C'mon David,' she said. 'Of course I am.'

The boy called David frowned and looked back at the other two.

'Who is she?' he asked them. They both shrugged.

'It's me!' she exclaimed. 'Jenny!'

Sarah snorted.

'Yeah, right. I don't think so.'

Paul put his hand on Jenny's shoulder.

They don't know you, Jen. It's like I said.

'Sarah, hey - really. It's me.'

Sarah pushed past her, dragging David and the other boy along with her. She turned back toward Jenny when they were a few yards past.

'Jenny's at home. And she'd never dress like that or talk like that.'

Jenny's mouth dropped open and she ran after them.

'Sarah, look, something's going on - I know this is weird, but I'm me - I'm Jenny.'

'Go away, ok?' Sarah replied harshly. 'Don't bug us - go home.'

'*What?*' Jenny screeched. 'Sarah, don't be such an idiot.'

Paul stepped in front of Jenny and looked at the three kids.

'I'm sorry - Sarah, was it?' he said.

She nodded. He reached out his hand toward David.

'I'm Paul Green. I think Jenny said your name was - David, right?'

David hesitated, frowning but when he finally shook Paul's hand, he smiled.

'Yeah - so how do you know Jenny?'

'Cousin from England. She's probably never mentioned me.'

David and Sarah both shook their heads. Paul stepped between Sarah and David, brushing against both of them.

'Jenny says you guys are her best friends. Especially you Sarah. She speaks highly of you.'

Sarah smiled and glanced back at Jenny, who was standing still, watching Paul.

'Yeah? Cool. But what's with your friend? Is she Ok?'

'Ok?' Jenny yelled. 'What's that supposed to mean?'

'I mean' Sarah said, looking her in the eye, 'that you're weird. Pretending to be Jenny - I just saw her at home.'

'No way - I'm Jenny.'

'No you're not - she doesn't look like you, act like you, or where freaky clothes like you!'

'Oh really?' Jenny said, looking at a tree above her. 'You want freaky? How about this?'

She pointed up at the snow-lined branches of the tree which started shaking hard. Snow poured down on the kids and Jenny looked behind her toward the field. She arched her arm at it and a large swath of snow lifted itself and soared toward Sarah and the others. Within moments they were buried up to their waists, staring at Jenny in fear.

Paul grabbed her and pulled her away, darting across the road and up a little side street to hide behind a small camper.

'Jenny! What's wrong with you! What the hell are you doing?'

'Me?'

'Yeah, you! We already know something's up around here, something's going on. Are you trying to get us in trouble? That was so stupid!'

She shook her head but remained quiet.

'So why'd you do that to them? I sure hope whoever's interfering with us takes care of that little mess you just made.'

'But Paul' she whispered, a tear dripping down her cheek. 'That was Sarah - she didn't know me.'

'I know, Jen - I know. And I'm sure it's on purpose. We're not meant to be here. It's all a trick.'

'So what should we do?'

'Leave.'

'*What?*'

'Leave. You know what happened when you phoned, and now you've seen first hand what happens when you run into people who know you. We've got to leave, and find our way through this, back to the common.'

'I don't want to,' she said, the tears flowing down her cheeks. 'I just want to go home. I want to see my mum and dad.'

'So do I. Really. But we can't.'

'But I'm already here. My house is just around the corner!'

'Yeah, and you know what'll happen if you go there.'

'Maybe not.'

'No maybe not - maybe it'll be worse. Sarah said you were at home.'

She looked up at him and wiped the tears away.

'That's true. God, Paul, what am I going to do?'

'Let's get out of here. Find the next gate, just go.'

She stood up and nodded.

'Yeah, ok, you're right. Let's try the park.'

'Why there?'

'It's where I left from. Maybe we can get back to the common the same way.'

'Worth a try,' he said. 'Just, look, if we see anyone you know, go the other way.'

'Ok.'

'And control yourself! I don't want to get killed!'

She glared at him and he held her gaze. A smile started to form on her face.

'I guess that was pretty stupid, huh?'

'Yeah,' he said. 'It was.'

She turned and led him back down the little street and across the road near where they had run into her friends. A large park lay across from it, rolling toward the Bow River. Jenny hopped the steel car barrier and they went across the field toward the trees on the other side. As they walked, Paul looked back at the houses that lined the street. A few of them had bright lights running up and down their gables and he was sure he saw a couple of snow men on one.

'This is it,' Jenny suddenly said.

'Is what?'

'The tree I jumped from.'

Paul looked up to its top.

'Wow. That's a long way up.'

'Yeah. Shall we?'

'What, jump?' he asked incredulously.

'Uh huh.'

'I wouldn't recommend it,' a booming voice said behind them.

They whirled around and saw an ancient man in a dark grey cloak staring at them, his eyes twinkling.

'Ornolt!' they yelled together, running over to him.

'Hello Paul, Jenny. Enjoying yourselves?'

'What?' Jenny exclaimed.

'It's a bit strange, here, isn't it?'

'Strange?' she replied. 'No one knows me! How can that be?'

'And why's there so much snow?' Ornolt replied. 'Or, as Paul just noticed, why do some people still have Christmas lights up?'

Jenny spun around and looked at where he was pointing and saw the glowing lights.

'Ornolt, what's going on?' she whispered.

He guided them over to the bench where he'd first watched her jump and made them sit down.

'It's as I told you both, when you started - find your way back to the common. It's the only way through.'

'So what's going on here?' Jenny asked.

'As much as I'd like to tell you, I can't. You shouldn't have tried to come here, as you can see.'

'So did you do this?' Paul asked.

Ornolt shook his head.

'No. All I'm allowed to tell you is that, while we're very impressed with your progress, you can't stay here. You've got to get going.'

'I know' Paul said, 'and Jenny's starting to. But can I ask you something?'

'Sure.'

'What *is* with the Christmas lights? And the snow, like you said.'

'Ah, well, that, I'm afraid, I can't explain. Take me. I know I'm three hundred years old or so. But to me, it feels like I'm only sixty years old - especially if I were to count the 'nights I've slept'. Yet I know when I was born, and I know what year it is now. The same thing is happening to you - you appear in certain places, at certain times, at which point things are real enough.

'Like today. You really did wake up in a box car, on a train, right? But I very much doubt you were in Hawaii yesterday. In fact, the way we bounce around, I doubt you were in Hawaii in the last few years!'

They stared at him in confusion.

'Why, Jenny, if you'd really been there two days ago, didn't your phone work? Why didn't anyone know your family lived here?'

Jenny had no idea and said so.

'That is one of the hardest things to learn. Just remember: you're not always where you think you are - *or when!*'

He stood up and stared off into the woods, nodding slightly.

'I'm sorry, I've got to go. There's lots more I'd like to tell you, but I can't - yet! So one more thing, ok?'

They both looked at him, waiting.

'You know how you were thinking about jumping out of that tree again?'

'Yes' Jenny said.

'Are your amulets hot? Warm even?'

They both shook their heads.

'Exactly. Gates are elusive things. Without your amulets, you have no idea where they are. Don't jump out of trees, step into fires, or do other such dangerous things unless your amulets absolutely say so.'

He turned and walked away. They started to go after him and then stopped. He was nowhere to be found - even his footsteps had gone.

'Wow,' Paul finally said.

'No kidding' Jenny said. 'I guess we better go. I just wish I could have seen my family.'

'Yeah, I know' he replied. 'But you will soon enough. Right now we've got to find a gate. Any ideas where we should go?'

'Let's walk toward the hotel. We haven't run in to any gates downtown, or here. Maybe there'll be something that way.'

They headed back to the road and started walking toward the Bow River Bridge, beyond which lay the road to the biggest hotel in Banff. They were talking intently about the strange morning, hardly paying attention to their surroundings when Jenny walked right into her father.

'Oh excuse me!' he said, smiling at them. 'I didn't see you there.'

Jenny tried her best to hide her feelings, yet the turmoil of seeing Sarah rushed back on her and she started to quiver. Paul knew, without her saying, who it was that they'd run in to and reached out to steady her. Before he could, Jenny's father stepped in front of him. He bent down, looked her in the eye, while holding her by her shoulders and whispered to her.

'You're doing fine, honey. Your mother and I are very proud of you. Keep it up.'

He stood up again and walked away, heading back the way they'd come, toward Jenny's house. She stared after him, wanting to run up and hug him but knew she couldn't. She smiled and stifled a small tear that ran down her cheek.

'C'mon Paul,' she said, regaining her composure. 'We've got to find our way out of here!'

Chapter 11

Her Resolve

Canace stared through the new amulet's core, smiled and handed it to her sister. Her sister tucked it into her shoulder bag, and held up her own amulet, promising to deliver it to the boy. Canace felt, for the first time in a long time, the urge to follow, to help, but could not. As her sister stepped through the gate, Canace saw something strange, a mist left behind, and with a sense of dread, realized it was the same purple as the boy's new amulet.

Jenny knew she had to leave Banff, that something had changed her home. She didn't yet understand why but she was sure her father knew who she was. Maybe others did as well but to her that no longer mattered. Ornolt had seemed pleased with them and so had her father. When this was all over, she'd explain herself to Sarah, and apologize to her and to David for burying them in all that snow.

Paul ran to catch up with her, confused by her sudden change in mood.

'Hey, what was that?' he asked, grabbing her arm.

'Well, I thought we better get going and figure out what Ornolt was so worried about.'

'But what about your father? You seemed so upset when you saw him and then all of a sudden you're smiling and walking away!'

'Didn't you hear what he said?' she asked

'Of course. He said 'excuse me',' Paul replied sarcastically.

'No, I meant after that,' she said.

'He didn't say much - he just kept going. He seemed in a hurry.'

Jenny stared at him, her mouth open and took a moment before replying.

'So you didn't hear what he said about being proud of me?'

'No,' he said, his eyes widening. 'I didn't. When did he say that?'

'Right away. He said I was doing great, to keep it up.'

'Wow. That's not what I heard at all. I heard him ask if he'd hurt you and then he said something about Banff, and took off.'

'That's just weird,' she said concentrating on his thoughts. 'He really did say that to you, didn't he?'

'Yeah,' he groused. 'And I wish you wouldn't do that to me. It's not fair - you know I can't read you.'

'Oh, sorry - I just can't help it.'

'Whatever. Just be careful, ok? Now what should we do? Why did we hear two different things from your father?'

'I think we'd better go back,' she said after a moment.

'Where?' Paul asked

'To Hawaii - I think maybe we should go back there to that guide that answered our questions. Maybe it will tell us.'

Paul nodded.

'So how do we get there? We can't very well climb back up that mountain and hope to find the other end of the gate!'

'No. Besides, we know the gates only go one way,' she added.

'True - that's what that Raven said.'

They arrived back at the old bridge over the Bow River and came to the T-shaped intersection. Jenny turned to head toward the Banff Springs Hotel when Paul stopped her. He was holding his amulet which was starting to warm.

Jenny grabbed hers and as she walked back towards him it began to heat up as well.

'Which way?' she said.

Paul took a few steps away from her and it cooled immediately. He came back and walked into the street.

'This way,' he said, pointing at the opposite side.

'But there's nothing there! Just, well, the administration office, some old park, and a hill leading to Sulpher Mountain!'

'See for yourself,' he said, going to the other side of the road.

As she crossed her amulet grew warmer still. They walked up the drive that ran around the ornate administration office, across the rock gardens on the other side and started into the brush on the far perimeter.

'Ok,' she said, 'Let's get back to Hawaii. All we have to do, I think, is imagine where we want to be and it'll take us there.'

Thinking hard about the places they had seen in Hawaii, they stepped into the hedge. A breeze started, warm and inviting, quite the opposite of what they would have felt in Banff. The prickly underbrush started to soften out and gradually changed to low lying ferns, from which tall, thin root systems rose up into the thick, grey, rippled trunks with long pointing leaves and black berries.

When the ground thawed and then got squishy, they knew they had passed into the gate. The air was so warm that they had to remove their cloaks. Banff was nowhere to be seen and they were traipsing through a deep rain forest. It didn't seem like Hawaii but it was warm.

They stopped to look around, trying to figure out where they were. The instant they did, the trees around them started to groan, turning a speckled grey. The trunks started to vanish, blending together into a solid wall of rock and when they looked back, they saw the passage they'd come through was closing, a barrier of rock hurtling toward them.

They turned and saw water and a beach ahead, so they took off, running toward it. They could hear the creaking, splintering cracks as the trees melted into rock. When their feet touched the sand they heard the slam of the rock as the gate snapped shut behind them and the amulets fell cool.

They were standing on a beach unlike any they had ever seen. It was jet black, made of coarse pebbles that rolled away from them as they walked. The sand ran back to jagged cliffs that looked like they had just been cut, with sharp outcroppings jutting from them at impossible angles. They could see many places where those outcroppings had fallen, large piles of rubble littering the beach. They looked down the sand and saw that it ran away from them to the horizon with no end of the rugged cliffs in sight. The ocean was calm in front of them and the sun beat down relentlessly, heating the black sand to an unbearable point.

'Oh my God!' cried Jenny. 'What's going on?'

'I thought we were going to be crushed,' Paul added. 'What kind of gate was that?'

'They seem to be getting more and more dangerous!'

'Water, fire, ice storms and crushing rock. At least the gates have been different every time!'

She glared at him.

'Well,' he continued. 'It *did* take us where we wanted to go.'

'This doesn't look like Hawaii to me,' she replied.

'Oh I don't know - this could easily be Hawaii - which is where we wanted to go. Remember what Ornolt said back there? This may be where we wanted, just not when.'

Jenny looked around then back at him.

'Are you saying this isn't, well, now?'

'I think so - something seems wrong - I just can't place it yet,' he said.

'But if that's true, how are we ever going to find our way back?'

Paul's eye's widened.

'Oh no, you're right. What if...'

He was cut off by a loud sound from far above them - an explosion, followed by a rushing of air. Looking up toward the top of the cliff they were horrified to see rocks, wood chips, dirt, even whole trees falling over the edge.

'Run!' yelled Jenny, grabbing his hand.

She sprang as fast as she could, pulling Paul along with her. In less than a second, they'd gone over a mile down the beach, easily moving out of range of the falling debris. Jenny stopped and looked back. She understood now what the sound had been. Slow moving red goo poured over the top of the cliff, leaving fire on everything it touched. A strong wind came up and blew sand toward them, making it difficult to see.

'Look Paul,' she shouted, pointing back. 'Lava!'

Holding his hand up to shield his eyes, he was stunned to see what was pouring onto the spot where they'd just been standing.

'What does it mean?' she asked him.

'It means we just heard an eruption, a minor one, and quite close by if the lava's already here. There's probably much worse coming!'

'So what do we do?'

'We leave, quickly. I think we better get as far away from that volcano as possible!'

Jenny reached for Paul's hand and, turning away from the volcano, they sprinted up the beach. They were no longer moving as fast as they had when they disappeared, although anyone watching them would never have believed what they were seeing - their hair was flying out behind them as they tore up the beach.

They stopped after about five minutes, completely exhausted, yet well away from the volcano - at least ten miles. They could see its summit belching steam and ash with small vents of lava pouring out the side.

When he caught his breath, Paul turned to Jenny.

'How do you make us run so fast?' he asked, before noticing how she looked. Her face was as white as a ghost and her eyes were wide with surprise.

'Hey, are you OK?'

'Yeah, I'm fine,' she replied, 'tired, but fine.'

'That was close, wasn't it?'

'Too close. I don't remember Hawaii ever looking like this!'

'Me too. Maybe this is one of the smaller islands - there should be others nearby.'

Jenny squinted against the wind and the sun, looking across the water.

'I don't see anything,' she said.

'Neither do I,' said Paul, 'which means this is probably a long, long time ago, before the islands all formed.'

Jenny looked back at him. 'Are you sure? We could just be on the far side of one.'

Paul shook his head. 'I don't think so. Eruptions like we just saw don't happen that way anymore.'

'How do you know?' she asked.

'Well, I sort of love volcanoes. I've been reading about them all my life.'

'Love them? Seems like a pretty dangerous thing to like!' she said.

'Well, I've never been near one, of course, but they're fascinating, really.'

They stood up and walked slowly away from the volcano. They'd run far past the cliffs and the sand ran back to the edge of the rainforest in a slow rise of rippling waves. Paul turned, headed over to a large driftwood log and sat down on it.

Jenny followed him and sat as well. She felt hungry so she opened her bag and looked in. She found an apple, some bread and a bottle of water.

'So' she said between bites. 'What's so different about that eruption?'

'Well,' he replied, 'it's pretty simple. Hawaii, at least the one in our time, has been building for a long time, and most of the islands are finished. There's some lava still there, but nothing like we just saw.'

'You can't be basing it on just that' she said.

'No,' he said, frowning, 'not just that. My other problem with this is that if it was the Hawaii of our time, there'd be geologists all over this place. This is way too interesting.'

'Oh no, you're right!' exclaimed Jenny. 'There aren't any people - we've gone over a long, long stretch of beach, and seen absolutely no sign of anyone.'

'So you believe me, then?' he asked.

'Maybe. But what'll we do? What if we're stuck here all by ourselves?'

'We've just got to find another a gate, ok?'

'But what if it takes us even further away?'

'What else can we do? I mean, I doubt the order would just abandon us here, would they?'

'Maybe they would. The gates have been pretty awful so far. That raven did say it was all up to us.'

'Yeah, but we weren't alone in Banff, were we? Ornolt was there, and I suspect others might have been as well.'

'So?'

'So I don't think they would just let us die' he said. 'I just don't.'

'Yeah, maybe,' she said. 'But what about those strange children we keep seeing?'

'What about them?'

'Maybe they're like us, only they can't find their way back.'

'I'm more worried about what's following us.'

She stared at him.

'What do you mean? Have you seen that weird thing again?'

'No,' he said, shaking his head. 'It's just a feeling. I don't think we were alone going through that gate. I thought we were followed.'

'You think something followed us through the gate? Is it here now?'

Paul closed his eyes and sat still for a few moments.

'No,' he said. 'At least, I can't feel anything other than you.'

'Maybe we out ran it? Or maybe there was nothing.'

She finished her apple and threw the core behind her.

'Hey' said Paul, 'Don't do that...'

'Do what?'

'Leave that core - what if some animal finds it, and comes looking for more?'

Forming a soundless O, she got up and went to retrieve it. She searched for some time before finding where it had landed. There was no sign of it anywhere, just the small impact mark and a little trail where it had rolled to a stop. She walked back over to Paul.

'Got it?' he asked.

'No - I couldn't find it.'

'Well, did you look where you threw it?'

She shot him an evil look.

'Of course. I found where it landed, and where it rolled - just, no core.'

'Show me,' he said.

She led him back to where the core had landed.

'Yet another mystery,' he murmured.

'Maybe. Or maybe it's simply that we can't leave things behind that come out of these bags.'

Paul nodded in agreement.

'I guess we better find some shelter - those clouds out over the ocean don't look friendly.'

'Hey, maybe we could make one - like that fireplace?'

'Do you think we could?'

'We'll never know unless we try. Let's make something small - like a beach hut.'

'Ok - I remember seeing a picture of one once, with a straw roof, and a small porch to sit on out of the sun. Let me show you.'

He put his hand on her shoulder and poured the image into her. She nodded and they stared together at an open patch of sand, well back from the water. An image started to wobble before them. The sand was flattening as if something really heavy was crushing it.

They thought harder about the hut - the bamboo walls it would have and the bright red material they would use for doors and curtains. The image solidified into a small building, grey to start and then it slowly bathed itself in color. The roof began to appear and they stared hard at its peak, watching the straw thatch itself together. The porch on the front was bathed in shade and had a small, bamboo rail around it.

'Wow,' Jenny said. 'That's so cool!'

'It sure is,' he replied, walking over to it and up the small steps to the porch. The clouds that they had seen were rolling away from them, and the sun's heat grew stronger. Jenny joined him in the shade of the porch and looked inside. It was completely empty.

'There's not much in there,' she said. 'I guess we didn't think of that.'

'That's ok,' he said. 'At least it'll keep us dry if it rains.'

She sat down on the porch floor and hunched her legs up, resting her head on them and staring at the ocean.

'So do you feel any different?' she asked.

'Than what?'

'Than at the start - you know, can you do more?'

'Yeah, maybe. My sense of things around me is definitely stronger. What about you?'

'I feel like I'm changing a lot. It's like this other part of me is getting stronger, you know?'

'Like the running?'

'Yeah, although that was starting already. It's more like a feeling of - belonging. I like the way I feel.'

'What about that blue mist around you - is that what's different?'

'Maybe - although I can't see what you're talking about.'

She was interrupted by a loud cracking sound from far down the beach and when they looked toward it, they saw another eruption had started, this one far bigger than the first.

Then they felt it - a dull rumble coming through the ground. It was starting to rock and they jumped up in alarm. As they did, the earthquake hit them with its full force. The cabin they'd made was shattered, the bamboo bursting apart and vanishing. In moments, everything they'd built was gone and they felt like they were standing on a mammoth trampoline while hundreds of people jumped on it. Sometimes the ground rose underneath them and sometimes it slipped sideways. They were flailing their arms about as they tried to keep their balance.

'Paul!' screamed Jenny, 'what's going on?'

'Earthquake, I think!' he yelled back, trying to steady himself.

'What do we do? Is it going to kill us?'

He stared at her and then at the trees, which seemed dangerously close. He began to wobble toward the beach, gesturing for her to follow.

'Paul! Wait!' she cried.

When she tried to follow him, the ground heaved up in front of her and knocked her back toward the trees. As she struggled to her feet, the ground shifted again and she heard a deep crash. She spun around and saw the trees swaying violently in the earthquake's grip, some of them leaning right towards her.

One of the trees split apart and its palm fronds scattered as it fell slowly down. Paul was well ahead of Jenny and turned to see where she was. He saw her struggling against the relentless waves of the earthquake, unable to gain her balance so he started back to help her.

With a horrendous groan and a crack, the ground underneath him split apart. What had once been solid ground was now a crumbling landslide, slipping into a deep, dark crevice. He tried to grab hold of the side to stop himself but it was too late.

He fell, plunging toward depths that he could not see. Just as he started to scream he landed with a splash in a wet pond far below the surface. The earthquake's shakes stopped and he swam over to the edge of the pond. He pulled himself out, rubbing his side where he'd hit the water.

Above him he saw a narrow shaft of light beaming down through a small opening. He couldn't tell how high it was but he was sure it was higher than he could climb. In the gloom that surrounded him, he saw that the walls were made of sharp rock that had just been ripped apart. He looked back up at the opening.

'Jenny! Hey! Help! Can you hear me? Jenny!'

When the earthquake finally stopped, Jenny picked herself up off the ground. Dusting off her shirt, she looked around for Paul. He was nowhere to be seen. She called out for him and stopped to listen. All she could hear was the distant rumbles of the volcano and the quiet lapping of the surf against the newly shaped beach.

Paul had vanished.

She held up her amulet and shielded it against the bright sun. It was glowing, a faint, soft blue. She couldn't see him but she remembered that he'd been running ahead of her toward the water, trying to escape the falling trees.

She rushed toward the water, fearing he might have fallen over into it and got hurt or drowned. The amulet's glow grew brighter as she ran and she didn't notice the gaping crevice in the sand ahead of her. Too late to stop, she slipped, arms flailing at the sides, and fell.

As soon as she felt herself falling, Jenny twisted in the air and looked down. She couldn't see anything and knew that wherever she was going, it was dark. She thought her landing wasn't likely to be soft and in a panic she willed herself not to hit and she felt her fall slowing down.

She looked up and saw the same shaft of light that Paul had seen. It was moving away from her and as her eyes adjusted, she looked back down and saw the approaching pond. Paul stood to one side of it and without stopping to think she floated over to him and settled on the ground beside him.

Paul was staring at her, his eyes wide in shock and amazement.

'Oh my God!' he exclaimed, running over and hugging her. 'Are you OK?'

'I think so,' she replied, 'but I never want to feel that horrible shaking again!'

Paul nodded, then stopped, looking at the hole high above them where the light poured through.

'Wait a second, how did you do that?' he asked.

'What?'

'Well, how you got here - you didn't fall, you floated. It looked like you were flying.'

Jenny looked back up at the light above them.

'I - I don't know,' she stammered. 'I just didn't want to hurt myself, so I slowed down.'

Paul looked at her with a gleam in his eye. 'Think, Jenny - how did you do it? Remember how you thought something was changing?'

'Yes,' she replied, 'but what is it?'

She thought about what had just happened. She'd been worried about Paul and had run to find him. As soon as she'd realized she'd fallen, she had stopped, without thinking.

'It's so strange - I didn't really decide to do it,' she started. 'I just, well, I knew I couldn't hit the ground from so high up, so I stopped.'

'But Jenny, *how* did you stop?' he insisted.

'I had to. There was no choice. I just...' she broke off, looking around. She could hear a voice, a girl's voice, whispering something. She walked away from Paul and she glanced at the cavern around them. Who was that? The voice faded away.

She picked up some loose gravel that was gathered at the edge of the underground pond and started throwing it into the water. She was throwing hard and the gravel rocks made an unnatural thwip sound as they cut the water.

What does it take she thought, *to smash that stick?*

'You already know, my sister,' the voice whispered again. 'You already can.'

She whipped around and looked at Paul who was just watching her. She concentrated on him and realized he hadn't heard anything. She threw another stone and shattered the stick.

'Do it again - hit it,' came the voice.

She tried and missed. How was it that sometimes it worked, others it didn't? The voice was gone and she threw the rest of the gravel stones angrily into the pool and stomped back to where Paul was sitting.

He watched her, trying to figure out what it was that let her do what she did. He couldn't hear the voices but could tell something was happening - he could see, as she paced back and forth throwing the gravel, that the mist around her had grown to an intense aura of power. It was swirling around her, rather than beaming out of her in a focused way. For one instant, when she'd made that stick explode, the aura had lashed out with her.

Then when she had thrown the gravel away in frustration, the aura had vanished, no longer under her control.

What is she missing? he thought. *What is it that comes and goes?*

She sat down beside him.

'I don't know,' she said, simply.

'Don't know what?' he asked.

'You asked me how I stopped from falling - how I do any of these things. The answer is I don't know. Sometimes I can and sometimes I can't.'

'Well,' he started, 'you told Ornolt that you've always been able to move things, right?'

'Yes' she said.

'You didn't tell him, but you have told me - since this started, since we got teamed up, you've been able to do it quite a bit more.'

She nodded, listening.

'I can't move things,' he continued, 'but I can imagine them. Like the hut we just made - that was a combination of what we can do, right?'

Again she nodded.

'When we did that, we were a little desperate, right?'

'Yes, that's right, and maybe that's the trick - when I was falling, I knew I had to stop, or I'd get hurt - maybe killed.'

Paul shook his head. 'I don't think that's quite it - why were you able to pour all that snow on your friends?'

She winced and sat back, puzzled. 'Yeah, that doesn't fit, does it?'

He shook his head.

'No, it doesn't.' He stood up and threw another stick out into the pond. He picked up a handful of gravel and handed some to Jenny.

'Let's have a contest - see who can hit it the most.'

Paul had an excellent arm so when he turned to the water, he hit the stick on his second shot. Jenny was impressed and stood up beside him. She tried to hit it as well and missed. Paul threw another and hit it again. She started to throw harder but missed every time.

She kept trying to concentrate on making the stick explode with the impact of her stone. She missed again, sending the stone far, far past the stick, almost to the other side of the pond. Paul looked at her, then back at the stick and calmly hit it again.

Jenny couldn't believe it and wound up to pulverize the stick. Just as she was about to let go, she heard the voice again.

'Just let it happen, sister. Use the wind! Be yourself!'

She relaxed, looked at the stick and threw the stone right at it. It split into several shards that drifted away from each other, riding the small, widening circular waves away from the impact.

Paul smiled and sat down. She looked at him in amazement.

'That was cool!' she said. 'Let's keep going!'

'No way - Looks like you're figuring this out. I'll have no chance. Besides, I think we should try and find our way out of here.'

'Ok,' she mumbled. 'Where to?'

He walked over to the other side of the pool where he thought he saw a cave. He stood looking into a wide crevice in the wall. It was dark and deep: no light penetrated it.

'There's a breeze coming from in there,' he said.

'Do you think it's a way out?' she asked.

'Maybe - but there's only one way to tell. The trouble is that it's too dark to see.'

'What if it's just another small shaft from the earthquake?'

'I'm fairly sure it is,' he replied, 'but, unless you can fly us both up there, we need to find another way out.'

He was trying to stare into the crevice and when he leaned in, Jenny saw his amulet spill out and its glow cast some light. She reached into her shirt, drew hers out, and held it close to his. The blue glow grew stronger and they could see that the crevice opened into a long, narrow tunnel that stretched into a dark, blue gloom.

They held the amulets up together and stepped into the tunnel. At first the walls were solid rock and sharp, clearly just ripped open by the earthquake. The tunnel was going steadily down, on a small incline and they could feel the cold, moist air moving against them.

By the light of the amulets they could only see twenty feet in front of them. All they saw was the continued line of the tunnel. The wall was starting to soften, the sign of rock that had been exposed for a long time. Embedded in it were thousands of small reflective crystals, a by-product of the volcanic chaos that had formed the walls.

They could see the tunnel curving down and to the right. The air was dripping wet like the exhaust of a humidifier. Jenny drew her free arm around her, holding her amulet out ahead as she turned the corner.

About half way around the bend they heard the sound of rushing water. An underground river was ahead of them, a deep runoff from a distant mountain. It had no smell other than its moisture.

They moved cautiously forward, not wanting to step into a trap, or fall into the river. They could clearly hear the rushing water although they couldn't yet see it. The walls around them were getting darker and less sparkly. Jenny held her amulet up to it and saw why: It was covered in a dark, moss-like growth.

'Paul,' she whispered. 'Look at this!'

'Moss,' he said. 'So?'

'And look at the sand - you know what it looks like?'

'No.'

'Like it would if it were underwater - look at the ripples!'

'But how could that be?'

'Tides!'

They rounded the final bend in the tunnel and came out on a small, dark underground beach. Its granular sand was hard and had the same underwater ripple.

'I think we shouldn't stay here long,' she said. 'We shouldn't be able to walk here.'

'I know - we've got to find a way out.'

The water was moving rapidly in the direction from which the air flowed.

'Looks like we've got to go that way,' he said.

'Following the river, right?' she asked.

They set off and Jenny felt herself being drawn in by the water's patterns. It was bubbly, which seemed wrong to her. She bent down to test how cold it was and was surprised by its warmth. Paul bent down to test the water as well.

'What do you think?' she said.

'It's being heated by something, isn't it?'

'Yeah, but what?'

'Well, maybe it's coming from far underground, and it's being heated by the lava underneath these rocks!'

Jenny wrinkled her nose up and shook her head.

'I've smelt hot spring water before - it's always got a smell of some sort - this doesn't.'

'Really? That might be trouble - what if this water is supposed to be on the surface?'

The walls around them were getting tighter and they had to walk on the edge of the river, occasionally stepping in. They came to a spot where the walls of rock completely surrounded the river, forcing them to walk right in it. A narrow opening, less than a foot high, spanned the river and the air they'd felt earlier was rushing through the gap.

The air began to change: while it was still moist, it was getting warm - the chill from the tunnels gone. The surface of the water started to evaporate, a light mist drifting away from it.

'Oh my god!' said Paul, realizing what this meant. 'We've got to get out of here!'

No sooner had the words come out of his mouth when they both felt the air warming behind them. They spun around and there - far, far up the dark, subterranean river was a red glow.

'Go!' Paul shouted, running toward the wall. He dove into the water and swam under it. Jenny followed and they were hurled along by the water. Far ahead of them they could see daylight and knew that if they just kept going, they would get there sooner than the lava.

They swam along and as the river widened, the current calmed and they slowed down. The water kept warming up.

'C'mon Paul, we've got to swim harder!' she screamed.

Paul was already ahead of her since he was such a strong swimmer. Jenny struggled to keep up to him. The water was getting hot and they felt their skin starting to burn. The daylight was close and Paul was almost there. Jenny swam as fast as she could, ignoring the pain. The river narrowed once more and the current picked up. Moments later they burst out of the face of a cliff and were washed into the ocean. They swam away from the river and up onto the shore.

As soon as they got there, Jenny grabbed Paul's hand and took off down the beach. A minute later she stopped, safely away from the river and the lava that was to follow.

She was completely out of breath and collapsed. Paul sat beside her, watching the display in the distance. The river was a long way away and the opening in the cliff face looked like a distant dot. Suddenly steam burst from it, followed by molten rock. The ocean fought it angrily, steam blasting from every point of contact.

Jenny looked like she was going to fall asleep so he tapped her on the shoulder.

'Hey, are you all right?' he asked.

'Yeah - fine - just, really tired. That was hard!'

Slow tears started down her face and Paul pulled her into a hug, waiting for them to stop.

'When will it end, Paul? That's what I don't understand!'

He was a long time answering. He wanted to tell her that he knew but he didn't. All he wanted to do was go home and sleep.

'I don't know,' he finally said. 'Maybe it'll be over soon...' he trailed off, looking out at the sea.

'It is kind of incredible how much trouble we keep getting in, isn't it?' she sniffed.

'Yeah,' he said, 'like we were meant to. Come to think of it, we probably are. That's what we're here for, isn't it?'

Jenny sat up and wiped the tears away.

'So what do we do next?' Paul asked.

Jenny looked out to sea at a bank of rapidly approaching storm clouds.

'Get to the trees. Those clouds don't look friendly at all!'

Paul looked where she was pointing. The clouds were angry, billowing thunder heads, rolling towards them at an astonishing speed. They could hear distant rumbles and felt the wind picking up.

'Why not build another shelter?'

'No time!' she cried, 'and what if it doesn't work?'

They stood up and ran up the beach toward the rainforest that lined its edge. They walked into the forest as the rain started. They pulled their cloaks over their heads while the storm pounded the canopy above, the water pouring down on them. Jenny saw a cluster of trees and rock ahead of them and guided them toward it.

Paul trailed after her and kept glancing up the beach, away from the lava. The rain had already soaked it and as it lashed down, driven in sheets by the wind, he saw a gap - a large, round gap that was moving toward the trees.

When they got there, they found they were on the edge of a large river; a normal, surface river, that flowed to the ocean in the opposite direction from which they'd come. The rain was beating down on it, forming thousands of deep drop marks as it vanished into the water.

The trees were tall and broad and just as the rain's fury hit them, they found one that appeared hollowed out, with more than enough room for them inside it. They rushed in and sat down, huddling together to wait out the storm.

'Something's out there Jen,' he whispered.

'What?'

'I saw something - like a bubble in the rain.'

She squinted out into the rain.

'I don't see anything.'

Paul closed his eyes and concentrated.

'I can't feel anything either,' he said. 'But I definitely saw something...'

Jenny leaned on him, her eyes slowly closing.

'You go to sleep,' he said. 'I'm just going to watch for a bit.'

'Thanks,' she whispered, lowering her head onto his shoulder.

Paul sat still, watching the bands of rain splash into the river. With each flash of lightening, he tried to see what was around them. After nearly twenty minutes of seeing nothing but the storm, his eyes grew heavy. He put his arm around Jenny and fell asleep.

Chapter 12

Reasoning With A Crocodile

Canace's sister returned to the boy's land, emerging from the gate in a cave, hidden from wondering eyes. As soon as she did, she felt a great pain in her side, and realized that something was burning her back. She hurled her shoulder bag away, and watched, in fascination, as the purple amulet emerged, and in a great whirl of wind and spark, split into two. The amulets before her where identical, a beautiful, glowing purple, and with great haste, she returned to their mountain-home, to tell Canace.

For the entire night, rain pounded down on the forest. Lightening lit up the sky, followed by loud, rolling thunder. The downpour lasted for hours and throughout it, wiped out by the day they'd just been through, the children slept.

Just as dawn broke over the eastern sky, a distant bird sang out and Jenny shifted before jolting awake. Paul's head, leaning on her shoulder, fell heavily onto her leg and he woke feeling groggy.

'Oh, Paul, I'm sorry!' Jenny said when she realized what had hit her.

'It's ok,' he mumbled, sitting up slowly.

It was a cold morning and even though they could see the sun brightening the tops of the taller trees, the land around them was still bathed in the cool dawn light. Jenny stood and stretched, looking around. The rain had soaked everything; even their clothes were damp from the moisture in the air.

She shivered as she stepped out of their tree-cave and drew her cloak tight. Paul followed her, doing the same and rubbing his shoulders to keep warm. His eyes still looked half shut like he was walking in a trance.

They were perched on the edge of a large, calm river, nestled in a patch of trees whose root systems made the trees look like they were suspended several feet off the ground. It was in just such a formation they'd slept the night before, one that had a natural rock face as an upper wall to fend off the weather.

The river was over one hundred feet wide and slow moving. The ocean that it flowed into wasn't far away and she could see the water of the river mixing with the ocean, changing color as it blended with the salt. The ocean had calmed down from the night before and its ripples sparkled in the sunlight.

'Isn't this beautiful, Paul!' Jenny exclaimed, stretching her arms out and yawning.

Paul grunted, looking around, but said nothing. He wanted to go back to sleep but knew there was no way Jenny would let him. She was getting more and more energy and moving around in a rhythmic way, watching the sun's early glints of light on the far side of the river. If Paul didn't know better, he'd swear he heard her singing but when he looked, her mouth was closed - just her feet seemed to be moving to the song.

He sighed and turned away, walking slowly along the bank of the river. He kicked at some pebbles, thinking about his home and the warmth of his own bed.

Why's she so happy? he thought, looking back at Jenny. Her arms were rising and falling in rhythm, dancing slowly for the sun. *I just want to go home. Doesn't she?*

He leaned against a tree and stared out into the river, scowling at how he felt. He watched Jenny still dancing and the frown faded as he thought about how great it was to have met her, to have found out about the order, even if it was going to be impossible to explain to his family and friends.

Jenny hopped over toward him, concentrating on what was gnawing at him.

'Hey, Paul,' she said, 'don't worry about it. We will.'

He looked at her sharply.

'Will what?' he groused.

'Get home. I'll come with you if you want, and help you explain what's happened!'

Paul's face fell even further and he glared at her.

'You know what - you should stay out of my head,' he snapped.

Her eyes widened.

'I'm sorry - I forgot. No one likes that, even those who know,' Jenny said. 'It's just - I know how you feel - really, I do.'

They kept walking. Jenny was looking at everything around them and Paul just shuffled along behind her, staring at the river. He was reminded of a time when he was young, three or four years of age, when his father had taken him fishing. He thought it might have been somewhere in France, in the north-east country side.

'It's not only home I miss,' he said suddenly, 'I miss...'

'You don't have to tell me' she said, putting a hand on his shoulder. 'It's like I can remember him too. He'd be so proud of you.'

Paul frowned and his eyes began to tear up, so he looked back out at the river.

'I asked you not to do that, Jen.'

'Before you came here, before you, um, met me, was it like this?' she asked, ignoring his request.

'All the time,' he sighed. 'I still think of him a lot.'

Jenny nodded and looked up into the trees. She could see some coconuts high in their canopy and wanted to get one of them down, to drink the milk they contained.

'You think of him even more now that we're here,' she said, heading over to one of the trees and kicking it.

He watched her, amused by the kick but still lingering on home, on his father.

'Yes, actually, much more. I keep looking around, hoping to hear his voice again, or maybe even see him.'

Jenny was shaking the tree, determined to get a coconut.

'Hey,' Paul said, 'not like that. You can do it without even touching it.'

She looked at him and then back at one of the coconuts. She gestured at it with one hand, in a sweeping motion. With a snap, it let go and went flying out into the river, where it landed about half way across.

Jenny looked back at Paul in amazement.

'You see?' he said, grinning.

She nodded, looking at the splash mark.

'It's like I said before,' he continued. 'You've always been able to do that. You just didn't know it.'

'Do you want one?' she asked.

He looked up at them.

'Um, sure, yeah.'

She raised her arm and pointed at one of the coconuts. It trembled and then broke free, hanging in the air. She cupped her hands around an imaginary ball and brought it down. As she did, the coconut floated down towards her. Paul saw the smile on her face as the coconut landed in her hands and she turned it over and over.

She turned and walked over to Paul, handing it to him.

'Wow,' she said, 'how did you know?'

'Because I can see it, all around you. That same blue mist. It's part of you.'

He looked down at the coconut, wondering how to open it. Jenny turned back to the tree, thinking about what he said. She looked back at the coconuts, picked one and imagined a rope tied around it. She tugged the imaginary rope and the coconut snapped loose, hurtling toward her. She caught it roughly, almost falling over and realized she hadn't done enough to control it; all she'd done was make it fall.

It was heavy and it sloshed under the weight of its milk. She turned it over slowly, looking for some way to break it open. It had an even surface - no obvious way in. She knocked on it, searching for the spot that sounded weakest.

Paul did the same with less enthusiasm.

'Maybe I should have stuck with the bag,' he grumbled.

Jenny looked over at him fruitlessly banging the coconut on a rock and rolled her eyes.

'Yeah well,' she said, sitting down beside him. 'These are as fresh as it gets. Watch this!'

She held her coconut between her knees and pointed her right index finger at the top of it. Paul watched, astonished, as she pushed her finger through its shell, making a perfect hole.

She withdrew her finger and handed the coconut to Paul. He thanked her and took a long sip. She grabbed the one she'd gotten for him and drank its contents. When she was done, she stood up and hurled the empty shell far out over the river.

Paul watched, still fascinated. 'I think you've really got it now, Jenny' he said.

She nodded and sat down again. 'I think so too. It's just, well...'

'I know,' he said. 'Remember?'

'Yup!' she said, smiling and leaping up. 'Now, come on, let's go back - you need more sleep!'

She turned and started back toward the tree cave, still practicing what she'd just found out. Paul lumbered along after her, thankful for the chance to sleep but surprised by what she was doing. A path was forming in front of her, the small sticks, rocks and dust moving aside as if pushed by an imaginary plow. Rocks kept rising out of the river, floating over to her and then bouncing high into the air toward the sea. Her eyes were darting from object to object as they rolled, bounced and flew about her.

When they reached the tree, Paul crept in and fell back asleep. Jenny saw a large boulder near the edge of the river on which the sun was beaming and decided to stretch out while Paul slept.

She climbed up and settled into the warmth of the sun. Her clothes were still damp from the night before and dried out as she drifted off into a light doze.

She lay still for about half an hour, enjoying the warmth and the tranquility. She could hear the water moving slowly past and birds calling to each other in the rain forest. What she found most peaceful of all was the total silence of her mind - other than Paul, there was no one here for her to avoid, no one to accidentally listen to.

She had nearly fallen asleep when she felt something on her chest getting warm. She thought she heard her brothers laughing and swatted at them. With a jolt she remembered where she was and sat up, holding her amulet up and staring at it. The glow stayed the same and so did its warmth. She moved it slowly back and forth, trying to find the guide.

The river was still and the breeze slight - not enough to move the leaves above her. She saw two birds circling out over the ocean but saw nothing on the surface. She turned to look inland, up the river. Its mangrove-lined banks curved out of sight and nothing moved. She grabbed her amulet again and felt it getting warmer. She looked back at Paul and saw his amulet dangling on the end of its chain. It wasn't touching him and his shallow snore kept a steady rhythm.

Something's definitely coming, she thought, *so be ready.*

She sat up, tensed, expecting absolutely anything.

Except the crocodile which burst from the river and lunged right at her.

She whirled to face it, held up her hand and screamed one word: 'FREEZE!'

It did. Right in midair. Its eyes went wide in shock, jittering back and forth, the rest of its body suspended and immobile.

Jenny crawled down from the rock, never taking her eyes off of it. Its mouth hung open and she could see the soft, moist depth of its throat. She hurried over to Paul and shook his shoulder to wake him.

He woke slowly, blinking his eyes and stretching. When he finally focused, he saw Jenny staring at him.

'Hey, c'mon, wake up!' she whispered.

'What time is it?' he asked.

'I've no idea - but you've got to get up now!'

'Why?' he said, sensing through his bleary mind that she was excited.

'Because I've found a guide!'

Paul jumped up.

'A guide! Where?'

Jenny pointed back at the rock.

'Oh my God!' Paul exclaimed. 'That's a ... a crocodile.'

Jenny smiled, nodding. 'It's not just a crocodile. My amulet warmed up as it approached. It's a guide, I'm sure of it.'

Paul scratched his head, looking at it and then back to her.

'How come it's just, well, floating there?'

'Oh,' she shrugged, 'it tried to attack me. I froze it.'

173

Paul stared at her. 'You what?'

'Froze it. I didn't want to get eaten!'

They walked back over and looked at it. It couldn't move anything except for its eyes which were following their steps with a look of indignation.

The two children stopped several yards back from it.

'So,' said Jenny, 'shall we release it, and see what it wants?'

'Oh sure,' Paul replied. 'Just let's get somewhere a little safer, shall we?'

They looked around and decided on climbing one of the nearby trees. The long, gnarly roots were easy to scale and they settled in high above the crocodile.

'OK,' Paul said, 'let's talk to it.'

Jenny looked back at it and smiled. The animal fell with a thud to the boulder where she had been sitting. It climbed to the top of the rock, shook its head and then looked up at them. Jenny wondered for a moment if she'd been wrong, since the crocodile just seemed angry, hungry, and wild.

Then it spoke.

'Well! That's a nice way to treat a guide!' it said in a booming voice that sounded like it was coming from inside a deep bottle.

'You didn't exactly give me much of a choice!' Jenny replied.

'What do you mean?' it demanded.

'Well, you burst out of the water like you meant to eat me!'

The crocodile laughed out loud.

'If I'd meant to eat you, my dear, you wouldn't be sitting there now!'

'Maybe not,' she replied. 'I've learned a lot.'

'Yes. So I noticed. But were I to bring my full power against you, you'd be gone.'

Paul put a hand on Jenny.

Leave it alone he thought.

She turned and stared at him.

There's more in front of us than you think he continued.

'Communicating already?' it said. 'Very good. Next time I sneak up on you, I'll have to use more stealth. I didn't surprise you nearly enough!'

'Yes you did - you scared me! I almost threw you out to sea!'

'Out to sea?' it said, genuinely alarmed. 'Oh, no, please don't do that. I don't like salt water much.'

'Can we come down?' Paul asked.

'Do you mean can you climb down or am I going to eat you?' the crocodile asked.

'Eat us,' Paul replied curtly.

'Then no, I never intended to eat you. You're too important for that.'

They climbed down and stood in front it.

'What do you mean, important?' Jenny asked.

'Oh come on!' it hissed. 'What do you think I mean? The Order isn't going to invest as much as it has testing you two just to have a stupid croc eat you, now is it?'

They both shook their heads, looking at the ground.

'I thought not,' it continued. 'Now then. We've got some important things to discuss.'

It had settled down on the rock, enjoying the heat of the sun.

'Why don't you two sit down there,' it finally said. 'And have something to eat - Paul, you seem hungry to me.'

Paul looked down at himself, wondering how the crocodile knew. It just smiled at him in a crooked way, as he sat down and reached in his bag. His hand emerged with a raisin bagel, slathered in honey.

'Ah,' said the crocodile, 'not something I would have chosen, but I understand they're quite delicious.'

Paul nodded and took a bite. Jenny didn't eat yet, preferring to keep a close eye on the croc.

'So what's so important?' she asked.

The crocodile looked at her, surprised by her question.

'Why just about everything, my dear. Haven't you noticed how the number of strange things that happen to you have been increasing lately?'

'Yes, I have. Going to Banff was maybe the weirdest thing that's ever happened. And this place,' she said, glancing around, 'I don't have any idea where we are.'

'Or when' it replied. 'Paul was right. You are no longer in the same time as you were when you were in Banff.'

'So how did you know?' it asked, turning to Paul.

'I didn't' he shrugged. 'Know, I mean. It's just that there were a lot of things that weren't right, and with what Ornolt said...'

'Ah yes, the Exeter. He's an interesting one. I'd love to spend more time with him. He gets to move around quite a bit. He's taken a fancy to you two.'

'What's that mean?' Jenny asked.

The crocodile shifted, to get the sun on its other side.

'It means that the Exeter has never before asked to visit new arrivals once their journey has started. We were shocked that he wanted to, and it says quite a bit about what he thinks of you.'

Paul and Jenny looked at each other.

The crocodile continued. 'Not that we blame him, really. You are a very interesting problem.'

'What do you mean, problem?' Paul demanded.

'Well, please don't take this the wrong way, Paul - you are a very gifted young man - believe me. It's her we're worried about.'

'What's wrong with me?' she asked.

'Oh nothing is wrong, Jenny. It's just that too much may be right, and that has us worried.'

'Who's us?' said Paul

'The Order, of course. I'm a member, in case you hadn't figured that out yet.'

'I did,' Jenny said. 'You seemed more annoyed than surprised when I froze you.'

The crocodile let out a low grunt of agreement. 'You've no idea how annoyed. I wanted to scare you, show the rest of them that you weren't what they all think you are!'

'Who do you think she is, then?' Paul asked.

'Well, Jenny has something very different about her, something that has never happened before in all our history.'

It paused, closing its eyes and its tail coiled around the boulder. When it looked back up, it stared at Paul.

'You have no doubt noticed, Paul, how many *abilities* Jenny has?'

Paul nodded.

'And have you noticed how quickly she's learning how to use them?'

Again, he nodded, remembering how easily she'd frozen the crocodile.

'So have we. No one has ever learned at the same rate as her. And no one has ever combined so many different skills at once.'

It paused, staring from one to another.

'Do you know why?' Jenny asked.

'No, but we do have a couple of pretty good guesses. Tell me, what was the strangest thing that happened to you in Banff?'

'Ornolt's visit?' Paul guessed.

'Nope.'

'The snowfall and the Christmas trees?' Jenny asked.

'Wrong again. C'mon, think about the people...'

'They didn't know her!' exclaimed Paul.

'Close...'

'Except one,' Jenny whispered. 'My father knew me.'

'Precisely,' it hissed, breathing out. 'Your father knew you.'

'But I thought you guys, you know, in The Order, did that to make me feel better.'

'Oh no. We didn't. He definitely knew you. And if you'd listened closely, you'd have realized that your mother did too.'

Jenny gasped. That was true - her father had said that they were both proud of her.

'He never said he knew her,' Paul said.

The crocodile-guide looked at him.

'Remember Paul, you and Jenny do not always see the same things. Jenny's father was one such instance.'

'Are you saying,' Paul continued, 'that he really did say those things to Jenny? When she bumped in to him?'

'Yes I am. And *he* didn't want you to see that.'

'Hey, wait a second!' Jenny burst out. 'Is my father a member of The Order?'

'That's hard to answer. Yes and no would probably be the best way to put it. You see, your father was once just as you are now, on a team, on an adventure, in a strange world, learning about some rather interesting abilities he had.'

Jenny stared at the crocodile with her mouth hanging open.

'He wasn't the same as you of course,' it continued. 'He could only do certain things, and learned at a more normal pace.'

'So he was a member, then?' Paul asked.

'No - just as you are not - yet,' it replied. 'You no doubt will be one day, but you're not there yet.'

'So what happened?' Jenny interrupted. 'Why did you say yes and no?'

'Because, Jenny, just when he made it through, just when he was going to join The Order, he gave it all up - he left.'

'What?' she exclaimed. 'Dad? Why would he do that?'

'Well, I don't know if this will make sense to you now, since you haven't been told everything about The Order. Be that as it may, the reason he left was your mother.'

'What about her?'

'He'd met her late in his training, and they'd developed a bit of an attachment. At least, that's all we thought it was.'

'Where did he meet her?' Paul asked.

'In Banff, of course. That's why they live there now.'

Jenny frowned.

'That's not right - they met in Munich. We didn't move to Banff until I was eight.'

'It's possible, of course, that they met before, but we're fairly sure it was there that it hit him.'

'What did?' Jenny asked.

'That the Exeter had missed her.'

Neither child said a word. The crocodile slithered off the rock and crawled into the shade of the boulder.

'I keep forgetting how hot the sun is at this time of year. Count yourselves lucky, you can control your own temperature!'

'So Jenny's mother could have been a member as well?' Paul asked.

'Maybe. We'll never know, since we never got to test her, or invite her to the training. Ornolt to this day isn't sure. He's been back to see her several times when she was a child, and just doesn't see it. She is quite gifted, however. She has a sensibility about others that you've inherited, Jenny.'

She was hardly listening. *Both her parents* kept going through her head. As if reading her mind, the crocodile continued:

'It's the fact that both of your parents could be members that makes you unique, Jenny. It's never happened before, because we have always prevented it.'

'Why?' Paul asked.

'Well, we didn't know what would happen. Would we get someone who was so dysfunctional that they couldn't survive? You both know how hard it was growing up, trying to hide what you could do.

'That was our biggest concern. There were a few who felt such a combination might be dangerous as well, but we've always dismissed them as being paranoid. That is,' he said, glancing at Jenny, 'until we saw you in action. Even old Aloysius Strumn is afraid of what you can do.'

'Strumn's not afraid of me' she said. 'He's an interesting person.'

'In what way?' the croc hissed. 'All he does is disrupt!'

'I think there's more to him than that,' she continued. 'He's helped us a lot.'

'Be careful around him. He's not trustworthy. He is a terrible man'

'But...'

'No buts, Jenny. Don't follow his lead - it'll ruin your life!'

'I, ok - I won't,' she stammered. 'I won't.'

The crocodile smiled, as much as it was able. 'I'm very glad to hear that.'

It moved out from the shadows of the rock, needing the sun's heat once more. In doing so it came closer to the children. Paul took a step back but Jenny did not, remaining still and staring at it.

'It's interesting, in fact, that you are the way you are, Jenny. Most children born to members of The Order have no special abilities at all. The talent seems to skip generations.

'In your family, Paul, there hasn't been a potential member for four generations. Quite a dry spell.'

'What about my brothers?' Jenny asked. 'Can they join too?'

The crocodile let out a low, hissing laugh.

'It's not a matter of joining. You either are or you are not. Your brothers are not. Your father was. Your mother might have been, although we'll never know now.'

Jenny could tell the crocodile was avoiding something important - she had been trying to read its mind the whole time that it had been talking and found that, like Strumn, there was nothing there to read - it was as if it didn't exist. However, unlike Strumn, there was a sense of fear about it.

'Ornolt said, when we talked in Banff, that The Order was worried about us - worried by how fast we were learning. That's not quite it, is it?' she asked.

'Well, I am impressed,' said the crocodile, 'Tell me, before I answer you, why you asked me that? What makes you think there's more?'

'You're frightened of something,' she said in a low voice.

'Very good. One day you'll have to tell me how you know that. But yes, I - we - are frightened of quite a few things.'

It smiled, shifting again in the sun. 'This is the part where I get to be guide.'

'You mean you weren't already?' asked Paul.

'Ignore me - that comment wasn't so much for you as it was for others who might be listening. Now then, do you remember what Aloysius Strumn said about this little adventure you're on?'

'He said a lot,' Jenny replied, 'but I really remember this one. He said not everything we see here is real, and then he said *separate the real from the placed.*'

'That's the quote I was looking for. Strumn has a talent for that, amongst other things. He can say rather a lot with almost no words at all. But let me add to that: Not everything you find placed here is our doing. Some things are quite beyond our control, or anyone else's for that matter.'

'Are you saying that we're in danger?' Paul asked. 'Is something trying to hurt us?'

'Indeed I am. Especially on this Island. As you've noticed, it's not exactly stable. You should probably get through a gate as soon as possible.'

'Will we be safe then?' Jenny asked.

'Of course not. You'll be safe from the dangers of this place, yes, but there are far worse things out there. Some of those things are better never faced.'

'I've had this strange feeling that we're being followed,' Paul said.

'Followed? By what?'

'I've never been able to see what it is. It's just a feeling. But a couple of times, I've noticed things missing.'

The croc looked at him and Paul felt a tingling in the back of his head.

'By missing, do you mean like a big bubble in the air? Like a small part of the world just isn't there?'

Paul and Jenny both nodded.

'That may be nothing,' it said. 'Maybe. But keep your eyes and senses on alert. If the feelings increase, get moving. Stay away from things like that until you know with what you're dealing.'

It turned to leave, heading back to the river.

'One thing bears repeating,' it said, pausing at the edge of the river. 'Some of those things out there are completely beyond our control. We can't help you if you do run into them.'

It slipped silently into the water and was gone.

Jenny and Paul walked back to the tree where they had slept and sat down on the rock that formed the back wall of their alcove. They were both on edge after the crocodile's warning.

'So what do you think we're going to find?' asked Jenny.

'I have no idea. I don't like the feeling of being followed. Of being hunted.'

'I think we can probably handle that now.'

Paul looked at her. 'What do you mean by that?'

'Well, look what I've learned to do!'

'Jenny,' he said, 'you've not seen anything yet. What if there really is something hunting us?'

'What, like invisible monsters?'

He glared at her.

'Seriously, listen to yourself. What if you suddenly forgot how to do this stuff? Like before. What if another, less friendly croc decides it's hungry?'

'I'm not going to forget!'

'Maybe, maybe not. The point is, I think we should be getting out of here quickly, and try to avoid whatever it is that's out there, as we were just warned.'

Jenny blew the hair off her face and looked at him.

'But it's so peaceful here - can't we just rest a couple of days, and then get going?'

'I'd rather not,' Paul replied. 'What if this Island really erupted, if it exploded the way volcanoes sometimes do - we'd be vaporized.'

Jenny gulped.

'Oh. You mean, yesterday...'

'... was a small burp for a volcano,' he finished for her. 'Listen to me - you can do some pretty amazing things, and hopefully you really can control them now. But if you get caught by a big volcano, I doubt you could do anything about it.'

'OK,' she said, 'then let's get out of here. All we need is a gate.'

They checked their amulets, which were cool and still at the end of their chains. They looked around, deciding which way to go. They knew they couldn't go back to where they'd come from the day before and decided against going into the rain forest since they wouldn't be able to run far or fast if something happened. That meant they had to cross the river and head along the island's shore.

The river widened as it approached the sea so they turned back inland, looking for a safer crossing. On the far side, they saw two crocodiles lumber toward the water, slip in, and head toward them. They moved back from the edge and made their way along the path that Jenny had made earlier that morning. They came to where they'd had the coconut milk. The river narrowed and disappeared ahead of them around a corner. When they approached the bend, they heard the rushing sound of a waterfall. The riverbank got steeper and was made of dark rock.

As they rounded the corner, they came across a tall, thin waterfall that cascaded down in flowing sheets. A pool formed at the bottom of it, surrounded by large boulders. The waterfall seemed impossibly high - like they'd reached the side of a hulking mountain that they hadn't noticed before. Climbing it would be difficult so they hoped there was some other way to cross.

While they were searching, their amulets began to warm and as they moved toward the waterfall, they got hotter.

They walked right to the edge and looked up at the cascading water. The sheets were thin but from the height they fell the water would pound them. They searched all around the base of the falls, trying to find the gate. They looked behind the large boulders and checked all the trees that surrounded them.

'Any ideas?' Paul asked, frustrated.

Jenny was holding the amulet and walking back and forth, trying to decide where it was warmest.

'I think it's the waterfall' she said, showing Paul what she'd found.

Paul stepped out onto a large rock at the base of the falls. The mist from where the water hit the pool soaked him. He looked back at her, and shrugged.

'Where should we go this time?' she asked.

'Somewhere dry!' he replied and stepped through the falls. Immediately, the glow in Jenny's amulet disappeared. Definitely the gate, she thought and she hurried after him, vanishing from sight.

Paul's idea of dry was a place Jenny would never have thought of.

Chapter 13

The Land of Dry Air

When her sister returned, Canace was deeply troubled. Her sister was still there, but something had changed, time no longer stood still. Canace drew up her strength, and for the first time in an age, left her home, returning with her sister to see the purple amulets. Canace could not approach them, their heat was fierce, but she could cause them to rise, and drift high into a crevice at the back of the cave, where they would remain safe, and hidden, for five thousand years.

When Jenny stepped through the waterfall, she felt the weight of the water slam into her head and shoulders. The force was hard enough that she nearly fell and she stumbled forward into the darkness behind them.

When she was through she felt the gate take hold and saw all light disappear. Her clothes were soaked by the waterfall but the air around her was getting tinder dry. She couldn't move her body, so she waited, watching the amulet's glow return. With a snap she was bathed in light and felt the sun's heat begin to bake her.

She blinked her eyes, trying to adjust to the bright light and took a breath. The air was hot and dry. She felt the water in her hair and clothes begin to evaporate. She saw Paul standing several yards ahead of her, looking over the edge of a smooth rock face toward a vast, dusty red plain that stretched away from them. It ran as far as she could see and it met the horizon.

'Where are we?' she asked Paul when she walked up beside him.

'Australia, I think.'

'Really?'

'Yeah, I'm pretty sure. It's where I wanted to go.'

'Why there? I mean here.'

'I have some cousins in Sydney. I thought we might try and contact distant relatives, to see if they'd been affected too.'

'Hey good idea. So do you know where we are in Australia?'

'Nope. I don't even know when.'

Jenny's face fell.

'What if we're not even there? Maybe the gate dropped us somewhere else.'

'I don't think so,' Paul said, shaking his head. 'Look down there - way out on the plain.'

Jenny squinted against the sun and saw dust rising behind a herd of animals.

'What are they?' she asked.

'Kangaroos. Look how they move!'

'They're hopping!'

'Yeah. And the only place in the world with kangaroos is Australia.'

He turned and headed back across the rock face and sat down in the shade of a low tree. Jenny watched the herd move away and then joined him.

'Maybe this is Sydney,' she said. 'Just, you know before it was built.'

'It could be. I don't know much about this country. Just what I've read.'

'Well that's more than me. I've never been any good at geography.'

Paul picked up a stick and started scratching the dusty ground in front of them.

'So we know we're in Australia, but we're not sure what part, or when. Not much of an improvement, is it?'

'We're still messing up with the gates,' she replied. 'It's like they don't quite listen or something.'

Paul kept scratching the ground, drawing random shapes and thinking to himself.

'Maybe they take both of us,' he said.

'You mean like the fireplace did?'

'Yeah. Maybe we both have to want to go to the same place for them to work. What were you thinking about when you stepped into the gate?'

'Well, the water hurt me, and I was worried about falling over before I got to the gate. Then I was thinking how nice shampoo and a blow dryer would be to fix my hair. Then the gate took hold.'

She paused.

'Doesn't make much sense, does it?' she finally asked.

'Nope. I guess it just focused on me. We should have asked that croc how to use them.'

'I wanted to ask it a bunch more things, especially about what it said about bubbles in the air, but that stuff about my Dad really threw me.'

Paul stood up and looked behind them. They were at the edge of a forest which looked cooler than where they were. He gave Jenny a hand up and motioned toward the forest.

'That was pretty weird, wasn't it?' he asked, as they set off. 'Did you have any idea?'

'Nope. I mean, he's always been the same, and never said anything to me about any trip like this!'

'I wonder if *he* knows where we are?' Paul asked.

'Or maybe mum does. Maybe they're looking for us.'

'Ah, probably not,' Paul said, stepping over a large tree trunk. 'If he knows what we're doing, he probably knows how it's supposed to end. Like the rest of them.'

Jenny concentrated on Paul for a moment.

'You seem a little bummed,' she said.

'It's just that I don't know exactly what's next. I'm tired, I want to go home, and we keep getting lost!'

'Yeah,' she said, nodding. 'And why am I changing so much?'

Paul stopped and looked back at her.

'You're not changing, you know - you're just learning how to control it better. Can you still move stuff?'

She looked back behind them at the log they'd stepped over. She pointed at it and it tore itself from the ground, and started to roll back down the hill.

'Looks like it,' she exclaimed. 'This is so cool!'

'I wish I could do that,' he mumbled, and then stopped. He crouched down and stared about. Jenny dropped beside him.

'What's wrong? What do you see?' she whispered.

'I think we're being watched.'

'Oh no, really? By what? Where?'

'That's just it - I can't tell where. It's that same feeling, like back in the snow.'

'I can't feel anything,' she said.

'I know. But I can. They're everywhere!'

'Are they moving?'

'Maybe. It's so weird - it's like they're coming and going. Here, let me show you.'

He reached out his hand and she took it. When she did, he flooded her with everything he was feeling. She looked around, still holding his hand and tried to concentrate on each spot where he felt something lurking. She got the faintest tingling sensation in the back of her mind before it flitted away.

'They know we're on to them,' Paul said. 'I think they've backed off!'

'Or maybe they're hiding another way!'

Paul stood back up.

'Maybe. So did you notice something just then?'

'Yup. When you showed me what was happening, I could follow what you felt. For a moment, we were both searching.'

'I wonder what else we can share?'

'Like what?' she asked.

'Well, what about the way I can talk to you? Maybe you can to me.'

Jenny frowned and looked at her hands.

'How?'

'Well, when I want to tell you something, or show you something, I have to sort of will my idea, what I see or think, to you. Unless you're snooping, of course.'

'And you have to be touching me, right?'

He nodded.

'Try it' he said.

Jenny reached out and took his hand.

Can you hear me? she thought.

'Imagine making me think what you think,' he said, oblivious to her attempt.

She concentrated hard and willed her words toward him. Suddenly their amulets flashed two bright pulses and she felt herself relax. She grabbed his hand again.

What about now? she thought.

'Yes!' he exclaimed. 'I got that! Try again!'

For the next few minutes they sat still, talking silently to each other. They found that they didn't have to be holding hands, any sort of contact worked. They stood with their backs to each other and described everything they saw.

'It's interesting,' Paul said. 'I'm only getting words from you. You said you get whole images from me.'

'It's like I experience what you are,' she said.

'Huh. Well, I guess we're still different from each other. I still can't read your thoughts, or move stuff!'

'Yeah, but this is a big change - now we can talk to each other without anyone else knowing!'

'That would be useful - if there were any people around,' he said.

'Hey, c'mon - we're getting there,' she said. 'We're starting to figure some of this out.'

He smiled.

'You're right - we are. I'm just tired.'

They started back up the path which rose two hundred yards above the plains. The dust from the kangaroo's passing had settled and they could see undivided fields as far as the eye could see.

The path they were on came to the rain forest which began to wrap around it. They kept going, following the path right into the trees. A gloom fell over them as the trees grew thicker and the sun punched through the canopy in dusty shafts.

Paul suddenly held up his hand and Jenny stopped. He was looking slowly around as Jenny crept over to him. He put a hand on her shoulder, and sent his voice to her.

I don't think we're alone.

Jenny snapped around, trying to sense what he did. Paul crouched down and gestured for her to do the same. They moved slowly toward a large tree until their backs were against it. Paul reached over slowly and grabbed Jenny's hand.

'Can you sense them?'

'No'

'I can. There's a lot of them. And it's way different than before. I don't yet know who, or where, but I'm sure we're being watched by people!'

Suddenly a spear whizzed through the air and slammed in to the tree above her. She screamed and dropped to the ground, as did Paul. From out of nowhere, several stocky, dark men appeared, pouncing on the children and tying them up.

'Jen, don't do a thing. Something else is here, and I think these men can protect us!'

She stared at him but took his advice, doing nothing.

One of the men shouted something at them, which neither of them understood. They looked up at their captors and realized that they had been taken by aboriginal warriors. They struggled to sit up and were grabbed immediately. Tied up as they were, they posed no threat and the warriors were confident that the children wouldn't get away.

They were roughly brought to their feet and gestured at to follow. The warriors set off into the forest, heading around and down the mountain, away from the path. Jenny and Paul struggled to keep up, their shoulder bags pinching uncomfortably into their sides as they walked.

'Where are we going?' Jenny asked, unable to understand what she read from their minds.

'I've no idea, but if I had to guess, I'd say it was to their village!'

For what seemed like hours they walked in silence. They never left the shadow of the rain forest's canopy which kept the sun from beating down on them. There was almost no breeze at all. The aboriginals walked single-file and often paused to look at the ground growth around them.

Some plants they would gather, stashing small amounts into shoulder slung sacks. Other plants were avoided, sometimes by several yards. Paul watched the sun glint off the tips of one plant which looked like it might be made of glass and made a mental note not to step on it. He looked over at Jenny and knew that she was frustrated; he could sense the anxiety that swirled in her mind.

'Jenny,' he said out loud, 'Don't worry, ok? I've got a great feeling about this.'

'Shhh!' she said, 'They'll hear you.'

'I bet they can't understand us,' he said. 'English is not yet the primary language here.'

Jenny slowed down, so that his hand, though bound, touched her back.

I think we should use this way she said silently to him, until we can be sure.

Ok, he replied, *I'm sensing a fear of us from them - something is upsetting them.*

Good! she thought, *they deserve it, making us walk tied up like this. Is this the way they treat all children*

'I doubt it!' he said out loud.

This drew the attention of their captors, who stopped and looked at them. One of them said something to Paul, of which only a few words stood out: 'Gumaring, ngarru muramba'. It meant nothing to him, even though he could sense they were taunting him.

Suddenly one of the taller men reached out and grabbed him. Jenny wanted to send him hurtling back but Paul whipped around, staring at her as soon as the man made contact.

'Jenny,' he said, 'I know what they're saying.'

'What?' she exclaimed.

'Really, I do. As soon as he grabbed me, I understood him. Watch this.'

Paul turned around and said something that sounded to Jenny like 'Muramba, jaju mija, nguu?'

Every one of the warriors stared at him in a hushed silence.

'How is it you speak now?' one of them asked in their language.

Paul stumbled slightly over his words, trying to make the sounds work.

'I was frightened. We are alone, we are just travelling...'

'... here? No *Gumaring* child travels here, young one. Especially alone. Now, be silent, and follow us.'

They started away again, gesturing for the children to follow them. Jenny stared in astonishment at Paul as they walked.

'What was that?' she whispered.

'I seem to have learned their language. When that man grabbed me, I felt this strange rush, like a spinning feeling, and then their words made sense.'

'C'mon Paul, how is that possible?'

The man following behind them poked Jenny in the shoulders, saying something that sounded to her like '*Yala, yurrgan gambil*'

Paul translated: 'He says 'young woman should be more respectful' - I think he means of me!'

Jenny smirked loudly which earned her another poke. Without thinking, she looked over at a sapling beside them and willed it to smack the man behind her. He yelped in pain, startled at the tree's sudden sting.

'Jenny!' Paul hissed, 'Be careful! If they knew you'd done that, they might kill us both!'

'I'm sorry! And I don't think they really could.'

'Well, think about this then: They know where they're going, and we don't. Let's just stay calm, and keep pretending to be lost children!'

They walked further, Jenny brooding on what had just happened.

'Paul, do you think you could teach me?' she asked suddenly.

'Teach you what?' he asked.

'Their language. You've been able to show me lots of things before, maybe we should try this!'

'Well, how?' he asked.

'I don't know, just, you know, send your thoughts the way you do.'

'Worth a shot,' he whispered.

He stopped and put his tied-up hands on her shoulders and told her silently to sit, cross her legs, hold her head in her hands, and pretend to be close to fainting.

'Don't worry,' Paul said to their captors, 'she just needs a minute. She'll be fine.'

He sat down beside her, and took her hands in his, looked in to her eyes, and said 'Like this.'

Immediately Jenny's mind was flooded with imagery, words, sounds, and smells - it was like she was growing up here, seeing the way they lived, what they ate, who they loved - and how they died. The experience swamped her. She felt like she was being pummeled and she was glad she was sitting when it suddenly ended.

Paul stood up again and looked down at her.

'Did it work?' he asked.

She answered in their language: 'Far more than you could know.'

She stood up and looked around. The aboriginal warriors didn't pay much attention to her knowing their language as they had assumed if Paul knew it she must as well. It was what she said next that alarmed them all.

'We have to keep moving. The *buyu*, the trees, will not protect us from the approaching *jigaru* storm - we must get to the village, to the *mija*! Quickly!'

'Jenny,' Paul exclaimed, in English, 'what did you just see?'

He sensed that she'd learned far more than just the language. She had a deep understanding of these people and he could feel her confidence rebuilding.

'Everything,' she replied. 'It's like I was born here. I don't know how, but I know where we are, where we're going, even why we're tied up!'

'Really! Why?' he asked, excitedly.

'It's our amulets - they look like sacred ornaments of theirs. They think we're thieves, that we stole them!'

'How do you know that?' he asked.

'Now that I know the language, their minds are easy to read. We are being taken to the village, to their leaders.'

'Do you think we should make a run for it?' he asked, 'Now that you know where we are and all.'

'No,' she replied. 'You were right about them - they will protect us. Let's just follow their lead.'

The rain forest started to level out and they could see a small lake in the distance, or a large river, surrounded by thinning rain forest. Smoke rose on the near side of the river and they assumed it came from the village they were traveling to.

Jenny's hands were getting uncomfortable so she asked if they might be untied.

'You will run, little *yipi*, if we do,' one of them replied.

'No, I won't,' she said earnestly. 'I'm only a child - how far would I get?'

The man who had spoken to her raised his eyebrows, looking at her carefully.

'We shall see. We will untie you. If you don't run, maybe we will untie your companion.'

As soon as her hands were untied she stretched her arms away from her to each side and bent over, unwinding her spine. She looked at them expectantly.

'Well,' she said, 'what about Paul?'

'Is that his name? Paul? A strange name. No, for now, he remains bound. Come.'

Paul looked at her enviously. 'Keep trying - my hands hurt too!'

While they walked, Jenny stared at his bonds. Then she got an idea. In this culture, a man whose bonds don't hold was not meant to be confined. So long as Paul didn't try to undo them, they would never tie him up again if the bonds let go.

'Stop!' she cried to all of them. 'Paul - hold out your hands.'

Paul looked at her, puzzled, but did as she said.

She stepped back, looking at each of the warriors.

'What does it mean if a man's bonds aren't strong enough to hold him?' she asked.

A few of them chuckled.

'It means, young one, that he is either stronger than his bonds, or his captor did not know what he was doing!'

They all burst out laughing and Paul felt foolish holding his hands up.

'Does it not also mean, in some cases, that he was never meant to be bound in the first place?'

They stopped laughing slowly, nodding.

'Yes, young *yipi*, it can mean that. However, he is still bound. Let us go, we don't want to get caught in the storm that approaches!'

'Paul,' said Jenny evenly, 'Spread your arms apart, show them.'

They all stopped, turning their attention back to Paul. He stared at her, wondering what she was up to. She nodded at his bound wrists and met his gaze.

Slowly, as he moved his arms apart, the bonds around his wrists unraveled and dropped to the ground. He stretched fully, smiling at her. This was the most subtle thing she'd done yet and he hadn't even seen the shimmering power around her this time, so carefully had she done it.

Waves of shock flashed across the faces of the warriors. Some started a low chant, while others merely stared.

'You're right,' she said in a commanding tone, 'Let's go - we need shelter. Neither of us will run.'

Making a ritual gesture to the ground, the *yapun jaju*, they set out.

Paul took Jenny's hand as they went

That was amazing he thought to her. *Thank you.*

The crocodile swam up the river toward the waterfall and its snout broke the surface as it looked around. Seeing the children safely gone, it swam to the shore and lazily pulled itself from the river. The animal looked into the forest and then closed its eyes. Its belly settled onto the sand and its breathing slowed. A shimmering mist appeared in front of it, emerging from the crocodile's body and gathered itself into a human shape. With the animal motionless, a man appeared, dressed in the clothes of the order. He reached down and patted the animal's head which still didn't move.

'Thank you for that,' he whispered, and walked away, toward the boulders that led out to the front of the water fall. He clambered across them until he stood where the children had stepped in. He drew his sleeve back off his right arm and reached through the water fall. It took him a few moments of searching and then he withdrew his arm, clutching his amulet in his hand. He unfurled the chain and put it around his neck and smiled as the familiar sense of presence enveloped him.

When he turned back toward the river bank, two more people, members of the order, emerged from the trees, standing well back from the sleeping crocodile.

'You really wore this fellow out, James.'

The man called James stepped off the rocks and walked over to them.

'I know. Quite a tough one, this time. The girl's powers almost knocked me out of the poor creature.'

'She is getting very strong, isn't she?'

'Stronger than I've ever seen. I don't think she knows yet what she can do, but the ease with which she froze my host was quite incredible.'

'So where are they now? Did you set the gate as we'd decided?'

'I did, but something happened. It changed its destination. I believe the boy has begun to figure out how they work, although she has not.'

'Interesting - we'll have to review that with the others. Are they safe?'

'I believe so. They've gone to Australia.'

'Which part? We'll have to get there soon.'

'They tried, I think, to go to Sydney. But something drew them north of it, and well before it.'

'Drew them? What do you mean?'

'It felt like the amulet was drawn to another. Was someone expecting them there?'

'Not that we know of. We'd better go back and find out.'

They held up their amulets, which began glowing. They stared at the trees, which began to wobble and then became transparent. The three people stepped forward, through the gate and walked into the common. They headed straight for the one they called Docent.

'We've got a problem,' he said to them as they approached.

'Yes, sir' James said. 'They went the wrong way.'

'They may have, but there's always a reason for where the gates emerge. Watch this.'

The stage flickered to life, and replayed the children's capture and subsequent use of the native language.

'What was that?'

'*That* was the problem. Mr Green, just by touch, learned their language, and I suspect Miss Greyson absorbed far more than that. We may be losing her.'

'How did they do that? Have you ever heard of such a thing?'

'I have, but never seen it. There was a story told, around the time of the building of Stonehenge, of a girl that could learn anything so long as she could touch it.'

'Was she one of us?'

'It's before my time, so I don't know for sure. But I don't think so, even though she knew an awful lot about us. I'm told she still sometimes appears, although never in front of us. We keep running into people who have encountered her.'

'And?'

'They are frightened of her. They describe her as confused, and angry. They say she has trouble speaking, doesn't know where she is.'

'You must have tried to find her. Where was she last seen? She might be able to help us with Miss Greyson.'

The Docent walked over and looked at the stage, watching the children heading toward the village.

'The girl was last seen in a church. Which has since been destroyed. There's been no reports of her since. I'm afraid we're on our own with this one.'

They were not far from the village and as they approached they could smell the smoke that rose from its fires. The smell was sweet as if made from sugar rather than wood. The ground beneath them was flat, interrupted by gnarled roots, jutting across the path in cris-crossed angles.

They spoke only briefly as they walked - a warning here about a root or rock, a comment there about an animal's trail. No one wanted to talk about the children, why they were here, or, more importantly, how it was that Paul had so easily dropped his bonds. It was clear that their captors were wary of them both, that something about Jenny and Paul upset them.

They approached the village from the woods and came to a fence around it made of a series of small saplings that had been sharpened at one end and stood point up, side by side. A small gate broke the otherwise forbidding wall of sharp points. The gate was not protected and when they walked through it, no one seemed to pay any attention.

The village was not big, no more than fifty small huts stood within. It had one larger hut with a clearing in front of it for gatherings and feasts. As they walked in, their captors started a low chant, using words that meant nothing.

'What's going on?' Paul asked Jenny.

'They're calling a gathering,' she replied. 'They have important news. I'm guessing that's us.'

People started coming out of the huts when they heard the call, and when they saw the children, a low murmur arose. They were shocked to see their condition, and started shouting angry accusations at the warriors - why were they so tired? So filthy? What was the reason for their capture?

The warriors defended themselves, demanding that everyone talk to the children, ask them why they were here, and most especially notice that they walked freely.

When they got to the large clearing in front of the main hut, the crowd had grown to include almost everyone in the village. A group of elders gathered in front and other tribesmen fanned out beside them.

The children were brought forward, where they were made to stand together, facing the elders.

'We found these children wandering on the edge of the open,' the leader of the warriors said. 'They were lost, and needed our assistance.'

He bowed toward the elder group as he spoke.

'They do not appear to be lost, *Jughu*,' an elder said. 'Nor do they appear in need of assistance!'

'But my hjnugu, you must know, when we found them, they were cowering on the ground before us.'

'We ducked!' Jenny exclaimed. 'You threw a spear at us!'

A shocked murmur rose from the gathered crowd.

'Not only that,' she continued in a plaintive, confused voice, 'you jumped on us, forced us to the ground, and tied us up! It really hurt!'

As more rumblings erupted from the observers, the elders held their hands up in unison.

'Why do you bring them before us?' one of them demanded. 'You should have left them where you found them!'

'They wear about their necks ornaments sacred to our people!' one warrior shouted. 'They must tell us how this can be, if they are not mere thieves!'

One of the elders stood and walked toward the children. He looked first at Jenny, then at Paul.

'Show me!' he commanded.

Jenny reached in to her shirt and brought out the amulet and held it cupped in her hands.

'Where did you get that!' the elder demanded.

'You would not believe me, my *hjnugu*, were I to tell you.'

At the use of the noble title, the elder stepped back, looking at her warily.

'How do you know that term?' he asked.

'I am from here, I am from you,' she replied, in a sing-song voice. 'I am not what I seem.'

She stepped back, letting go of the amulet. It remained suspended in front of her, and slowly rose, its necklace rising off her as it did.

'These are not your *Jylagu*, your sooth - they are our bonds!'

The amulet floated up above her and hovered nearly two feet above her head. Jenny looked over at Paul and said in English: 'let yours go too, Paul'

He drew his amulet out and it rose above him just like Jenny's. She took his hand and drawing him with her, stepped back. The amulets remained in midair, slowly circling each other and glowing an intense blue.

'What trickery is this?' demanded another of the elders.

Jenny stepped up and held out her hands, below the amulets.

'None at all, *hjnugu*, they are bound to us! Your warriors accused us of stealing - I meant only to show you we have not.'

The amulets settled back into Jenny's hands. She turned and handed Paul's back to him. He watched the whole episode and tried to gauge their reaction.

'An interesting trick,' the first elder said. 'But why should we believe you?'

'Will you permit us to show you how they keep us from harm and yet bind us together?' Paul asked.

'Yes, young *gumaring*, please do.'

Paul gestured toward Jenny.

'Take her, with her amulet, and hide her, wherever you like, in this village. I will walk straight to her, using my amulet as a guide!'

An excited buzz ran through the crowd.

'How can this be?' one of them asked.

'Take her,' Paul replied, 'and watch.'

He walked over to the elder and hid his eyes in his robes. A laugh erupted around him as Jenny was hustled off, smiling at Paul's idea.

After a few minutes, a man returned and whispered in Paul's ear.

'Try now, *gumaring*, you'll not find her.'

Paul looked up and saw he was still surrounded by most of the village. He held up the amulet, and said in English:

'Ok, then, this is where we go on a walk, and think about a nice bed, and maybe we'll find Jenny!'

To everyone around him, it sounded like he was saying a prayer. In their language, he then said:

'The amulet binds us. It keeps us together. The amulet is only one, divided into two halves for us to carry. My half can only light the way to my partner!'

He held it high and showed its almost non-existent glow. While he held it up, he searched for Jenny, trying to sense her emotion, her anxiety. It wasn't hard - they'd taken her back to the gate house and she was thinking about it in as much detail as she could, making it easy for him to pick up.

He started walking toward the gate and as he did, the amulet's blue core grew in intensity.

'Look!' he cried, watching the reaction, 'it knows where to go!'

A low chant started amongst those who could see the amulet. It was obvious to them that the amulet obeyed Paul's command and that it was showing him where to go. He walked steadily toward the gate-house, opened its door and grabbed Jenny as she burst out.

He put his hands on her shoulders and silently said say what I say now

Together, they turned to the elders who had followed and said: 'They guide us. They are part of us. We are bound to them.'

After a moment's silence, one of the elders stepped forward.

'It is clear these are not ours, nor those of our ancestors. We hope you can accept our apology for the way you have been treated!'

Jenny and Paul both smiled at him.

'Of course,' said Paul graciously.

'What can we offer you?' another said.

'Sleep!' they both said together.

'We have travelled a long way today and are tired and hungry,' Paul continued.

'Then tonight you shall rest,' the elder said. 'Please, stay here with us until you recover your strength. Rest, eat, and bathe - you are welcome amongst us.'

Jenny smiled at Paul. He'd been right all along, these were people to be trusted, who would help and he'd understood them perfectly in a way that, despite her deep knowledge of them, she never could.

Chapter 14

The Storm

When they returned to their home, Canace felt her sister's exhaustion. Canace carried her to her bed, and laid her down, bringing her food and water. Her sister smiled and ate, then fell asleep, and when she awoke, her face bore the marks of their passage through time. Canace knew that her sister was leaving, that the moment would come when she was to face all the world alone.

After a brief supper, the children were shown to a guest hut that stood near the entrance to the village. They whispered their thanks and went in, where they found two thick mats on the floor, covered by a bright orange material. Jenny sat down on the edge of one and pulled her boots and socks off, before leaning back and wiggling her toes.

'I can't believe we're here!' she said.

'I know what you mean,' Paul replied, balling his cloak up to make a pillow. 'I've never been through anything like it. The way we learnt their language...'

He yawned, kicking his boots away and curled up. The storm that had threatened them had blown itself out and they could see, through the small window, the red glow of sunset bouncing off the underbellies of the clouds.

Jenny waited for him to continue and when he didn't, she turned and found him fast asleep. Copying his use of the cloak, she lay back on hers and drifted off, enjoying the warm breeze that blew in.

Paul woke up the next morning with the sun's rays beaming down on him through their window. He sat up and stretched, taking a moment to remember where he was. He could feel the heat radiating from the thatched roof and knew they were in for a scorching hot day.

Jenny had once again risen before him and was nowhere to be found. He pulled his boots on, which had lightened into tall sandals and headed out past the curtain of their door. Her clothes, freshly cleaned, were hanging on the wall of their hut and her boots lay beneath them. He scratched his head, looking around for her. He followed the path back toward the center of the village and when he got there, he found a large circle of people sitting, eating and talking.

They wore colorful jewelry and light clothing - the men mostly in loin clothes and the women in loose-fitting sarongs. Sitting in a small group to one side was Jenny, dressed in a bright yellow and black sarong. Her hair was wet and tied back in a pony tail and she was trying to eat a piece of fruit and tell a story at the same time.

Paul went over and sat down beside her.

'Well, good morning sleepy head,' she said.

'Hi. Where'd you get those clothes?' Paul asked.

'From Njgura,' she said, pointing to a woman sitting across from her. 'They're her daughter's. She took me down to the river to wash up, and lent me these while mine dry.'

'Sounds nice,' he said.

'It was. Here, eat some of this, and then I'll take you down - you could use a bath!'

Paul looked down at himself and smiled. His clothes were filthy and he could see a layer of dust on his skin. He took the fruit she offered him and sat down, biting into it. Everyone else in the circle looked at him but said nothing.

'He sleeps too much,' Jenny said to them.

'My son is the same,' Njgura said. 'It takes a stick to raise him.'

'Don't get any ideas,' Paul whispered to Jenny.

When he was done, Paul thanked them for his food and Jenny led him toward the river.

'You won't believe how good the water feels,' she said.

'Yeah, I bet I would - I feel all shriveled - parched.'

The path they were walking on was hard packed clay, had the same dark red color in it that they'd seen on the plains. Jenny's feet stood out against it.

'I guess I don't really need my boots, huh?' Paul said.

'Nope. No one wears shoes around here.'

He reached down, pulled his off and tossed them at the edge of the river. He dipped a toe in the water and winced.

'Oh my God!' he exclaimed.

'What?'

'Did you actually swim in this?'

'Yeah. What's the matter?'

'Well, it's freezing! How could you stand it?'

'I don't know - it didn't seem that cold. Plus I kept my clothes on, to wash them. Maybe they helped?'

He cast a doubting look at her and then stepped back in, wading up to his knees.

'I'm sorry,' he said, bolting out. 'There's no way I'm swimming in this. I'll kill myself!'

Jenny hiked her sarong up and walked slowly in. She turned and looked back at him.

'It's not that bad, you wimp.'

'Shut up - it's like ice!

She reached down, cupped some water and splashed it on her face.

'I guess you're not that tough, huh?' she said, wading out and climbing up onto a large boulder.

He glared at her and splashed back in. He started to shiver and stared out. He could see a current of clear water flowing past him, toward the center of the river, where it mixed with the murky depths.

'Hurry up!' she called to him. 'Or I'll push you!'

'Yeah right,' he replied, still grimacing. 'I'll just take my time, thank you very much.'

She raised her hand and he felt a gentle push on his back.

'Hey cut it out!' he yelled. 'I'm going!'

He took one last look back at her and dove out into the current. When he hit, the warm water smothered him and he started laughing before he reached the surface.

'Nice!' he called out. 'Did they do that to you?'

Jenny was laughing so hard she nearly fell of the boulder.

'Yup!' she giggled. 'It's way warmer over there - see where all the foot prints are?'

Paul looked where she was pointing, about twenty feet away. The shore slopped down to the river and he could see a couple of pans near the bank - this was where most people went in. He swam toward it and when it got shallow enough, he stood up. He pulled his shirt off, rinsing it in the water. Jenny climbed down and walked over, still grinning.

He rolled his shirt up in a ball and flung it at her, hoping to soak her. She held her hand up in front of her and the shirt slammed into an invisible barrier and fell to the ground.

'Uh-oh,' she sang. 'You dropped you shirt in the mud!'

'Give it here, you show off.'

She threw it back to him and he leaned down to rinse it off. She watched his amulet as it skirted the water's surface. When it hit, it left no mark, passing through the water without splashing, without making ripples. Unaware of what she was watching, Paul threw his shirt back to her and dove out into the deeper water. He coasted down and then back up, watching the surface approach.

When he broke it, he felt a tension waft over him and he looked back toward Jenny. She was standing up straight and still, staring beyond him into the river. She gestured for him to swim to shore.

'What is it?' he called out.

'Just get over here,' she hissed.

He turned to look where she was and saw a large splash on the far side of the river, followed by a dark shape flowing toward him. He whirled around and swam as hard as he could toward her.

'C'mon,' she urged, 'Something's coming!'

He kicked his feet, moving as fast as he could. He looked up at her and saw her raising her hands, the blue aura gathering around her. Suddenly she shot both arms forward and he heard a mad thrashing behind him as something rose out of the water.

He scrambled up on shore and turned to look. Hanging in midair, still fighting her grip, was a massive crocodile - far larger than their guide from ancient Hawaii. She flicked her arm and sent the beast flailing out into the center of the river, where it splashed heavily into the water and darted away.

'Oh my God!' Paul exclaimed.

'Did it hurt you?' she asked, looking down at his legs.

'No, no - I'm fine. But, oh my God! Jenny, that was terrifying!'

'That was too close,' she said, breaking into a tremble. 'I didn't know what it was. And I was so scared - if I lost you right now, I...'

He smiled at her.

'But you didn't. And now that's two I owe you. You keep being that fast, and we'll be fine!'

She sat down and stared across the river, toward the crocs that were pulling themselves back out of the water.

'Here's your shirt, by the way' she said, holding it out.

He took it and pulled her back up, climbing up the boulder she'd sat on earlier. He draped the shirt over the front and watched the steam rise from it as it dried.

'Hey,' he said. 'Turn around - I want to lay my trousers out too.'

She did and he pulled his pants off, laying them in the sun next to his shirt. He leaned over and they sat, back to back, listening to their surroundings.

'Do you think anyone saw that?' he asked.

'I hope not!' she whispered. 'Pretty hard to explain.'

'No kidding. Since neither of us can. And you know, last night, with the amulets? I thought you were pushing it then.'

'Yeah, but they didn't believe it. They thought it was a trick.'

He nodded.

'Weird, isn't it. If you did that in front of my friends, they'd be shocked. Here, it didn't seem that big a deal.'

'I know. And if you hadn't thought of that hide and seek game...'

They fell silent, letting the sun warm them. Paul leaned forward, to flip his clothes and Jenny nearly fell off their perch.

'Serves you right,' he snorted. 'After what you just did.'

'I can't believe you fell for that!' she laughed. 'Can you actually imagine swimming in water that cold? You probably *would* kill yourself!'

'Yeah, well, you tricked me, standing in it like that.'

'I could hardly stand it. Couldn't you tell?'

He reached down and felt his shirt. It was dry enough, so he pulled it back on. He slipped down off the rock and grabbed his pants.

'C'mon - let's go hang these up in the sun with yours - they'll never dry here.'

He stopped, staring across the river. Jenny turned, sensing his unease and looked in the same direction. Standing on the other side, beyond the basking crocodiles, just in front of the trees, were two children. They had pale faces and colorless hair and were dressed exactly like members of the order. They each had amulets on which were glowing a bright orange.

They looked at Paul and Jenny, held their hands up and waved. Smiles splashed across their faces, before they turned and walked back into the woods, fading away and vanishing in a pale orange mist.

'Did you see that?' Paul whispered.

'Yeah. What do you think they're telling us this time?'

He looked at her, a frown on his face.

'Nothing, I think. They just seemed happy - glad to see us.'

'You mean you could sense them?'

'A little - can't you? Like in Hawaii - remember, or on the train - didn't you feel them?'

'No - the only time I ever understood them was when Midori talked to me...'

'What?' he exclaimed. 'You've never told me you'd spoken to them!'

'Well, you never asked,' she stammered. 'But maybe I should have. It was just before Halloween, before my jump. I got in trouble at school, and when I ran away, Midori came to see me.'

'So who is she?'

'I don't think she knows anymore. She said some really weird stuff.'

'Tell me!' he urged.

'I think I can do better. Remember what we were practicing? Let's see if I can show you.'

She held out her hand and when he took it, he was flooded with her memory - he felt the humiliation she'd suffered in the playground and then saw the phantom that was Midori come into the woods and stand below Jenny, speaking on the wind. Her words surrounded him just as they had Jenny and he stumbled, nearly falling over.

'Hey, are you ok?' Jenny asked.

He shook his head to clear it and looked back at her.

'Wow. How'd you get so good at that?'

'I didn't. I think these are pulling us closer,' she said, holding up her amulet.

'That - that was unbelievable.'

He sat down, still rubbing his eyes.

'No wonder Mum freaked out.'

She sat down beside him.

'It is pretty weird, isn't it? So what do you think Midori meant?'

'God, Jen, I ... You know, I don't think she was supposed to talk to you.'

'What?'

'It just doesn't feel right. It's like these strangers that keep helping us? They're not supposed to - they're not even supposed to be here.'

She nodded and leaned down to grab his boots.

'I thought that too, before. But it must mean something.'

'Yeah, it must. We've got to figure out what, though.'

He took his boots from her and they walked back up the path toward the village. When they got to their hut, Paul hung his pants up to dry and they headed back toward the main clearing, where a small group of children was playing. Two women sat to one side, watching and they smiled as Paul and Jenny arrived.

'Where is everyone?' Jenny asked.

'The men are hunting, or looking. The women and older children are also searching for the things we need.'

A commotion across the clearing caught her attention and she ran over to break up a fight.

'What are they looking for?' Paul asked the other woman.

She looked at him suspiciously.

'They are worried about others.'

'Others? What others?'

'Other tribes. Sometimes they try to drive us from here. It is a good spot.'

Jenny nodded, remembering what she had learned of their culture. These were a peaceful people but they were fiercely territorial and had special corridors of land on which people could freely walk and other areas that belonged to a tribe. Those boundaries were not always respected, which caused short, violent conflicts.

'You were swimming?' one of the woman asked Paul. 'Your hair looks wet.'

'Yes' he nodded. 'It was - cold at first.'

Jenny couldn't hide her smile and the two women laughed loudly.

'Everyone gets taken there first!' the first woman said. 'But, we never swim at this time of day - too dangerous. There are crocodiles that travel up the river.'

'Yes, we saw them,' Jenny said. 'But we weren't in the water then.'

'It sounded like you were,' the woman said. 'We heard a large splash, and thought perhaps a *gupa* was taken.'

'Really? That's what that sound was?' Paul asked.

'It happens sometimes when they come to drink.'

The women turned away, forced to break up another skirmish and Paul and Jenny wandered back toward the main gate.

'I guess we got away with it,' Paul whispered.

'Yeah, but that was close, wasn't it?'

'Could have been. I wonder what they would have done if they saw you?'

'I don't know - they'd probably think it was witchcraft, or something.'

'Well they might just be right. Like I said, we still don't know what it is yet either.'

Jenny looked out into the forest where she thought she could hear voices, carried on the wind.

'Do you hear that?' she asked him.

Paul paused and listened.

'I think so. It almost sounds like yelling, doesn't it?'

'Think we should go see?'

'Maybe we should. Let's go get our boots.'

They hurried to their hut and changed back into their clothes. When they returned to the gate, the shouting was louder so they ran into the woods. After a few minutes, Paul held his hand up.

'They're just ahead,' he whispered. 'See?'

Jenny peered through the trees and saw what he meant. Two groups of aboriginal men, one of which was from their tribe, stood face to face, glaring at each other and yelling. The children crept forward until the words were clear and stopped to listen.

'You know nothing of them!'

'They are *gumaring* - white children - you must get rid of them.'

'They speak our language, and know our ways!'

'How can that be? No *gumaring* knows such things.'

'They sleep in our village, eat our food - we will protect them.'

'But you didn't see what we saw! They appeared out of nowhere! They aren't natural!'

Jenny drew back behind a dense bush and pulled Paul down.

'What do we do?' she whispered. 'They saw us come out of the gate!'

'All we can do is show them we're harmless,' Paul said. 'Follow me.'

'Wait - what are you going to do?'

'Trust me. Just do what I do.'

She frowned but realized he'd been right about them so far. He stepped forward, walking toward the group. As he got close to them, he started shuffling his feet, bending over as if looking for something on the ground. Jenny followed behind him, reaching in to her shoulder bag and grabbing her walking stick. She used it to search the leaves and ground cover, intentionally making a lot of noise.

Suddenly both groups stopped talking and looked toward the children. Paul felt a wall of tension come from them and saw one reaching for a spear.

'Look out, Jen,' he whispered, still leaning over.

She looked up just as the man hoisted the spear and threw it at them. Paul ducked and Jenny swatted it aside with her walking stick.

'Hey,' she called out, trying to sound frightened. 'Why did you do that?'

'You shouldn't be here!' one of the new tribe shouted back. 'You are dangerous!'

Paul motioned Jenny back, and walked toward the speaker.

'Dangerous? Us? We're just children.'

The new group made the same gesture they'd seen the day before, right after Paul had escaped his bonds.

'You are the *yapun jaju*, the strangers who know our ways.'

Jenny stared at the one who had just spoken.

'You are called Jgun Whi-Kal'd, aren't you?' she asked.

'How could you know that?' he demanded, stepping toward her.

Jenny thought hard about what she had learned of their culture and knew, despite her age, that she had to defend herself. She stepped forward and met his glare.

'You should be far more respectful, Kal'd, if you want to learn something of strangers.'

Some of the other warriors began to snicker and Paul relaxed, sensing their slow acceptance of her.

'They are traveling, and are knowledgeable of our ways,' one of their hosts said. 'They are no threat, just peaceful guests.'

'I cannot accept that' Kal'd said, still glaring at the children. 'They are not natural. What of their appearance yesterday?'

Paul stepped forward and reached out to Kal'd, who frowned, slowly touching Paul's outstretched hand.

'We're different, no question,' Paul said, willing Kal'd to relax. 'But that's all we are. We're just traveling, trying to learn.'

The way he said it, the pitch of his voice, had a calming effect on everyone.

'Come,' he continued. 'Let's go back to the village - we will tell you about our journey.'

Their hosts looked at each other in alarm and Jenny realized that such an invitation was rare.

'Is that all right?' she asked them. 'If they come too?'

'I think so, yes, young *yipi*, it is. Paul has a good idea.'

They set off toward the village, with their hosts leading and Paul talking to the new group. Jenny trailed after them, listening to their thoughts. They were slowly accepting that the children really weren't a threat but when she concentrated on Kal'd, she found the reason he was so hostile: He was the only one who'd seen them emerge.

When they reached the village, they could hear gales of laughter and as they walked in, they saw lots of the children running between the huts, playing a chase game. As they reached the main clearing, people began to gather, wondering why there were foreign tribesmen with them.

Jenny pulled Paul aside when they approached their hut.

'I'm going to change back into my sarong,' she said.

'Too hot?' Paul smirked.

'No - I think it relaxes them a bit.'

'Well, what about me, then?'

'You're fine - maybe get rid of the boots. They see you as our leader, I guess because you're a boy.'

'Really?'

'Yeah - and besides, if I have to do anything, they won't expect it from me.'

Paul nodded, seeing what she meant. Dressed as she was, with her pale skin and flaming red hair, she was a glaring contrast to them. He waited while she ran in to change and when she emerged, they headed back to the group. When they got there, they found the other tribe's warriors seated in a semicircle across from the elders. They were smoking a long pipe and engaged in a deep conversation. As the children walked up, they stopped, looking up.

One of them turned, offering them the pipe.

'Come, *gumaring*, share our smoke!'

Jenny held her hands up and smiled.

'No thank you, Jliko - my parents wouldn't like it!'

The man, Jliko, was startled by her use of his name but the elders smiled.

'You see?' one of them said. 'They are so interesting. They know us by name, as soon as they see us. It is so welcome!'

Paul sat down and held out his hand.

'May I?' he asked, gesturing at the pipe.

He took it and stared at the glow in the end of the pipe. He tried to smile and took a small drag. He closed his eyes, willing himself not to cough and slowly breathed out.

'Paul!' Jenny whispered. 'Where'd you learn to do that?'

The elders around her grinned.

'Perhaps, Jenny,' one said, using her name for the first time, 'you should not be surprised when you find that there are things you do not know about others!'

Jenny sat down next to Paul, smoothing out the folds of her sarong.

'I have come to learn that, my *hjnugu*, you must have noticed,' she replied.

'Yes, young one, you have - but still,' he paused, not wanting to continue.

'But what?' she asked.

'You hide a great power from us. We all can sense it. There were stories told here earlier.'

Paul looked up in alarm and Jenny probed his mind, seeing that he only meant the amulets. She drew hers out from underneath her dress.

It was glowing brightly, since Paul was right beside her.

'It is not such a great power,' she said, taking it off and handing it to him.

He turned it over, and held it up to the sun, looking at the light that came through it. He weighed it in his hand and then examined the thin, strong chain of gold that held it around her neck. He turned to a young man that sat behind him and barked a gruff order.

The young man got up, went into the large hut and came back with a closed, woven basket. He placed it in front of the elder and returned to his seat. The elder handed Jenny's amulet back and looked at her.

'This is why our warriors were so suspicious of you yesterday,' he said and opened the basket.

Paul and Jenny gasped at what lay inside it.

Two matched amulets glowed from the basket, a deep ruby red. Their chains were almost identical to Jenny and Paul's, and the gold overlay was exactly the same. There was no question: These amulets had belonged to members of the order.

Paul reached for it and was immediately stopped by the elder.

'Do not try to touch them, they are - protected,' he said, fumbling for the right words. He picked up a stick and slowly moved the end of it toward the ruby amulets. At about six inches away, the stick burst into flame.

'You see?' he said, looking at the children. 'They protect themselves, as they protect us.'

Jenny stared at the ruby amulets, trying to get a sense of what she'd just seen, of the shield that was glowing around them, shimmering in a way that made the image of the amulets wobble in and out of focus.

'May I try?' she said, looking up at the elder. 'To touch them?'

'No one ever has. But if you don't mind burning your hand, go ahead.'

Jenny held her hand out toward the amulets. The shimmering field thickened as her hand approached. She could feel the heat on her hand increasing and drew back. Holding her hands together, palms up in front of the basket, she concentrated on the amulets, willing them to come to her. The field around them vanished and the amulets slowly floated up out of the basket and settled in her hands.

Cries of shock rang out from the gathered crowd as she turned them over and over, looking for a sign of where they had come from.

'How long have you had them?' she asked.

'The story goes that they have been here for many, many generations,' one elder finally replied.

Another continued: 'They have never, before this day, been taken from the basket.'

'Where did they come from?' Paul asked.

'The story says that wanderers of our ancestors found them, in a hut just like this one. We do not know where they came from.'

Jenny turned to Paul and held one out. He took it and immediately sat down in shock.

'What is it Paul?' Jenny asked.

He was staring into the ruby amulet, his eyes slowly rocking back and forth. When he looked up, he had a glazed look on his face and he held out one hand to Jenny. She took it and he flooded her with images, old, old images, of travels, of learning, of gates. These were the memories of the two whose amulets these were and Jenny closed her eyes, drifting into them.

The ruby amulets had not stirred from their basket for nearly three thousand years. They belonged to two brothers, men who had been bound to the amulets in what is now northern Europe. The brothers were taken through their first gate on the summer solstice, to an open field, where others like them, others bound to amulets, gathered in outdoor stone temples. Their clothes had changed when they went through the gate, becoming the same as those they met - the dark, flowing cloak over grey pants and shirts, with black, sturdy boots to walk in.

The people at the temple taught them the use of the gates and invited them to return each year on the solstice to share the stories of their lives. The brothers had tried to return home but their families rejected them, frightened of what they had become. They became explorers, using the gates to travel to remote locations, letting the amulets decide where to take them.

As they traveled, they became more and more aware of everyone around them and they learned how to sense people's feelings and presence. For forty years, they studied new worlds, new people and shared their knowledge at the stone temples. Despite the joy of discovery, of companionship with the others like them, an increasing sense of doubt crept into them, as if they were in a trap.

Every time they stepped through the gates, they felt pursued as if something was traveling with them. They couldn't see anything but their fear grew. They decided not to travel back on the solstice, not to share any more of their experiences. They started searching for their pursuers, willing the gates to take them to the source of their fears.

As they traveled, they found nothing, and they felt like they were too late. Only once, when they emerged high on a mountain top, did they find anything. The peak of the mountain had a cave in it, and when they approached the cave, they couldn't go in - a translucent, shimmering barrier surrounded it.

When they touched the barrier, they felt a shock pour through them and the glow of their amulets dimmed. They ran back from it, feeling the amulet's power return, along with an increased sense of a trap. They were surrounded by something they couldn't see. They opened a gate, wanting to get as far away from the cave as possible and the amulets took them to the northern rainforests of Australia.

They decided never to go through the gates again and began to wander south, where they met their first aboriginal tribe. Using the skills they had learned from their past travels, they befriended them and were slowly accepted. They didn't tell their hosts anything about their past or where they had come from, simply calling themselves *yapun jaju*.

When their sense of the trap still didn't fade, they decided to remove their amulets. They made a small basket for them and took them off, placing them side by side and closing the lid. Their sense of others around them vanished and they were left with a feeling of great loneliness. The trap had gone but so had everything else they'd learned to love.

They lived for another two years with the tribe, helping to build villages and to hunt. They never opened the basket again, instead keeping it between their mats in the hut they slept in. They died on the same night, on the southern summer solstice and the tribe buried them as their own.

Their name for themselves, *yapun jaju*, passed from generation to generation, along with the amulets. Its origin faded, changing over the years until it came to mean 'the strangers who know our ways'. The ruby amulets remained in the basket, with the tribe, until the children arrived, three thousand years later.

Jenny opened her eyes and stared at Paul.

'What should we do?' she whispered, in English, still holding one of the ruby amulets.

'What do you mean?'

'About these amulets - should we take them back?'

'To the order? I don't think so. I'm sure they know they're here. And if we take them, the tribe will think we really are thieves, after all.'

'Should we tell them about the brothers? Where the amulets came from?'

Paul shook his head slowly.

'Too hard to explain, right?' she continued.

'Way too hard. I'd rather talk to Ornolt about it first.'

'Yeah, good idea.'

She turned back to the elders and held the ruby amulet out.

'Would you like to see it?' she asked.

The elder nodded and reached out. Jenny saw the amulet flash, a small pulse from the ruby core that lingered all along the chain and felt a wave of heat begin pouring from it. Paul felt the same and they darted the ruby amulets back into the basket. The elder snapped his hand back and glared at the children.

'What trickery is this?' he demanded. 'They burn us, yet you are unharmed.'

'It is difficult to explain, my *hjnugu*' Paul started, as the crowd began to rumble in discontent. 'It is because we are bound to our amulets. They are connected to each other.'

'You must tell us how you became bound.'

'We were found,' Paul replied. 'The amulets found us, we didn't find them.'

'Where did this happen? Why do ours not bind with anyone?'

'It happened near our home,' Paul lied. 'And these two amulets - they have been bound already. They never will again.'

'Never?' the elder said, his face falling.

'I don't think so,' Paul continued. 'Although Jenny and I are young - we still have a lot more to learn about the amulets.'

Jenny looked at the basket.

'They are bound to you, in a way,' she said. 'If you keep them safe, they will protect you.'

The people gathered around them murmured their agreement and the elder signaled to the young man who'd brought the basket out. He stood and picked it up, returning it to the large hut that housed them.

The elder stood up and signaled to his right.

'We should welcome our friends,' he announced. 'Let us eat!'

Instantly food started to appear, carried from distant fires to the center of the gathering. Their guests ate first, according to their customs, followed by the elders, and then the rest of the tribe.

The warriors from the other tribe gathered around Paul and Jenny, talking with them in low voices as the feast continued. A drum sounded across the grounds, followed by a low, ringing blast from a didgeridoo.

'Dancing!' Jenny exclaimed. 'I love dancing!'

'Not me,' Paul whispered. 'I suck. I trip over my feet all the time.'

He looked at the grounds filling up with people stomping, dancing and hooting as the sound enveloped them.

'Are you going to be ok with this?' he asked.

Jenny's feet were already tapping.

'Yeah, what do you mean?'

'Well, I was just thinking of Hawaii again, remember? The crowds?'

'This is way different,' she smiled, standing up and starting to sway. 'Everyone's happy - everyone wants to dance!'

She reached down and pulled Paul up.

'And so do I,' she continued, pulling him toward the throng.

Paul followed her, trying to match her step - the graceful way she moved amongst the dancers, and tripped over a root. He landed hard, dusted himself off and headed back to sit near the elders. He watched Jenny and saw her arms rising in unison with the others, how she danced forward and back to the rhythm of the drums. She danced around the circle and he lost sight of her momentarily, before her bright red hair and white skin caught his eye on the other side.

'She may stand out,' an elder chuckled to him, 'but she is very good - you will have to be careful with her!'

'I didn't know she could,' he replied. 'She's having a lot of fun.'

'And you?' the old man asked.

'I wouldn't trade it for a thing - this is a wonderful place.'

He looked back toward the hut that held the ruby amulets and the elder followed his gaze.

'They thought so too,' Paul continued.

'Perhaps that is why they protect us still.'

A distant rumble interrupted him and they turned to see lightning flash across the sky, far across the river. Each time the lightning appeared, the thunder's deep boom came sooner.

The wind picked up, blowing the sparks from their fire toward the forest. The dancers heard the thunder and realized a storm was coming. They moved quickly, quietly, without alarm and covered the fires to quell them. The food was packed up and the instruments put inside the huts.

Even though the wind was blowing strongly and the first drops of rain were starting to fall, no one sought shelter. The other tribe's warriors returned from the dance to sit with the elders and the pipe was passed between them once more. They looked up when drops of rain hit them, wiping water from their brow but otherwise ignored it.

Paul and Jenny sat with them and kept looking from their faces to the approaching storm. Jenny was having trouble sitting still and kept fidgeting with her amulet. Paul could feel the total lack of fear around him and did his best to feel the same.

A sudden bright flash of lightening sizzled into the river right outside the village. The thunder exploded above them even before the bolt had faded and crackled across the sky for several long moments. Shrieks erupted and the people started to hurry to their huts.

The wind was rushing across the river's valley and as it approached the village, it turned back on itself.

'It is the wind that spins!' a man shouted, pointing back at the river. 'We must get to the trees!'

Jenny turned and looked where he was pointing and heard a low roar, like an angry fire, bearing down on them. She could hear loud crashes, snapping trees and hissing wind as the tornado approached.

'Jenny!' Paul screamed. 'Run! We've got to get away from here!'

She turned toward him, squinting against the rain that beat down on her and started to reach her hand out.

'No, my sister, not like that.'

She snapped around looking for the voice, the girl from her nightmares.

'Do not run, sister. Remember who you are!'

Jenny staggered over and Paul caught her, feeling the same ancient presence he had on the snow covered mountain.

'Jenny!' he cried. 'What's wrong?'

'You are the wind, my sister,' came the voice. 'Always remember that!'

Jenny stood up and looked at Paul.

'Keep them calm, Paul,' she said, her voice echoing with a melodic undertone. 'Keep them away from me!'

She walked out to the middle of the open grounds and stared at the approaching funnel of the twister. It was bearing down hard and fast on the village and they heard the water being whipped up by its tail. Paul could see the cold, blue aura gathering around her, swirling together into a powerful force. She slowly raised her hands, fingers up, palms facing the oncoming fury and braced.

Paul saw the power race from her and attack the storm. The twister faltered and then split, becoming several smaller but equally dangerous columns of spinning rage. Jenny watched each one carefully, gauging where it was going.

The tribe noticed what she was doing, seeing the storm stop at the outskirts of their village and tried to figure out how she did it. A humming bolt of lightning hit just beyond the walls to the east and sparks shot away from an exploding tree. The people screamed with fear, knowing the force of the wind could take them at any moment.

As the various tails of the twister rushed toward them, they were met with an opposing, unyielding force. Paul looked over at Jenny and was astounded by what he saw. She had one arm outstretched in front of her and another rose above her head, its palm facing the sky. She was slowing turning on the spot, caught in a nearly-frozen pirouette. She radiated a massive power, pushing the storm back from the village.

A bubble formed around the village, through which the rain, wind and lightening could not pass. The bubble was colossal and brought an eerie calm to its interior. More of the tribe began to emerge from their huts and stood staring at the reason for the storm's deflection.

Jenny continued her dance with the storm, never stopping the slow spin and they could see the barrier of the bubble being strengthened as she passed. Her hands moved as if smoothing the inside of a distant surface, reinforcing it against the storm.

On the river's side of the village, a powerful funnel was trying furiously to break through. Every time Jenny faced it, her arms buckled and she strained to force it back. She never blinked or even seemed to breathe as she turned, facing the storm's fury and holding it at bay.

The villagers walked toward her, forming a wide circle around her and watched her with a mix of fear and fascination. Her arms started moving at a frantic pace, strengthening the barrier against a growing force that only she could feel.

Paul walked over and stood beside her, watching the crowd and beckoning them to stay back. He could tell that Jenny wasn't aware of them and to him she seemed barely present - something else, the power that surrounded her, had taken over. He looked at her face as her slow spin came around and saw her eyes had filled with the same, luminescent blue as their amulets. Her pupils were bulging, dilated almost entirely across her eyeballs and Paul looked away, afraid of what he might see beyond them.

Suddenly a roaring fireball exploded beyond the village as another bolt of lightning hit a tree. Sparks from it showered down on them, passing through the bubble without slowing. Paul wanted to turn and run but couldn't bring himself to leave Jenny. The villagers rushed to put out the small fires that ignited where they fell.

Jenny didn't react and kept holding off the storm, turning on her spot. The river was in a frenzy and the trees beyond the village, beyond the bubble, were bending over almost to the ground. Yet in the village, the air was impossibly calm, and the tribesmen stood listening to the rage beyond.

In the distance, past the river, Paul could see a break coming. The wind was dying down and like a wall, the end of the storm came across the river, the light behind it bursting out on them. Jenny's pace slowed with it and as the wind abated, her arms returned to her side.

As the last gasp of the storm passed and the fading daylight returned, she finally stood still. Paul watched in shock as she looked once around the village, the still standing, safe village and faltered, her legs buckling under her. She collapsed to the ground, exhausted, unconscious and didn't move.

Chapter 15

Recovery and Warning

When Canace returned from gathering food, she found her
sister on her bed, her arms folded across her lifeless body, a
smile left on her face. Canace leaned over her and wept, and
when she looked up, and dried her eyes, she saw that something
was missing, that her sister's amulet, that had been with them
since they had first awoke in their mountain-home, had
vanished.

The gathered crowd fell silent, staring at Jenny's motionless body. No one moved and no one said a word. Then slowly, one by one, they began to chant, a low, melodic chant that spread across the deepening circle of tribes people. They were praying, believing that the children were Gods, that they had a divine power. They had all witnessed her fight against the wind that spins, the *hfujga* and had seen her win.

They prayed for the Gods to restore her strength and waited for her to spring back up.

'Jenny!' Paul screamed over the chant. He ran over to her and crouched down, cradling her head in his arms.

'Wake up,' he whispered. 'C'mon, please wake up.'

She didn't move, her arms hung limply at her side and her breathing was slow and shallow. Paul put a hand on her forehead and concentrated on her. He found nothing, no sense of her presence, no sense of anything at all. If it wasn't for her breathing, he wouldn't have known she was alive.

'Jenny,' he cried, a tear starting down his face, 'don't go - please come back.'

He started rocking back and forth, trying to get through to her. He kept his hand on her forehead and sent his voice silently to her. *Come back, Jen. Please. Don't leave me here alone.*

The crowd began to move forward, to close in on the children and the chant grew louder again. Paul looked up at one of the elders.

'What should I do?' he said. 'I don't know what's wrong!'

The elder crouched down and looked at Jenny's face and held an outstretched finger in front of her nose.

'She breathes,' he said. 'She is still with us.'

'But why won't she wake up?' Paul asked.

'Perhaps she is speaking to the others' he replied, joining back in with the steady chant.

'What others? What do you mean?'

Paul looked at their faces, saw the smiles and felt the adoration that poured from them.

'What do you mean?' he asked again.

'She was sent to protect us. She is more than the *Yapun Jaju*. She is the daughter of the Gods.'

A gnawing fear crept over Paul while he watched the people around them. They didn't know what was wrong with Jenny and if they really thought she was a God, they wouldn't think she needed any help at all.

'Please!' he cried. 'We've got to help her - something's wrong!'

He struggled, trying to pick her up.

'Paul - what are you doing?'

'I think we should take her to our hut. Can you...'

A large man approached the children and knelt down. He looked at Paul and then scooped Jenny up in his arms. Paul walked with him back to the hut, the crowd following after, still chanting their prayer. When they got there, the man carried her through the door and lowered her onto her mat. She didn't move and lay exactly as they had placed her. The man bowed his head and left.

Paul leaned down and felt the tears welling up again. He rolled her cloak up and tucked it under her head and then shifted her onto her side, the way he had seen her sleep before. Her amulet lay on the mattress at the end of its chain, glowing brightly. He grabbed his cloak from his bed and spread it over her as a blanket. He sat beside her and stared out the window, before leaning over again with his hand on her forehead.

Come back Jen - I don't know what to do. Come back.

There was no reply and she still didn't stir. He could hear the quiet murmur of the people outside the hut and began to tremble. Without her knowledge of the tribe, he had no idea what to say to them and he sat in a ball, the panic settling over him.

He held his amulet up and stared into its core.

'Where are you?' he whispered to it. 'Why won't you help me?'

'Paul!' a voice called from outside, 'are you there?'

He looked up and out the window. The chant had died down and he could hear people talking in hushed tones, waiting for him. He looked back at Jenny.

'What should I do?' he said out loud.

215

From all around him came a voice, one that sounded just like the girl Jenny had seen in Banff. He thought it might be the wind and he strained to hear.

'Go, Paul. Do what you know you must.'

He darted his eyes around, trying to find the source and thought he saw a fading green mist in the darkened corner of the hut. The crowd outside was growing louder and with one last touch on her forehead, Paul stood up and walked slowly out to them. He went over to the small bench in front of their hut and sat down.

'Is she well?' an elder asked, sitting beside him. 'She is asleep?'

Paul looked at him and tried to think of what to say.

'I don't know,' he murmured. 'She is asleep, yes, but I don't know what's happened.'

'You look tired, Paul,' a young man named Ylujs said. 'I'll get you fruit, water.'

'We must speak of what she did,' the elder continued. 'My eyes saw something no one has ever seen before. That wind that twists was strong tonight. Many should have died.

'This,' he continued, waving his hand toward the village, 'should not be here anymore.'

He paused, waiting for the chant around him to die down.

'Your sister performed a miracle - She held back the wind - the whole storm.'

'She is my ... friend,' Paul answered. 'Not my sister. And I'm not sure what we saw tonight. I don't know what's happened to her.'

'We all saw the same thing, Paul - we saw what she used to hold off the storm.'

Paul's head snapped up and he stared at the elder.

'What did you see?'

'It was like the light of early morning - a mist that seemed to come from her. It shot itself from her and fought the wind.'

Paul's sense of dread continued to grow and he began to wonder if the blue mist had harmed Jenny.

'You saw that too,' he said. 'So did I.'

'What do you think it was?' asked Ylujs, returning with Paul's food.

'I've seen it before, when we were in trouble. They can sense danger to Jenny and me.'

'Who can?' the elder asked.

Paul held his amulet up, an idea taking shape in his mind.

'These. They not only bind us, they protect us.'

A collective whisper rolled through the crowd, accompanied by nodding heads.

'It's the only thing I can think of.'

He stood and stared into the amulet's blue glow.

'I should stay with her,' he said, walking toward the door.

The elder agreed and stood as well.

'When she wakes, perhaps she will tell us,' he said. 'Come, let us leave now. Paul needs to sleep.'

Paul went into the hut, sat down beside Jenny and stared out the window. The silence grew as the people left and he felt entirely alone and frightened. He crept across to his mat and curled up, staring at her face.

'Come back, Jen,' he whispered, staring at her until his eyes drifted shut.

The night was silent after the storm's defeat and the air was still. Paul had a fitful sleep, filled with dreams of amulets, storms and crashing waves of water. The moon was a small crescent and cast dim rays over the huts.

When the village was finally asleep, a tall, thin figure crept out of the woods, darting in a slouched position to the edge of the wall. He kept low to the ground, crouching to hide his height and approached the gate. With his back against the wooden poles, he peered around the edge and watched for movement. The moon cast a pale light on his long, gaunt face and he hunched down further.

Sure that no one had seen him, he slipped into the village and made his way between the huts, stopping outside of each one and listening. He checked every hut, pausing a long time in front of the large one that held the ruby amulets. As he crossed the large dance space where Jenny had faced the wind that twists, the moon lit him further and his grey slacks and shirt made him look like a phantom.

He traced the steps from where she had fallen to the hut where the children slept. He paused for a long moment in the doorway, before turning and sitting on the bench. He slouched over, his head in his hands and stared at the ground. His legs twitched slowly and he looked back up, breathing in deeply. He stood and, checking once more that no one was watching him, disappeared into the children's hut.

He waited while his eyes adjusted to the darkness, before crouching down beside Jenny. He could see her face lit up by her amulet's blue glow and he searched it for any sign of activity. Finding none, he slowly reached his hand out, placing it on her forehead.

'How could they leave her like this?' he muttered, sitting back. He turned toward Paul, whose back was facing him and crept over.

'Paul!' he whispered, shaking him. 'Hey, Paul, wake up!'

Paul's body uncurled slowly, stretching out.

'Go away,' he breathed, relaxing back in to his dream.

'No, Paul,' the tall man whispered. 'I need your help.'

Paul's eyes snapped open and he shot back away from the man, nearly crashing in to the hut's wall.

'Who's there?' he cried.

'Shhhh!' the man hissed. 'You'll wake the whole village.'

Paul stared at the crouching figure and watched the man's hands begin to tremble.

'Is that you?' he said. 'Strumn?'

'It is. Are you Ok?'

'Uhm, yeah, sure I guess. What are you doing here?'

'I'm here to help. Jennifer will need all she can get.'

Paul crept forward and looked at Jenny.

'Do you know what's wrong with her?'

'I've a good idea, yes. But I can't help her here.'

'Why not?' Paul asked.

'It will take too long. We've got to get her away from here.'

'What are you talking about?'

Strumn sat back down on Jenny's mat and held his hand to her head.

'Can you sense her?' he asked Paul.

Paul concentrated on her and then reached out a hand, touching her head as well.

'No,' he whispered after a long moment. 'What's happened?'

'It is difficult to explain. Tell me, did anything about her change before this happened? You might have thought she was, how to say it, older?'

'Yes, you're right,' Paul said, nodding. 'Right before she fought the storm, something happened. I thought there was someone else there.'

'Exactly. Now look, we've got to go soon. Someone or something else was there.'

He bent down and gathered Jenny in his arms and stood up, his head nearly reaching the lower part of the peaked roof.

'Get your things, and hers, and follow me.'

Paul pulled his boots on, then grabbed Jenny's cloak, slacks, boots and shirt, stuffed them in her bag and slung it with his over his shoulder.

'Where are we going?' he whispered to Strumn.

'I know of a cave, not too far from here. But we have to get there on foot, which will be difficult in the dark.'

'Why there?'

'It may take some doing to revive her,' he replied. 'And we must make sure we're not disturbed while we do.'

'By what?' Paul asked, his voice wavering.

'That's part of the problem. I'm not sure what. Something's definitely there, and after last night, well, let's just say we need to avoid being seen.'

He shifted Jenny in his arms and walked out the door with Paul following close behind. They walked swiftly out the gate, across the clearing and disappeared into the woods. Strumn paused to look back at the village and Paul felt something cold pass by him.

'What was that?' he asked.

'Never mind. The villagers mustn't stay here.'

Strumn set off into the woods, using his long legs to set a harsh pace and Paul struggled to keep up.

'Why can't they stay? What have you done now?'

'It's what I do, you know that. I disrupt. They must move on, or perish.'

'Perish!' Paul exclaimed. 'I don't understand you.'

'Few do,' Strumn grunted. 'It is the way of things.'

Paul frowned and looked back through the trees. The village was no longer in sight.

'Why must they move on?' he asked.

'There are people coming, ancestors of yours actually, who will destroy this place. I have tried to convince them to leave.'

'By doing what?'

Strumn stopped and looked back.

'I have removed those amulets. The ruby ones. Without them and with your disappearance, the tribe will be spooked.'

'But wait, they'll think we stole them!'

'They might, yes. Or they might think that the Gods have returned for you, them and Jennifer.'

He started walking again, stepping so lightly the ground made no noise.

'It doesn't really matter what they think,' he continued. 'So long as they move on. Which I hope they will.'

They walked in silence, the few moon rays that fell lighting their way. Strumn slowed his pace, tiring under Jenny's weight. They were going steadily downhill and the trees grew larger and thicker as they went.

'Why did you come and get us?' Paul suddenly asked. 'Why not someone from the order?'

'I've wondered that myself,' Strumn replied. 'They must know you're here and I can't believe they wouldn't have seen what she just did. If so, they must know how risky it is to leave her like this.'

'It is?' Paul gasped.

'Oh absolutely. She took a massive chance, and it nearly over ran her. We've still got a lot of work ahead of us.'

'So why would they leave us there? Why don't they help?'

'Ask them,' Strumn snapped. 'They have no use for me, so I'm a little shocked I'm having to clean up their messes.'

'Can I ask you something personnel?'

Strumn paused, looking around.

'In a moment. We're nearly there. Look out for a sudden drop - we're approaching the edge of a cliff, and it's tough to find in the dark.'

Paul's eyes widened and he crept forward, seeing the trees becoming sparse.

'I think it's just ahead,' he said. 'Look there.'

'Good, yes, that's it. Now, to the left. Look for a gentle slope.'

They moved slowly along and found a break in the trees that led down the edge of the cliff. Strumn hoisted Jenny over his shoulder and picked his way carefully down the narrow path. Paul followed and saw him turn back into the cliff, disappearing. When he caught up, Paul saw the dark mouth of a cave and as he stepped in, he saw Strumn lower Jenny to the ground.

'So what did you want to ask me?' he said, looking Paul in the eye.

'Why do you hate them so much,' Paul replied. 'The order, that is.'

'Actually I don't. But they hate me, there's no doubt of that. They don't trust me, they despise what I do, and they probably wish I had died long ago.'

His face twitched into a crooked smile and he sat down beside Jenny.

'But enough about that. Come, sit down here, and let's start bringing her back.'

Paul hurried over and sat down across from him.

'What should I do?'

Strumn didn't answer right away and instead reached a hand into his robe and drew out an amulet. It was glowing as brightly as the children's and as he took it off and placed it on her chest, its glow increased. He fished around in his right pocket and brought out the two ruby amulets and placed them next to his.

'Do the same, please,' he said. 'We're going to need all the power we can get.'

Paul slipped his off and felt a wave of anxiety rush over him. Resisting the urge to put it back on, he balled the chain up and placed it beside the others and moved her's next to them. Strumn leaned over and stared at the children's blue amulets.

'Fascinating,' he murmured, running his fingers over the engraved gold bands.

'What is?' Paul said. 'What are you talking about?'

'Nothing, please forgive me,' he replied. 'Now what I want you do to is talk to her. It is likely that yours is the only voice she can hear.'

'What should I say?'

'Your name, that you're here, that you need her to come back. Tell her you're not finished yet.'

Strumn's arms were beginning to twitch and he glanced nervously around.

'Is something wrong?' Paul asked.

'Of course. Something is always wrong. Ignore it - just concentrate on your friend - let's get her back.'

Paul leaned forward and took Jenny's hand in his.

'Hey Jen,' he whispered. 'Can you hear me? It's Paul.'

'Not like that,' Strumn said. 'Use your inner voice.'

'Will it work?'

'I hope so. It's far more powerful than the spoken word, believe me.'

Paul began silently talking, telling Jenny where they were, using his name as much as he could and listening for a response. Strumn placed one hand on her head and one on the amulets and held himself still. He closed his eyes and stiffened. His amulet's yellow glow dimmed, as did the ruby amulets but the children's blue glow increased. A mist drifted from them, traveling across Jenny's body. It grew in radiance, bathing the whole cave in a warm blue light, before it slowly settled into her.

Paul kept talking and thought he heard a reply. Jenny's eyes started to move, rolling back and forth across her closed lids. Strumn withdrew his hands, opened his eyes and looked at Paul.

'It's starting to work,' he said, before reaching for his amulet.

He stood up and put the gold chain around his neck, tucking the amulet back in his robe. His legs were twitching violently and he had difficulty standing. He put his hand on Jenny's forehead once more and listened. Suddenly he turned away from the children. He grabbed the two ruby amulets and held them up toward the back of the cave. They flashed once, a brilliant red flash, before he whisked them into his pocket.

'The rest is up to you,' he growled, turning back to Paul. 'Don't leave here until she is fully restored. If you do, they will catch you!'

He walked toward the mouth of the cave and looked out.

'But wait,' Paul said, running over to him. 'You can't leave us here!'

'I most certainly can. I must, or we'll all be in more trouble than we can manage. And don't leave your amulet unattended like that!'

Paul rushed back and grabbed his amulet, whipping its chain back around his neck. Strumn walked back over and looked down at him.

'There's something else happening, Paul. You've noticed it, haven't you?'

'You mean that feeling of being followed?'

'That's correct. More properly you are being *hunted*. It is the reason that I have come here to help you. You must not be caught, or they may kill you.'

'Who might?'

'The creatures that are pursuing you. You represent a threat to them - the pair of you do. I don't know what it is, and I don't even know which form is chasing you. But you absolutely have got to stay ahead of them.'

Paul looked back at Jenny.

'What about her? I can't carry her.'

'You won't have to - she is already on her way back.'

'Have you seen them before? These creatures?'

'I have, though rarely. There's something important that you must convince Jennifer of: She is far, far stronger than them. I can tell you're frightened, and I bet she is as well. But trust me, they wield nowhere near the power that she does.'

He moved over to Jenny and placed a hand on her forehead once more.

'She's close,' he said. 'Stay with her, and remember what I've said. She may be afraid to ever use her gifts again after this, and you must convince her to.'

'But what if this happens again?' Paul asked. 'How do I stop it?'

'That trick will have to wait. For now, just small bursts - no fighting off tornados.'

He walked back toward the cave mouth.

'Can I ask you one more thing?' Paul said.

Strumn looked back at him.

'Go ahead.'

'Why are you helping us? Especially when the order won't?'

'That's even harder to explain. It's because I have met her sister.'

'She doesn't have one, though!'

'That's what's so hard to explain. She hasn't met her yet. But I have. Over five hundred years ago.'

He turned and strode out into the dark.

'Good luck, Paul!' he called back.

Paul stood at the entrance to the cave and stared out, hoping Strumn would come back. The moon had set and with sunrise still hours away, the air was nearly black. There was no breeze and he could hear lots of strange sounds - insects and creatures he did not know.

He felt a familiar tingling in the back of his head, the first sign of someone approaching and stiffened. The feeling left him and he stood as still as he could, waiting for it to return.

When it didn't, he turned and headed back toward Jenny, watching the glow on her amulet increase as he approached. Her eyes were moving slowly but her breathing was unchanged and no other muscles moved.

He sat down beside her, put his hand on her head again and listened.

Hey Jen he thought. *Are you ok?*

Of course! came the reply. *Why wouldn't I be?*

'Can you talk?' he asked out loud. She didn't move so he repeated his question with his inner voice.

Yeah, can't you hear me?

No. You're not moving, you're not talking.

What do you mean? I am so!

Paul frowned at her.

Describe where we are he thought.

Ok, we're sitting in a... I think, maybe we're standing. Or swimming?

That doesn't make sense, Jen. C'mon - dig your way out - come back to me.

He watched the movement in her eyes increase and saw her nostrils flare as she struggled to wake up. Her breathing increased and then she moaned, rolling over onto her side. Paul put his hand on her shoulder and shook her.

'Hey, Jenny! Wake up!'

He saw her eyes open and stare at the glowing core of their amulets. She stretched and sat up.

'Where are we?' she whispered, her voice hoarse.

'In a cave, in the middle of the night, a long way from the village.'

'Oh my God - the village - Is it all right?'

'Yeah - you were great. You saved it.'

'But, then, how did I get here?'

'You collapsed, and then I sort of didn't know what to do. You'll never believe who helped me.'

She stared at him, concentrating.

'Strumn?' she exclaimed. 'Why would he help? Why didn't Ornolt? Or someone from the order?'

'I don't know exactly,' Paul muttered angrily.

'Well what did he do,' she said, ignoring his discomfort. 'Tell me everything. Did he disrupt us, do you think?'

Paul stood up, walked toward the cave's mouth and tensed as the tingling returned.

'Hey, what's wrong?' Jenny asked, standing up and stumbling over to him.

'Oh man, my leg hurts,' she cried. 'It feels like it's been ripped off and sewn back on.'

'That's gross!' Paul said. 'You probably just slept funny. You couldn't move - I had to shift you around.'

'Really? Well, thanks then. So what's wrong?'

'I think something's out there, only I can't see a thing.'

Jenny limped over and stood beside him and when she glanced around she felt the same thing.

'Yeah, you're right, something is there! What should we do?'

'I say wait until morning. Hopefully we'll be safe in here.'

Jenny nodded and they walked to the back of the cave and sat down.

'I put your stuff in your bag,' Paul said, pointing at where it lay. Jenny reached for it, and pulled out her clothes, boots, and a dried sandwich. She ate it in one bite, and then reached in for another.

'I'm famished!' she exclaimed between mouthfuls.

'I'm not surprised,' he replied. 'It must have been really hard, fighting that storm.'

She stared at him, thinking back.

'You know, it wasn't. The hardest part was the end. It's like, whatever was helping me didn't want to let go.'

'Really?'

'Yeah, it was so scary. I thought I was dead.'

'For awhile, so did I. You just didn't seem to be there. But you were breathing.'

'Well, one thing's for sure - I'm never trying that again!'

'Oh, that reminds me' Paul said, sitting up. 'Strumn left me with a warning. For both of us.'

'What?'

'Here' he said putting his hand on her shoulder. He shared everything that had happened with Strumn, including the way the amulets had brought her back.

'Wow,' Jenny breathed. 'We're in trouble.'

'Not if we stay ahead of them. That's what Strumn said. We have to keep away from whatever's hunting us.'

'But wait - isn't the order watching us the whole time?

'I thought so too. But if they are, why didn't they rescue us? Why leave it to Strumn?'

'I don't know,' she replied. 'I guess we'll have to ask them, when we find the common.'

'If we find it, you mean.'

'Oh c'mon - we will! I can't believe they'd let this keep going on forever.'

Paul looked at her over his scrunched up knees but said nothing. The first signs of the new day started splashing across the sky and Jenny stood up.

'Guess I better change,' she said. 'Turn around.'

When she was done, she folded her sarong and put it in her bag. They walked back to the mouth of the cave. They were facing east, looking over a long, rolling stretch of rain forest that made its way to the sea. When there was enough light to see the ground around them, they crept out of the cave and descended the rest of the way down the trail into the dense forest.

'How's the leg?' Paul asked. 'Do you need to rest?'

'No thanks - it's fine.'

The forest that surrounded them was beautiful and varied. Long, slender tree trunks sprung up everywhere - some white, others a speckled, greenish brown and they reached up to a canopy of broad leaves with spiky ends that layered themselves in yellow and green patches. As they walked, they saw all sorts of wildlife - birds, snakes and even the occasional prehistoric dragon - small creatures about one and a half feet long that clung to the sides of trees, searching for bugs.

Spread sparsely amongst the slender trees were much thicker, shorter trees with frozen tentacles for roots which rose over furry brown bark to a crowning ball of leaves with hundreds of long green shoots sticking out.

Every time the children stopped to look at the exotic trees, the tingling feeling would return and they'd set off again, looking behind them as they went. After nearly two hours of walking, they came to the edge of a dusty grass plain. They could see the forest spring up on the other side, several miles away.

They set out toward it and felt the sun bake down on them. As they had before in Hawaii, they slung their cloaks over themselves, using them to reflect the sun's heat.

'Paul,' Jenny said, after five minutes of walking through the grass. 'What's that over there?'

She was pointing to the north, where a dust cloud was rising.

'I don't know,' he said, shading his eyes with his hands. 'But it looks like it's moving.'

'Towards us?'

'Yeah maybe. And, hang on - can you hear something?'

She stood still, staring at the approaching dust.

'Sort of a thumping sound, isn't it?'

'We should turn around,' he said, heading back toward the trees.

Jenny followed and as the dust cloud increased and the thumping turned into a thunderous pounding, Jenny grabbed his hand and sprinted back into the woods.

'C'mon, up this tree,' Paul said, scrambling up a thick, gnarly trunk. He reached back and helped her up onto the branch beside him.

'You ok with the running?' he asked.

'Yeah, don't worry - I won't do anything stupid,' she replied. 'So what is that out there?'

They could see small brown dots at the front of the cloud and when it drew close, they saw that they were being approached by a herd of kangaroos.

'Wow - that's so cool!' Jenny exclaimed. 'I've always wanted to see them!'

'Me too. I'm just glad we're up here and they're down there. They're really big!'

The herd thundered past and after the dust settled, the children climbed down and headed back out onto the plains. Jenny reached into her bag, found a bottle of water and took a long drink, before handing it to Paul. After about an hour and a half of baking in the sun's heat, they reached the far side of the plain. They headed in, feeling the cool depths of the woods surround them.

At first glance, the rain forest was no different than it had been on the other side. There were a few more trees, and the ground level growth was much thicker. Jenny tried to point out as many different plants as she could remember, including some that were poisonous, or deadly sharp.

'So what do you think Strumn meant?' she asked when they came to a flatter area.

'About what?'

'About my sister. He must have been wrong.'

'Well, what was it you told me you heard in your dream? Or on the mountain in the snow?'

Jenny sucked in her breath.

'That voice - it called me sister.'

She looked at him and then back the way they had come.

'This is just so weird, Paul.'

'Yeah, I know,' he replied. He looked at her face, watching a frown fall across it.

'What's wrong?' he asked.

'Me. Strumn. My five hundred year old sister. I'm a freak.'

'Jen, cut it out. If you're a freak, so am I, and I just don't believe that.'

She started off again, tromping away before turning back to him.

'Sorry,' she said. 'I just, sometimes I don't like what's happening to me.'

Paul walked along beside her, scraping the ground with his walking stick.

'But you're ok, right?'

'Yeah,' she said, 'I'll be fine.'

They started off again, Jenny leading them, still moving over the same rough terrain. The sounds of the forest continued, getting louder as the density of the woods increased. The wind picked up, rustling the canopy above.

The sky beyond darkened as rain clouds billowed together, rolling over them and blocking the sun. The children had become used to this afternoon ritual with the gentle rain falls that cooled the land for the evening. They searched around for shelter and, finding nothing but the trees around them, clambered up onto a large boulder and gathered their cloaks around them.

The rain began to fall, spluttering down as the clouds let go, followed by a deluge of water. The wind was light and there was no thunder or lightening, just the gentle drone of the rain. Jenny peaked out from under her cloak and saw that everything was getting soaked - birds were hunkered into tree crevices, waiting it out.

Several yards away from them, the rain splashed off a large object, the water bouncing away from it. Jenny frowned, staring at the splashing water and couldn't see a thing. The water was just stopping in midair. She realized that if the water wasn't hitting it, it would be invisible.

She reached out slowly and took Paul's hand.

Can you hear me? she thought.

Yes, he replied.

Look very slowly around, until you're looking ahead of me. Maybe thirty feet.

Paul did as she said, sensing her anxiety. He saw the same effect, the hulking, bubble shaped area where the rain couldn't go.

What do you think it is?

I don't know she thought back, *but I think it's watching us.*

So do I he thought, *and I think it's what we've been sensing all along. It looks like those things we saw before.*

Only way bigger she thought back.

The rain continued to steadily fall and the apparition across from them sat motionless. Jenny looked at the canopy above and pointed at a large, broad leaf, causing it to fall, drifting down toward what sat there.

She guided the leaf down and placed it on top of the strange bubble. The leaf came to rest on something solid and the pattern in the rain shifted, brushing off the leaf with a translucent, muscle-bound arm.

Whatever was sitting across from them was definitely alive.

Paul she thought, *what happens when the rain stops?*

What do you mean?

We won't be able to see it anymore!

Concentrate on it now, try to get a sense of what's there - once the rain stops, it'll be the only way.

She cast her mind out, toward the apparition, trying to sense anything. After a few moments, she felt a strange tingling but nothing more. She looked away from the object, and tried to find the tingling again. It took a while but she was finally able. She tried a few more times, while the rain continued to fall.

It took another ten minutes for the cloud burst to end. The children sat still, watching their strange companion. When the rain did end, they could no longer see it but they could sense it.

'It's moving, Paul,' she said.

'I know - the tingle has moved.'

'Yeah - sort of like hide and seek, isn't it?'

'Yup. The same feeling. It's just over there,' he said, pointing ahead of them.

Jenny looked where he was pointing, and felt something cold come toward them.

'What's that?' she asked.

'Anger. I think it knows we can sense it.'

She shuddered and slid down off the boulder.

'I think we should get out of here - get to the coast as soon as we can.'

'Ok.'

She turned and started off, heading right for whatever it was that was shadowing them.

'Jenny!' Paul hissed. 'What are you doing?'

'Well, the coast is this way. If we start avoiding it, it'll know for sure that we can see it.'

'Oh,' he trailed off.

As she walked toward it, it moved. When she went past, Paul felt the apparition following them.

They continued like this for another ten minutes, their cloaks drying as they went, with the strange figure tracking them.

Suddenly their amulets started to heat up and as they did, the children sensed more than one of their mysterious stalkers arriving.

'Jenny!' Paul cried. 'A gate!'

She held her amulet up, stepping in one direction and then another.

'This way!' she yelled.

They started running but found their way blocked by one of the strange objects.

'Should I move it?' she asked.

'How?' he said.

'You know, make it move?'

'I - I don't think so. Then they'll really know!'

Jenny looked at him, trembling.

'They probably already do - we just stopped in front of it!'

Paul's eyes widened, realizing their mistake.

'Oh no! Let's get out of here!'

They took off, following their ever-warming amulets. The creatures were following closely and the children could feel their anger and knew that there were at least ten of them trying to catch them.

'We've got to find that gate!' Jenny cried.

The amulets were getting unbearably hot and just ahead of them they saw a thick clump of trees. They ran over to investigate and found a deep hole, about five feet wide.

'This has to be it!' she yelled.

'I agree!' he replied, 'and those things are coming right at us!'

Jenny picked up a rock and dropped it in. A few moments later she heard a distant splash.

'Oh no!' she said. 'A well. This is going to be awful!'

'No choice!' Paul said, hopping over, Jenny close behind him.

They fell into the dark shaft of the well, waiting for the gate to take over and whisk them away from whatever it was that was chasing them. It never happened and after they splashed down in the water, they bobbed back to the surface.

'Where's the gate?' Jenny asked.

'I've no idea!' said Paul.

'Maybe the amulets were wrong!'

Chapter 16

The Talomni

Canace never sought her sister's amulet, and felt a great urge for rest. She sealed the door to their mountain home with rock, letting the snow reclaim the peak, and took herself to the chamber of crystal veins. She sealed the passage that led down to the chamber as she went, leaving behind her on the wall the inscription from their amulets. With nothing but the glow of the crystal, she lay down, and fell asleep, waiting for the right moment to awake.

'This is worse than I feared.'

The man they called the Docent paced back and forth in front of the stage, pulling so hard on his beard that he winced.

On the stage, Jenny lay asleep in the cave, with Paul and Strumn crouching over her.

'What is *he* doing there?' Ucheen demanded.

Chantal watched from her seat, staring at the amulets that had been placed on her chest.

'There's a lot we don't know here,' she finally said. 'Strumn's presence is not normal. What he's doing is not a disruption - it's a rescue.'

The Docent turned toward her.

'Explain, please.'

'She is not asleep. She could not possibly have been the one to turn that storm. They, Paul and Strumn, are trying to bring her back.'

'So who, if not Miss Greyson, did we just watch?'

'Physically? Definitely Miss Greyson. But she had a lot of help. I fear that whoever or whatever is chasing those two children are now going to be doubly interested.'

She tilted her head sideways, watching the Docent thinking.

'Her amulet?' he mused.

'Maybe. There's something about them - remember when they were bound?'

'I do. But I don't think that's quite it. What about those visitors they keep having? Some of us have been able to see them, and they look a bit like us.'

Chantal nodded.

'Another strong possibility.'

She looked back at the stage as the amulets on Jenny's chest began to glow.

'Where did old Aloysius learn that, I wonder?'

Several sets of eyebrows rose at her use of his first name.

'And why does he have three amulets?' Sasha added. 'What's he been up to?'

The glowing amulets dimmed and they watched Strumn as he put his hand on her forehead and then smile.

'He seems to have done it, she's ...'

Strumn looked up from Jenny and scowled at them, right through the stage. As he picked up the two ruby amulets, he held them up for every one watching to see and then smiled at them. With a bright red flash the image on the stage disappeared, replaced by a mirror image of the common and all those in it.

'What on earth was that!' the Docent roared. 'Get them back at once!'

Several members stepped forward, holding up their amulets toward the stage and concentrating. For several minutes, the stage refused to listen, flashing back over the children's journey. When they finally did stabilize it, the children were standing at the edge of the plain, watching the approaching herd of kangaroos.

'We've just missed a lot!'

'What happened?'

'Where's Strumn?'

'And what's that?'

This last question, one of a torrent that poured down from the seats of the common, drew everyone's attention. Standing behind the children, almost completely translucent, was a huge, round object. They wouldn't have been able to see it, except for the dust carried on the open plain's wind.

'That is a massive problem.'

The Docent looked at Chantal as he spoke.

'Agreed,' she replied. 'We haven't seen them in many centuries. We must get them out of there. The next gate must rescue them, whatever the consequences to the girl's future with us.'

'I will place it myself,' the Docent said. 'This will be tricky, as they mustn't be followed.'

'Don't bring them directly here. You must be sure first.'

The Docent frowned and tilted his head toward her. He turned away from the stage and walked out past the infinite fire, fading away into the gate.

As soon as she splashed into the water and realized the gate wasn't here, Jenny started shaking with fear. Paul splashed down right beside her and they bobbed up and down in the cool water. There were no sides to the well, no ladders to climb up and their feet were not touching the bottom.

'What are we going to do?' she cried.

'We've got to get out of here,' Paul replied. 'The trouble is, how? We can't climb out, and even if we could, those things are up there waiting for us.'

Jenny looked up and saw the sun beaming down from far above them. She could sense the strange tingling somewhere near the top and screamed when she saw the light from the sun ripple.

'They're coming down Paul!'

Paul looked up, confirming what she'd said.

'Jenny - block them. I've got to find the gate.'

'With what?' she said.

'I don't know - what did you use to block that storm? Do that again.'

Jenny swam to the edge of the well and found a rock sticking out, enough to hold on to. With her free hand she pointed up at the top.

'Stay there, whatever you are!' she yelled.

Paul saw her power shimmering but it wasn't strongly focused, something was wrong. He looked at her and saw her trembling. She was scared and it was affecting her ability.

'Jenny, relax,' he said in a soothing voice. 'You know you can do it.'

'But I might get hurt again!'

'No, this is different - not nearly so difficult, ok?'

'Are you sure?'

'Absolutely - you're far stronger than they are, or they'd have caught us long ago. Remember what Strumn said.'

He saw her face relax and then the aura around her intensified and shot from her outstretched arm toward the top of the well. It stopped there, forming a round, swirling barrier just below the top.

It's appearance had a strange effect. The swirling barrier was sparking, in different spots, and every time it did, the sense of anger from above increased as the creatures were trying to get past and couldn't.

Jenny looked over at him.

'I don't want to do this for very long!' she cried. 'Please find it soon!'

Paul held up his amulet. It was still hot, so they must still be close to the gate. When he held it higher, it cooled. With a sense of dread, he held it down, under the water, where it heated up further.

'You're not going to believe this!' he said.

'What?' she said, still blasting the top of the well.

'The gate is under water.'

'Oh that's just great. I hate that kind,' she fumed.

'So do I,' said Paul, 'but we've got no choice. C'mon - let's go.'

He took a deep breath and dove under water. As soon as he did, the amulet cooled and its glow disappeared. He was traveling through the gate. *Get us out of here* he thought to himself.

Jenny saw him dive but saw no air bubbles or splash. She looked at her amulet, which was no longer glowing, so she took a deep breath and dove in after him. She thought she heard an angry howl from above as she released the barrier but was unable to check.

She swam down and felt the rushing sensation as the gate took hold. The blue glow in her amulet returned and she could see light coming from below her.

She felt the urge for air and fumbled for her amulet. It was bubbling, as she expected but the bubbles were floating down, toward the light. She stuffed her amulet in her mouth and swam toward it.

Moments later she burst through the surface. She realized that the gate had turned them around and released them heading up to a new water surface. This water was different from anything she'd ever swum in before. It was thick, muddy and had leaves growing on it. As soon as she took the amulet out of her mouth and smelled the air, she realized why: they'd been dropped in a swamp.

'Oh yuck,' she cried, 'why this?'

'I was going to ask you the same thing,' said Paul, standing beside her. 'C'mon, the land is fairly firm here.'

She swam over and pulled herself out and when she looked at Paul, she smiled.

'What's so funny?' he asked.

'You! You're filthy and there's leaves stuck to you!'

'Well, so are you. And you're hair looks like a big, long, muddy mop!' he replied.

'Shut up' she grinned, wiping most of the muck off and shaking her hair out. 'So why did we end up here?'

'I don't know. I wasn't thinking of anything other then finding my way through the gate,' he replied.

'Me too. There has to be some other reason.'

Paul looked around.

'Maybe,' he said, 'but I don't want to stay here - it smells awful. Let's see if we can find our way out.'

He grabbed his walking stick from his bag and started using it to poke around for a solid path. Going at a cautious pace, they started weaving their way through the swamp, heading for a distant forest. Paul stayed in the lead, drawing on his experience hiking in England's northern moors.

Jenny picked at her hair as they walked, dragging her fingers through it to release the dried muck that pasted it together. Their cloaks, clothes and boots cleaned themselves, adjusting to the cooler temperature by thickening out.

They were approaching the edge of the forest and the smell was starting to fall behind. They were standing on a rock shelf that wrapped all the way around the swamp before stretching out of sight beyond the far edge. The trees were almost all conifers - pines and cedars with just a few maples and birch sprinkled throughout. The forest wasn't dense and they could see small clumps of snow in the darker depths.

'Wherever we are, it looks like winter's just ended,' Jenny said.

'I've been thinking that too. The air is still cool - you can smell things melting,' he replied.

They started walking along the edge of the rock, looking for a clear way through the woods.

'I still don't know why we ended up in a swamp,' she said, 'since neither of us were thinking of this.'

'You weren't the only ones there, though, were you?' a booming voice said.

They whirled around. Out of the trees came an impossibly old man, walking with a gnarled cane. His face was partially hidden behind a hood that draped lazily over him, turning into a grey, threadbare cloak as it passed over his shoulders. He had several rings on his fingers, and while his skin was dry and wrinkled, his eyes had a spark to them that belied his years.

'There was something else with you, wasn't there, when you went through?' the old man continued.

Jenny stared at the old man, concentrating on him and felt a wall of strength and confidence radiating from him.

'You're more than a guide, aren't you?' she asked.

'Indeed, Miss Greyson, I am. I'm one of those who have been observing you, helping to monitor those around you, and trying, as best we can, to understand what we have been seeing,' he replied.

'Why have you come to us now?' Jenny asked eagerly, 'Have we finished? Do we get to go back?'

'No, not yet. A situation has arisen which is incredibly dangerous - one we couldn't let you face alone.'

'Worse than what happened to me back in that village?' Jenny asked.

The old man fixed his gaze on her and she felt a gnawing pull in the back of her head.

'We will address that later,' he said, his face darkening. 'What happened to you was unprecedented, and your recovery even more so. You should not have survived that.'

'What to you mean?' she whispered.

'You're right to be alarmed, Miss Greyson. This has not happened before, and Strumn's involvement makes things far more complicated. Please, both of you, listen carefully, follow me, and let's figure out if there's any way to avoid the trap that's been laid for you!'

'What trap?' Paul asked.

'I'm not yet sure,' the old man replied as he set off into the woods. 'We may even be wrong. Let me explain. The order has been around for centuries, as you no doubt surmised when you were shown those amulets in Australia. We do not make our presence known to our fellow man, as it leads to problems that are difficult to control. But we most definitely do make it known to others that share this world with us.'

'Is that what Strumn was talking about?' Jenny blurted, her eyes darting back and forth.

He held his hand up.

'Indeed, Miss Greyson, Aloysius Strumn was speaking of this, although the manner in which he presented his arguments were as flawed as the rest of his existence. You will understand, please, that Strumn's entire manner, and means of life, are considered an outrage in our world. We do not accept him, nor what he does.'

He had stopped while saying this, clearly upset at what had gone on between Strumn and the children.

'Can't you stop him?' Paul asked.

'No, we can't, although we do have the physical means. It would make us appear too weak.'

He set off again, still talking.

'But that is not what I am here for. You will have plenty of opportunity, over the next few years, to spend time with us and study what it means to be part of the order.'

236

He paused and looked at both of them.

'And I really hope you do. You have shown yourselves to be very, very gifted, much more so than any of us thought. As a result, you seem to keep getting out of the increasingly challenging situations we place before you. I should like you to know that most new arrivals hardly make it through two gates before we have seen all we need to see. You two are quite different, and you, Miss Greyson, are something we haven't seen before.

'We'll return to that later however, once this is over. I only tell you this as a means of introduction to our problem, one that I must help you with. These gifts of yours have drawn the attention of creatures of a most unsavory sort. They see you as something of a threat, and I believe they are right.'

His look left them and he turned his head, staring into the depths of the woods. The children followed his gaze.

'Because of what they sense about you, they do not want you to succeed in your efforts to join the order. In fact,' he said leaning over toward them and whispering, 'I believe they do not want you to survive at all!'

Jenny's eyes grew wide in shock and Paul frowned at the old man.

'Why would they think that?' Jenny finally said, 'We're just children - we're no threat!'

'Ah, but Miss Greyson, you most definitely are. Have you any idea what just happened to the two of you, before you found your way in to the swamp?'

They shook their heads.

'Then let me explain it for you. You two were being hunted, tracked in fact, by Talomni, creatures that live on the outside of society, watching all the time for opportunities. They are a strange sort, the Talomni, as you have found out.'

'But what did we ever do to them?' Paul asked.

'Well, it isn't so much what you did to them, but what you might do. They saw Miss Greyson's performance against the tornado, which, may I say, was rather unwise. They had already been pursuing you, though we really weren't sure. In hindsight we should have been as close to you as Strumn was - perhaps we could have drawn their attention. Be that as it may, after the storm, they and whoever else they work with, decided to bring you down. That is the only way of explaining how many of them were there.

'But then, you did something that no one else has done before. You were able to see them. They are very xenophobic, and do not like anyone to be aware of their presence.'

'But that was an accident,' Jenny said. 'Without the rain, we wouldn't have seen them.'

'Not so. You knew you were being followed. You have all along, so on some level, you knew they were there. And they could sense that. Most of the members of the order cannot detect them, at least not on our own. That both of you could, and figured out how as quickly as you did, disturbed them.'

He paused, looking around again, before setting off in a new direction.

'But they didn't catch us, did they?' Jenny said.

'Not yet,' he responded, 'but, why, do you suppose, the gate brought you here, if neither of you was thinking about a swamp?'

The children looked at each other and shrugged.

'I'm not sure,' said Paul. 'We still haven't got the hang of the gates, so we just thought we'd made another mistake.'

'It was no mistake, though you are right, your use of the gates is in need of improvement. You were not the ones in control of the gate, nor were you the only ones to pass through it.'

Jenny started looking around, searching out in the swamp and among the trees. As she looked up one large pine, the familiar tingling sensation returned.

'We're not alone,' she whispered.

The old man looked around, then back at her.

'Where, Jennifer?' he hissed.

'See that large white pine to your right? There's one of those creatures in the branches, two thirds of the way up.'

'Then we must be very careful. That one is probably the one that came through the gate with you and is probably trying to keep itself hidden from you. Do not let it know that you are aware of its presence.'

The old man shifted on his feet and gestured for them to follow.

'Can I ask you something?' Paul said.

'Certainly, Mr. Green.'

'Do you have a name? Like Ornolt, I mean?'

The old man chuckled. 'Of course, please forgive me for not introducing myself. My name is, like so many others, not easily said out loud. Here give me your hands, you probably can understand me that way.'

They each held out a hand and he took them. Immediately, a long musical tone started, wavering, bending, sometimes hissing to a stop and other times bursting like a drum, filling their minds. The melody repeated, layering in details as it went. The old man let go, smiling.

The children were smiling too. A name like music was completely new to them, but told them so much more. This man was very old, as they thought and his name's song spoke of being over six hundred years old. He was a master teacher within the order, and carried the title 'Docent Miltabardo'.

'You may call me that, when you need to call my name out loud,' Miltabardo said, following their thoughts.

'Now come along, if we really are being watched, then no doubt others have been called. When there are sufficient numbers of them, they will try to attack, of that there can be no doubt!'

He shifted his cane to his other hand, which he grasped firmly as he walked into the woods, still moving away from the watching Talomni. The children silently followed him.

The woods had many noises to them. The trees creaked as they moved in the wind, which blew slowly from the north. It was a crisp, cold wind and they gathered their cloaks about themselves to ward it off. Miltabardo set a steady pace, following the gently rising slope of the land. The sun was starting to get low in the sky and their stomachs were growling.

After another hour, they came to a small grass clearing. Miltabardo held up his hand and the children stopped, watching him. He walked to the center of the clearing, poking the ground with his cane. He scratched a large circle in the dirt, perhaps two feet in diameter. He drew himself up, took a deep breath of air and blew out. The circle burst into flame and Paul jumped backward. Jenny put her arm around him and whispered something.

Miltabardo turned, concentrated on Paul and walked over.

'I have it under control, Paul,' he said. 'Don't worry.'

Paul looked at him then back at the fire.

'Now if you would be so kind,' he continued, 'I think we'll need something to sleep in.'

Jenny looked at Paul and shrugged.

'I'm sorry, Docent, what should we do?' she asked.

He smiled at her.

'Remember, I have seen or heard almost all of the voyage on which you two have been. You kept yourselves warm on that train in an interesting way and for a while there, you had a wonderfully private beach hut, didn't you?'

The children smiled, understanding what he wanted.

'I'm too old for that sort of thing now,' he continued. 'Let's see how much further you've come.'

'I think Paul would be happier with a proper fireplace,' she said. 'I like them made of stone.'

Paul grinned at her.

'If you have that much control, Miss Greyson, I shall be truly impressed.'

Jenny turned to Paul, took his hand and sent an image of a log cabin into his mind, with a large vaulted ceiling over a living room, a small bedroom and bathroom on one floor, and a two person loft above that. They both looked back at the clearing concentrating on the image.

A shimmering began around the edge of the field causing Miltabardo to jump up and rush from the field. The image started to take shape - large, dark logs were forming, intertwining together to form walls with a beautiful cedar shake roof above them and a small stone chimney up one side. Windows appeared next and a door, with a small covered porch running up to it. The building occupied most of the clearing and, as glass formed in the windows, a small column of smoke rose from the chimney.

Paul and Jenny let go of each other's hands and stepped back, admiring the cozy cabin that stood in front of them. Miltabardo walked up behind them, placing a hand on each of their shoulders.

'In all my long years,' he said, 'I have never seen such an impressive display, from anyone, let alone new arrivals. Come, let us see if you are as good with interiors as you are with structure!'

He walked up the small steps and opened the door. Inside, two small sofas angled in front of a warm and crackling fire, a dark carpet on the otherwise shining hardwood floor in front of them. Behind the sofas was a small dining table, with four chairs around it, and a kitchen opened beyond that. The doors to the bathroom and lower bedroom stood either side of a pine ship's ladder that rose to the loft above.

'This is a familiar place to you, isn't it, Jennifer?' he said.

'Yeah. My parent's best friends have a cabin just like this near Jasper.'

'I thought so. Wonderful detail, though - you two must have a powerful bond with your amulets to communicate so well.'

He stepped in, hung his cane near the door and walked over to one of the sofas, sitting down slowly, with the care of someone suddenly fragile. His smile was broadly splashed on his face and as the children came in and closed the door, he sighed.

'This is the first time we've been able to do so much detail' Jenny said, following him in.

Miltabardo smiled looking up at her from his seat.

'You've always known how children. Just remember, you did it this time, not because you had to, or because I asked you to. You did it because you could - you made it happen. Now then, I'd like a little nap before supper. I'll cook tonight, something I'm very fond of. I suggest you two get cleaned up.

'That is,' he said with a chuckle, 'if you remembered a tub!'

With that, he closed his eyes and was instantly asleep. Over the next hour both children showered and changed into pajamas, housecoats and slippers. When Miltabardo awoke, he found them sitting in front of the fire playing a card game, deep in thought.

'This looks a little too perfect,' he said watching them. 'Enjoy it while you can. Tomorrow I expect will be something different entirely. Now then - do either of you like pasta?'

He rose and headed to the kitchen.

'As you may have gathered from my name, I am of Italian descent. I am going to prepare a meal for you that I have been perfecting these last two hundred years!'

Dinner was a mushroom based pasta and although Jenny would never have touched a mushroom before, she couldn't believe how good they actually tasted. Miltabardo insisted that the meal was not complete without wine and told them they could have a little, so long as they told no one.

After they ate he gathered them around the fire and sat down.

'Now, let us go through one or two more things before tomorrow. I expect that the Talomni know exactly where we are. They will not bother us here, they do not like enclosed buildings like this, for reasons I do not yet know. Tonight we will sleep soundly and then tomorrow we'll try and find our way out of this land.

'You haven't yet asked but I'm sure you have thought it. Why is it that I, or others in the order, don't just remove us from this place?'

Both children nodded and waited.

'When the first members of the order found each other, it was not a well organized group, the way it is now. It was almost an accident. The first amulets were discovered nearly five thousand years ago in the land we now call Mexico. In the mountainous part of that country there are many, many caves. Explorers of the time found those first two amulets, and took them back to their village. They couldn't touch the cores, finding them too hot to hold, but they could carry the basket they lay in.

'Some years later, two children from the village - brothers - were playing near where the amulets were stored. They found them and were able to pick them up. As soon as they did, they were paired off, just as you two are now. They left the village soon after, wandering the North American continent.

'They soon started to recognize certain things that we take for granted in the amulets. They glow near each other, they provide things we need, like food, water, air, etc, and they locate and open the gates. This, in particular, is very important, and is the means by which we move as far and as quickly as we do.

'You will find as you grow older that you can place the gates wherever you want, have them take you wherever and within limits *whenever* you want to go. These original two holders of the amulets had no special abilities to start with but noticed almost as soon as they bound with their amulets that there were things they could see around them that others couldn't.

'The details of the time are of course sketchy but the story passed down to us says that the brothers wandered north where they ran in to a skilled jeweler. This man was so taken by their amulets that he fashioned replicas and when one of the boys put one on the replica started to glow and then became so hot he had to remove it. When he placed it back on the table the new amulet split in two and vanished. He tried again with a second replica with no result this time but when his brother tried the new amulet started to glow, got hot and split, vanishing just as before.

'The jeweler made yet another replica, and this one, no matter what they tried, would not come to life. It has since become evident that the amulets pick their wearers, not the other way round, which by the way is how you come to wear yours. Over the centuries the amulets became much more careful who they chose as bearers. Intelligence, self-awareness, compassion, these all became qualities the amulets sought out.'

'So why do the amulets bind with us? Why do they even exist?' Paul asked.

'We're not sure why they exist. Where did those two in the cave come from?' Miltabardo replied. 'We have no idea. But we believe they bind with us so that we may better see the world around us, and help guide our species through its hidden dangers.'

'Dangers?' Jenny said.

'Indeed. As you've already seen. There are many such creatures and threats mind, but some are much more interested in us than others. Take the Talomni, for example - we have never been able to communicate with them and I doubt we ever will, but we have tried.

'Every time we do, we seem to tell them something of ourselves and get nothing in return. The result is that they know about the gates and when we're going to use them, and we don't even know how to find them. That is,' he said looking at the children, 'until you two figured it out.

'These creatures also do not seem to like us. There's always a sense of aggression from them when we encounter them, though we know not why. Tomorrow, I expect that we will walk into something they have devised for us - there's a reason they brought us here.'

He paused and looked at the children, sensing their fear building.

'Don't worry though - with your ability, Miss Greyson, I doubt any harm could come to us. And with your sense of others Mr. Green, we may just learn something new about them.'

He finished talking and sat staring into the fire before finally rising.

'Enough for tonight. I am exhausted, as I'm sure are you. Get a good night's sleep - we'll start as early as we can in the morning.'

The children watched him head into his room and moved toward the loft. As they climbed the ladder they heard the floor behind them creak. They scrambled up to the top and looked back down. Standing on the floor, everywhere, were children. The children appeared to be from all over the world and from many different periods in history. They were dressed in variations of the clothes of the order, some much simpler than others, clearly from ancient times. They were all completely pale - the only things of any color were the amulets around their necks.

Jenny stood at the rail looking down on the children. They were all silently staring at her, smiling gently. More of them stood outside the cabin looking right at her. Paul stood beside her and took her hand. He looked around and sent the feelings he was sensing from them to Jenny - anticipation, excitement, hope, support and encouragement. It was as if the pale children knew what was coming and wanted to be with them. After a few moments of silent watching, Jenny bowed toward them and they slowly started to fade.

When they were gone the two children climbed into bed without saying a word. They slept soundly, dreaming of pasta, of ancient amulets, of children watching and warm fires. When they woke, Miltabardo was already up and had breakfast ready for them.

After they ate, they changed back into their hiking clothes. With one last look about, they walked out of the cabin and closed the door. When they were a safe distance away, Jenny turned back to the cabin and glared at it. Paul and Miltabardo both saw the power shimmer around her and then shoot toward the cabin. In just a few moments there was nothing left to show that it had ever been there.

Docent Miltabardo raised his eyebrows. It was the first time he'd had a chance to see the aura around her, the shimmering power and it was much stronger than he had ever seen in anyone else.

'We're not supposed to leave stuff behind, right?' she asked.

Miltabardo patted her on the shoulder. 'A lesson it took me some years to learn. Indeed, we do not. Now, do either of you know where we should go?'

With no clear choice in mind he was interested to see what the two children came up with. Jenny suggested they continue walking away from the swamp as they had been doing the day before. With no objection from Paul or Miltabardo, they set off.

After they left the clearing and headed back into the forest, Jenny remembered something that had bothered her just before they went to sleep.

'Docent?' she asked.

'Yes, Miss Greyson?'

'There's something you didn't quite answer last night when you were telling us about why we're here where the Talomni brought us. You didn't tell us why the order can't just pull us out.'

Miltabardo stopped and looked at her quizzically.

'Did I not?' he said, 'Ah well, perhaps it slipped my mind, as things tend to do more often of late. The reason is quite simple. You've already seen it. We travel by the gates and the Talomni know that. If we just use a gate, they may accompany us without our knowing it. It would not do to have them find us. To have them find our Gathering Common.'

He paused, looking at them.

'We must find another way out of here, more than likely on our feet.'

He continued walking, taking the lead. Jenny followed with Paul lagging behind. When he'd fallen significantly far back Miltabardo stopped and waited for him.

'Mr. Green, is there something troubling you?'

Paul nodded. 'I was just thinking - how will we know, just walking, when it is safe to use the gates again? I mean, what if they just follow us until we don't think they're with us?'

Miltabardo smiled - a grim smile that spoke of something more troubling than that.

'There may be another possibility,' he said. 'Though I am not yet sure if what I suspect is true.'

Jenny drew a sharp breath. She'd been trying to read the Docent and was starting to have some success.

'You think we're on an Island!' she blurted out.

He whirled on her with a stern, angry look on his face.

'I would strongly advise against that!' he said fiercely. 'It does not do to use an advantage such as yours over other members of the order!'

Then his face softened. He continued: 'However, you are right. That is what I was thinking. We were brought somewhere under the direction of the Talomni, somewhere that must offer them an advantage.'

'Then, Docent,' Paul said, 'I believe we should stop walking. I think we should make ourselves comfortable here and wait for the Talomni to come to us!'

Miltabardo thought briefly about it before agreeing. He held his hands out, palms down, and slowly waved them over the ground in front. The ground shimmered as something heavy started to form. Stout legs rose from it and then a molded bench appeared on top, with a wooden backing. When he was done, he sat, gesturing for the children to join him.

They looked slowly about, listening to the woods. They could hear the calls of many birds and the rustling of the brush as squirrels or chipmunks moved past. There was no wind and the sky above the trees was a clear, deep blue. They sat still for a long while.

Waiting.

Jenny felt uneasy. The birds had stopped singing. She looked about and could not see any of them. She pointed this out to the others who agreed that something definitely was wrong. She and Paul started casting their mind's eyes about, trying to find the sign of the Talomni. It didn't take long. Paul found several approaching them from his side. Jenny found many more on her side, coming along the ground and through the trees.

Miltabardo looked alarmed, unable to see them, or sense them. Paul asked if he could try something on the Docent, try to teach him. Miltabardo agreed. Paul put his hands on his shoulders sending a stream of memory, images of their Australian encounter, into his mind. The Docent looked about wide-eyed now understanding how Paul and Jenny did it. He quickly saw what they saw and was surprised at how many of the Talomni were surrounding them.

Jenny stood up facing the ring. There was a cold, concentrated look on her face, preparing herself for the creature's attack.

'Jenny!' Paul said excitedly, 'I have an idea!'

'What is it,' she said, her voice rushed, like it was carried on a swift wind.

'They know we can't see them, although they may be starting to realize we're aware of them. Now that we can detect them, there's an easy way to make them visible!'

Jenny's concentration broke as she looked over at him.

'How?' she asked.

Paul pointed to their left at a dark pool.

'Mud.'

Jenny grinned and turned toward the pool of mud, raising her arms. The mud rose and drifted toward her in a brown haze. She gathered her arms in, concentrating the mist, and then spun, facing the Talomni, sending it hurtling toward where they were massing.

The effect was immediate and terrifying. The mud coated the creatures as the rain had. Unlike the rain, it stuck. The Talomni were hideous. They had enormous, round bodies, with two muscular arms protruding from the sides and two from the top. There was no head. On the front of the round body there appeared to be openings where eyes and mouths might exist.

The Talomni did not have legs - rather their bodies were supported on tentacles that made them look like giant octopi.

As soon as the mud coated them they started thrashing madly, trying to remove it. Jenny and Paul slowly walked toward them. The Talomni realized that not only was the mud not coming off but the children could see them. Several of the front creatures rushed at them and a loud, menacing hiss filled the air.

Jenny whipped her arm forward, snapping them back to the others and crashing them together. The Talomni began to bellow and hiss. They advanced on them. Jenny stood still with her arms folded across her chest, staring at them.

Docent Miltabardo had watched with fascination as the children walked toward the creatures but jumped up as soon as Jenny hit the first ones. Her power was immense, far beyond any he had seen before. He knew that while she probably could destroy every one of the creatures gathered here, there were many more of them and they would hunt her relentlessly.

He darted over and put a hand on her shoulder.

'Miss Greyson, you must not kill them. You would only start a long, difficult battle, one which might result in the death of several members of the order, and perhaps even yourself!'

'Then what should I do?' she said, 'They're coming for us!'

'Just hold them off. We must try something else.'

'Ok,' she said

She brought her arms up again. Instead of trying to hit them, she started plucking trees, logs, rocks, anything large that she could find and floating them toward the Talomni. They stopped. They watched as the items floated toward them.

Jenny continued darting her eyes around, pointing into the woods. From all directions, logs were floating toward them, gathering and hovering around the Talomni. Suddenly she raised her arms and slammed them toward the ground. The hovering logs immediately turned upright in the air and shot to the ground, piercing it and forming a fence all around the Talomni. The rocks then hovered above them suspended in the air.

Jenny walked to the edge of the cage she'd created and looked in. The Talomni were wrapping their tentacles around the logs, trying to pull them down. Paul and Miltabardo watched as Jenny surrounded the fence with her powerful aura, making it impenetrable.

She looked over at Paul and gestured toward them. He walked up to the fence and as one of the Talomni's tentacles wrapped again around a log he grabbed it. Immediately he was flooded with fear, anger, hate and something else - their language.

He released the tentacle and stood back. The Talomni were still thrashing about in the cage as Paul walked to Jenny. She held her hand out and he took it, passing what he had just learned to her. She staggered over but recovered before the shield around the Talomni failed.

The two of them then turned to the Talomni and let out a piercing screech which cascaded down to a slow hiss. Every one of the Talomni stopped moving. The creature's arms relaxed and their tentacles dropped back to the ground where they sat quietly twitching.

They did not understand how what they heard could be possible: The children were speaking to them, in their own tongue.

Jenny turned and walked away from the enclosure. Paul glanced once more at the Talomni and then followed her. The Talomni were watching in a trance as they returned to Miltabardo, who was once again sitting on the bench. Paul sat down beside him. Jenny turned back to the enclosure.

'We are leaving now,' she hissed in their language. 'I am going to release you. If you do not try to harm us or follow us, I will leave you alone. If you try anything else, you will be destroyed.'

The creatures started shifting impatiently on their tentacles and a swift, low hissing erupted, as they discussed what she had said. After a few moments one of the Talomni near the front of the cage shook its arms and said one word:

'Agreed.'

Jenny raised her arms and as she did, the trees that formed the barrier rose into the air and drifted away into the woods. The Docent rose and turned, erasing his bench, then took the two children's hands and walked away from the Talomni. Soon there was no signs of the creatures and the children's amulets started to warm up. The blue glow that came from them whirled and pulsed about them.

Jenny and Paul watched in amazement as the entire forest around them dissolved with a rushing sound of wind and vanished. In its place, now occupied by hundreds of people, were the seats of the Gathering Common.

Their journey was over.

Chapter 17

The Order

The two young boys were almost always in trouble, caught by their curiosity. The basket was forbidden - every one who touched it was burnt, but they weren't afraid. They reached in, grabbed the glowing purple amulets, and put them on. Staring about in wide-eyed wonder, they suddenly flinched - without seeing who it was, they knew someone was coming. They crept out the back of the village, and never returned, caught by the wonder of the world newly open to their discovery.

The children blinked and looked around. The people that surrounded them were all dressed in matching robes and they all had amulets around their necks. Some were in pairs and some shone on their own but every amulet present was pulsing - the light growing brighter then dimmer. Many of the people stood, arms crossed and glaring, as the gate snapped shut behind them.

Miltabardo let go of their hands and stepped away from them and his robes changed from their threadbare grey to a much richer, fuller cloth becoming black with blue inlays, hanging loosely about him. They were standing on the stage and the Docent turned and smiled at them.

'Welcome back,' he whispered, 'Let's see how we did.'

He turned and walked to the side of the stage, moving slowly down the small steps at the edge. He walked over to a group of people gathered in front of the fire. He held his arms up in greeting, then quickly dropped them, frowning as he did.

Paul and Jenny stood still and tried to hear what was being said. Faint bits of conversation drifted over to them but the words were lost.

'Can you hear anything?' Jenny asked him.

Paul shook his head.

'Not a thing. But they don't look happy.'

'Maybe they're mad at us,' she replied.

Paul didn't answer, instead stepping forward and looking at the people lining the rows of seats. He tried to get a sense of what they were feeling and found nothing, just a cold emptiness. He turned and walked back to Jenny.

'I can't tell what they feel,' he said. 'It's like they're not even here.'

The Docent's voice rose in anger and the children heard him clearly.

'What are you talking about?' he demanded. 'I was there. I saw what they meant to do. If these two hadn't acted as quickly as they did, well, we wouldn't be here now.'

Two of the people near the Docent crossed their arms, their heads slowly shaking. The children stepped closer to hear what was being said.

'Docent, you could not see everything the way we could here. These two were being hunted by an entire horde! What explanation do you have for that?'

'None yet,' Miltabardo replied. 'But that doesn't mean there isn't one.'

'Of course not.'

They all turned toward the voice. A woman with long black hair, as straight as silk, looked back them. She had been sitting in the front row, watching, and stood up as the Docent spoke.

'There is an explanation,' she continued. 'It's just that I doubt there are many here who would remember it.'

Several voices rose at once but the Docent held his hands up, waiting for her to continue.

'Go ahead, Chantal. What do you think we just saw, besides the Talomni.'

'How old are you, my friend?' she asked in return. 'Do you remember our first gathering place? Before we fled here?'

A puzzled look crossed his face and he looked down at the ground.

'I didn't think so,' she continued. 'The creatures that just tried to capture those two have been waiting a long time. And they won't mind waiting a little longer.'

Miltabardo looked up at the children and then back at Chantal.

'You are referring to the old solstice gatherings. We would meet there, perhaps every 10 years. I remember it.'

Chantal smiled.

'I am my friend. I suppose I was wrong - you do remember.'

She turned and looked up at the rest of the order, all waiting.

'What we have just seen,' she said, in a booming voice, 'is from our distant past. It is a reminder, to those of us that remember, that we must be careful not to reveal ourselves - not to get caught.'

Paul suddenly felt fear creeping down from the surrounding seats. He turned and whispered this to Jenny. Several of the people in the first row saw him and pointed up at them.

'What are they saying?' one of them demanded. 'You, Paul - what did you just say?'

Paul looked over at Miltabardo, a questioning look on his face.

'Go ahead, Paul,' said the Docent.

'I was trying to tell Jenny what I feel around us.'

'Why?' a voice asked from the seats.

'Well, it's just, I thought we were supposed to.'

A small hiss to the left of the stage announced another arrival through the gates. The children looked over and smiled as Ornolt stepped into view. He nodded back at them.

'In fact,' Paul continued, 'Ornolt told us we had to, and that rude bird said we absolutely had to.'

'Be careful who you call rude,' another voice said. 'That was no bird.'

'You are right,' Ornolt said. 'You were told to act together.'

He turned to look up at the seats.

'It's a good thing they did, don't you think? They'd probably be dead now if they hadn't!'

Several voices murmured at each other.

'So what did you tell her?' the original person asked. 'What do you feel around you?'

'Uhm, fear, I suppose,' Paul replied.

Paul's sense of those around him was growing stronger and along with fear, he felt anger. He had said something that upset them, though he had no idea what. Jenny stood still and quiet beside him. He reached over and grabbed her hand.

Can you get anything from them he thought.

No - it's like Strumn was, or Miltabardo - they're silent.

Several members suddenly stood up, glaring at the children.

'Did you know they can talk to each other without speaking?' they said, turning toward Chantal and Miltabardo.

'I suspected it,' Miltabardo answered.

Ornolt had a frown on his face and he walked toward the group.

'Again, I ask - what's wrong with that? You say it like it's never happened before. Lots of us can do that. Ucheen, if I recall correctly, you can do such a thing.'

Ucheen snorted.

'Yes, *Exeter*, but I can't knock down trees with my mind. I can't learn a language just by touching someone. Something's clearly not right here.'

Miltabardo stepped toward the centre of the common and held his arms up.

'Enough, everyone. The children are strong, of that there can be no argument. Jennifer, especially, is gifted with several talents, but that does not mean something's wrong.'

'I disagree,' Ucheen replied. 'Since you can remember back to our original gathering place, can you remember anyone ever being like this?'

'In a sense, yes. And we'll get to that. But do remember that her father, and perhaps her mother, are like us. That's definitely never happened before.'

The man named James, who had been the children's crocodile guide stepped over to the group.

'There may be something more, sir. After I told the children this, there was a palpable change in the feeling around them. Not quite fear, more like - anticipation.'

Jenny looked at Paul and shrugged. She didn't remember any such thing.

'Did you get a sense of where it might have come from?' Miltabardo asked.

'No sir. My host had limits to its patience. I couldn't be as alert as I would have liked.'

The docent rubbed his beard and then looked over at Chantal.

'Perhaps we'll find out more in a minute. Shall we get on with their *Vitoc?*'

Many heads began nodding at once, including Chantal's. Ornolt stepped toward the center of the common and turned to face the children.

'You are finished the first part of your journey together,' he said solemnly. 'It will soon be time to reflect on it, and then to return home.'

Jenny smiled, excited about going home and talking to her father about everything that had happened, about what she'd learned.

'But first,' Ornolt continued, 'the greeting ceremony. May I have your bags please, and your walking sticks.'

They handed the bags over and passed him the sticks. He took them over to the infinite fire, which still burned to the left of the stage in its circle of rectangular rocks. He placed the walking sticks in it, where they dissolved into the flames, washing over the logs, before finally vanishing. The fire crackled and sparked, before settling back into its original form.

Ornolt returned and held his hands out to Jenny and Paul. They walked to the front of the stage, where Ornolt had them sit with their legs dangling over the edge. Then he turned and walked over to Chantal and Miltabardo. The three of them sat down in the front row of seats and stared back at the children.

'What you have been through together,' Ornolt said, 'has been a marvelous start, and a dangerous one. We would like to share that with you, all of us would like to experience what you have. We will do that now.'

A hush fell over the entire common and every member of the order stared at them, their eyes unmoving, hardly even blinking. Jenny and Paul felt lightheaded and the space around them began to blur, like a fog was drifting between them and the rest of the order. Jenny felt a pressure on her head, an itch, and raised her hands, rubbing her hair frantically. She tried to look at Paul and saw he was doing the same. A feeling of nausea began to rise in her throat and she felt herself growing faint.

As the feeling increased, she thought she felt a tingling in the back of her head, one that she had felt before. She started to feel like they were floating down an invisible river, even though they were still sitting on the edge of the stage. She began to feel sicker still. She stared through misty eyes at the people sitting in the common, wishing the feeling would end.

Paul reached out a hand and grabbed hers. He tried to calm her, so they both could fight against the strange, unseen river. The tingling in her head rose to a roar, and she started to curl up against it.

Feels like a gate, doesn't it came Paul's thoughts.

No! It's horrible - it's like being sick!

Paul forced himself to look at her, and saw the pain written on her face.

Sick? Really?

She nodded her head weakly.

Not for you she thought.

The pain doubled itself and the glow of the amulets around them increased.

No. Try and relax - just let it happen.

Jenny closed her eyes and tried to settle into the feeling around her. She took a long, slow breath and let it out.

It's getting worse! she thought.

Maybe it won't last much longer.

Paul had closed his eyes again, absorbing how Jenny felt. Suddenly he snapped them open and looked at her. His sense of her had changed and he felt the same presence he'd felt on the snow-blasted mountain - the second, ancient memory.

Jenny? Are you OK?

'No,' she answered out loud, her voice once again laced with a melodic undertone, 'I'm not. This must end.'

She slipped back on the stage and stood up.

'Please stop this!' she called out, her voice so loud that some of the people in the front row flinched.

The amulets that hung around their necks increased in intensity but no one said a thing. Jenny walked back over to Paul and sat down beside him, putting her arm around his shoulders.

Hang on she thought.

The blue mist that he saw around her returned and as its brightness increased, it moved to wrap around him as well. As it did, the feeling of being on a river subsided. Many of the members of the order leapt to their feet and pointed at them. Paul could see the edge of the mist rippling and he felt Jenny fighting back, the other presence in her growing stronger.

Miltabardo and Chantal stood up as well and stepped toward the children, both frowning at Jenny.

'Please,' Jenny said again, 'Make this stop.'

'You must share with us,' Chantal replied. She glanced at Miltabardo and the two of them wrapped one hand around their amulets and raised the others, pointing palm out toward Jenny.

Paul saw a massive ripple in the mist, like a bubble pushing inward and the arm around his shoulder flinched and tightened. Jenny started to moan, sounding both angry and in pain. She closed her eyes and Paul thought he heard her say something, whispering, in a language he didn't recognize.

She opened her eyes and looked at Paul. Paul's eyes widened in shock at what he saw - the same expansion of her pupil across her eyes, the same blue color as their amulets, just like he'd seen at the storm, before she had collapsed.

'We will end this now,' she growled and stood up, folding her arms across her chest.

Miltabardo saw the change in her, saw the color of her eyes. He let go of his amulet, and turned to Chantal.

'Perhaps we had better stop,' he whispered. 'I've no idea who is standing in front of us.'

'It's just the girl,' Chantal snapped. She stepped forward again and several other members of the order followed her.

Jenny glared at them all, drew in a deep breath and then flung both her hands forward. The blue mist whipped away from her, toward the standing members and they crashed back in their seats. Jenny turned her eyes toward the rows behind her, and the mist moved toward them. They all sat down at once and the pulsing in their amulets stopped.

Jenny turned and walked back over to Paul and sat down beside him. She leaned up against him and closed her eyes. Paul felt the ancient presence withdraw and in its place Jenny's familiar feeling returned.

'You ok?' he whispered.

'Yes,' she said back. 'It's ok this time. Just tired.'

Paul looked around at the members of the order. They all sat perfectly still, no one speaking, staring at the children. Paul started to stand up but Jenny held him back.

'Not yet,' she said, 'still tired.'

Ornolt was the first to move. He stood up from where he was seated and walked slowly toward where the children sat on the edge of the stage. He put one hand on Jenny's knee and looked at her.

'Jenny,' he said. 'Open your eyes.'

She did, and looked back at him. Her eyes, though watery, had returned to their normal shape and color.

'What did you just do?' he said.

'I don't know,' she mumbled.

Several people in the rows of seats started murmuring, but their words didn't make it to the stage.

'Well figure it out quickly,' he whispered. 'You've terrified most of the people here.'

Jenny jumped as if she been hit with an electric shock and stared around her.

'It just felt so awful,' she said. 'The pain was so bad - I thought I was going to get sick.'

Miltabardo joined them.

'Sick?' he asked. 'You should not have felt that. What about you Paul?'

'It just felt like a gate,' he said, drawing nods from the people who could hear him.

'But it didn't for her,' he continued. 'I knew how bad she felt. She couldn't have stood that for very long. Why did you do that, anyways?'

Miltabardo sighed and started to pace back and forth.

'It has always been our custom to share in the experiences of each other. We can bond with each other because of the amulets, although that bond is nowhere near as strong as what you two share.'

'It lets us see what you saw,' Ornolt added. 'It lets us learn from what you have been through, and lets us figure out how to help you in the future.'

Jenny looked at Ornolt.

'Did it work?' she asked.

'Not really,' he replied. 'You stopped it too soon.'

'Maybe there's another way,' Paul said. 'I can share our journey with the Docent, as I have before, and then he could show you?'

Miltabardo smiled.

'That sounds like a plan worth trying,' he said, holding out his hands.

'Maybe you should sit down,' Jenny said. 'This is a weird experience.'

Miltabardo nodded and walked back to his seat. Paul followed and when the Docent held out his hands, Paul grasped them and whispered 'Like this.'

The Docent slumped over and Paul held him firmly. For nearly twenty seconds they remained that way, before Paul slowly lowered his hands. Miltabardo drew in several long breathes and then sat back up.

'Weird, Jennifer, does not begin to describe that!' he smiled. 'It felt like I was actually there!'

He stood up and turned toward the seats.

'I have what we need, and will share it with you shortly. Perhaps we'll let the children go home first?'

Agreement and disagreement rained down from the seats.

'What about what just happened?' several people began. 'We must know how she did that!'

'I doubt we will ever know exactly how,' Miltabardo replied. 'But I assure you, she meant absolutely no harm.'

'How can you be so sure?'

'Because Paul just shared with me how she felt. He also shared a rather vivid recollection of her stopping that storm. The power she can wield is immense, so I think we actually just got off rather lucky just now. All she wanted was for the feeling to stop.'

Jenny sat on the stage, still feeling tired, and listened as the debate continued. Finally she stood up, walked over to Paul and whispered something in his ear. He smiled and waited for a break in the debate.

'For anyone who's still wondering about her, maybe you should just come down and meet her.'

No one moved, looking at the Docent instead.

'A fine idea,' he said. 'Why don't we get these children something to eat, and let's just talk a bit. We'll save the formalities for later.'

Paul turned away from the Docent, heading for Ucheen and two of his colleagues. Ucheen stood with his arms folded and glared at him as he approached.

'You don't like her, do you?' Paul asked.

'That's not it,' Ucheen replied. 'I don't know her at all. I don't know what she is.'

'But I can tell you don't like her. Your anger is pouring off of you.'

'How would you know what I really feel? Earlier you said you felt fear, now anger?'

Miltabardo, overhearing the conversation, walked over.

'Something wrong, gentlemen?'

'No sir,' Paul replied. 'I just thought Ucheen and his friends should come over - talk to us a bit.'

'Do you know how old I am?' Ucheen asked Paul.

'Sorry?'

'How old am I?'

'Uhm - I really couldn't say.'

'Ok, then where am I from?'

Paul frowned, but didn't answer.

'I thought not. I'm sorry, Paul, you seem like a nice kid, but you make a lot of assumptions about me, about my feelings, without knowing the first thing about me.'

'Ucheen,' Miltabardo interrupted. 'You really think, given what you have seen of him, that he's just a kid?'

'Yes, sir. He's not one of us, not yet.'

'Not yet, as you know, is irrelevant. You are born one of us. You just learn more as you grow up. Paul knows exactly how you feel - that is part of his gift.'

Miltabardo glanced at the other two that stood beside Ucheen.

'What about you, Masi? Do you think the same thing?'

'Not the same sir, no. I'm the first to admit what the girl just did was very frightening... very - unexpected. But I'm not angry at her, or at Paul here.'

'Look, it's not about anger,' Ucheen said. 'I just don't think, as I've been saying for the last few days, that we should let things go as fast as they are. Neither one of these two is ready for what they can do, nor are they ready for what awaits them.'

Miltabardo smiled.

'That is very true. It was for all of us too. And we'll help them with that, just as we did for you. Come, talk to Jennifer.'

Ucheen stood firm, his arms still crossed.

'She doesn't bite,' Paul said, putting his hand on Ucheen's shoulder.

Ucheen relaxed, his arms dropped and a small smile cracked one side of his mouth.

'Ok,' he said, following Paul. 'But don't think I didn't notice what you just did.'

For the next hour, the children were swarmed by members of the order, each keen to ask them something about their journey, about their experience. Several people asked about the way Jenny had broken free of the vitoc, which she tried as best as she could to explain. As the talking died down, Chantal walked away from the crowd and stood in front of the stage, watching them.

Docent Miltabardo walked over and stood beside Chantal. The other members of the order saw this and returned to their seats. Ornolt stood with the two children and waited. Miltabardo held up his hands and turned toward the children. When he did, a low chant filled the air, coming from all around them. They looked at the assembly and saw everyone studying them, their mouths closed, and their amulets pulsing strongly.

'Jennifer Greyson. Paul Green. You are formally invited to undergo the training necessary to become members of our Ordered Family. You have shown yourselves to be fully capable of the challenges ahead; indeed, more than capable.'

Paul put his arm around Jenny's shoulders and they were both smiling at him as he spoke.

'Each member of this group will have a chance to review the experiences you've just been through. You have provided us with a great gift already, the means by which we might locate the Talomni, and for that we are profoundly grateful. We will attempt to improve upon it when you return, and are able to teach us their language.

'But that is still ahead of us. For now, we must temporarily part company.'

He paused, looking at both of them.

'Each of you will go to your own home, and return, as much as possible, to your own lives.'

The children looked at each other with apprehension.

'When you do get home, you will not remember us.'

'Or each other.'

'Or any of what you have just been through.'

Jenny gasped and was about to ask why when Ornolt put a hand on her shoulder.

'Don't worry, Jenny, it's not for long. It's the only way we know that will work.'

She turned to him, a questioning, pleading look on her face. The chant that surrounded them had ceased when the Docent had stopped speaking and a lingering silence hung in the air. After a moment, Ornolt continued:

'You'll understand when you return to us, which you no doubt will do,' he said, and then looked up at the stirring crowd.

'Alright then everyone, it is time!' the Docent said, clapping his hands twice.

With a few last words, the members of the order rose and started walking away, chatting to themselves. As they reached the edge of the common, they started to fade, and vanished from sight. Minutes later, only Ornolt, Jenny and Paul remained.

'Well that certainly was an amazing introduction,' Ornolt said enthusiastically.

'Yeah, I guess,' said Jenny. 'Although I don't understand why I won't remember any of this when I go home! I don't want to forget you, or Paul or anything!'

A tear formed and ran slowly down her cheek. Ornolt reached into his robes, and brought out an ornate facial handkerchief, with which he dabbed her tears.

'Come, let me tell you why things need to be this way.'

They sat down close together, and looked up at him.

'I'm going to take each one of you back, and as you've just been told, you will not remember any of what has happened to you - for a small while.'

The children looked at him with dread and he held up his hands.

'Don't worry, it won't be permanent. You will remember all of this, slowly, bit by bit, over the next year or so. It is important that you return to your normal lives first, and have the order return to you gradually. If we did it any other way, you could not possibly adjust to being home again. Believe me, we know this the hard way.'

'So, when I go home,' said Jenny, 'you're saying that I will have forgotten everything? All that I've learned, everyone I've met, even Paul?'

'Not quite, Jenny,' he said. 'You will know all of it, it's just that you won't have access to it right away. Think of it as a safety measure. Can you imagine what life would be like for you back home if you had all these powers of yours right away? Someone would do something that upset you and you'd react, or perhaps you'd see a chance to save someone else from some danger.

'Or perhaps,' he said with a wink, 'you won't like the weather one day and decide to change it!'

He laughed and then, seeing that the children took no consolation from this, continued:

'No, it's better that what you have learned, and the abilities you have mastered come to you very slowly.'

'When will I remember Jen?' asked Paul.

'I cannot say when, exactly, but it will certainly be before you come back here.'

'Can we visit each other, when we're home?' asked Jenny.

'Once you remember each other, yes, of course. In fact, I'm sure you will, otherwise, you never would make it back here.'

Paul gasped and took Jenny's hand, sending a flood of images into her, images of his home in London, his mother, his grandparents, their house, even the square where he and his friends played.

'Will I be the same as I was before?' Jenny asked, turning back to Ornolt.

'How do you mean?' he replied.

'Before I came here, I didn't like stuff - the mind reading got me in trouble a lot, you know? People avoided me.'

Ornolt sat thinking for a moment.

'Then yes, probably, though not for long - maybe a day or so. The confidence that you have built here is usually the first part to come back - it makes the other memories easier to absorb.'

He stood.

'Now, come, I think we'd better go. This will feel a little... strange.'

The children stood, looking at each other, not saying anything. Jenny still felt waves of sadness at leaving Paul and eager excitement at seeing her family and friends again. Ornolt stood in front of them and drew a large circle on the floor. He turned to Paul.

'You first - just stand here.'

Paul gave Jenny a lingering hug, and, looking at her the whole time, he slowly stepped into the circle. The Exeter placed his hand on Paul's forehead.

'Home, now, and remember us when you can!'

Paul started to fade from view, shimmering and then he was gone.

'You're next, Jenny,' said Ornolt gently.

She stepped forward and looked at Ornolt. He repeated the same thing with her. He stepped back and Jenny felt suddenly confused. She could see Ornolt watching her, although his face was changing, aging rapidly and stepping back from her as everything around him began to blur. The light faded and then burst up in intensity, the air warmed and Jenny found herself standing back in Banff, in the park near her home.

It was a beautiful summer's day and she could hear the sounds of children laughing and playing. She felt dizzy and reached out to steady herself on the tree standing next to her. She shook her head and looked around. A game of park tag was in full progress.

Sarah came running up to her and poked her in the back.

'Got you at last!' she shouted triumphantly.

Jenny looked around at her.

'Sarah?' she said questioningly.

'Yeah, you silly ...'

Sarah stopped and looked at Jenny. Her face was pale and she looked exhausted.

'Are you all right?' Sarah asked.

Jenny blinked, trying to regain her composure.

'Yeah, no problem - just a little dizzy. I'm going to go home, I think.'

Sarah looked concerned.

'Do you want me to come with you?' she asked.

'No, thanks, you keep playing - I'll see you later.'

'Hey,' said Sarah, reaching out for something hanging around Jenny's neck. 'Where did you get this? It's really pretty!'

Jenny looked down and saw her amulet. She picked it up in her hand, turning it over and over, smiling as an image of two amulets, floating in the air, flashed through her mind and then was gone.

'I don't remember.'

Sarah frowned at her.

'Maybe you better go home - you don't seem yourself at all.'

Jenny nodded and turned to leave, walking slowly back along the path toward the park entrance and her street. She noticed an ancient old man, in dark grey robes with a white beard watching her from the other side of the park. He was trying his best not to stare but she knew he was anyway. She kept walking, too weary to care.

Ornolt stood, satisfied that she would be fine and walked away from her, back into the trees, fading from view as he went.

It took Jenny a long time to walk home. She couldn't believe how tired she felt. She knew that they'd had a lengthy game of park tag but that had never bothered her so much before. She walked slowly up her street, looking at the many wonderful gardens that grew along it, including her own. Her parents were great gardeners and knew how to make the oddest plants flourish together.

She walked up to her house and stood on the porch. She had the strangest feeling about standing there, like she shouldn't open the door. She shook her head again, opened it and went in.

She took her running shoes off and headed into the back, where she could hear dishes rattling about. She was feeling much better and when she stepped into the kitchen, she saw her father, bent over something on the table.

'Hi Dad,' she said, coming in.

'Oh hi, kiddo, how are ...' he stopped when he saw her.

Jenny was certain she saw a strange blue glow reflect in his eyes when he saw the new necklace, with its ornament on the end.

He paused and breathed in slowly.

'So how did it go?' he said finally.

The memory of a tall, curly haired boy flickered in front of her and then was gone. She looked over at him, smiled and sat down heavily in a breakfast chair.

'Great,' she said. 'What a long game!'

www.ingramcontent.com/pod-product-compliance
Lightning Source LLC
Chambersburg PA
CBHW071136170626
46809CB00002B/645